Under the
Light of the Sun

Casey A. Telling

Under the Light of the Sun

Chronicles of Emeraldia: Book 2

Casey A. Telling

Praise for

Into the Blood of the Sun

"An awesome adventure... The story of the battle between good and evil is the dominant theme in the history of mankind. Alliances, both false and true; battles, fierce and bloody; and powers, mystical and mighty, are the same elements found in Tolkien, C. S. Lewis, etc... Casey Telling has created some unique characters in this tale which has no dearth of violence... The importance of the Creator versus the Dark One conflict precludes any subtlety to the spiritual aspect of this novel... *Into the Blood of the Sun* is a self-published book... better than many traditionally published books I have read-including the quality of the editing.

— Donald James Parker, author of *All the Voices of the Wind*, posted review on Amazon.com

"*Into the Blood of the Sun* does what a fantasy novel should do. It leads the reader to imagine themselves (or associate themselves with) a hero fighting the forces of evil, in a world where the lines between good and evil are clearly drawn, the will of the creator and the will of the people are on your side, glory and honor are attainable, and the world is just different enough from the reader's own for her to suspend disbelief....This reader found Telling's style enjoyable and appropriate to the tone and genre of the novel. His writing is literate and able, and carries the tale...He does a good job of balancing detailed description with fast-moving action and lively dialogue."

— Reviewer for the Mark Sullivan Associates, NY, NY.

DEDICATION

Once again I would like to express my deep appreciation for all of the support and encouragement shown for this work by my wonderful wife, Elvera. She not only provided an excellent model for the character, Veranna, but has proven invaluable for her input on crafting the story and making it far richer than it would have been without her contributions. May the Creator's blessings be upon you, my love.

ACKNOWLEDGEMENTS

I am very grateful for all of those people who have been so generous with their encouragement and comments upon my work. Many who read my first book, *Into the Blood of the Sun*, demanded more and I am pleased with being able to provide this second book.

My sister's-in-law Rita, Erna and Helene provided great feedback. I wish to thank Ms. Jodi Lantz for her valuable advice. Her experiences as an author (*The Khaki Mafia*, with Robin Moore) provided many insights into the publishing world.

To those people from my place of employment whom I acknowledged in my first book, I would like to add: Stan Knapp, Laurie Klos, Tina Fox, Karen Hill, Nicole Boudreaux, James Mason, MD, Ron Graff, MD, Shari Fernandes, Misty Beardsley, Alicia Rowley, Rita Sue Grage, Paula Villars, Leslie Leonard, Debbie Keifert, Carmen McCulloch, Linda Heritage, Bob Schu, Anne Fields, Mary Ann Odne and Scott Hubbell.

I would also like to thank my sister-in-law, Christy, for her help in getting my first book into the local library system, and J. Renni Storm for the cover illustration input she provided. My thanks also go to Alicia and Asana Miranda for their excellent work on the cover art.

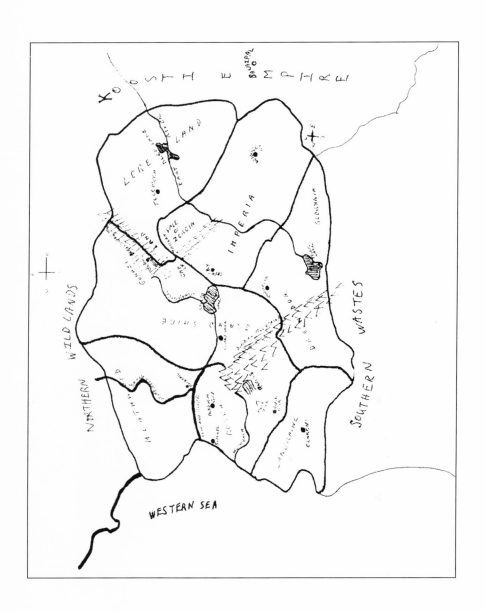

CHAPTER ONE

VILE PASSIONS

R ed-orange flames leaped up from jagged fissures in the mountain's side. Lightning flashed out of roiling clouds, sending its thunder booming through the range. The light faded quickly, leaving the night to be illuminated by a single fire at the center of a large hollow atop one of the lesser mountains.

That single fire wrapped around the dais of an altar made of finely cut stones. Its diameter was easily thirty feet, as was the height of an obelisk located at the back of the altar. On the dais danced a woman, her bronze skin shining brightly with tiger stripes painted from head to toe. Three-score more people danced around the dais, their unclothed bodies glowing like bronze ingots fresh from the furnace.

On rock outcrops high on the surrounding slopes, dragons roared at the sky, sending their colored flames into the clouds. The largest beast, a shiny-scaled, black monster, dropped down to the floor of the hollow and opened its massive jaws. The woman on the dais raised her arms straight up and the dragon bowed down its horrid head.

The woman made a slashing motion across her throat and pointed toward a cave opening at the back of the hollow. Four men from the group of people dancing around the dais ran into the cave, then emerged carrying a man whose wrists and legs were tightly bound. His hair and clothing had all been removed, revealing long, infected welts across his torso. They brought him to the foot of the dais and held him up for the woman to look down into his eyes.

The man did not even notice her bare body, for her eyes held his attention as she leaned over his face. Her hair was a dark curtain around her head, and her eyes rolled back in their sockets as she incanted a spell. Flame shot up again from rends in the slopes, and lightning crackled amidst the clouds. The woman snapped up straight, her left arm raised to the sky with the hand clenched into a tight fist. Her right hand pointed directly at the dragon on the floor of the hollow. The four men carried the bound man over to the dragon, his screams unnoticeable against the noises of the people. The dragon opened its huge jaws and the four men tossed the captive into its throat. With one swift gulp the dragon swallowed him whole. Furious movements could be seen along the dragon's belly, and then they ceased abruptly. The beast raised it's head and blew red-orange fire from its nostrils into the sky.

The people circled the dais as they shouted, writhing in their mania, until the woman on the dais pointed at the cave again. This time, the men brought out a tall woman whose red hair had been shaved off. Her swollen breasts and abdomen revealed that she had recently given birth, and her back and legs showed thousands of nettle punctures. Her blue eyes were locked in terror onto the eyes of the woman on the dais. She screamed as the woman bent over her, but her voice failed as they threw her into the dragon's maws. One spasmodic jerk was all that could be seen against the dragon's belly.

The dragon beat its mighty wings and lifted into the air, returning to its rocky perch on the craggy slopes. Another dragon, a red one, replaced it on the floor of the hollow. Two more captives, a man and a woman, were brought and thrown into its jaws. It flew up and a brown dragon replaced it. This cycle repeated until all twenty-four captives were given over to the dragons.

The woman on the dais whirled and danced around in ecstasy. She came to a sudden stop at the front of the dais and held up her hands as she cried, "So shall it be for all who oppose DeAndre, and his sister, the Great Lady of the Koosti, LeAnre. Look upon yen-Kragar and his family, and learn!"

She turned and pointed at the obelisk. Yen-Kragar, four of his wives, and five of their sons hung from ragged prongs penetrating out through their chests. Their bodies bore the marks of excruciating tortures, and their empty eye sockets testified to the blindness of death.

The woman, LeAnre, addressed the others once more. "yen-Kragar has been vanquished to the abode of the Dark One, as have four of his wives and his five sons. No more shall his line ever rule the Koosti, nor will they cause us trouble ever again." Wild cheering broke out among the people.

"I, LeAnre, the Great Lady of the Koosti, tell you that we shall never be subject to anyone again, save the Dark One, who gives us victory over our enemies.

"Chief among our foes will be the Emeraldians. We have not forgotten how they refused our forefathers, and opposed our worship of the Dark Master. Millennia of time shall make no difference for our revenge. The Dark One shall reward us for bringing all the Seven Lands under his control.

"The Empress of Emeraldia, like her ancestors, has the aid of the Genazi. They are unchanged since the days of old, still as pathetic in their devotion to the idiot deity they call 'Creator'. The empress aligns herself with that weakling, too. But when she bows down to my brother, and takes her place in his harem, she will know the true extent of her errors.

"The ancient ones sought to obliterate the inhabitants of the Seven Lands, entirely. But that was a mistaken notion, even if one we can sympathize with. No, we must maintain some of the population for slave labor, and some for breeding purposes. They shall be as cattle, and we shall be the herdsmen. Our dragons will need more and more food as their numbers grow. What better supply could be given them than the sweet meat of our enemies? We will build an army of warriors and dragons that will dominate all the lands of this world.

"We celebrate our victory over yen-Kragar and begin our conquest of all things. As your Great Lady, I command you to bring forth warriors. You men of the Koosti, take pleasure in your women, and see to it that their wombs are filled with your offspring. You women, see to it that you do not fail to bring forth children to serve the Koosti. Our warriors shall begin the conquest of other lands and bring the captives to be our slaves. Use the captive slave women not only for pleasure, but to increase the number of workers and slave warriors.

"These are the commands of your Great Lady. Fulfill them, and you will be true followers of our Dark Lord."

The people swirled and yelled in frenzied abandon. LeAnre danced across the dais again, then dove into the throng of people below. All regard for caste or modesty was gone; the orgy had begun.

CHAPTER TWO

UNTO THE SUN

The early morning sun shed its golden beams onto the ancient capital of the Emeraldian Empire. Tolemera bustled with activity, the streets full of both foot and wheeled traffic. Since the day that duke Weyland had been removed from power, the city experienced rapid growth in commerce, business ventures and the birth rate. New hope and pride gave even the lowliest an incentive to move forward, especially when one of them was invited to share the dinner table with the empress and her lords. Sincere care and action flowed from the Emerald Throne, leaving both noble and commoner feeling confident and vital to the betterment of the realm.

Kreida sprang through the halls, having cleaned up after her morning workout, and headed for the dining hall. The empress, Veranna, who was more like a sister to the volatile Genazi woman, would be there with the inner circle of leaders sworn to the Emerald Throne. Tomius, the leader of the Genazi and Lord of Imperia, would also be there with his wife, Laura. The two had not been in Tolemera since Veranna's coronation, over a year ago. Imperia had required a lot of reorganizing since Dalmar's downfall, and even the Hammerhand needed a break.

Kreida gave Laura and Tomius hugs before sitting down. "You two sure look great after the journey here. Noble life must be agreeing with you."

"Ha!" snorted Tomius. "Organizing the Genazi was easy, by comparison. I assume that you are familiar with the nauseating cycle of council meetings that take place in a castle?"

She held up her hands to ward off some unseen force. "Gag me and beat me, but I refuse to attend more than one a week. I still have a bruise on my leg where Veranna kicked me under the table to wake me up. They were discussing money things and I just could not keep my eyes open. I tried several cups of strong, black tea, but then I could not sleep. It made me really cranky for a few days." She looked around the room, then asked Laura, "Where is the kaffe urn, and where is our haughty little leader?"

Laura chuckled. "Kreida, there is a better chance that the sun will stop shining than that you will change." She pointed at something behind Kreida. "There is your kaffe, and your breakfast as well."

Kreida's eyes popped wide open, and her face took on an angry mien. "What are you...Have you no shame, girl? What will people think when they see you plodding along like some serving wench? I'll get my own food before I see the empress of the empire dolling out rations!"

Veranna smiled in reply, then carefully set Kreida's breakfast on the table. "We have spoken about this before, and I have not changed my mind. If the Creator can serve us such wonderful gifts, I don't see why I can't serve my fellow man, too. Are you arguing that I am somehow above the Creator?"

The young Genazi princess took a quick drink of her kaffe. She yelped as the hot liquid burned her tongue. "Blast! Now look at what you've made me do."

Karsten, seated to her right, leaned forward on the table with both elbows and said, "If you keep your mouth closed the pain will go away more quickly."

She gave him a dirty look and slumped in her chair.

Veranna sat next to Karsten and said grace, and before long a great deal of small talk livened the room. "Karsten, how far along on your chronicles are you?"

A bright twinkle came into his eye as he replied to his fiancée. "The work is progressing quite well. With all of the accounts I have collected regarding your later years at the Academy, and down to the day of your coronation, there is no lack of information about the rise of New Emeraldia." He gave Kreida a quick smirk. "Of course, Kreida's account will need to be edited for language."

Kreida smiled sardonically. "For someone who can't seem to decide on a wedding date, those are mighty boastful words. Tell me, after you actually have the ceremony, are you going to delay getting down to business, and claim that you are simply waiting for the right moment?"

Veranna and Karsten both frowned, but the rest of the table laughed. Yanbre, feigning indignation, said to Karsten, "Sir, how can you accuse such a literate lady of poor choice of words! Why, I'd be willing to bet that you will be able to find at least three whole sentences in her writing."

Kreida threw a pancake at him as laughter erupted again. Veranna held up her hand and asked for them to be quiet, then said, very matter-of-factly, "I will say it once more, since Kreida does not seem to have heard me the previous hundred times. We cannot set an exact date until Tesra returns, and the nobles have needed this time to get their fiefs in order. Plus, they will require a good deal of time for travel since many live at the far ends of the empire." She sat up straight and smiled. "Now that this matter is cleared up I am going to enjoy my breakfast and friends, and then take the rest of the day off for personal needs. Kreida, Laura, would you like to join me for some shopping in town? We could then have lunch at a wonderful café I've found."

Laura agreed enthusiastically, but Kreida sneered. "Are you talking about that hole-in-the-wall with outdoor seating? The one run by the guy named 'Dufuss'?"

Veranna tried to maintain her smile, even as her teeth ground together. "His name is 'Dufer', and deserves our respect. Simply because you are expected to act like a lady is no reason to behave like a barbarian. He is a kindly old man, so don't address him as 'dumpling' any more. Besides, he has some of the best chefs in the empire."

"Fine, fine." Kreida rolled her eyes and stuffed a forkful of eggs into her mouth.

Yanbre seized the moment to change the subject. "Your highness, Karsten and I will be reviewing the trade policies that have been in place for many years, and will give you a briefing tomorrow morning. Your meeting with the various guild leaders is tomorrow afternoon, so you should be well prepared."

"Thank you, Yanbre. Just thinking about having to sift through all of the policies and politics is enough to make me ill. I'm sorry that I put it off for so long."

Karsten put his hand on hers. "Don't worry about it, my love. We'll be with you and make sure that the meeting remains calm and productive. Some of the guildsmen are jealous of the contracts they have had with the throne, and do not want their exclusivity threatened. Not a few grew fat under Weyland, and pretended not to notice his atrocious deeds. They will presume that you will continue with business as usual."

Tomius shook his head. "I've been dealing with the same problem in Imperia. The guild merchants operate from the assumption that they are the only ones who can provide goods and tradesmen. They believe it is their right to have all the business flow through their organizations."

Veranna pushed away from the table and sprang to her feet. "That will just have to wait until tomorrow. Today, I'm not going to worry about anything. I am going to enjoy myself and relax."

An hour later, Veranna, Kreida and Laura casually made their way from store to store. The empress wanted to find some quality fabrics for her wedding gown, while Laura searched for sturdy, but attractive clothing that Tomius could wear through a typical day in court. She and Kreida were a great help to Veranna. They were familiar with weaving and knew how to pick among the fabrics for first-rate work. Accessories and gifts were also on Veranna's list. The two other women were a great help picking the right items for the occasion.

Sitting at an outdoor table of a café, Veranna reviewed the day's finds. "Kreida, I must say that I am very impressed with your knowledge of materials, and your bartering abilities. How did you acquire such skills?"

As Kreida's mouth was stuffed full of her meal, Laura replied for her. "People from outside of our culture often make the assumption that we are illiterate and crude. I suppose that they have seen only one side of us, and can easily make that mistake." She paused and gave Kreida a withering look. "But the reality is far different. Since we were considered to be near outlaws by the Erains, we had to conduct trade through the black markets. The fabric that Tesra used to make your travel clothes was made by us, and common jewelry and insignias, made by our smiths, are highly competitive in the marketplaces."

Kreida sloshed down her food with a swig of ale. "One of the reasons that our fabrics are so much better than the lowland hacks is that our winters are longer and harder. The weavers have a lot of time to concentrate on their work. And, our animals grow strong, thick winter coats that help make for sturdy fabric. The two materials we don't produce, silk and satin, are so expensive that most people see our products as good alternatives."

Veranna just stared wide-eyed at her for a moment. "Kreida, you've been hiding from me the fact that you have a reasonable side. I would never have guessed that you know so much about the markets."

"What good is it when you have knife-work taking up your time? Besides, being a warrior gets me more time around the men. I know a lot about that craft, too."

Veranna rolled her eyes and sighed. "Kreida, I won't ask which market you learned that craft in." She was interrupted when a woman passed by and bowed, while another presented her newborn baby to her.

"If you don't mind, your highness, I've named her after you."

Veranna was taken aback a bit. "Why, madam, I am greatly honored. May I hold her?"

"Yes, your highness."

Veranna pulled back the blanket and looked on the child's face. "She has such pretty blue eyes, madam, and a strong chin. She shall make you very proud."

"She does, your highness, and I hope that she takes after you in more than name only."

Veranna waved the comment away. "I hope that she turns out better. I've got some not-so-honorable weaknesses that require constant attention." She thanked the woman for letting her hold the baby, and then looked at Laura. "Thank the Creator that she did not name the girl 'Kreida,' or we'd have no end of trouble."

Kreida gave her a dirty look. "For someone who has so much trouble simply getting out of bed in the morning, I wouldn't talk."

Enjoying the chance to tease her, Veranna put on an innocent face and said, "At least I know which bed I'll be waking up in."

Kreida responded with a lurid grin. "You're really feeling frustrated, aren't you?"

Laura laughed softly, but Veranna scowled as she tried to think of a good retort. "You...you," but was cut off in mid sentence. An elderly looking man dressed in a rough, gray robe, stood outside the short picket fence surrounding the seating area, his dark, intense eyes fixed on Veranna. He pointed at her and spoke through his bushy mustache and beard.

"Thrice the harvest, then new moon.
Stoke the fire and store the boon.
Days far off, to see their dawn;
Midnight's soul has come to spawn."

Kreida sprang up and pulled out her knife. Before she could blink, the man jabbed his staff into her forearm, hitting a nerve. She dropped the knife and yelped, holding her arm. Laura drew her back from the fence.

Veranna rose slowly and did not take her eyes off the man. She felt little fear, and a strange sense of familiarity nagged at her. "Injuring one of my servants is a crime against the throne. But you have injured my friend, as well. She pulled her knife first, so you had just cause. Now, sir, state your name and business, or you will find yourself giving me just cause."

The man did not flinch. He and Veranna locked eyes for a moment before he said, "Heed the words; negligence is fatal."

Before Veranna could respond, the man turned away and disappeared into the crowd. "Kreida, did you see where the man went? I swear, my eyes must be playing tricks on me; I couldn't keep track of him."

The young Genazi woman's face burned with shame. "Are you kidding? I couldn't even hold on to my own knife, let alone watch the old geezer wander in the square. He surprised me with his speed. He'd better be really quick the next time we meet, or I'll cut off his..."

Laura purposely cleared her throat and gave Kreida a warning glare. "I'll have no more talk like that, young lady, especially since you are a member of the imperial court. Now, let me take a look at that arm."

Veranna could find no trace of the man. As she turned back to her companions, she noticed a group of onlookers wondering what had happened. "Everyone, please..." she had to wait for them to complete their bows, "...please, there is nothing to fear. No one has been hurt or threatened. It was just an unusual exchange with an eccentric..."

A strong voice cutting through the hustle and bustle of the city square interrupted her. "Make way for her highness's servants! Make way!"

One of the guard captains, selected by Yanbre, swiftly led his squad up to the café and bowed. "Your Highness, are you alright? We had a report that someone attacked you."

"I am perfectly fine, Captain Cody. No one attacked me. The Lady Kreida pulled her knife on a man whose style seemed aggressive, but no one was hurt."

"Did you get a good look at the man, your highness?"

"Yes. I don't think I could ever forget how his eyes burned into me. Look for someone middle-aged, with dark brown eyes and bushy gray beard. He was wearing a buckskin top and pants, with a thick gray robe tied around his waist. He also had an oak staff. I repeat: He did nothing wrong except act a bit rude. I just want to talk with him."

The captain bowed, and said, "Yes, your highness," then turned to his men. "You heard what her highness said. Pair up, and start patrolling the streets. This is not a matter for an arrest. Report any sighting immediately. Dismissed."

"That's just great!" Kreida folded her arms across her chest and gave Veranna an angry look. "Not only do you choose a café full of inane niceties, but then you have trysts with degenerate quacks. Anymore little surprises planned for this circus?"

Veranna ignored the outburst and closed her eyes in thought. "I can't recall all of the riddle that the old man said. Do either of you remember it?"

Laura looked at Kreida, then shrugged. "We were so startled that we did not pay much attention. It's a Genazi drawback; we react too quickly before we take in what is going on."

Veranna gave Kreida a hard look. "Yes, I know." Her face changed to a curious frown as something tugged on her dress. A little girl with bright blond hair and blue eyes stood smiling sweetly up at her. "Elly! What are you doing here? I have not seen you for months."

The girl curtsied and beamed with delight. "I know. That's why I wanted to say hello."

"That is very kind of you, Elly. Remember, anytime you want to visit me, all you need to do is come to the castle and ask for me."

"My Mommy says that I shouldn't bother you since you have so many things to do."

"Well, your mother is right. But I can always find time for an old friend." Veranna sat down and placed Elly on her lap. "Have you had lunch?" When the girl shook her head 'yes', Veranna asked, "Well, then, how about joining my friends, and me, for dessert?"

The girl's eyes lit up. "Can my cousin, Alicia, have some, too?"

"Of course. Is she here?"

"Uh huh. Alicia, come over here."

A girl about four years older than Elly carefully made her way between the tables and stopped in front of Veranna, then did a quick curtsy. "Good afternoon, your highness, my ladies." Her brown eyes and hair added to her serious diction and posture. "I hope that you have all recovered from the frightening incident of a few minutes ago."

The three women wondered for a moment if the girl might not be the hostess of a noble event. Veranna replied in kind.

"Thank you very much for your concern, my lady. We are all doing very well. Elly mentioned that the two of you are cousins."

"That is correct, your highness. Our fathers are brothers."

Laura gave her a motherly smile. "We can see that quality runs in your family. Are your parents of noble birth?"

"No, my lady, but they insist that we learn our manners."

Elly's eyes sparkled as she covered her mouth and giggled. Veranna was puzzled. "Why are you giggling, Elly?"

She pointed at Alicia, and said, "I know one of her secrets, when she forgot her manners."

Alicia's face went red, and she frowned. "Elly, this is not the time or..."

Elly blurted out, "She likes a boy, and gave him a kiss, already!"

All three women put hands to their mouths and pretended to gasp. Alicia turned scarlet from the neck up, but could not abandon being the center of attention. Veranna gave her a wink before speaking to Elly.

"I am surprised at you, Elly. That was a big secret. You should tell her that you are sorry for doing that."

The little girl could not help giggling as she apologized.

Alicia rolled her eyes and looked away, but Kreida brought her attention back to the group.

"Hey, kid, is this swain of yours strong and handsome?"

Alicia ignored Elly and answered Kreida's question with forced dignity. "Yes, my lady. I think he's..."

Elly blurted out again. "He's skinny and weird. All he ever wants to do is look at bugs and books. My brother throws him into the pond all the time."

"That's good for him." Kreida flexed her arm muscles. "It'll make him strong."

Veranna gave Kreida a scowl. "Don't say such things. It sounds like the children are picking on the boy. He just has other interests than they."

Kreida looked at her as though she was crazy. "Wake up, girl. The kid is a wimp and needs prodding to get over it. Building strength requires tough measures." She pointed at Alicia. "Don't you go babying him with sweet words of comfort, or he will always be pushed around. Kick his butt, if need be, and get him out of his weakling ways."

Veranna began an angry retort, but Laura raised her voice and called for the owner. "Mr. Dufer, what are you serving for desert, today?"

A plump, balding man in his later sixties came to the table and gave a short bow. "Today's selection, my ladies, is raspberry shortcake."

Veranna took Laura's cue and dropped the previous topic. "That sounds wonderful. Please bring us five servings."

"Yes, your highness."

Before he could leave, Kreida rubbed his belly and said, "Make sure that my helping is as much as you would choose, dumpling."

He frowned at her and headed back to the kitchen.

Veranna sat Elly in another chair, then pulled one up to the table for Alicia. "Kreida, why do you always have to embarrass people?"

"He loves it. He's so fat that he probably does not get any attention from his wife, so he's more than ready to get some from another woman."

"I am surprised that one of those inattentive wives hasn't given you a lesson about flirting with her husband. Treybal may be a patient man, but you should not presume upon his leniency. He may explode with jealousy." Veranna scowled at her when Kreida just laughed in reply. She decided to turn to someone more mature. "Alicia, what is your young man's name?"

"Jeremy."

"That sounds like a strong name. Why don't you bring him up to the castle and let me meet him?"

The girl smiled and shook her head. "I'll try. He's been collecting rock samples, lately, so I don't know exactly when I'll see him next."

"Whenever you have a chance will be fine. Ah, here comes our dessert."

Veranna saw that Mr. Dufer had been more than generous with the helpings, and before long, everyone but Kreida felt stuffed. When Dufer returned with the bill, Veranna snatched it up. "It's my treat, today," and signed it to the castle account.

Stepping onto the sidewalk, Veranna scanned the square for any sign of the old man, and then looked up. She froze in mid-step, her eyes riveted on a strange sight in the sky. The sun shone bright yellow, but its descending rays formed into expanding rings, making it look like a huge funnel, with the sun at the far end. They were of different colors and caused turmoil when they reached the ground.

A fully laden apple tree grew out of the ground and stretched toward the sky. The sun rings struck the tree, shaking it. Many of the apples fell to the ground and were eaten by worms, mice and crows, but a few survived on each major branch and ripened. People from near and far picked and ate them. As they walked away, the paths under their feet blossomed with verdant grass and flowers. The colored circles emanating from the sun landed on the new growth. Some rings brought nurturing, while others seared the plants. One ring drew back after colliding with the tree. It spread out and began consuming the sky, turning darker as it radiated in all directions.

Suddenly, Veranna's foot touched down on the sidewalk. She nearly fell onto the stones due to the interrupted contact. Laura caught her arm and steadied her.

"Veranna, are you alright? You look as though you've just awoken from a deep sleep."

"Yes...no, I mean, I don't know what just happened. I was looking around the square for the old man, and then saw the sun emitting strange light. It was very similar to what happened on the day of battle against Dalmar. I must have seen a vision that lasted for a few minutes, but when I came out of it, I had only completed one step. It is very odd."

"That figures," quipped Kreida. "You can't satisfy a man, sleep halfway through the morning, serve food like a tavern wench, and give a girl bad advice about her wimpy friend. Is it any wonder you'd have weird visions?"

"Or friends, for that matter." Veranna felt annoyed with Kreida's attempt at humor, but was too distracted by the vision to engage her in an exchange. "Let's return to the castle; I will share with you the contents of the vision, then."

She gave Elly a quick kiss, and Alicia a polite handshake before heading back to the castle at a brisk pace. Both the old man and the vision filled her with such a sense of foreboding that she could think of nothing else. *After all these months of hard work, I finally take a day of rest and have two bizarre events. What is going on under the light of the sun?*

CHAPTER THREE

BOARD WITH THE PAST

T he city of Clarens, in Langraine, pulsed with activity. Traders, merchants and financiers shared the public spaces with farmers selling their wares and musicians performing songs. An overcast sky threatened rain, but the people paid it no mind.

Tesra, the only Mother of the Academy known to have survived Duke Weyland's attack on the school, was feeling her age in spite of the day's festivities. She had returned to Clarens to revive the Academy, bringing a handful of the students back after their enslavement under Weyland, and the former emperor, Dalmar Gelangweil. For over a year they scurried like ants to get the institution running again, and with the help of four freed Sisters, she was able to announce the graduation of three students. Leighana, Didi and a young lady named Anita had passed their required advancement exams, but due to their age and the lack of faculty to instruct on the necessary spectrum of topics, they would have to wait longer than usual to earn the title of Sister. Four more years of instruction and instructing, and they would receive their Sisterhood rings.

The aging Mother felt uneasy for no reason that she could pinpoint. The expectations of the young ladies echoed through the Academy halls, and visiting dignitaries were full of thanks and enthusiasm that the school would be supplying qualified personnel for their offices. None of the surrounding exuberance alleviated her sense of apprehension. *Maybe I'm simply unsure of the quality of the work done since we returned. Oh, Veranna, dearer than daughter, how I wish you were here!*

She strode through the main entry and was greeted with loud cheering and applause. Theodore Lenarde, Baron of Langraine, bowed and shook her hand. She had gotten used to people bowing to her, and knew that it would be useless to try and stop it. As the adopted mother of the empress, she was treated as royalty, also.

Soldiers of the young Army of Langraine stood along the walkway leading to the podium, and Rockhounds occupied the first row of seats brought in for the graduation ceremony. The men were battle-hardened veterans, and lent an air of dignity to the proceedings.

Tesra reached the podium and bowed to the crowd. She estimated that there were at least fifteen hundred people sitting and standing along the open area between the building and gate. After letting the crowd quiet down, she turned and bowed to the two-dozen young ladies seated together to her left.

"Dear ladies of the Academy," and then to the dignitaries, "...my lord, Baron Lenarde, and all the rest of our distinguished guests and fellow citizens, allow me to express, on behalf of this ancient institution, the utmost gratitude for your generous support. Your time, monies and skills have been invaluable for getting us up and running. The Creator has certainly been most gracious in His supply of wonderful people to aid us in this time of great need. May He be praised for His mercy and kindness."

She turned and made a sweeping gesture toward the buildings behind her. Looking up, the red and black tiles of the roofs caught her eye. They needed tending, but only for the sake of appearance. They were as sound as when first installed two millennia ago. "These buildings have housed and trained some of the finest minds ever to have graced the empire. Our schools for public instruction vie for our graduates to join their staffs, and noble lords seek them for their courts. These are amazing testimonies to the quality that this Academy has been able to achieve. The greatest example of this is our dear empress, Veranna. She has expressed her love and thanks for this school many times, and no less are her thanks for the people of Clarens.

"You who are graduating to the preliminary level of Sisterhood know the gravity of such a position. You will enjoy great respect throughout the empire, but only because you will be expected to provide top-notch quality in all that you do. Your riches will not be gold or status, but a sharp mind bent on serving your Creator. This can only happen as you serve those whom He has created, with the gifts He has supplied.

"Our work of restoration is far from through, and we can be thankful that we are, at least, on the path to recovery. It will take years to replace that which has been lost, and some things can never be replaced. As Sisters you shall have the heavy burden of setting the standards for years to come, and will be pressed to the limits. Let us hope that…"

The city alarm bells suddenly clanged in furious warning. Smoke billowed up from the walls of the city, and some of the bells suddenly ceased. Screams echoed down the streets, and people ran for cover.

Baron Lenarde jumped out of his seat and ran for his carriage. The soldiers mounted their horses and formed a protective wall around him as he sped for the City Center. Total confusion gripped the crowd, and they looked to Tesra for guidance. The Rockhounds went to work quieting them down and maintaining order.

Tesra froze in place as the reason for the alarms became visible. Barely audible, she gasped a prayer. "Dear Creator, have mercy upon us." Her eyes were as wide as saucers, and she screamed, "Dragons!! Get inside, now! Leighana, Didi, get them inside, right away! Rockhounds, to me!"

Many thought she must be joking, but a blast of red fire over their heads sent them scrambling into the building through any opening they could find.

Six red dragons circled in the air above the school, roaring with the delight of attack. One of the Rockhounds, a young man of less than thirty years, drew an arrow and fired upward. The arrow bounced off of a thick scale on the dragon's neck. The huge beast then dove straight down and spewed a line of fire that consumed him. Terrible was his cry of pain, sending the people into an unruly panic.

The dragons attacked anything that moved. Blast after blast slammed into the roof and walls of the school buildings, but they had no affect. The dragons increased the terror factor by chanting a poem of dire cruelty.

Sharp be tooth, and claw, and nail;
Eyes that bore and make hearts fail.
Tails that swing, and fear inspire.
We'll burn your bones with raging fire!

Two of the dragons dove down and flew close to the ground. By the time they beat their wings to rise high into the air again, five of the people had been scooped into their bellies.

Tesra tried to get the crazed crowd inside more quickly, even using a stick to prod them along. Fireballs landed all around, setting trees, bushes and grass ablaze. At the far end of the lawn, one of the hideous beasts landed and began hopping toward the entrance. It fired anything that would burn, and raced to catch the people at the rear of the crowd.

The elderly Mother of the Academy grabbed a bow from a Rockhound, then held out her hand for an arrow. After a couple of seconds, she gave him a stern look and growled, "Quit dozing, and give me an arrow, or we will be dragon fodder!"

The man hesitated, so Tesra snatched the quiver from his shoulder. She understood his reluctance to use them, for they were ancient, tempered-steel shafts used for ceremonial purposes. But ceremony would just have to submit to necessity. She drew back on the string, sighted, and then let the shaft fly.

The dragon was so absorbed in reckless destruction that it never knew what hit him. The arrow penetrated deep into its eye, and the monster exploded in a huge fireball. The blast knocked out a section of the school's wall, and shattered windows as far as three blocks away. A putrid, sulfurous smell resulted from the flames, gagging many people.

Tesra's grim voice could be heard over the cheering for the dragon's demise. "Blessed be the Creator! Rockhounds, to me!" The last of the crowd jammed in to the building, allowing the Hounds a chance to assist her. "Use your metal arrows and shoot for the eyes, or the hollow of the breast. Quickly! They will be angry, now."

Sure enough, the red beasts ceased their taunting and began roaring curses in their own foul tongue. Tesra stood where they could see her; she wanted to draw them in close for the archers. Three dragons plummeted toward her. "Hold until the last moment, when they can't avoid being hit." She directed the Hounds to fire simultaneously, with one group of three firing at the dragon on the left, one group on the one to the right, while she took the one in the middle.

Streams of fire poured forth from the dragons' nostrils, causing sweat to run into the eyes of the Hounds. Tesra wiped her brow on her sleeve and called out, "One...two...three...fire!"

Away flew the arrows. The dragon on the left, and the one in the middle, both exploded into huge fireballs. The dragon on the right pulled up sharply and avoided the arrows, beating its wings hard to gain altitude and exposing its belly to its enemies. Tesra ignored the heat from the fireballs and quickly drew another arrow. The dragon had just cleared the top of the buildings and was relaying information to its fellows, when Tesra sent her arrow upward. It pierced between the plates of armored hide and sank deep into its heart. The fire of its explosion lit the sky brighter than the sun. Another of the dragons was so close that it, too, burst into flames. The last dragon let out a deafening roar of frustration, and then flew away to the east.

The alarm bells ceased, so Tesra and the Rockhounds inspected the buildings and grounds, while others marked the areas where people had been killed. All that remained of the victims was a fine ash.

Tesra tried to recall all she had ever heard about dragons, when she saw two young men starting to shovel the ashes. A memory crystallized in her mind. "Wait!" They halted as she made her way over to them. "Ancient lore tells us that breathing the dust of those burned by dragons will have serious consequences. They used to call it 'spawn fever', since those affected would suffer high fevers, and their skin would harden into thick scales. Insane brutality preceded death, and many had to be killed to keep them from rampaging through a crowd. If left to themselves, they transformed into dragon spawn."

The two young men looked at one another, then backed away from the ashes. Before they could run off, Tesra put a hand on each man's shoulder.

"Do not worry; all you need do is sprinkle water onto the ashes, scrape them up with the underlying dirt, and put it in a bag with no holes. Throw it onto a hot fire and let it burn. It will be harmless, then."

She walked along the front of the buildings, inspecting all of the areas hit by dragon fire. Anything made of wood was destroyed, but the brickwork suffered virtually no damage. Moving hastily through the entryway, she dolled out instructions to the Rockhounds and Leighana, telling them to clear the grounds of all unnecessary people.

"I am heading for the roof; I want to see if it has been damaged."

A young Rockhound, named Joel, snorted, "Are you kidding? The dragons were blasting away at the roof constantly."

"Get busy with your duties, before I start blasting away at you."

The lightning on her brow sent him running to assist the jam of people exiting the building.

Staring at the roof she could see little damage , and the char scraped away easily. Support beams below the tiles showed no sign of damage, and were not even warm, while the surrounding trees and wooden buildings had disintegrated without taking direct blasts.

Two hours later she was in Baron Lenarde's office. "Dragons have not been reported in the Lands for over two thousand years, Ted. Most of us had adopted the notion that they were creatures of myth, or poetic devices. Now, reality has stepped in and removed all of these flawed theories, as well as a number of our fellow citizens."

The baron sat across the desk with his hands covering his face, and sighed. "It would have been far worse if you had not been here. As it is, the gate tower is destroyed, and the people are wondering if today is a sign of the end of the world."

"I understand their fear, but it is misplaced. The dragons are a sign of a beginning, not an end. It would be more precise to say that they signal a revival. Veranna has taken the Emerald Throne and begun the restoration of Emeraldia. That empire was one of divine blessing, but also one that the lord of evil attacked relentlessly. Veranna's ancestors held evil in check by exercising the rare gifts given them by the Creator, and established policies of piety and knowledge. The Academies were instituted for such purposes, and play an integral role in defending the good.

"The dragons were sent to destroy the Academy. Whoever sent them has not done their homework, though. The buildings are made of what the ancients called 'dragon stone'. Now we know why; only exposed wood and metal were damaged."

"Did you know of this material beforehand? We could have used it on other buildings."

"I just found out about it after the attack today. The secret archives in the Academy record many things, and it took me over an hour to dig up information about the dragon stone material. It was developed by the ancient genii because of all the problems they were having at that time with dragons. It looks like both sides have a lot of catching up to do."

Lenarde rose from his chair and came around to the front of his desk. "I hope that we have enough time to refit our buildings with this dragon stone before anymore of those beasts return. But you have come here for another reason, I take it."

"Correct. I must leave immediately for Tolemera. I need to take the information about the dragon stone to Veranna, and see if we can't decipher how to make it. The documents are full of strange symbols and procedures that my feeble brain won't be able to work out in time."

The baron chuckled. "Really? Then how do you explain the total drubbing you gave me in our last game of chess?"

"Well, that's only due to familiarity." She gave him a satisfied smile. "This is a technical matter that I am not well versed in, Ted. Veranna's mind is growing every day and can assimilate new information much more rapidly. I'm hoping that you can spare me a unit of cavalry, along with some Rockhounds, to speed me to Tolemera. You can't refit your buildings unless we figure out how to make the stone."

"You are a demanding old biddy, but I suppose there's really not much choice. We have to prepare for trouble. I'll notify the Rockhounds to be ready to go at dawn, tomorrow. Since Treybal now serves the empress, Brian Bilmerger has taken over the leadership of the Hounds. He's a good man."

"Oooo, and he's very handsome, too! Sounds like a good arrangement. Have one of them pick me up at Charle's and Kate's house, first thing in the morning."

"As you wish. Do you still want to get together, after dinner, for a game?"

"Yes; it'll take my mind off of all these serious matters. See you at sixth watch."

Back at the Academy, she sorted and selected files to take with her to Tolemera. In spite of the pressing circumstances, she felt great joy at the thought of seeing her beloved Veranna, the empress who was like her very own daughter.

Baron Lenarde was in top form for the chess game. His patience had grown with age, and he was able to restrain himself from risky, speculative attacks. Preoccupied with the events of the day, and not used to Ted's subtle maneuvering, Tesra found her most powerful piece, the queen, in an inescapable trap. She looked up at Ted, shaking her head slowly in disbelief.

"That should not have been possible. I can't believe that I was so careless." She offered her hand, which he shook with understated satisfaction.

"Tesra, its been a long time since I've enjoyed a moment like this. You will join me in a bit of celebration, won't you?"

Still in disbelief, she agreed without really thinking about it, while Ted called for a round of brandy to be served for all in the lounge. He raised his glass in salute, then downed it in one swift gulp. Tesra sipped from her glass, but couldn't take her eyes from the board. Her queen stood alone, attacked on all sides. She could see no way to extricate the Lady safely. A cold chill ran up her spine as an image of Veranna formed in her mind's eye. Seated on the Emerald Throne, killers poised to strike and drench the dais with her blood. She had no way to escape.

"Tesra; Tesra, are you alright? You look so pale. Has losing affected you that much?"

"No!" She shoved her chair back and rose in a huff, but caught hold of herself when she saw the hurt and concern on his face. "I'm sorry, Ted, for being so gruff. The dragon attack still concerns me, since I know it is only the beginning of woes. I expect that the easterners loosed them upon us, and are readying for war. We must not be slow in our own preparations. I advise you to build defensive positions along the harbor entries, and begin monitoring the ports.

"The eastern lands are vast, and made up of many tribes and kingdoms. Yen Kragar was well on his way to consolidating them, but it looks like LeAnre y'Dob, and her brother, have taken over the task. I hope I'm wrong, but I would not be surprised if they sent a fleet of warships south, around the Prongs of the Continent, to attack the coastlands to the west. That would be horrible, truly horrible. They know no mercy, only lust; we must fight with everything we have."

She looked at the chessboard once more before leaving, and Ted tried to calm her anxieties.

"Even though you resigned the game, there was still a lot of play left in the position. You might yet have found a way to reach parity."

"You are too good a player to let me do that, Ted. All that I'd accomplish would be a futile carnage before a crushing defeat. Besides, its late, and I need to rise early, tomorrow."

The baron gave her a hug before she departed, and promised to give her a return match whenever she wished.

But all she could think of was Veranna, surrounded by vicious enemies, and no escape in sight.

CHAPTER FOUR

SILENT ASSASSINS; LOUD AND CLEAR

The Empress of the Emeraldian Empire sat back on her throne, patiently waiting for the Merchant Guild accountant to finish his report. She tried to concentrate on the numbers he listed, but his monotone voice and dull cadence made it difficult. When he finally sat down, she wondered if it was late evening. A quick look at the eastern windows dispelled the notion.

"Thank you, Master Scriboe, for your report. It was very...thorough."

The other fifteen men and women wagged their heads and downed generous amounts of kaffe. Sitting in a half-circle, not far from the steps of the dais, they waited for Veranna to continue.

"It is obvious that this year's harvest has been the best that any of us can remember, and that the banks are recording greater deposits than they could have ever hoped. Lord Eifer, how do you explain these results, and do you see this as a singularity, or a continuing trend?"

The fat, balding man waved his hand dismissively and failed to look at her. For almost fifty years he had been involved with trade, and given a noble title by the former Duke of Loreland. His influence was felt throughout the empire, and beyond.

"As for the harvest, you must keep in mind that there are many factors that must converge at the right time in order to bring about a good crop. The idiot farmers may think that they have done something wonderful, but really, its mostly decent weather.

"Many of the people feel optimistic about the future now that Duke Weyland is gone, and believe that it is a good time to invest their money in the banks. They also fancy that they know something about business, and have rushed into setting up their own enterprises. I am sure that most will be begging from the gutters before long, especially since the guilds control a good number of the trades and market outlets."

Karsten and Yanbre both edged forward on their seats, ready to give the man an earful about his attitude, but Veranna restrained them with a quick glance.

"Are you saying, Lord Eifer, that the harvest is merely a fluke, and that the people are so stupid that they don't realize they are making a mistake trying to set up their own businesses?"

"Essentially."

"Have you calculated the consequences should even one in ten of them prove successful?"

"No, but then, it really wouldn't be worth the effort. The guilds will see to increasing the economy."

"Ah, I see. And these guilds, they all function under your auspices?"

He yawned, and then, in a very patronizing tone, said, "Yes. The guild structure has served us quite well."

Anger flashed in Karsten's eyes, and he rebuked Eifer, sharply.

"You will address the empress as 'Your Highness' or 'My Lady'."

Eifer's eyes widened in contempt for a second, and then he resumed his flat stare at the floor. "As you wish...Your Highness."

Veranna was as surprised at Karsten's tone at Eifer, and gained boldness from his support. "Lord Eifer, does it not make sense to encourage the people in their endeavors? I get the impression that you want to control everything in the business sector."

"That is not correct...Your Highness. My colleagues, and I, simply want to ensure that there is a high level of order in these matters. Quality is the result of standardization."

"Possibly, but it can also lead to suffocation. Weyland pursued such policies, and you have profited by them to the detriment of the people. You have become fascists if you think that your own group is the only one with the necessary skills to administer the markets. I'll have you know that just yesterday I visited several of these new businesses and found their goods and services to be excellent. Are you going to sit there and tell me that they must submit to you if they wish to remain in business?"

Eifer sighed, a teacher having to tolerate a slow, petulant student. "Not to me personally...Your Highness...but to the guilds. We've been at these tasks for hundreds of years. The wheel has been turning adequately, so why add another spoke?"

From in back of the group, a man stood and waved his hand for attention. "Your Highness, may I speak?"

Veranna beckoned him forward, noting his weather-beaten skin, and hands covered with thick calluses. His clothing was not fine, but strong and practical.

"Do you have something to add to this discussion, Mister...?"

"Gellint is my name, Your Highness, Stivant Gellint. I am here to represent the independent businesses that this man, here..."

"You refer to Lord Eifer?"

"Yes, Your Highness. Well, he wants to squash us before we can get going. If we don't join the guilds, he, and his henchmen, sees to it that we don't have a chance. Some of us have had our tools confiscated and our shops vandalized by his cutthroats."

Karsten and Yanbre could feel Veranna's anger rising with every second. Gellint's sincerity contrasted sharply with Eifer's duplicity.

"Lord Eifer, are these charges true?"

"I've never met this commoner before, but I can tell you that my men have done nothing illegal to him, or to any of his group. I can say that guild representatives stopped some illegal dealings, for we have had authority to regulate trades for many years."

"Who granted you this authority?"

"The late duke's father."

"One moment, please." She leaned over and conversed first with Karsten, then with Yanbre. Sitting straight and tall on her throne, she pronounced, "From this moment on, the guilds shall not have the authority to police non-members. Competition in the marketplace will be the standard, not coercion. All confiscated materials shall be returned to their rightful owners, immediately.

Failure to do so will result in criminal prosecution. So say I, Veranna, Empress of Emeraldia. You are dismissed."

Eifer's face went scarlet. He bowed hastily before leading his group out the doorway. But Gellint stayed and thanked Veranna.

"Master Gellint, I am sorry that you and your associates have gone through such troubles with the guilds. There are many good ones, but these seem to have lost sight of their purpose. May the Creator grant you much happiness as you strive to achieve your goals. Go in peace."

Hat in hand, he bowed low and left the room.

"Whew!" The young empress stood and stretched her limbs, then gave Karsten a hug. "I thought Eifer was going to pop a seam when you chastised him about etiquette."

The young lord, raised by the Genazi, looked into her eyes and smiled. "He's not used to having anyone tell him anything. Under Weyland, he had a free hand to do as he pleased. All the more so since the two of them are consumed by power and greed. I couldn't stand to see him mistreat you in that way."

In his sardonic manner, Yanbre said, "It is fortunate that there were no pieces of wood nearby when you spoke with him; they would have burst into flames. I wonder, however, how it is that they feel so bold as to challenge your will, and be insulting as they do so."

"Ha, ha, ha, ha!"

The craggy, cackling laughter ripped through the court. From behind a large column stepped the strange man Veranna had encountered the day before. Yanbre called for the guards and drew his sword.

Using a staff, the strange man effortlessly relieved the guards of their spears and knocked the wind out of them, sending them to the floor. More guards rushed in from the corridor, but Veranna ordered them to stand down before they could engage the man. She stepped to the edge of the dais and addressed him.

"You, sir, have now injured my servants on two occasions. Yesterday, I was disposed to great leniency since you obviously meant no harm, and were simply defending yourself. Today, you have violated the rules of the court and used a weapon against my guards. I will have an explanation of your conduct, and judge your case now."

A mocking smile came to the man's face as he sauntered toward the dais. "Oh, that was good, very good! I haven't heard such royal style in ages. As to your guards, the only thing injured is their pride."

She silently agreed with the man, but spoke for the benefit of the guards. "Their only failure was in misjudging your abilities. I will not be so slow, and command you to announce your name and purpose. Otherwise, we will jail you until you reveal them."

After performing an exaggerated bow, the man chuckled. "Yes, Your Highness. My name is Denny Strorfer, and what I've been doing is trying to get some sense into your head."

"All you've given me is a riddle, and two incidents involving my servants."

Strorfer rolled his eyes and groaned. "For someone trained at the Academy, and mentored by the great Tesra, you are pretty thick at times."

Veranna smiled at the remark. "You sound like her in ways, and my intuition tells me you mean no harm. Forgive me if I am slow in grasping your sparse messages, but you don't look like someone of depth."

"Shoddy clothes, shoddy mind?"

She laughed. "No, it's more like shoddy clothes, deranged mind."

They all laughed, dispelling some of the tension.

"Now, Mister Strorfer, what is your purpose here at court?"

Laying aside all mirth, he stood straight and pointed his finger at her. "To wake you up!"

His words shook the ancient hall, leaving a gnawing silence. Veranna felt no fear of the man, but his words filled her with foreboding.

"Wake us up? To what?"

"To your sloth and ignorance."

Feeling a touch indignant, Veranna's posture and voice became more regal than she realized. "I'll have you know that we have been working night and day to bring order to the Lands. Lords Karsten and Yanbre have been tireless in their research and training, helping us to learn from the past, and prepare for the future."

The man's voice was flat, as he said, "Commendable."

"I take it you don't approve."

"Of course, I do! But you are so limited in your view of what to do." He held up his hand for silence as she started to respond. "Come down to the floor level; I'll show you what I mean."

She hesitated a moment, then stepped down from the dais, against Yanbre's protest. Strorfer snapped his fingers at one of the guards, motioning for him to give Veranna his staff.

"Do you know how to handle that?"

"Yes. Tesra, whom you seem to know, was my trainer."

"Good. Remember her teaching. En guard!"

Strorfer jabbed his staff at her chest. She blocked the blow and swung at his shins. He simultaneously blocked her blow and countered toward her face. Only the fact that she had learned proper form saved her face from being struck, her staff's end being positioned exactly to ward off his attack.

"Hold!" he cried, and stepped back. "Why did not my staff strike you?"

"Obviously, my own staff was in place to deflect yours."

Strorfer's left hand squeezed into a hard fist as he said, "Now, you've got it! Heed the riddle."

He turned and moved through the doors before they realized it. Yanbre ran down the center aisle and into the hallway, then returned.

"He's gone."

Karsten put his arms around Veranna, and lifted her chin until their eyes met. "My love, are you alright?"

She felt as though she was in a fog bank.

"Yes...yes, I'm alright. I am just trying to figure out what Strorfer was talking about. He obviously thinks it very important for us to know. The staff lesson has a far deeper meaning than we realize." She adjusted her gown and straightened her hair. "I need to sit and think, Karsten. Would you mind looking through the census lists for anyone named 'Strorfer'?"

"Not at all, my love. I'm doubtful of finding anything in those lists, but I'll let you know at lunchtime." He gave her a kiss and headed for the archives.

Hearing Yanbre checking his weapons, she turned and asked his opinion of Strorfer.

"He is certainly strange in his manner, but I sense no hostility toward you or anyone else. I would have to describe him as eccentric, similar to some of the best artists I've encountered. One thing is clear: He has a sharp mind."

"That is my conclusion, as well. Tell your guards that we do not see him as a threat, but that we just want them to keep an eye open as far as his whereabouts."

"Yes, Your Highness. You know, he reminds me of someone."

"Who?"

"You."

CHAPTER FIVE

INN THE KNOW

Two weeks after leaving Clarens, Tesra stepped through the doorway of the Red Tailor, in Grandshire. Her imperial escort went for lodging in Duke Heilson's castle, but she wanted the company of old friends.

"Tesra!" An ugly hulk of a man rose from his seat in the dining area and gave her a hug. "It's wonderful to see 'ya, but I thought you were gonna be in Clarens to get the school up and running again."

She patted his burly chest and sat down at one of the dining tables.

"Jerry, I am just passing through on my way to Tolemera. Some things came up that I wish to discuss with Veranna. Besides, she is due to be married, and won't have the ceremony until I arrive. I imagine that she is feeling desperate after waiting all this time."

Another woman, Rita, wife of the innkeeper, entered the dining area and noticed Tesra. She hurried over to give her a hug.

"Hello, Tesra. It's been quite a while since you stopped here. How have you been?"

"Oh, as well as can be expected at my age. The Academy is now operational, so I figured that I'd best be getting back to Tolemera for Veranna's wedding."

Rita's eyes glowed with excitement. "I received an invitation a couple of months ago, along with a personal note from Veranna, asking me to be in her wedding party. I've already got everything packed and ready to go. May I travel with you?"

Concern flashed across Tesra's face, and Rita wondered if she had disturbed her in some way.

"Tesra, what is wrong?"

After a moment's consideration, Tesra motioned for them to move closer. "I am concerned for your safety, my dear. I would love to have you as a traveling companion, but it could prove to be very dangerous."

Rita looked at her face and saw no indication of humor. "What are you talking about? We have not had any trouble since Veranna ascended the throne."

"The two are somehow related."

"Tesra, you are being obscure. We might be able to help if we know what is troubling you."

The wizened Mother of the Academy let out a deep sigh, and quietly said, "Clarens, and the Academy, especially, have been attacked by red dragons."

The only thing that the other two could say was, "You're kidding."

"I am deadly serious. A number of people were killed, and damage to the city gates was extensive. One of the dragons survived and flew away, most likely to report on our handling of the situation.

"Do you recall any of the stories of strange events following the battle with Dalmar's forces? While there was a lot of exaggeration on some points, others were literally true. LeAnre y'Dob, whom you met in this very room, is the co-regent of the Koosti, and summoned a black dragon to fly her away from the field of battle. The Koosti are as merciless as a school of starving piranhas, and practice the black arts."

Rita shook her head and held up her hands. "Wait a moment. Are you saying that dragons are not just creatures of the imagination, to scare people?"

"Indeed, I am. I have seen and killed some."

"But, Tesra, if what you say is true, where have these creatures been for the last two thousand years?"

Tesra shifted into her academic mentoring mode. "That is a fair question, and one that has occupied some of the greatest minds in our history. Have you ever imagined yourself in a different set of circumstances than you actually experienced? Of course, we all have. Were they necessarily impossible? No, for when you make a decision and do something, you set in motion an entire set of reactions, and you have no control over many of those consequences. This is due to the very nature of reality.

"Now, suppose that you have a number of reality's strictures removed, such as time, place, or the force that pulls things to the ground. You would be able to do things that others, in this world, would say were incredible or miraculous. The dragons may have been sealed up behind the Curtain of Power or prevented from entering this land for some reason by the Creator. Kreida, in fact, witnessed this on the battlefield, when Veranna suddenly appeared, out of nowhere, right by her side."

Rita rested an elbow on the table and grabbed a glass of wine from a passing servant's tray. After a long swig, she looked at Jerry and shrugged her shoulders.

"I haven't heard that account before. Most of the stories had to do with Veranna's uncanny fighting abilities."

"Yeah," grunted Jerry, "the duke's men were totally amazed at her speed and precision."

"And so they should be." Tesra turned to a serving girl and requested a cup of kaffe before continuing. "Veranna is the key to all of the change that has been taking place, whether good or ill. Maybe you've noticed that the black markets are not able to undersell the official markets. Lower taxes and a sense of life have encouraged the people to pursue business ventures of their own."

Rita shook her head in agreement. "That is true. Our profit margin has increased, allowing us to hire a couple of extra workers. I get to take the evenings off, now."

"You are looking well, dear." Tesra then lowered her voice. "But, Veranna is also the reason for the presence of new evils. During the battle with Dalmar, LeAnre led the practitioners of the black arts in forcing Veranna to open the curtain to the higher realms, where the fearsome creatures dwell. LeAnre, and her minions, could not do this on their own. Only Veranna had the authority to do so. The Creator, for the sake of improving life in this world, granted her forebears this authority. Foolishness led to this power being used to summon evil creatures.

"Who knows what will happen next? Along with the evil ones, many good things will have come through, also."

"Like what?" asked Rita.

"If the ancient records be true, then great minds, as well as warriors, will rise up in the Lands. Conditions may change rapidly in this world." She looked out the window at all the people, horses and wagons moving along. "If Veranna, and her line, were to be extinguished, this world would be under a dark cloud of evil that would have no end in sight. We would be worse than the savage eastern realms. They do not realize it, but Veranna helps to keep them from insane evil. Look at the Sudryni. For centuries they hated the Emeraldians, and practiced darkness. Veranna's noble and sympathetic ways brought change to them. The Baroness, Camilla, swore fealty to Veranna, and has begun the transformation of her culture. Veranna helped bring the light of the Creator into their hearts and minds."

After emptying her kaffe cup, Tesra asked one of the serving girls to hail a carriage. Rita asked Tesra if she would be staying in the city for a while, and the older woman shook her head no.

"I may just be staying the night, and leave early in the morning. Please have someone wake me at the sixth hour. For now, I must pay the duke a visit and fill him in on what is happening. None of us can afford to walk in the darkness; we must go forth under the light of the sun."

CHAPTER SIX

PLANS INCONCEIVABLE

Candle and firelight flickered off the limestone walls of the ancient Koosti palace. Streams and slaves, whose blood still stained the chalky stone, had carved it out over the centuries. But time had left the builders of the main corridors in oblivion.

The evening sun sent its orange glow down one of the many-mirrored shafts to light up the inner chamber of LeAnre y'Dob's section of the palace. Her bright, bronze skin blended with the light, making her virtually indistinguishable from any other object in the room. Only her eyes stood out, aflame with blue-hot anger.

Pacing back and forth, she suddenly fell into one of the divans in the center of the room, and pounded her fists into the cushions.

"It cannot be! It must not! I have not come so far only to fail at the crux. It is my destiny to rule, and rule I will!"

Kaesean, her long-time lover and servant, sat and put his arm around her.

"LeAnre, my Great Lady, do not fear. You shall have as many children as you wish. It is all in the Dark One's will. He has his own schedule and is simply waiting for the right moment, when it will be the most effective."

"Oh, shut up, you fool! Don't you think I know all that already? The Dark One revealed it to me, the High Priestess, not to a lower-class brute such as you."

Kaesean's eyes flashed with anger, but he held his tongue. He'd seen her in this mood before, and knew that it would subside in due time. Then would come the gifts, and most likely another step up in the social hierarchy.

"My love, what did your brother say to you?"

Glaring at the floor, she spat back at him, "Only what I'd have said in his place." She closed her eyes and calmed her breathing. "He says that if I do not conceive within a month's time, he will be forced to command me to his own bed and assure the elders that I am capable of bearing a child. Otherwise, all of my inheritance will pass to him by default, and one of his daughters will be installed as High Priestess. He'd have no choice but to keep me in his harem as a lowly servant, or sacrifice me to the dragons for my shortcomings."

Kaesean hugged her close and spoke soothingly. "My love, I am confident that everything will turn out well. You will rule the Koosti with a mighty hand, as will your descendants. Tell me what you would have me do."

She cleared her mind and contemplated her options.

"Everything depends on being able to conceive a child. You will have no other duties until then. Every day, you will be attending me in my bed. When you are spent and need rest, you will bring my harem men to me. And, I shall not color my skin again until I am pregnant."

He stared at her in disbelief. "That is the mark of our people. You could be slain as a traitor if you are found out! And if you have any more challenges, your skin may be weak."

She sighed and shook her head. "I am not worried about the challengers. My prowess has kept them down to less than one per week. The last woman was the best by far, and gave me a thrilling contest. My skin suffered little damage from her nails, even though I felt great pain. In spite of that, I was able to break her back precisely, so that she could not move, but still felt my knife as I cut out and consumed her liver. Her eyes were also firm and tasty."

Kaesean shook his head in agreement. "Yes, she died well, and did her family great honor. I've noticed that you haven't received any more challenges since then."

"That's right, and my eyes and liver will stay with me until I die. But I will pass my strength and vision on to those from my own body, not to my brother's."

"I can't wait until the day comes when you meet the Emeraldian woman, and take her liver."

"Neither can I, but my brother wants to use her for a while, first. After I've crushed her soul, she will long for me to dispatch her to our Dark Lord. She won't die like our own cultured women, for she is a barbarian. All the more reason to make her death very slow."

They sat facing the fire, dreaming of the day when they would realize their goals. After several minutes, LeAnre lay back on the divan and pulled Kaesean close to her.

"Come, my darling; you must help me conceive. When you are through, I want you to speak with the army commanders and see how long before we may embark to take Emeraldia. But, before you go," and here she gave him a hard stare, "you need to send in three guards. I must conceive, or all of our plans will be mere mist."

Ambition left little room for jealousy, but Kaesean still felt a twinge of insult that she would be using other men to attain her goals. Such was their culture that he dismissed the emotion easily. And he did not want to risk a deadly, or debilitating, challenge match. If LeAnre failed, so did he.

The army commanders assured him that they would be ready in a month, and that their covert units had already departed for key targets throughout Emeraldia. The barbarian Emeraldians would be without their leaders, and before long, without their land.

He signaled a slave to bring his cart and run him over to his home. His concubines had not had the pleasure of his company for a couple of days, and day dreaming about running his blade through Emeraldians had aroused his sensual appetites. He just wished that he could be there to see the assassins annihilate their enemy's leaders. Hopefully, he would receive a detailed account of the killings from the associates they'd located in that strange land. It would be so glorious.

CHAPTER SEVEN

CROSS CURRENTS

Lord Eifer sat in a plush chair not far from the room's fireplace. Surrounded by gilded candlesticks and tables, he enjoyed a lifestyle more opulent than many of the nobles could boast. Not only were his belongings expensive, they were exotic, too. Teacups from Rumia, drapes from Chewl, and the Beeyay rugs gave the impression that the far corners of the world had come together on Eifer's estate.

His servants were as varied and exotic as the accessories. A tall, sensually built woman with wheat blond hair, named Raeki, was busy serving Gelani tea, and her bright yellow eyes, with vertical pupils, quickly scanned every person in the room to see if they had need of drink or dessert. Another slave, a short, petite girl with fire-red hair and soft, slanted black eyes, moved behind the chairs, ready with cushions, pipes, tobacco and brandy.

The elderly businessman didn't care so much for his guests as he did for business. He had learned long ago that a rich setting and treatment could sway even seasoned merchants, especially if they believed they would share those riches.

Addressing the seven guests sitting in a circle around a low table, Eifer barely controlled his anger.

"This girl comes out of nowhere and expects me to just sit and listen to her drivel about business matters. She did not even have sense enough to demand a share in the gross incomes of the guilds. "Putting on a sick caricature of a smile, he mockingly said, "She wants us to be nice and fair to everyone, and to operate according to these rules by our own choice. Or, she will enforce them by imperial edict."

Zelfer Gorig, a tall, lean man with graying brown hair, set down his pipe and grabbed another pastry from the blond slave woman. He gave no heed to the fact that he'd already consumed the portions intended for at least four of the other guests.

"Tell me, Eifer, what is your make of this girl? I've had to crack down on my servants since she came to power. They have taken up slogans about being able to transcend their caste and be noticed. Some have even threatened appealing to the throne for justice."

"Throw them into the streets!" Avaricia Colenly's jaw was set hard, and her right hand squeezed on a butter knife so tightly that her knuckles turned white. Her smooth complexion and brown hair would have seemed soft were it not for the stern mien ruling her face. She had made her fortune in textiles by means of tough competition and ways of cornering the market that she refused to delineate. "If you let them, they will spread their silly notions until it's impossible to find a servant who knows how to work. 'Nice' is for lesser minds; we must rule the masses to keep order."

A short, pale-faced man with bulging eyes sat across from her, shaking his head. "Ave, Eifer and I have been trying to get it into your head how to solve that problem." Lenin Skiro snapped his fingers, and the red-haired girl knew instantly to put a lighted cigar in his hand. "What you need to do is import servants who have been taken as hostages or slaves in other lands, where it is still the custom. Tell them that you have their family members enslaved somewhere else, and that you will punish them for their mistakes and bad behavior. Make them feel that they are suffering valiantly for the sake of their family, and they will give you few problems."

Another woman, sitting on his right, leaned forward and brushed her black hair away from her face. Her porcelain skin seemed set into a slight smile, regardless of her mood, and her voice was light. But her sapphire-blue eyes were as cold as ice. "Where were you able to obtain such slaves, Lenin?"

His reply brought no surprise to any of them. "I bought them from yen-Kragar, Lucy."

Lucy plopped back in her chair and looked at the ceiling. "A fat lot of good that'll do us now. Yen-Kragar, and his family, is five feet under in, or as, a manure pile."

Eifer gave her a sinister smile and raised his brandy glass in salute to Lenin. "Our dear Master Lenin has found an excellent opportunity for a contract renewal with yen-Kragar's successors; a most excellent contract, indeed."

Avaricia eyed him suspiciously. "What does that mean?"

Metamorphosing into the consummate businessman, Eifer calmly addressed an aide sitting silently near the wall. "Wilson, come here and answer Mistress Colenly's question."

In a high-pitched voice, more like an adolescent boy's, Wilson laid out the manner in which one could obtain slaves. His wedge-shaped face and large ears were bereft of emotion, as though long years of adaptation had molded him into resignation to his lot in life.

"My Lords Eifer and Skiro, have negotiated a contract whereby they may obtain as many slaves as they wish. They are willing to sell them to you at great discount, provided that you agree to one particular provision."

If Avaricia and Lucy had had fur on their backs, it would have stood up straight. Their eyes gleamed as they waited for Wilson to continue.

"You will be required to aid us, and our associates, in deposing the new empress."

Everyone but Eifer and Skiro seemed frozen in ice. Lucy shattered it with a sudden outburst.

"Hah! And just how do you propose to do that? The vast majority of the people love her, and would gladly throw themselves on an enemy's spear if they thought that might help her. And various other countries, in particular those to the north, have rushed to establish friendly ties with her. Some have even sent proposals of marriage. And make no mistake about it, she is more than adept at analyzing even the smallest bits of information, even if her overly optimistic opinions regarding people make her seem naïve."

Eifer simply chuckled. "My dear Lucy, you seem to have missed the point. We are not going to do much of anything, except direct the markets and supply a few needs. Our associates will take care of the problems with the throne." He took another swig of brandy and snapped his fingers for Raeki to come near. Caressing her feline form, he said to Lucy, "All we do is enjoy the rewards of keeping our ends of the bargain. I've heard you complain about the shortage of decent prostitutes for your business houses. If you join with us, you'll be able to have the best females from multitudes of different lands. Imagine the profits you could realize with a troupe of whores like Raeki, here."

Lucy considered his proposal for a moment, then looked at the faces of the others for confirmation.

"Very well. I suspect that I speak for us all in agreeing to the terms. But I will require a pledge on your part."

Eifer and Skiro frowned, then shrugged. Eifer gestured for her to continue.

"I require the use of this slave, Raeki, for at least two weeks. I want to see if these foreign women really know how to please men, before I purchase any."

Eifer laughed. "Oh Lucy, you have never seen the like. I am confident that she will do well, so I expect thirty percent of the profits you make with her. But there had better not be any damage, or I'll charge you the full price for a replacement."

"That is acceptable. I will leave, now."

Eifer clapped his hands twice, and the door opened. A servant bowed low and entered the room. "Have the guests' carriages brought around to the entry." The man bowed again and hurried off to do his duty. To Raeki, he said, "You will go with Mistress Lucy, and do whatever she says. If I hear even the least complaint from her regarding you, I will give you severe punishments, as well as have your mother and sisters beaten. Understood?"

Raeki's yellow eyes burned, and her cheeks purpled, but she knew better than to resist. She went down on her knees, leaned over, and kissed his feet. She screamed when Lucy grabbed her hair and dragged her toward the door.

"I haven't got all day, you idiot. Get moving!"

Raeki desperately gained her feet and sprang through the door. Breathing hard, she bowed as Lucy moved through the doorway, but her head snapped back from a sharp slap on her cheek.

"Follow closely, and don't slow me down. Inefficiency will cost you dearly."

Tears came to Raeki's eyes, but she held them in check. All she could do now was obey, and leave the tears for later.

CHAPTER EIGHT

DEAD END

Late in the evening, Karsten escorted Veranna to her chambers. The evening was filled with the joy of discovery as they listened to several presentations regarding the ancient empire of Emeraldia. They had both delivered expositions, with nobles and commoners in attendance, and the social time following was filled with good wine, song and dance. Veranna found herself dancing with a city street sweeper, then with the Earl of Rosea, and then with a brick mason. She saved the last dance for Karsten, and the two of them glided over the floor in total harmony with the quick waltz beat.

Karsten gave her a gentle kiss, and reminded her that it wouldn't be long before he would carry her across the threshold. "Until then, my love, you'll just have to use your own two feet."

Her smile lit up the corridor, and she did a quick curtsy. "Aye, my lord, and I hope my feet don't grow sore with the waiting."

"That makes two of us. Until then, my lady, sleep well." He bowed and started to turn away, then turned back to her. "I'm going to get my desk in order before I turn in. Don't stay up too late reading; we've a full day, tomorrow."

Veranna nodded and opened her door. "Yes, Sir. Make sure that you get a good night's sleep, also. And don't worry too much about your desk; it'll be there waiting for you in the morning, as usual."

He shook his head and smiled stoically. "It does seem inescapable. Good night, love."

"Good night, my dear." Closing her door slowly, she gave him one last lingering smile before he went down the hall. She released the doorknob and danced across the room to a tune that only she heard. Her clothes fell to the floor as she headed into the bathing room, and after an elegant pirouette, she hopped into the bathtub. The soothing, hot water felt just right. She thanked the Creator for all of His blessings and prayed that her wedding day would speed its coming.

It was nearly midnight when Karsten finally pushed back from his desk. Even if anything remained undone, he'd know exactly how much was left and where it was.

He snuffed the candles and closed the door, the lock clicking sharply in the deserted hallway. A chill breeze wafted through, coming from the direction of the banquet room. The servants must have opened a window while cleaning. He found it wide open on the northern wall. The iron lock was old, but the servants should have noticed any trouble, especially since pieces of it were lying on the floor. It was odd that the lock didn't seem to have been broken from the inside. Gouges in the stone of the outer sill were fresh, and something had been inserted under the metal frame of the window in order to turn the lock handle.

Looking closely at the wall beneath the window he saw two short pieces of dark thread snagged on the stone. On the floor, the window debris and the dust indicated that whoever came through the window had proceeded into the main corridor. Drawing his knife, he followed the trail, stretching his senses for any sign of an intruder. He counted thirty paces before it came to mind that he hadn't encountered any of the routine guard patrols. A few more paces and he saw blood spots on the floor and walls. The spots turned into smears as he approached an intersection of hallways. The smears were drying and hard to see against the dark stone of the floor, but enough sheen remained for him to see that a trail wound around the corner and into the hallway on the left. He readied his knife and sprang around the corner to surprise an opponent, but none were present.

He followed the blood trail down to where it disappeared under a door on the left. Turning the knob slowly, he whipped the door open and jumped inside. Again, no opponent, but one of the castle guards lay in a pool of blood, his back stiff and his eyes gone. His hand clasped the handle of his sword, but he'd not had a chance to draw it.

Karsten took the sword and examined the floor for a clue as to where the killer had gone. A footprint, outlined in blood, pointed down the hall to the left, toward the personal chambers. His heart beat faster, but he forced himself to concentrate.

Moving into the hallway again, he cat-footed to the next intersection, and slowly peeked around the corner. There were fewer sconces in this hallway, but he was able to discern a faint footprint heading down the hall and into the shadows. He took a deep breath and let it out slowly, then went around the corner. It wouldn't be much further until he reached the guest chambers, and Veranna's chambers were just a short distance further down.

A soft swishing sound made him duck instinctively. The next instant, an eight-pointed throwing star sank into the wood of the wall just behind his head. He sprang to the other side of the hall as two more of the deadly stars flew by. He caught a glimpse of movement, something dark against dark. Charging forward, he brought his sword up and, without thinking, deflected another star in midair. His Genazi war cry echoed through the halls as he swung his sword at a crouching form cloaked in black.

A scimitar appeared out of the blackness and deflected his blow. Karsten brought his blade around and dodged to his right, barely evading the counter strike. With a series of quick jabs, he forced his opponent back and into a portion of the corridor where the light was greater.

Only the eyes of his opponent could be seen. Dark blue, with a malicious glint, they lusted for his blood. A voice hissed through the mask covering his face. "A Genazi pig, eh? All the better; I will take your eyes and savor every bite!"

Karsten understood the words, for they were similar to the Genazi tongue. But a strange brogue and cadence told him that it was a tongue different from Genazi.

"Koosti, you will have nothing of mine. I will send you to your dark master, empty of all honor."

He lunged forward and pressed his attack. The Koosti killer had no chance to counter, and when he raised his blade to block an overhead blow, Karsten's foot pounded into his gut and caused him to drop his sword. The Genazi warrior then brought his own sword around in one blinding motion, and sliced through the throat of the Koosti, nearly decapitating him.

He bent down to see if the killer carried any papers, and another star grazed his right earlobe. He sprang toward where the object came from and tripped over another black-clad killer. Rolling to his feet, he brought up his sword and carefully moved closer to his attacker.

Hatred shone in the killer's eyes, along with grudging respect. The High Lady's assassins were among the best and had earned prestige working against the dreaded Ravens Blades, the fanatical assassins under the Gelangweils.

Karsten attacked and maneuvered the assassin toward the body of his fallen comrade, hoping to trip him up, but the assassin hopped around, as agile as an acrobat. Back and forth they went, lunging, parrying and calculating. Each responded with automatic, technical precision until Karsten found the advantage he needed.

In the Battle of the Vale, Karsten had fought against many of the eastern soldiers. He learned that they often resorted to a stylized system of clockwise movement and upward slashes meant to disable an opponent. They would then try to break their opponent's back and gouge out their eyes. Karsten feigned joining the clockwise pattern, bringing on the formal response from his opponent. Just before the clash of swords, Karsten altered the arc of his swing and cut into the forearm of the assassin. The man screamed, but it was cut short by a blow that landed square on his nose. He was knocked backward and tripped over his fallen comrade, but rolled to his feet. His right arm was nearly useless, so he pulled out his dagger with his left hand, and waited for Karsten's next attack.

The young Genazi lord could see his opponent bleeding profusely, and tried to use reason. "Surrender now and we may be able to save your life."

Utter contempt came through the Koosti's voice. "My life will end in honor, you Genazi midden!"

Karsten's voice came back sterner than stone. "So be it." He swung his blade in a tight arc at the assassin's neck. The man ducked, and then hopped over Karsten's blade as it swept toward his knees. Aiming for the stomach, Karsten was surprised when the assassin jumped straight onto the point of the sword. In one last desperate attempt, the assassin brought down his knife and stabbed at Karsten's throat.

Karsten's forward momentum brought the tip of the sword clear through the killer. The reduction in distance caused his foe's knife strike to miss its mark, and the blade bit into Karsten's shoulder blade. It burned like fire, but he pulled his sword out of the killer and swung again, cleaving the killer's head in two.

He took a moment to search the dead man, hoping to find some clue regarding their orders, but found nothing. He moved further down the hall and found another black-clad figure working feverishly to pick the door lock to Kreida's room. He rushed forward and swung hard at the man's shoulder. The killer swept upward with his scimitar and turned the blow, but the impact knocked the weapon from his hand. Karsten brought his blade around to sever the man's arm from his shoulder, but another black form grabbed his wrist.

Karsten ducked and twisted his wrist free, but his sword flew off and down the hall. He snapped up straight and drove his elbow into the attacker's chest, knocking him back. Instinct moved him to dodge to the side, and the other attacker's knife grazed his right shoulder. Karsten snapped a kick into his side and slammed him back into Kreida's door, then turned in time to engage the other killer.

The Koosti killers held a high view of their prowess with knives, believing that all others were beneath their contempt. Their pride overlooked the fact that the Genazi were superb with the knife, and they did not know that Karsten was the Champion of the Genazi.

Just as the two engaged in the intricate dance of blades, they were surprised when Kreida's door banged open. It pounded into the other assassin and sent him to the floor. More light flooded into the hallway, as did Kreida's war cry when she saw Karsten battling the two black figures. Although dressed only in a short, sheer nightgown she sprang into the contest and pounced on the nearest attacker.

Karsten's blows, and surprise at Kreida's savage onslaught, left the attacker vulnerable to her blade. Up it came in a tight arc and sliced through his throat and into his brain.

She turned and saw Karsten locked in close combat. Both men were trained in the art of unarmed fighting, and fought furiously for an advantage. Karsten ducked a punch and countered with a blow to his opponent's abdomen. The man was well conditioned and absorbed the blow, but it caused him to pause in his defensive routine. It was just enough for Karsten to slip in a quick uppercut to the bottom of his chin. The man's head snapped back, disorienting him for a second. All he could do was try to grab Karsten and restrict his movement.

But it was no use. A straight punch landed on his forehead, sending him backward. A split second later another blow landed on his nose. He tried to duck and cover, but the toe of Karsten's boot smashed into his groin. A right hook connected with the side of his face and he knew that he was losing consciousness. In one last act of desperation, he bit down on the poison capsule implanted under his tongue and preserved his honor. They would not take him captive.

Just as Karsten started to search the assassin for information, Yanbre came around the corner with three of his guards. From further down the hallway, Veranna ran up and surveyed the scene.

"Karsten! Are you all right? Karsten, tell me you're not hurt. Did they poison you? What happened...?"

He placed a finger over her mouth and wrapped an arm around her. "I'm fine, Veranna, really. Just calm down and..."

She looked at his face and felt the blood soaking into the back of his shirt. Glancing at the figure on the floor, she yelled, "Is this the one who did this to you?" She spun free of his grasp and kicked the fallen assassin in the stomach. "How dare you! Tell me why you are here. Tell me!"

Karsten and Yanbre each grabbed one of her arms and gently moved her back. Yanbre kept his voice calm. "He is dead, your highness. Please try to calm down."

"Calm down! Assassins try to kill my fiancée and who knows whom else, and you tell me to calm down? How many more of these wretched pigs are there running around the grounds? And where were the guards?"

Yanbre had no good answer, especially when she was in this mood. "I'm sorry, your highness. I can say that I have guards posted and searching for information regarding how the assassins got in."

Karsten started to speak, but she shushed him. "Don't talk; just get to the infirmary. You have lost a lot of blood, your lip is cracked open bigger than a canyon, and you've got a big bump on your forehead."

Karsten couldn't help but be amused at her reaction. "I was just going to say..."

"You were just going to say, 'Yes dear,' and get moving to the infirmary. Kreida?"

"What?"

Veranna saw her standing in her bedroom doorway. The light from the room shined through her skimpy nighty, silhouetting her form like a prostitute wanting to attract business. Veranna was taken aback.

"Girl, at least get your robe on. What do you think you're doing, traipsing around the castle like that? Hurry up, and wake the healers."

Kreida gave her a sarcastically sweet smile. "Why, I'm fine, your royal hiney. I've just had a man try to cut my guts out and had to kill him, but I'm just fine!" She stomped into her room and put on her robe, then went to rouse the healers.

Veranna grabbed Karsten's arm and pulled him down the hall. "C'mon, let's get going."

All that he could do was talk over his shoulder as Veranna scuttled him down the hall.

"Yanbre, look at one of the windows in the banquet hall. You'll see how they got in." They disappeared around the corner.

Yanbre shook his head and smiled. He'd never seen Veranna so flustered before. When it came to Karsten, she was like a tigress defending her cubs.

They arrived at the infirmary before any of the others. She sat him on a table and lit all of the candles and lamps she could find. Pulling off his shirt, she shuddered and gasped when she saw his wounds.

"How could you be so careless? Why didn't you summon the guards?" From a basin of previously boiled water she wrung out a towel and began cleaning away the blood.

"Veranna, I know you are upset, but I am going to be fine. The assassins weren't sent for me, they were coming after you. I just happened to interrupt their plans."

Kreida walked in with the healer. "Yeah, and you interrupted my sleep. Couldn't you have sliced these guys up a bit more quietly?"

Veranna's face flashed anger, but when she heard Karsten laugh at the comment, she realized that Kreida was simply trying to lighten the atmosphere. Karsten followed suit.

"I don't know, Kreida. I guess I've gotten a bit rusty when it comes to quick, quiet kills. I'll try to be more considerate next time."

They all laughed, and Veranna resumed cleaning his wounds.

"I'm sorry, Kreida, for being so short with you. Thank you for being there when Karsten needed you."

"Oh, forget it. It was good to be able to get in some practice. With the new moon up tonight, I hadn't really gotten to sleep yet."

Yanbre entered the room and reported that no other assassins had been found, and that he and Treybal found a trail leading back to the castle wall. A rope ladder was hidden in the bushes, and the trail disappeared into the traffic of the city.

"These assassins were definitely from one of the eastern tribes, but it is difficult to say which one. No documents or identifying symbols could be found."

Veranna had expected as much, so she only half-heard his report. The healer did a good job of stitching Karsten's wounds, but the large one on his back still oozed blood. She daubed it again with pure water and placed both hands over it. Closing her eyes, she said a quick prayer, and a faint green light glowed from her hands.

Yanbre did not see the light, but he felt the presence of a soothing power through the armor he wore. "What was that? I felt something. Did anyone else feel something?"

Veranna shook her head as though waking from a nap. "I felt nothing, Yanbre. Do you think it was something bad?"

Before he could answer he moved to hold Karsten up. He had gone to sleep and nearly fell off of the table. Kreida and the healer helped to move him further onto the table.

"I felt something, your highness, but it made me feel calm and peaceful. Maybe I'm just relieved that no one else was hurt."

She smiled. "So am I. Kreida, would you help me get Karsten to his room?"

"Hah! Are you kidding? I can't wait to see the look on your face when you get him in bed."

Veranna's face turned crimson, but she spoke to Yanbre. "If you hear Kreida begging for her life, just ignore it."

He laughed as he left the room. "As you wish, your highness."

Karsten was barely awake as the two women walked him down the hall to his room. They laid him on his bed, and Veranna found a nightshirt for him. Kreida's face twisted up in curiosity.

"By the way you carried on, I thought he had a serious wound on his back."

Veranna wasn't in the mood for frivolity. "Don't be juvenile, Kreida, please. It is a terrible gash; he'll need a good deal of recovery time."

"I can just see it now; you're going to be one of those wives who treats her husband like a spoiled little boy."

"Kreida, I declare, you have no..." She looked at Karsten's wound and froze. "Thank the Creator!" The wound was closed and not bleeding at all. It looked as though the stitches would be ready for removal the next day. "Kreida, this is wonderful. The Blessed One has shown him mercy. Isn't it awesome to know that the Creator has done this right before our very eyes!"

Kreida was astonished, but deflected the comment away. "Yeah, it's great to know. But when you're Genazi, you just have to get used to it. Now, let's get this little boy's shirt on and cover him with some blankets before he dies from freezing."

"Yes, ma'am!"

He was soon snuggled into bed and fast asleep. Veranna snuffed all but one candle, then moved back to brush her hand lightly over his head. *Sleep well my hero. May the Creator bless me with you for the rest of my days.* She closed the door and walked down the hall to her own room. Rounding a corner, she saw the guards removing the last of the dead assassins.

In her room she said a prayer for the dead, and prayed that the Creator would give her the strength to face the challenges of the days to come. *Dear Creator, what will be around all of those corners?*

CHAPTER NINE

ENEMIES AT BAY

The pounding of drums carried across the bay, rumbling like a storm approaching. The people of Morelock looked out at the fleet of oncoming ships, puzzled. Commercial vessels were common, but huge galleys, powered by slaves, hadn't entered the harbor for hundreds of years. In fact, since Clarens had been a Free Zone of the empire, warships had not been necessary.

High Admiral Mirjah stood on the deck of his flagship and watched the shore approach. He was amazed at the lack of fortifications and soldiers. Since he had taken up the knife as a little boy, every nation and tribe in the east tried to build impregnable buttresses to keep out enemies.

The admiral flexed his hard muscles and stretched. If it weren't for the weapons training he would have compromised his lean build and been an easy target for anyone wanting to challenge him in an honor duel. Since coming under the suzerainty of the Koosti, he was considered something of an oddity. He refused to wear the capes and robes so typical among them. Besides, sixty years of habit were hard to break. Uniforms of shirts and pants proved far more practical at sea, and they allowed a better compliment to his fine-chiseled features.

Morelock resolved into an unimpressive town in the early morning light. No large buildings of industry, habitation, or any distinguishing landmarks. Fishnets lay drying on the shore and chimneys put out thin streams of smoke that carried the smells of meats, eggs and breads being prepared.

Mirjah hoped that subduing the town wouldn't involve too much killing or destruction, for captives could replace the slaves lost in battle and prepare a breakfast for him that would be a welcome change from the stored foods of the galley.

The sound of alarm bells ringing carried across the water. Men scurried along the docks, readying bows and swords. Smoke from fire pits billowed up, and women and children fled east into the countryside.

Mirjah went below for a touch-up on his grooming, leaving his subcommander, Admiral H'rasbani, to carry out the conquest of the negligible town. Cargo vessels with two-score troops and their horses headed for the shore near the inlet's mouth a quarter of a mile away to each side of the town. Mounting up, the troops signaled the admiral that they were ready. H'rasbani gauged the ships distance from the docks and nodded to his signalman to have the soldiers move toward the town.

On the docks a large, burly man shouted orders. A score of longbows rose up and took aim at the approaching ships, with six tar throwers ready to sling their fiery loads. A dozen men in armor took up positions on each side of the town where the road would limit the enemy horsemen since the terrain was thickly wooded.

The burly man turned to his men for one last word. "Listen up, men. We are the first line of defense for our land on this side of the empire. The Baron and his advisors in Clarens doubted that we would be attacked, but Tesra, the Mother of the Academy who lived in the west, warned them that this day would come.

"Remember, our goal is to slow them down, and not to try to defeat them on our own. The Baron will need time to call up the army and get the people into the city. We will pull back and race for the city at the last moment. May the Creator give us strength."

H'rasbani casually gestured to his lieutenant to begin the assault. A moment later, a hundred arrows rushed out at the docks. The defenders raised their shields and crouched behind any cover they could find, but one of the arrows struck a young man in his calf. He cried out in pain and hurriedly pulled his leg further under cover.

One gray-haired archer yelled to their leader, Paul Sowndent, that one of their fellows was injured. Paul yelled back a quick set of instructions. "Jurgen, get to Davey and staunch the wound. He needs to be able to fire with the rest of us. Johnny."

"Aye, Paul?"

"Prepare to let the tar fly. Archers, we've got a huge supply of arrows, and our bows have greater range. Keep firing, so that our catapults can deliver the fire bombs." He waited for a minute lull in the enemy's rain of arrows, and then cried out, "Fire!" Their shafts raced toward the enemy archers, taking out several on the first volley.

H'rasbani yelled at his men when they failed to return fire, and ordered them to resume. The one closest to him stood and drew back his string, but just before firing, an arrow flew down and into his eye. His own arrow jumped off his bow and penetrated deep into H'rasbani's chest. The hapless admiral fell back and thudded onto the deck.

Sowndent yelled, "Catapults, release!"

Fifteen flaming fireballs streaked toward the three ships at the front of the formation. Four of them missed and hissed out in the water, but the other eleven landed on their targets. The fireballs were designed to splatter and ignite a large section, and soon the ships were ablaze. One ship exploded when its oil supply ignited, and the flaming debris spread to other ships nearby. The sailors were forced to fight the fires, and many of them fell to the incoming arrows.

Mirjah came on deck, hotter than the flames around him. Barking orders, he quickly had the archers firing again, and set the slave rowers to a quicker beat. The galley smashed into the dock protruding furthest into the water. The easterners leaped onto it, crouching behind shields. Soon there was a score of them on the dock, set into an attack formation.

From the north and south of the town, the enemy horsemen rode hard and bore down on the defenders. The townsmen's arrows had taken out a number of the foreigners, but there were just too many. Out came the swords, and gruesome, close-quarter fighting ensued.

Sowndent suddenly yelled, "Now!" The defenders torched the heavy barricades erected on the docks. Dry and oily, the wood caught fire immediately, blocking the easterners approach to the town.

Mirjah screamed for the attack squads to get to shore on boats, or by swimming. If some of the ships were lost to flame, so be it. His own ship was lost, but he would have his personal things transferred by slaves before they abandoned it. All he wanted now was to take the eyes of these townsmen.

After Sowndent and his men repulsed the first line of attackers he called a retreat. They made no effort to conceal the fact that they were withdrawing. Running up the gradual slope to the main part of the town, the archers continued firing at the easterners.

Mirjah fumed at his captains. "I want captives! Dead men are no good for information or for entertaining torture."

Dozens of longboats reached the shore to both sides of the blazing docks. Foot and horse soldiers quickly scrambled into formation and sped after the townsmen. In minutes, they were into the town and searching out any inhabitants, but puzzled by the fact that none could be found.

On a rise to the east of Moorlock, Sowndent and four archers said their farewells to the town. Paul closed his eyes and quietly said, "Fire."

The archer's bows twanged and sent their flaming arrows off toward the four corners of the town. A few seconds later, building after building exploded into huge fireballs. The force of the blasts rocked the ships entering the bay, and the surrounding forest swayed. The townsmen climbed onto their horses and headed for Clarens.

Mirjah stood rooted to the deck of his burning ship. None of the masters who had planned this mission had ever mentioned that these people were capable of such tactics. With few exceptions, Emeraldians were sentimental weaklings given over to the idea of individual worth.

By the time that the admiral's tent was erected, his commanders reported to him as he sat at his freshly set table for breakfast. Over seven hundred men had been lost in the landing and taking of the town, which was now a smoking heap of rubble that would not help replenish their supplies. No enemy bodies had been found, and the town left few indicators of recent, large-scale occupation.

Mirjah pounded a fist on his table. "They must have known we were coming and set this trap. We must not underestimate them again. When we attack this city called 'Clarens,' we will use full force from the start. Give the order that we will march on the morning of the second day from now. Do not bother me for the rest of the day." His officers bowed and then went about their duties.

The Admiral had been given a map of the Seven Lands purchased in the city of Neidburg, Imperia, and he studied it closely while dining on dragon meat. Two of the fearsome blue beasts had engaged in a contest for dominance and each suffered deadly wounds. The Koosti leaders declared the carcasses sacred, and that the people should consume them for dragon strength. Mirjah had not noticed any increase in strength, but he definitely enjoyed the flavor.

After considering the terrain of western Emeraldia, he decided that heading south would be the lesser of evils once they conquered Clarens. They would pass the Dividing Mountains and swing north to join the battle against Grandshire. It was a reasonable course, but taking Grandshire might prove exceedingly difficult. A fifth of his force had been eliminated by a handful of rustics; how would he fare against bona fide soldiers when they attacked Clarens? The three armies landing further up the coast had better do their jobs and hem in the enemy on the north and west before he could take a stab at Grandshire.

The Great Lady wished to bypass the Land called Imperia and hasten to Grandshire. This would allow her to squeeze Loreland and take Tolemera. The rest of this barbarian empire would rapidly fall into her hands. All that was left was to see that their allies in this strange empire did their jobs. After this campaign ended, even they could be disposed of.

CHAPTER TEN

PAST AND PRESENT

Duke Heilson set his flagon onto the end table and took a deep breath, the last three hours seeming like three days. Prince Naim of Volonya, continued pressing his case for a merger of their lands, and failed to appreciate the legal ramifications involved.

"Joel, please, I have given you my answer and ask you to respect it. I am not going to change my mind, and will handle my own affairs, thank you."

Joel Naim was a tall, slender man who had recently celebrated his thirtieth birthday. Light brown hair and brown eyes set in a placid face were unremarkable, but he was clearly an ambitious man.

"I am not trying to take over your affairs, Russell; I just want you to understand the difficult position you're facing. At your age you should already have a grown heir to succeed you. But you don't have any legitimate children who can satisfy the legal requirements. Were we to consolidate our realms, the issue could be solved advantageously for both of us. You would be able to enjoy a retirement far beyond your dreams, and I would be able to provide a successor to the duchy. Financially, we would be the envy of the empire."

Heilson groaned. "Joel, when I am ready to produce an heir, I will. Besides, this Theresa McFaye of yours cannot provide you an heir, so that is a moot point."

"Theresa and I are not married, so I can still find a wife from a royal household to fulfill that function. She can even be ugly and do the job."

Heilson chuckled and shook his head. "Ah, Joel, you are playing with fire if you think Theresa will just look the other way when you seek a wife. If you think that she is jealous now, just wait until you even hint at courting another woman."

Naim downed the last of his wine. "Pah! Theresa will do as I tell her so don't worry about that. Besides, she is a hired servant, so she can be fired if she gets too uppity."

"You are not being realistic, Joel. She has been managing your affairs for a few years and is responsible for increasing your wealth to a level you'd not have thought possible. Not only that, but she is a graduate of the Academy, in Clarens, and should be familiar with the empress. That is an inside connection you could exploit to great advantage."

"Now you are not being realistic, Russell. Theresa hates the empress. Apparently there is some old grudge between them that she can't let die."

"That's unfortunate; Empress Veranna is a woman like no other."

"That is the problem. Theresa wants to believe that she has no equal. She feels that the Academy slighted her by not showing her the same attention as Veranna."

"Have you met the empress?"

"No."

"You'll understand Theresa's attitude when you do."

"All the same, I'm not going to let Theresa's problems rule me. I'm still the master of my own..."

The door opened suddenly and Theresa whisked into the room. She smiled at the duke and did a perfunctory curtsy.

"Good morning, my lord." Each word was precise and quick. Before either of the men could respond she gave Naim a stern look that made him cringe. "Already drinking, eh? And, I noticed that you've still not seen to the documents I laid out for you before breakfast. Are you wanting your fief to degenerate right in front of your eyes, or do you simply desire to show the duke how to be lazy?"

Theresa was shorter than Naim, but at five-seven she seemed to tower over him. Her face was pretty, with blue-gray eyes and thick blonde hair. But the severe character of her posture and gaze overshadowed her attractive qualities.

The prince gave Heilson a glance and stood up straight. "Theresa, you are out of line. I am your prince, and you will show proper respect when..."

Her voice cut through his sentence like an axe. "No more of this foolish talk. If it weren't for me you would have seen your petty lands repossessed by the Guild Banks, and you would be begging in the streets for crumbs." She put on a smile and curtsied to the duke again. "Please forgive the intrusion, my lord, but the prince has his duties to attend to. Come, Joel."

She strode through the door without looking to see if he was following, knowing that he would. All he could do was grimace and fall in behind her.

Tesra plodded along, growing grumpier with every step. She had wanted to leave Grandshire over a week ago, but the duke asked her to stay on until after a business counsel meeting in which she would serve as the moderator. She was anxious to see Veranna, but would just have to be satisfied with sending her a message by pigeon.

The meeting chamber was filled with business people and a few nobles. Lord Ferdinand, the right-hand man of duke Roland, of Starhaven, sat at the far end of the table, while Tesra and duke Heilson took seats in the middle.

Tesra called the meeting to order and requested that Heilson begin. He laid out the issues and goals, as well as the policies set down by the empress. Concluding his presentation he challenged them to achieve higher standards in their work and to reduce unethical business practices.

Before he sat down a man with graying hair and blue eyes objected. The duke was not surprised, for that was the man's job. Steven Reby was often hired by the guilds to represent them.

"My lord, we must protest the throne's intrusion into the markets. We've had a system in place for hundreds of years and don't see that changing things now will do any good."

The duke answered levelly, "That viewpoint will satisfy you because it serves your needs uniquely. But growth in the markets will not take place if you strangle competition. People need to have the opportunity to try before you rule them out. Your way offers them no chance for success or failure."

A young woman sitting directly across from Tesra smiled at the duke and leaned forward to reveal an ample amount of bosom. "My lord, that is not really true. Anyone can join the guilds and work their way up. Our vineyard employs nearly two hundred workers, all of whom could potentially run their own vineyard."

Heilson knew that the guildsmen had invited this woman, Jodi Talnz, for the specific purpose of distracting him. He had sampled her wines, and more, on many occasions. Tall, slender, well endowed and pretty of face, she swept back her red-blonde curls and fixed her gleaming blue eyes upon him.

"Lady Talnz, I appreciate the theory you have put forth and have used it, myself. But honesty compels us to ask whether we have ever seen it happen. I daresay that none of your servants has ever moved on to start a vineyard of his or her own. Guild memberships are too expensive for them and the start-up costs are prohibitive."

She gave him a coy smile. "Are you saying that you are dissatisfied with my wares, my lord?"

He felt his face reddening. "Not at all, my lady. But that is not the issue. What you need to understand is that the empress has decreed that the markets shall follow the pattern of Langraine. Clarens has done very well with its Free Zone status, and the system of class envy we've been living under fosters discontent. That hurts us all."

Lord Roland sat back in his chair and stared at Jodi. "What the duke says is true. In Starhaven we have enjoyed a great deal of success with an open opportunity approach. The guilds have adjusted and realize that they benefit from the arrangement, too. It might do you well to visit your fellows in Starhaven and speak with them."

The guild representative laid his documents on the table and stood. "My lords, we don't need to travel to out-of-the-way towns to understand what is going on right under our noses. If the throne will not recognize our authority in these matters, we may need to ignore the throne."

Menacingly calm, Tesra looked him in the eye. "Ignorance would not be bliss, sir. The empress desires peaceful harmony, but knows when to use force to uphold the law. She has the wisdom of the Creator behind her decisions, as well."

Reby paused to look over his contingent. "Are you threatening us, my lady?"

"Not at all, lord Reby. I am simply saying that your threatening behavior against the throne will be met with serious action. If you practice treasonous ways you will receive the punishment due traitors. The Law of the Creator supports the throne in such circumstances."

Naim shifted uneasily in his seat. Under Theresa's guidance Volonya had profited greatly by supporting the present guild structures, and their new allies certainly would not appreciate the trade practices being changed to a less favorable arrangement. He had been able to acquire numerous servants from the eastern realms through the guilds, and the markets for construction had never been better. The number of servants and slaves needed housing, and the farmers were hard pressed to meet the demand for food. A number of the foreign women were pregnant, so the population would be increasing all the more.

The meeting adjourned on a tense note, the guild representatives resentful of anyone wanting to regulate their operations. Tesra walked to a window overlooking the city below, while the rest of them exited. Prince Naim gathered up his materials and turned to leave when Theresa walked in and closed the door behind her.

"How did it go, Joel? Did you argue the points I told you to?"

The prince kept his eyes on the table. "No, Theresa, there was no time for any other matters than those the duke laid out."

Theresa placed her hands on her hips and spoke in an icy tone. "So, once more you have been derelict in your assignment." When he failed to look her in the eye she slapped him hard across the face. "You incompetent coward. I should have let you rot into oblivion and never sold my services to Volonya. How you could ever have inherited the title of prince, I'll never know; fortunately, I won't have to worry about that much longer. Our partners will see you for what you are and roast you for their dogs. I may be tempted to undertake that project myself if you don't learn…"

Tesra stepped away from the window. Theresa nearly jumped out of her skin and ran behind Naim.

"You are not one to talk when it comes to learning, Theresa McFaye. You still have not learned what makes for noble character, nor how to be thankful for all the blessings given by your Creator."

The prince looked at them, wondering what they were talking about. Theresa's eyes were wild with fear and her panting made it difficult for her to speak.

"Joel, don't let her touch me! She gave me a beating once before, and I did nothing to provoke her. She is mad, and is against me for some reason."

Tesra's voice rumbled like thunder. "Reason is not a word suitable for your vocabulary, girl! You failed to use it when you came to my home, and you ignore it in the manner in which you treat your prince."

Naim had been on the verge of a retort, but Tesra's last remark surprised him. He moved out of the way as she stepped forward.

"It seems that you have learned nothing when it comes to your empress, also. In your limited outlook on life you have passed up a friendship that would have blessed you throughout all your days. But no, you have a grudge that you wish to settle. You could not stand to see Veranna excel, so now you seek to do her harm.

"You have erred in your thinking once more. I will have the full story now or you shall rot in jail for many years. You might even wind up being executed. It will all depend on your character."

Theresa moved to the other side of the table and glanced at the door. "I don't have to tell you anything. I am a member of a ruling prince's entourage and may not be assaulted."

Tesra grinned. "Your studies in the law were obviously incomplete. That does not surprise me since it parallels your other qualities. I am a member of the imperial family and the Ambassador-at-Large for the throne. As a Mother of the Academy I am also a servant of the courts. You have no immunity from prosecution, and I am ordering your arrest and interrogation immediately. More than likely you'll be cleaning out the kitchen grease pits tonight."

Theresa's breathing became labored and she yelled at the prince. "Don't just stand there, you idiot! Go get the duke and have him take this mad woman away."

"Theresa, it's no use trying to hide anymore. If you tell them what's going on we may be able to avoid serious punishment."

Anger took over where fear left off. "You pitiful coward. What good would it do to suffer in their jails only to have the Lady take our eyes! I'll not give in to this old woman's threats or your weakness. I am a daughter of Dalmar Gelangweil and will yet rule this land."

Tesra shook her head slowly and went for the door. Suddenly, the window glass shattered and three gray-clad attackers swung into the room. Tesra threw the door open and yelled for the guards, then sprang back to shove the prince out of the path of two death stars aimed at his head. Grabbing his sword she dodged more of the deadly stars and closed on the foremost attacker. He was an excellent swordsman, but Tesra fought with furious speed. In seconds he fell to her blade.

The prince hid under the table and edged toward the door.

The second killer pressed Tesra back, but his skill failed him when he faltered in his defense. Tesra's blade found the opening and slid through with lightning speed, slicing into his left thigh. The pain froze his muscles for a moment and Tesra bludgeoned him with the hilt of her sword, knocking him to the floor. She looked across the room and saw the third attacker holding a knife to Theresa's throat, while the prince ran out of the room just before a guard entered.

The attacker looked at Tesra with mixed loathing and respect. "Gyar kan quetol ye monyea. Yen fiayra crites (I see that you deserve respect. My mission is done)." In one swift motion he stabbed his blade into Theresa's back. A sharp yelp came from her and her body went rigid. Before Tesra or the guard could close the distance the killer gouged out Theresa's eyes and slit her throat. He joined her on the floor a second later after biting down on something in his mouth.

Tesra looked out the window to see if any more of the assassins were readying to attack. Before she turned away the alarm bells and horns sounded. Soldiers scurried to man the walls and in the city the people rushed to finish their business and take cover.

"Take me to the duke," she barked at the guard, then grabbed Naim by the wrist and pulled him along with her.

They found the duke in an observation tower on the south wall, gazing out onto the horizon. Still clutching Naim's wrist, Tesra reported the assassin's attack, then asked about the alarms.

The duke looked shaken, but resolute. "If you look to the south you'll see a large dust cloud rising. My advisors estimate a force of more than twenty thousand approaching. We don't have any reports regarding who they are, but what you've said about the assassins leaves me with little doubt. I've received several other reports about attacks on my officers. Over thirty of them are dead, verses a dozen assassins."

Tesra shoved Naim forward and forced him to his knees. "Tell the duke what you know and you may avoid torture and death."

Heilson was shocked by Tesra's words and tone. He was shocked even more as the prince related what he knew of the assassins.

"My lord, I should have been stronger and resisted Theresa's counsel, but I fear that I am the cause of these attacks. Theresa, before I knew it, began meeting with a Koosti spy who filled her head with ideas of how high she could rise in their empire if she showed her loyalty by helping them to infiltrate the Seven Lands. That is why we have been doing so much building. They have come by the thousands over the last four years and settled in their own communities.

"When I mentioned to Theresa that their numbers filled me with unease she said that they would prove loyal, and that they had a right to live just like anyone else. They now have settlements in all the Lands. Theresa loved the fact that they groveled at her feet, but I can see now that it was all a sham."

The duke wanted to slice off his head right there, but could do nothing but stare in disbelief. "You fool! You pathetic fool! Your weakness of mind shall be the death of us all." His rage threatened to overtake him totally, and with one swift swing he knocked Naim to the floor. "Guards! Lock him in the dungeon."

Tesra ran over to Naim before the guards could haul him away. "Wait! I want some information first. I want to know where this army to the south is coming from."

Naim had to flex his jaw several times before he could speak. "These come from the land known as 'Slucia', which is on the far side of the Koosti kingdom. They were scheduled to attack Clarens before seizing the passes through the mountains. Rosea also was to be occupied. Starhaven has probably already fallen to the northern arm of their forces."

The look on Tesra's face made him back up against the guards. She abruptly turned back to the duke and then looked out to the south. "I doubt that they have taken Clarens, but have laid siege. We must send out messages to the other Lands and warn them of this threat. If my assumption is correct, they will be coming from the north and west to cut off any assistance we might otherwise expect. We need to shore up the river batteries and get the fletchers busy. Also, we will need to ready cavalry sorties; these attackers will be poorly armed as far as horses."

The duke nodded to an aide to see to her instructions, then drew his sword and inspected it. "I had hoped and prayed that this blade would not taste blood ever again. But you seem to have a knack for bringing trouble with you."

"Let's just say that the Creator has directed me to where the trouble will be taking place. By the way, I assume that you have kept up your reserve stores?"

"Yes, and then some. The harvest was three times greater than usual, so we have enough provisions to last for a long time. We can always get fresh fish from the river."

"Good. It will be harder for our enemies to re-supply, and this will bring them to make rash decisions. We must exploit this advantage. They will also find it harder to obtain fuel for making fire once they consume the materials outlying the city. What of our own supplies of fuel?"

The duke smiled. "Hah! The castle and the city both sit on massive coal beds. Dark oil is also abundant and is used for fireballs. After a few of their soldiers get crisped they will concentrate on taking out the catapults."

"We must plan on that contingency. If we reduce their numbers faster than we loose our own, we will reach the point where we can take the initiative and attack. They have erred in attacking after harvest; the farms will have sold their goods and have little to pillage."

The duke sighed heavily. "I just hope that those in the villages make their way into the city; these Koosti are beyond barbaric when it comes to prisoners. They'll get so desperate that they'll eat the bark off of the trees."

Tesra's eyes widened as an idea came to mind. "Have the farmers herded in their livestock to the markets yet?"

The duke was puzzled by her question. "Yes, but what has that got to do with your preparations?"

"A great deal. Here's what I want you to do."

A wicked smile came over the duke's face as she laid out her plan.

CHAPTER ELEVEN

TRAGEDY AND TREMBLING

South of Grandshire lay the fief of Starhaven. Rolling grasslands and woods stretched away as far as the eye could see, and the brilliant blue sky looked more like a painting with high, puffy clouds rolling along.

But young Duke Roland could see only red as he surveyed the terrain around his encampment. His enemies had not bothered to pursue them this far out since they had a greater objective in mind further north. He had no doubt that Grandshire would be their next target.

The last week had come on like a nightmare. A flood of attackers from surrounding villages besieged the castle and city before he could organize a defense. The city dwellers fell to the knives and swords of the invaders, with many stripped of their clothing and led away in chains. The younger women and girls were their chief desire, while the older women and men were put to death without a second thought. The younger men and boys' screams still resonated in his mind from when they were publicly castrated and dragged away to holding pens. The worst was when his mother was caught in the hallway. She delayed abandoning the castle in order to help some servants escape the easterners, which proved her undoing. Before she could flee into one of the secret passages, they caught her. Roland watched helplessly from a far wall as she was dragged into the courtyard, scalped and had her eyes and liver removed. While still barely alive they threw her onto a fire and cheered.

Roland cursed himself for not being by her side. The terrible scenes, and her horrible cries, were burned indelibly into his mind. Were it not for the fact that his family's chief counselor, Yargen Yiyay, had troopers restrain him Roland would have charged into the fray and been crushed. He resented Yargen's interference, but his parents had taught him the necessity of cool reason. He would accomplish his vengeance on these mongrel dogs and survive to pursue them to the far corners of the world. The slightest copper penny in the hidden reserves would not be spared.

"Yargen."

"Yes, my lord?" The middle-aged counselor's blue eyes opened wide at the rock-hard tone in Roland's voice.

The young duke stood tall, his muscles taut as he gripped his sword. "We leave at dusk, and will head for Genazi country. I want everyone alert. We'll be moving swiftly and must watch for any traps of the enemy. When, and if, we reach Tolemera, I'm sure that the empress will not hesitate to supply us with enough troops to win back our land. Everyone but the sentries should get what rest they can before we leave."

"As you command, my lord." Yargen relayed Roland's commands and contemplated their situation, wondering if his hair could grow any grayer. He was gratified that Roland had matured in the last few years. He had shown great promise even as a little child and worked hard to develop his mind and physical qualities. Banners won during the many fencing contests Roland participated in lined the walls of the family castle. The training had paid off, saving his life many times in combat, and a vital turning point came when he met the new empress. She impressed him greatly with her wisdom and skill, especially so since they were roughly the same age. The two of them now faced the challenge of an era to preserve the empire. Their youth would be sacrificed for its survival.

Veranna awoke, bounded from her bed and hurriedly swept on her robe before heading out of her room. In the pre-dawn quiet her slippers slapped against the stone of the corridor floor. A guard trotted over, bowed and asked if something was wrong. She waved him off and told him to have Yanbre gather the leaders in the conference hall in an hour. Fumbling with a set of keys, she finally found the one for Kreida's door. The door banged open, then bounced off the wall. She did not even notice as she stretched out her senses to locate Kreida. The Genazi princess was in her bathtub with her head submerged as she lay on her back. Veranna reached down and grabbed her hair, nearly lifting her out of the water. Kreida screamed and wiped her eyes.

"What in the name of Wahweh's shrine are you doing?!"

"Kreida, hurry up and dry off; I've had a dream that was more than a dream. We've got to act quickly."

"Well, couldn't you have just tapped me on the shoulder? Only men are allowed to grab me by the hair when I'm bathing. And did the guard see you like that? Your breasts are bouncing out of that nightgown like two wild horses in a corral."

Veranna looked down at her front and gasped. "Blast!" In her rush to find Kreida she had forgotten to tie her nightgown closed. "The guard will think I am a total ninny. Thank goodness the hallway is dark. But never mind; I need you in the conference hall in an hour."

"An hour? I'll miss the weapons training with the guards!"

"Too bad. Besides, anymore training with those men and Treybal will be tying you to a post just to make sure that you don't get into trouble."

"Hah! Let him try and I'll make sure that he doesn't walk for two months."

Veranna just shook her head. "I am going to get dressed and see about some food for the meeting. Don't be late."

"And don't you be ridiculous; I'll be ready in ten minutes and you'll still be getting your bosom in order. I'm sure the guards will be more attentive from now on."

Veranna feigned a sweet smile. "Well, then, we won't have to worry about you ever distracting them." With that she hurried back to her own room, anxious to organize her thoughts and share them with the others.

An hour later she paced around the conference room as her advisers filtered in. Meetings usually took place at the tenth hour, after training and breakfast. The break in schedule would have them all curious.

"Everyone, please sit down." She did not wait for Karsten to help her with her chair, and took a long swallow of kaffe as the others sat. "You all know that it took a bit of doing before I finally accepted the facts regarding my ancestry. This was especially true about my dreams. The Creator was showing me things to come and I failed to recognize them for what they were. However, I've had my first such dream after many months and I cannot risk ignoring it."

Kreida washed down a biscuit with a swig of tea. "Oh yeah? I have dreams all the time and you call me a 'sensualist;' my dreams involve real people."

Yanbre said flatly, "Yes, but the empress' dreams are not recollections."

Karsten and Treybal chuckled, while Kreida frowned at Yanbre. "Just what are you implying with that..."

Veranna clapped her hands, bringing everyone's attention to her. "Please, this is serious. I need you to hear what I have to say."

Kreida rolled her eyes. "Okay, fine; let's hear it."

Veranna frowned at her but refused to get into an exchange. "I believe that this dream deals with the empire as a whole. I was standing on a mound in a field, enjoying a pleasant day, when suddenly I saw swarms of large black and bronze ants crawling around. They tore down the grain stalks and killed or subdued any other insects or animals in their way. The local ants were turned into slaves, with huge master ants pushing them to work harder and harder. I looked up and saw Tesra a little ways away on another mound. The ants were after her, climbing up the mound in large numbers. The same happened to Baron Lenarde, who was on another mound. Starhaven and Neidburg went through the same thing.

"Pushing the ants into a frenzy was a giant queen that followed the orders of an even larger warrior ant. The warrior sent swarms to attack mounds far away, and left us to the queen. I couldn't stamp them out quickly enough and they started crawling up my legs, biting all the way. That was when I woke up and ran to find Kreida. What do you think it means?"

Kreida shrugged and rolled her eyes again. "You ate something sour before going to bed." When Veranna showed irritation at the comment, Kreida rushed to explain herself. "C'mon; if I told you I'd had a dream or vision that scared me, would you run to see if a catastrophe was headed our way? Of course not; without more to go on I'd say that right now we are doing pretty well."

Veranna scowled and asked if anyone else had any input. Karsten reached over and held her hand.

"My love, Kreida may have the manners of a goat, but she does have a point. We can't address something that is so obscure. Until we receive some solid information it would be reckless to get upset over the unknown."

Yanbre voiced his agreement. His confident and fatherly tone helped calm her anxious spirit. "Such dreams are disturbing, to say the least, and we know that you have a gift from the Creator that has helped us before. The dream is suggestive, but we don't know enough to reach a conclusion. In the meantime I'll increase the guard watches and send out patrols to scout the countryside."

Veranna felt a small measure of reassurance, but a nagging doubt could not be dispelled. "Thank you, Yanbre. The hard part is not knowing when something will happen; I just hope that we are prepared."

Kreida stuffed another biscuit into her mouth and made an expansive gesture with her hands. "You've got an entire empire behind you, girl, and they've been overstocked with this year's harvest. There's even a new moon festival planned for this evening. Relax, and realize that you are worked up over nothing."

A knock came on the door, and a page entered with some notes. He bowed and laid them on the table before Veranna. "Excuse me, your highness, but Master Qyecors said to bring these messages to you immediately."

Qyecors was the man Yanbre had chosen as their head of intelligence gathering. That an urgent message from him had to be delivered at that moment gave Veranna a sense of dread. "Thank you, Trevan." The page bowed and departed as Veranna studied the papers and noticed that they were transcribed from code used by the imperial pigeon service. Qyecors had interpreted the condensed notes and printed the contents in large characters. Her eyes went wide and she held her breath. "This is terrible! Clarens, Grandshire, Imperia, Fontbalm and Rosebloom have all sent messages that they are under attack. The coastal regions are taken over, and Starhaven has fallen. Lord Roland reports that his mother was tortured and cannibalized by easterners carrying Koosti standards, and Tesra says that Grandshire is completely surrounded, but that they are managing to hold their own for now. Imperia is under siege, and Clarens, too. She says that red dragons attacked the Academy."

Karsten, stunned by the reports, asked quietly, "Is there any report about Loreland, or any indication of activity to the north?"

"No. All that Lord Bearson, Tomius' lieutenant in Imperia, says is that several days ago a large portion of the invaders headed north from there."

Yanbre stood and paced a moment. "If they are headed this way then we only have a day or two before we are under siege. We must use every moment wisely."

The young empress felt overwhelmed. "I'm open to suggestions."

Karsten tried to comfort her by being decisive. "We must evacuate the city and surrounding areas. As we've seen before these easterners will destroy anyone, and anything, just for the fun of it. Many would be taken as slaves or cannibalized. They must get moving right away and not worry about possessions."

Kreida snorted, "And just where will they go with winter around the corner? Do you expect them to hide in holes in the ground?"

Yanbre abruptly ceased pacing as an idea formed in his mind. "That is exactly what they will do." When both Kreida and Veranna gave him puzzled frowns he hurried to explain himself. "The foothills of the Boar's Spine Mountains have more than enough caves to hold the people, and when the Resistance used them we stockpiled a great store of provisions. The caves are easily defended, especially with Genazi only a few hours west of them."

Tomius shook his head in agreement, as did Karsten, while Veranna sighed with relief. "So be it. We will also need to draft all males sixteen years of age and older for the defense of the castle and city, with some of the women and girls for support service. And, Tomius?"

"Yes, your highness?"

"Send word to the Genazi that they will be needed, and that a legion of them are to march immediately to the aid of Grandshire. Kreida will command them."

Tomius's eyebrows rose, but he responded with a simple, "Aye, your highness."

Stunned, Kreida nearly fell out of her seat. "Are you insane?" She pointed at Treybal and shook her head. "Who is going to take care of this numb skull while I'm gone? He can hardly put one foot in front of the other if I don't show him how."

Treybal put his arm around her shoulders and spoke softly. "Don't worry, my little *zache.*" A *zache* was a doll that the Genazi gave to small children. The children protected and tended them with fierce loyalty, even to the time when they passed them on to their children or grandchildren. "You need only worry about getting back soon so that we can finally be wed. Don't get reckless or do anything that'll cause me grief."

Veranna smiled warmly. Kreida and Treybal were like family, and even though she put on a hard, rascally front, it was easy to see that Kreida loved Treybal deeply. "I am sorry, Kreida, but you are the only Genazi I can spare for this mission. Tomius will be planning the liberation of Imperia, and Karsten will be leading a company to locate Lord Roland."

Karsten blinked. "I will?"

"Yes; he's likely wondering where to turn in the wilderness. He and those with him are probably exhausted and hungry. You're the best scout and tracker among the Genazi, so you stand the best chance of finding them."

"As you wish, my love." He pulled her out of her chair and gave her a long hug.

She whispered in his ear, "Be careful, my dear. I promised Kreida that we would be married and her friends forever. You can't make a liar out of me."

He smiled and gave her a kiss. "In that case I'll try extra hard. I'll get my squad ready and be off before lunch."

"Thank you, my love." She tried to put on a brave smile, but tears came to the corners of her eyes. He bowed and departed, gesturing for Kreida to come with him. Once they were gone, Veranna laid out strategies for Treybal and Yanbre. "Treybal, you and your Rockhounds are going to be our special attack unit. The Koosti will no doubt surround the city, especially the castle, and think that nothing can be done about it. You will show them just how wrong they are. As you know, the castle is our ally and has secret openings and attributes which Yanbre has been finding accidentally, and I've been finding out through studying the ancient records. You will strike the Koosti silently, after nightfall, and return to the castle before morning. You and your men will wear the special armor of Yanbre and his knights. The helmet visor will allow you to see at night while the rest of the armor will hide you like ghosts. We want to put fear in them from the start."

"Yes, your highness, I understand. They will be so jittery that they won't know what to do."

"Thank you, Treybal. Remember, Kreida is like a sister to me, so I will be keeping an eye on you while she is away."

He laughed. "With Kreida away, I will have a chance to catch my breath. Battle will be almost boring by comparison." His face and voice went serious. "She had better return to me, or I don't know what I'll do. She is already such a large part of me."

Veranna placed a hand on his shoulder and spoke soothingly. "I know what you mean. If anything happens to Karsten I will feel that part of me has died. We will simply have to trust that the Creator will guard them well."

He bowed and smiled. "You are right, but I will still be in knots until she returns. I will simply have to lose myself in the mission to keep from worrying." He turned and strode from the hall, anxious to prepare his men.

Veranna stared after him for a moment, lost in thought. Yanbre's armor clinked and she shook her head. "I am sorry, Yanbre; I did not mean to ignore you. I was distracted for a moment."

"No apology necessary, your highness; I have a wife and children whom I love dearly." He paused before continuing. "One of the principles of combat is mobility. If we keep the troops inside the castle walls we may have a strong defense, but we will be greatly hindered as far as maneuverability is concerned."

"True; as in a game of chess, the side with the greater range of motion generally wins. Defense too often leads to stagnation."

"Exactly. That is why I would like to propose that we leave simply an adequate force to defend the castle, and take the rest of the army to run raids on the enemy. We can strike with great effectiveness and catch them off-guard by choosing our points of attack. Re-supply and healers can come from the western hills."

"An excellent plan, Yanbre. This time, don't be so eager to dive into the enemy; you may get yourself trapped and killed. Remember, there is no disgrace in retreat if it is executed according to a plan. We can't afford to lose any of our troops, while the enemy has more than enough to spare. Be very careful."

He bowed and gave her a reassuring smile. "We will do our best, your highness. Make sure that you stay safe, too. We pawns don't want to fight a battle only to return and find that we have lost our queen."

"Not pawns, Yanbre, but princes in service to our Creator. Go with His grace."

"Thank you, your highness." He gave her a short bow and headed for the guardhouse.

Veranna dismissed the attendants and turned back to gather her documents, but a tingle of surprise went down her spine and her senses perked up. A friendly cackle sounded from the far end of the table, bringing her head up to see Denny Strorfere sitting with his feet resting on the table.

"Mister Strorfere, you always seem to show up without warning. A simple knock on the door would be sufficient."

"Would it? Sufficient for whom? I'd have to hassle with your guards and go through all of that protocol nonsense. By the time I got to speak with you the world would have ended."

Veranna could not help but laugh. "What won't happen until world's end is your penchant for obscurity."

"I've never had trouble with others understanding me before."

"And the fish will have a difficult time telling the bird what water is like."

Stroerfere turned serious and put his feet on the floor. Leaning forward on the table he asked calmly, "Why is that?"

Veranna sat next to him, a thrill of realization bringing a warm smile over her face. "Well, the fish has no way of judging his world against that of the bird's. It is limited to its own environment and language."

"And you think this applies to me?"

"Only to a very limited degree. We speak the same language and share a common environment with similar bodies. But your existence is not at all common."

"You have become nearly tedious in your logic."

"That is an odd statement from someone who advanced the science of logic so much in his own day."

He feigned amazement. "I see that not all forms of knowledge were obliterated by the Erains. What else do you know?"

"Not nearly enough. However, I love to read, and one of the first things I read when I came to Tolemera was the third volume of the *Analecta Emperia Emeraldia*. The empress, Carolina, was blessed with the rise of the Talents, men and women of exceptional intelligence and curiosity. She even married one. You seem to fit the description of the leader of the Talents: Dennayaon Forest."

"You remind me of Carolina; mentally bright and very beautiful."

Veranna smiled appreciatively. "Neither of which are my doing. My lord, why are you here? Obviously, since only the Creator can restore life, He must have sent you. Apart from a few riddles the only other thing you bring is enigma."

He barked a short laugh. "You even sound like Carolina. To put it simply, I don't know. The existence I've experienced since my being taken from this world is like a seed in the ground. The Creator arranged my sprouting out just as He arranged your birth at the precise moment He knew would bring the right consequences. My expertise was in fashioning counter-measures to dragons. Perhaps that is why He sent me to you; have you experienced any dragons lately?"

"As a matter of fact, we have. At the last battle with the Gelangweils, a huge, black dragon helped our current foe, the Koosti Great Lady, to escape capture. And, some red dragons attacked the Academy, in Clarens."

He mused for a moment. "Yes, it all fits. I believe that was when I came back. You opened the Curtain of Power and did not realize that doing so allowed many evils to enter the world, making your situation both better and worse."

"How so? I was under the impression that my ancestors were gifted by the Creator to do good. How can evil come from a good source?"

"Sometimes it is simply unavoidable. Consider the ability to think. Is it good or evil?"

"Good."

"But we constantly witness the results of evil thoughts. Your powers are good, but they open the Curtain and allow evil things to escape along with the good. The evil entities manifest more quickly than the good, and that is where I come in. I will help you fight the dragons."

Veranna shook her head in disbelief. "How could anyone have known this chain of events? I feel as though I've entered one of the story books."

"No, you've simply had history catch up with you. There is a hard road ahead; however, if you defeat these Koosti you will gain a time of peace since they have a slow reproduction rate. They subdue other tribes for fighters and will drain much of the east for this war. But that will only happen if you manage to defeat them now, in the present."

"We won the last battle only because the Creator aided us. I pray that He will do so once more. Swarms of easterners, dragons and strange old men are hard enough to deal with; leading an empire has so many facets that I wonder at times if I'll have a moment to breathe."

"No one with a lick of sense would think that being a ruler is easy. However, if you always keep in mind that you are a servant of the Creator it will not be so hard to bear. His designs are far beyond what we could ever imagine."

She gave him a wry smile. "That much is obvious."

He chuckled and shrugged, but Veranna arose and continued before he could respond. "We are in great need and can use your abilities. Since you swore an oath to the Emerald Throne once before, I ask you to do so again, Lord Forest."

He kneeled and held up his right hand in pledge. "Knowing what the afterlife is like allows me to swear this life without fear. So be it; I plight myself to the throne of Emeraldia, and will give you total fealty."

She gave him a short bow. "Thank you. My first command is that you don't simply disappear as before."

He barked out a laugh and stood. "That won't be possible now that I'm sworn to the throne. So much for a quiet retirement."

A somber look overtook her face and Veranna seemed far away for a moment. "*Quiet* is a word that is becoming more alien to me every day. It seems that I just cannot avoid being interrupted by someone, or something."

As though in confirmation of her words the castle alarm bells clanged furiously. Boots could be heard stomping through the corridors as signal horns blared four double blasts indicating trouble in the city.

Lord Forest felt a thrill run through him as Veranna transformed from a sophisticated lady into a goddess of war, casting aside all regrets.

"My Lord Forest, join Yanbre in the tower and let him know that you are now sworn to the throne. He will give you further instructions. I'll join you in a minute; I must change into more suitable clothing."

She did not delay for formalities, but sped to her quarters. Passing a window in the southern wall of the corridor her attention was drawn to the sky. Conical rings of light radiated down from the sun, pounding the land and city. She recalled her vision from the marketplace and knew that any thoughts of half-measures or compromise were futile.

CHAPTER TWELVE

SIEVE AND SIEGE

A thick column of smoke rose into the sky as fire consumed a large building on the northern side of Tolemera. Men and women jumped from the second and third stories to escape the intense heat, meeting their fate on the stone of the sidewalks and streets. Those fighting the fire soon resigned themselves to simply protecting the surrounding buildings.

Yanbre directed a company of cavalry to assist in transporting the injured to the main Healing House back in the castle compound. He was nearly knocked out of his saddle as a thick, heavy arrow impacted his breastplate. Quickly regaining his balance he deflected another arrow with his sword. On the street, civilians started dropping as a rain of arrows flew down from nearby rooftops. A large, swarthy looking man darted out from an alley to Yanbre's right and thrust a long spear into the chest of Yanbre's horse. The horse reared in agony and threw Yanbre from his saddle. Swarms of easterners issued from buildings along the street and rushed toward him, swords raised in attack.

Anger boiled up inside Yanbre as he barely rolled clear of the first sword swung at him. He got onto his knees in time to block the follow-up blow, and in one feline move he slammed his fist into the inner thigh of his attacker. The man bellowed in pain, giving Yanbre a split second to regain his feet. Without pause he lopped off the easterners' sword arm, and then ran him through.

A dozen more attackers screamed battle cries as they rushed to engage him. He and his knights had to consolidate their defense or be individually cut down. He feigned retreat, sent his thoughts to Veranna through his armor, and then ran at his foes. Surprised, they were unable to reset their attack. In seconds two of them fell to his sword. A third sprang in front of him but his timing was his fate. An arrow, meant for Yanbre, went right through the man's back and protruded out of his chest. He fell and tripped up two of his comrades.

Four of Yanbre's knights fought through their foes to join him in the middle of the street. Communicating with them through their special armor, he warned them to watch out for the archers on top of the buildings, and then posted them to assist civilians trying to escape the scene. A moment later a blaring of horns sounded down the street, accompanied by the thunder of horse's hooves on the cobblestones. Treybal rode at the front of the castle guards and Rockhounds armed with crossbows. While they engaged the easterners, Treybal and Yanbre hurriedly worked out a plan. They agreed that Yanbre's knights would lead teams of guards and Rockhounds since they were able to communicate through their armor. Within seconds the knights each had three men assisting them in charging the buildings occupied by the enemy. They pushed their foes back steadily, but civilians were falling to arrows shot from atop the buildings.

Crossbows slung over their shoulders, the Rockhounds scaled the sides of the buildings like flies. Guards on the streets provided some covering fire as two more squads of guards arrived to assist. An enemy archer popped up over the rim of a nearby building and aimed quickly at a Rockhound scaling the building across the street. From below, the guards loosed their arrows at the enemy, but too late. The enemy's arrow flew straight into the Rockhounds right ribcage. He screamed with pain but saw his attacker pierced with two arrows and fall to the ground. Feeling blood flowing down his torso he knew that he would soon pass out and fall to his death. With his last strength he edged toward a nearby window and fell through, hitting the floor on his right side. The arrow broke, but the pain sent him into a daze and thought he saw a lion with yellow eyes and flowing mane looking down on him.

Another Rockhound slowly peered over the top rim of the building from which the enemy archer fell. On the opposite side of the roof he spotted three crouching figures readying to fire. With all of the noise from below, the three did not hear him when he swung his leg up and over the rim to roll onto the roof. On his feet quickly he brought his crossbow to bear on the furthest enemy archer. Concentrating on his target, he crossed the roof and screamed a war cry about twenty feet away from the nearest enemy. All three of them bolted upright and turned to face him. The furthest one felt the crossbow arrow slam into his chest and knock him off the roof to the street below. The other two had no chance to get off a shot at the Rockhound before his sword bit into their limbs. A second later and their lifeless bodies littered the roof. The Rockhound grabbed one of their bows, all of their remaining arrows, and fired at the enemy archers on the nearby buildings. Before long, several Rockhounds repeated the technique on other buildings and eliminated the threat to the troops on the street. The enemy now had to beware of arrows from above.

Yanbre directed his troops to start searching the buildings from which enemy soldiers issued. Two city blocks were cordoned off as reinforcements arrived. The oddest of them was Lord Forest, who strolled up to Yanbre as if going for a walk in a park.

"Hey, Yanbre, my good man, the empress said I was to assist you. Have you left any of the fun for me?"

Forest's offbeat humor and countenance gave Yanbre a moment's chuckle. "Certainly, sir. We are storming a few buildings, and I'm sure that the most fun will be in a point position. Would that be acceptable?"

Forest smiled and rubbed his hands together. "That would be lovely. If you don't mind, I'll start with this one right across the intersection." He maintained his smile but his eyes were intense as he walked up to the front of the building. More than once, enemy archers fired at him from lower story windows. Forest simply snatched the arrows from the air and tossed them to the ground without taking his eyes off the front door.

Four guards stationed themselves to the sides of the door, and at Forest's signal the largest of them jumped in front and kicked it just below the handle. It moved inward several inches and stopped. The guard jumped back just in time to avoid a sword thrust at him from inside. Two guards threw themselves at the door, knocking the barricade and enemies back from the doorway. Forest leaped through, now armed with a two-foot long oak stick in each hand. An enemy slashed at him with his sword, but Forest deftly sidestepped and swung his other stick and struck the man right between the eyes, knocking him out. More guards rushed in through the door and engaged the enemy. Surprised, and unable to maneuver adequately, the easterners were forced back into the inner hallways and rooms of the building. Those who attempted to escape through side doors or windows fell to the arrows of the Rockhounds outside.

Forest's voice could be heard above the din. "Search every nook and cranny! I don't want any of these rats to have a chance to escape. I'm heading up to the third floor to find the Rockhound that fell in through the window. Secure the rest of the building and bind the prisoners. They might try to torch the place, so be ready with water." He bounded up the central stairway to the third floor and halted at the corner of the hallway. Readying his sticks he sprang around the corner to surprise an enemy, but was surprised himself when he saw the bodies of dead enemies strewn along the hallway. None of the guards had gone up the stairs ahead of him, and the wounded Rockhound would not have been able to accomplish such a feat. Forest made his way slowly through each room and found more dead. A number of civilians must have fought valiantly to survive, but in vain. Most had their eyes poked out.

He reached the last room on the right, where he figured the Rockhound must be, slammed the door open and jumped inside. A shrill cat's cry pierced the room as a keen blade whisked out of the shadows. Forest jerked his head back just enough to evade the knife, but it cut off part of his beard. He was more startled by his attacker, a tall, blond female with creamy brown skin and yellow eyes with vertical pupils. He fended off several more attacks as he pushed his memory for information. The woman made a minute mistake in the pattern of her defense and allowed him to deliver a sharp blow to her knife-hand wrist. She let out a yelp as the knife flew across the room. She jumped back out of range and eyed Forest with wonder and fear, then moved cautiously toward the Rockhound lying unconscious on the floor, trying to calculate whether she could grab his knife from its sheath and get set for an attack before her opponent could stop her.

Finally, Forest's memory delivered up what he needed. "*Yiree! Nedoh meown,*" (Peace! Do no harm.).

The woman's eyes went wide and she froze. A second later she went down on one knee with her head bowed.

Forest tapped her twice on her left shoulder. "*Porteh!*" (Arise). "You have nothing to fear from me. What is your name?"

The woman rose and studied him for a moment. "I Reiki. How you know my talking? You talk like masters."

"I *am* a master."

"You very much funny. I know all masters of my people. Never see you."

"You would need to look at the very old skins to find my name." He handed her one of his fighting sticks. "If you look closely you will see that it bears the mark of Clawson Pantare. He gave me these sticks when I became a master."

Reiki started to laugh, but halted when she saw that he spoke seriously. Counting silently on her fingers, she snorted loudly. "Ke Pantare live thousands moons before." She then laughed teasingly. "You not so old, only ugly."

Forest frowned and growled, "Wrong on both accounts." He knelt next to the fallen Rockhound and gave his wounds a quick inspection. The broken arrow had been pushed through and removed, and a heavy bandage was wrapped around his chest and back. His breathing was shallow, but even, and his pulse steady. "You've done a good job tending this Rockhound. He should survive if we get him back to the castle infirmary. You take the lead while I carry him. Don't trip over the bodies you've left lying around."

Reiki sneered at the corpses. "Hah! Koosti dung make no more trip me."

As they entered the hallway they encountered guards searching the building. All of the enemy had been eliminated and the guards rushed to extract their wounded. A low, flatbed wagon with a bed of straw sat in front of the building, piled with those unable to walk. Forest laid the Rockhound gently onto the straw and motioned for Reiki to climb in as well. He sat next to the driver and ordered him to proceed to the castle at once. The driver, unsure about Forest, looked to Yanbre for confirmation and received a quick nod. A second later the horses pulled them down the street at a fast trot. Once inside the castle loading dock large carts took the wounded to the infirmary.

Veranna was there, making her way from bed to bed, consoling the wounded and thanking them for their valor. Those with serious wounds typically lay unconscious, oblivious to her and to their own pain. The healers set limbs and staunched flows of blood, but could save only a few. Tears filled her eyes, as she looked on those willing to die for their fellows. She went to the closest and placed her left hand on his forehead, and her right hand over his wound. Bowing her head in prayer, a green-tinted nimbus glowed from her right hand. The wounded man took a deep breath, then exhaled sharply and fell into a deep sleep. Veranna repeated this event with all of the seriously wounded, leaving the healers amazed.

Forest nodded and smiled. "Your highness, I see that you are learning the gifts of your ancestors. Have you had instruction in the healing process?"

She blinked as though emerging from deep water. "Lord Forest, I, uh...why no, I have not had any training. It just came to me when assassins wounded Lord Karsten. It was as though another window opened inside my heart and mind."

Forest's voice turned sad as he recalled images from the past. "You don't know just how true that comment is." Silence fell between them for a moment, but Forest suddenly clapped his hands and smiled. "Well, enough of that for now; we should be thankful that we have a healer among us." He paused and took Reiki by the hand and drew her forward. "Your highness, let me introduce you to Reiki, of the Felinii Pride."

Veranna looked upon the foreign woman and was intrigued, and surprised when she fell to her knees and bowed her head to the floor. Confused by this demonstration of humility, Veranna kept her eyes on her while speaking to Forest.

"Is this your idea of a joke, my lord? If so, it is poorly timed."

Forest chuckled softly. "It is no joke, your highness. The Felinii are not creatures of myth, and had dealings with the fathers of the forefathers of Emeraldia. They even fought alongside one another against the ancestors of the Koosti and Sudryni. However, the Felinii were nomadic and gradually moved far to the east of the Koosti lands while the Emeraldians moved west. When I was a young man I dwelt among them for three years and learned their ways. I even convinced them to let me learn their stick fighting techniques."

The empress gave Reiki another inspection and told her to rise. The Felinii woman was dressed in common servant's clothing and bore no jewelry or insignia of any kind except a small tattoo behind her left ear. It was a snake tied into a knot.

"I have seen this mark before, Reiki, and it is one that causes great suspicion. We have found many of our enemies wearing it."

Reiki lowered her eyes and nodded. "I sorry..." and here she turned to Forest and asked him a question. He said the word 'highness' and she shook her head, then turned back to Veranna. "I sorry, highness; mark not choice for me."

"How did you come to have it placed on you?"

"Koosti pigs slave me and uh..." She looked at the ceiling and shook her hands in frustration. "Koosti give me to Eifer for gold."

Veranna's eyes widened as she held up her hand for silence. "Do not speak of this again until we are through dealing with the enemy in the city. My maid will see you to quarters in the meantime." She clapped her hands twice and her maid, a short, grandmotherly looking lady in her middle years, came in from the hallway. "Mrs. Gruntun, please take Reiki to the guest chambers and see to her needs. Until we know more about her she is to be treated as a dignitary. It will be an hour or two before I send for her. Thank you."

Mrs. Gruntun gave her a short bow. "Yes, your highness." She then turned to Reiki and curtsied. "Would my lady follow me, please?"

Reiki bowed to Veranna, then turned and bowed to Forest before exiting the room behind Mrs. Gruntun.

A humored frown came over Veranna's face as she addressed Forest. "My lord, please keep in mind that too many surprises can become boring by repetition." He simply grinned and shrugged. Looking at the number of wounded people still being brought into the infirmary, anger flared up in the young empress. "We must get to the tower and see how things are going outside."

Forest had to trot to catch up with her as she made her way through the halls and up the stairs. Gazing out toward the city center they could no longer see flames jumping into the sky. A heavy, black column of smoke wafting over the city and castle grounds burned both eyes and nose.

Veranna coughed and tried to spit out the noxious fumes. "I've seen buildings burned before, but nothing like this. What was that one made of; dung and tar?"

Forest put a handkerchief over his nose and wiped his eyes. "Even that combination wouldn't smell so foul. I wonder if the Koosti haven't come up with a new tactic."

Veranna closed her eyes and covered her nose for a few moments. "Yanbre just told me that he is rounding up the city people and directing them back to the castle. It seems that the smoke is disabling them. Lord Forest, I'll need you to help get the people organized as they arrive. Yanbre, Karsten and Kreida will be heading away from the city with the army, so I will be counting on your help." Before he could respond she turned to one of the guards nearby. "Corporal, tell Lord Yanbre's lieutenant to start moving the army northwest of the city and await him on the plain."

"Aye, your highness." The tall, muscular man ran down the stairs as fast as his feet could move.

"Lord Forest, I believe you are correct about the fire. The Koosti have concocted a diversion and weapon. We have to spend time fighting the fire and will be weakened from nausea."

"Yes. That means that they want the city and castle to remain intact since they won't have to destroy as much to get at us. They may even hope to take us alive and unconscious."

Veranna shivered. "That would be a fate worse than death. Victory is not an option; it is a requirement." She closed her eyes and put her fingers to her temples. A moment later she gazed into the southwestern sky and muttered the word 'hurry'. Turning back to Forest, she gestured for him to follow her down to the courtyard. "Yanbre has returned. I want to get his report before he leaves with the army, and I'm expecting some help with reconnaissance."

He gave her a quizzical look, but said nothing as he followed her to the courtyard. Yanbre could be heard shouting orders and directing the city people to shelter on the castle grounds. Scores of people moved through the gate clutching their scant remains. Many were still in shock over the loss of loved ones or life fortunes. Veranna took a few minutes to move among them and give consolation. Tears still in her eyes, she approached Yanbre and asked for his report.

"Your highness, the Koosti fighters were simply a cover to try and take out as many of us as possible. It seems that they wanted the building to burn unhindered. Whatever was in there sure caused us difficulty. The heat became more intense after the wood burned away, and a large, black mound of tar-like goo kept smoldering regardless of how much water we tossed onto it. Several guards passed out from the fumes."

Veranna absentmindedly brushed hair away from her face as she gave him a brief looking over. "I am glad to see that you are not injured, Yanbre. The Koosti may suffer from a lack of organization, but they are fearsome warriors."

Forest scoffed at her concern. "Hah! He has the Talents of his forefathers, your highness. His distant grandfather was the best swordsman I ever knew, and Yanbre would do him proud."

She smiled briefly. "He is a wonder. I am sorry to have to send him out with the army again so soon. Yanbre, the mess has prepared some saddle rations for you and your men. Make sure that you keep up your strength. We'll stay with our plan for now, but if you see the need for a change make sure to contact me right away."

"Yes, your highness. Make sure that you stay safe in the castle. It is your ally; who knows what secrets it will reveal to protect you." He gave Forest a skeptical frown. "It is doubtful that you ever knew either of my grandfathers. They both died when I was very young, and I cannot recall any reports of them as swordsmen."

Forest simply shrugged his shoulders. "I am sure that you are correct, but you are incorrect, as well."

Just then, Karsten and Kreida joined them, leading their horses out of the stables. Forest looked at Karsten before speaking to Yanbre again. "Is this your son, Yanbre?"

"No, my lord, but we think that there may be some family connection that accounts for our appearance being so similar."

Forest snorted and shook his head dismissively. "Hmmm, it could just be bad luck."

Both Yanbre and Karsten started to reply, but Veranna laughed and gave Karsten a hug and kiss. "You terrible little boys shouldn't be so mean to each other. Lord Forest, I think they are both very handsome. And, Karsten is our official chronicler of the court."

Forest feigned being impressed. "Oh, a bookworm, eh? Maybe you and Yanbre are related. We should call you 'yawn-bore'."

Kreida pointed at Veranna and Karsten and burst out, "You should see these two together. Their idea of fun is digging through old papers and discussing strange words. Then, little miss prudicious here, instead of jumping on his lap, goes and fetches tea. It's frustrating as everything watching them. Can you conceive of them married? Not to mention any other conceiving."

Karsten and Veranna blushed. The young Genazi lord tried to ignore Kreida. "I have an idea, your highness. When this is all over why don't we have their tongues cut out? We can think of it as a service to humanity."

Veranna glared at Kreida as she tried to think of an appropriate rejoinder, when suddenly a voice sounded in her mind. She raised her hands to signal silence as she closed her eyes. "It's the eagles; I've summoned them to help us find the enemy's movements."

Kreida rolled her eyes and muttered, "Not the little birdies, again!"

A cheer went up from the castle guards and servants when they spotted two large eagles approaching from the southwest. The larger of the two headed straight for Veranna and fanned out its wings for a landing. The empress pointed to a nearby horse hitch and the eagle set down easily. With its wings stretched out to each side it lowered its head in a bow and let out a soft scream. Veranna gently put her hand under its beak and lifted its head up to look her directly in the eye.

A panoramic view from high in the sky opened up in her mind. She recognized the landscape as one about five hours southeast of Tolemera. Below was a forest of dark trees in motion. The eagle spoke in her mind as they circled lower.

"Many two-foots with shiny talons. Many two-foots on four-foots. Huge two-foot aerie toward dawn not let these two-foots in. Aerie still circled by them. Wing lizards with fire burn many small aeries."

Veranna felt as though waking from a dream. "The eagle says that the enemy is about five hours away, and that Neidburg is still holding them off. Dragons are part of the attack on the city and have burned a number of buildings. The army is as large as a forest, but they do not have that many cavalry."

Yanbre bowed quickly and jumped into his saddle. "Five hours will give us precious little time to get ready before the enemy arrives, so we'd best be away, your highness."

She tried to put on a confident tone, but her voice was full of emotional strain. "Be very careful, Yanbre, all of you, and don't do anything foolish. I will ask the eagles to provide one of their own to help Karsten locate Lord Roland, and then Kreida will help him eliminate the Koosti from Starhaven. By that time I should receive updates on Grandshire and Clarens. I am hoping to put up such a fight here that the Koosti will divert their soldiers from Neidburg to assist them. That will give Tomius a chance to break the siege."

Kreida gave her a hug and tried to reassure her. "Don't worry about us; Genazi can take care of themselves. You are going to be the one to take care since the eastern scum will send their greatest force here. We'll try to be back as soon as possible."

The eagle's eyes went wide as Karsten stepped up to Veranna and gave her a tender hug and kiss. "My love, let your men do the fighting, and remember that pain and sorrow there will be. You cannot avoid it. Look forward to our wedding day." Another quick kiss and he mounted his horse.

Tears filled Veranna's eyes and her lips were pursed. All she could say was, "I pray that the Creator will protect you, my dear."

Yanbre signaled the bugler, who blew three sharp blasts, and a second later the cavalry moved through the gate. The young empress watched the last soldier pass by and said a silent prayer for them. Those closest to her might never return, and her heart trembled. A thought from the eagle penetrated her distress.

"The one you touched beaks with is your mate?"

"Yes, we will be mated after this battle is over."

"Have no fear; his wings are strong and his talons sharp. Your aerie will be full of chicks."

Veranna smiled and thanked him. "We will provide food for all of you so that you do not have to use time for hunting. Be strong, and may the winds lift you up."

The magnificent bird bowed and then flew off to the south, the guards raising their spears in salute.

"My lord Forest, I must see to the welfare of the city folk here, but I will need you to assist me when I speak with the Felinii woman in about an hour. In the meantime I want you to coordinate with Master Treybal regarding the nocturnal raids on the Koosti."

He bowed and spoke softly. "Little has changed since the beginning of the world. It will give you resolve to remember that you serve the Creator, and that all will finally turn out for the best."

After a brief nod and smile, Veranna climbed the stairs to the top of the wall to look out on the land. The wretched smoke from the city poured into the air, and the wind blew some toward the castle. It stung the eyes and throat, but the most alarming symptom was fatigue. She had never before felt short of breath after climbing these stairs. However, all she wanted now was to sit and rest. *We can't be caught in slumber or the result will be the sleep of death.* She then returned to the main level of the castle and found a guard leaning against the wall, half asleep. "Sergeant, wake up."

The man shook his head and opened his eyes. Seeing Veranna, he came to attention and apologized. "No need to apologize, Sergeant; the smoke from the city causes fatigue and drowsiness. I want you to go around and make sure that everyone is awake. In fact, assign a page to make rounds every hour just for that purpose. We must maintain our vigilance."

He quickly bowed, his face still red with embarrassment. "Aye, your highness. I'll get right on it."

"Thank you, Sergeant. If something urgent comes up I'll be in the guest wing." She turned and headed down the corridor, bothered by how the wind scattered the smoke into nothing. Were she and her comrades simply a spark from an old fire whose smoke would vanish in the winds of time?

CHAPTER THIRTEEN

NAUGHTY GIRL

High stood the ziggurat atop the palace of the Koosti. Built both into and out of the native rock in the hillside, the palace and its grounds dwarfed the city of Banaipal that held nearly a hundred thousand people. With its massive thirty foot wall that ran from the east to the west in a half circle around the palace compound, the ruling Koosti left no doubt regarding their total dominance of the eastern lands. The various dragons flying to and from the palace added another degree of terrible awe to the might of LeAnre y'Dob and her brother, DeAndre, the Potentate of the eastern tribes.

LeAnre stood before the tall, bronze doors at the entry to her brother's ruling chamber. The air was cool, but sweat trickled down her sides as she waited for the gong to sound announcing her presence. The faces of the guards were as hard as the stone walls, and being clothed in a short, cotton wrap-around made her feel as common as the lowliest slave. Her brother was a stickler for tradition, and tradition demanded that subjects approach the Potentate with the greatest humility. It gnawed at her pride that she, the Great Lady of the Koosti, had to denigrate herself before her own brother. But his anger was growing at her inability to conceive a child, and she did not want to provoke him in any way.

The gong sounded, echoing through the corridors until the doors stood wide open. LeAnre fixed her gaze on the raised platform before her. DeAndre sat on a cushioned chair, wearing his typical purple robe and headband, but no shoes. To his right his bodyguards and administrators waited for his slightest requirement, and to his left sat his concubines on multi-colored pillows. The higher ranking concubines sat closest to DeAndre and wore long robes while the lesser ones sat behind them and wore simple wraps like LeAnre's. The chief concubine, a tall, red haired, perfectly proportioned woman with blue-gray eyes, stared at LeAnre. Haughty malice emanated from her face, a smirk that nearly turned LeAnre's legs to jelly, for the woman had born LeAnre's brother two children, a beautiful daughter and a strong son. If LeAnre did not bear a child soon she would be relegated to the ranks of the lesser concubines since a woman of the royal lines who did not bear a child was a severe disgrace. The chief concubine would become her ruler, and her brother would be forced to either ignore her for the rest of her life or try to impregnate her. Even then she would only rise to the level of a higher caste concubine, and could never marry.

She approached the platform and looked down at the floor. A guard stepped in front of her and held up his hand. At a nod from DeAndre he moved out of her way and she laid herself prostrate on the cold marble just close enough to kiss his feet.

"Gracious Sovereign, your humble servant begs you to recognize her. I have come as you commanded."

DeAndre was not a tall or heavy man, but his voice sounded as though it came from the great deep. His brow furrowed as he appraised her for a moment.

"You are testing my patience, sister."

LeAnre's heart skipped a beat; he called her 'sister'. He might be given to mercy. "I am sorry, my Great Sovereign. How may I serve you to show that my heart is truly devoted to your will?" She could not stop the trembling in her voice, and was thankful that she was not standing lest her legs give way.

DeAndre's voice grew loud and stern. "By doing as I have commanded you. By now your belly should be swollen with child, but it is as thin as a pleasure woman's. Time is growing short for you to fulfill your duty."

"Great Sovereign, I will bear a child. The Dark Lord promised this, as you well know. His will..."

DeAndre's reply cut her sentence like a broadax. "Do not presume to tell me what I do or don't know! The Dark One promised me that our family would rule these lands forever, including that of the Emeraldians. You fail to heed him by refusing to provide an heir to your office. Our family has ruled all aspects of our kingdom since before the writing of records. As high priestess you should realize your obligations."

LeAnre kissed his feet several more times. "I will fulfill all my duty, my Great Sovereign. I am your most loyal subject and will serve your glory for all my days."

DeAndre snorted, his muscles tensing under his bright bronze skin. Disdain laced every word he spoke. "Since you are my sister I will give you one more moon to prove yourself, but that is all. Stand up."

She bolted to her feet, tears of relief seeping out the corners of her eyes. She went as stiff as ice at the cold change that came over him.

"There has been a criminal charge put forward against you. It is said that you have refused to take the bronze, the very sign of our people. Is this so?"

She nearly swooned. Looking away, her voice was hardly to be heard, as she said, "No, my master."

His face went deadpan as he nodded at his chief concubine. The woman arose, walked in front of LeAnre and grabbed her simple garment in both hands at the bosom. In one swift motion she ripped the fabric away and exposed LeAnre for all to see. Around her belly, breasts, thighs and back were patches of skin where the bronze color had dulled.

DeAndre sighed, and several of his concubines hissed their disgust. After what seemed an eternal moment of silence, he spoke softly, a volcano on the verge of eruption.

"You have lied to me, sister."

LeAnre opened her mouth to reply, but had no opportunity. The chief concubine's right hand slammed into her cheek and sent her to the floor. Instinctively she tried to roll away, desperate to escape her brother's fury. Hands clamped down on her ankles, restricting her movement, and a second later she heard the familiar sound of a *paiche*, the ancient flagella of her people, whisking through the air. She shrieked as her lower back and buttocks felt the whip bite into her flesh. Not having used the bronzing vat for some time, her skin split open and blood flowed from her wounds.

The chief concubine looked to DeAndre for directions and smiled with grim delight as he ordered two more blows. She directed the concubines holding LeAnre's ankles to turn her over onto her back, and then brought the paiche down with full force across her torso from the left shoulder to the right hip. LeAnre felt as though her body was on fire and split in half. Delirious, she was totally unaware that the chief concubine walked around to her other side. The paiche slapped across her body from the other shoulder to her left hip. She had no strength to scream, and went flaccid as she slipped into unconsciousness.

DeAndre sighed and closed his eyes, calming his pulse. After a moment he looked at his chief concubine. "You have done well, Ghijay. She is now marked for all to see her shame. However, she is my sister, and I cannot help giving her another chance. Since she has not obeyed and produced an heir, I want you to take charge of her and see to it that she conceives within two moon times. If she does not, then assign her to the lowest concubines.

"Since she wears shame on her very body she will never again serve as high priestess or ruler over the Koosti, even if she bears a child. Remove her to your chambers, and then join me in mine. This has given me great distress." He arose from his chair and all but the closest guards fell to their knees until he left the room.

Ghijay smiled and directed the lower concubines to carry LeAnre to a locked room in the pleasure wing. Walking with them, she spoke to another concubine who served as her maid. "Rendi, use the *orgay* ointment on her wounds; we can't have her blood despoiling the palace." Rendi bowed as Ghijay turned and headed toward the Potentate's chambers, walking in satisfied delight, knowing that her vengeance was all but complete. LeAnre had taken great pleasure in consuming Ghijay's mother's eyes, and now she would pay for it with a lifetime of total misery. She would bear no children; the Koosti idiots couldn't bring themselves to admit that the bronzing solutions interfered with conception, and LeAnre would be in the vats at least once a week. The only skin that would be unable to absorb the dye would be the scarring along her body; the orgay ointment would see to that. The scars would bulge like knotted cords on her torso.

She put her hand on the door to DeAndre's private chambers and stopped. Her jaw hardened as she recalled her life before the Koosti ravaged her people, when she assisted her wonderful father in his duties as a provincial chief. Gone were the days of worship at the high shrine of Wahweh, the Creator, and watching her people prosper in their land. Gone too were the days of merriment in the royal park in Woodglen, the premiere city of the Deeri. All of it was now past, trampled under by these brutal dogs called Koosti. Only the Felinni had come to their aid, but it proved too much for them. They retreated to more distant lands and surrendered the children of the leader of the Pride to the Koosti in payment for resisting them. And where were they now? Only one son remained, and the others were sold in slavery to distant allies of the Koosti.

The one whom the Deeri counted their greatest ally had deserted them. Wahweh, the Creator, had done nothing to stop the Koosti's rampage. It must be that the Dark One truly was the master of the world. The thought made her feel emptier than a hollowed-out log.

She shook her head and cleared her mind. All she could do now was fight for her future, and that meant keeping DeAndre happy. She had no equal when it came to satisfying a man, but it was growing complicated since he started treating her with devoted tenderness. She actually enjoyed his presence and touch.

DeAndre looked up as she entered the bedchamber. His sad face fled at the meeting of their eyes. "Ah, my tender doe, happy am I to have you here. This day has been full of great grief."

Still several feet away, she undid her robe, tossed it to one of the lower concubines on the floor around the bed, then slowly turned a full circle and gave him a sensual gaze. Removing his robe she shoved him playfully onto the bed and lay on top of him, kissing him repeatedly on his neck and face.

"My great master, I will help you forget your grief. Think only of me, and our children. Imagine how happy you make me, and how Emeraldia will prostrate itself before you. Its empress will be unable to do anything other than even your slightest desire."

His breathing became quicker, and in one synchronized maneuver he rolled her over onto the bed and stared into her eyes, full of primal desire.

"Nor will she resist you in the least, my unmatchable queen."

Held together by bonds stronger than chains, the moon rose on their love. The light of day would reveal their world all the more.

CHAPTER FOURTEEN

AGONY AND ECSTASY

Smoke obscured the late afternoon sun as Tesra and Duke Heilson looked out at the southern plain of Grandshire. The trees and bushes were gone, and the Koosti army was less like a thriving hill of ants and more like limp weeds scattered round. The smoke waned each hour as the city fires were extinguished, and the Koosti campfires and smithies added little to the haze.

"The maggots are running low on supplies." Heilson stood motionless as he tried to count the number of enemy per camp place. "If I remember my numbers correctly there is only a little more than half of their army left. Before long they will strip the ground of every blade of grass if they don't get resupplied."

Tesra studied the enemy camp, trying to glean every bit of information possible. A grim smile grew slowly on her face. "The poor vermin are probably wondering where their supply and reinforcements are. No doubt Clarens has proved far more difficult to take then they imagined. They can't spare any troops or supplies lest Baron Lenarde's forces break out and slaughter them."

Heilson's eyes smoldered. "I can't think of a more beautiful sight. We have lost almost a fourth of our own troops and three-dozen buildings. Amazingly, the ancient buildings survive better than the newer ones."

"Didn't I tell you so? They are made of dragon stone, just like many in Clarens. The Koosti have no knowledge of it, and we know only because of the ancient records. We will need one of the ancient Talents, however, to reveal how it is made.

"But right now I want to use something far more ancient against our foes. Is the barge ready?"

The duke nodded, great satisfaction showing in his voice. "Indeed it is, and the archers are in place. Let us walk around to the west wall for a good look." He held out his arm for her to take, and as they walked, the troops were cheered.

Although weary from many long engagements, the soldiers stood proudly at their posts while saluting Tesra and the duke. Heilson had proven himself a fighter instead of a soft, self-aggrandizing noble, and Tesra was nicknamed 'the Wonder' by them. Her skill and endurance amazed them as she put down one foe after another, and her tactical solutions to problems gave them great confidence in her leadership. They had made the enemy pay six for one and discouraged them from direct confrontation en masse. As Tesra had predicted, the enemy moved more troops to attempt breaking into the city through the river gates. Amassed on both banks, the easterners awaited the arrival of a floating battering ram from downstream.

Tesra and Heilson halted at a bend in the wall where they could see the river gate and the Koosti forces. A sentry warned them to watch out for random arrow shots, while another handed Heilson a yellow signal flag. "My lord, all is ready."

Heilson then handed the flag to Tesra. "This is your plan, so we would be honored to have you signal its start. May the Creator give us relief from all our enemies."

"Thank you, my lord, I would be happy to do so."

Raising her flag, she waited for the other signalers to raise theirs and saw all four held high. In one swift chop, she brought the flag down and twirled it several times. The other signalers brought theirs down and a multitude of voices sounded out a defiant cheer. Archers arose and sent their arrows at the enemy formations along the banks while a heavy iron chain clanked on the river gate. The gate lifted and a long, wide barge floated out from the city. On each side were six archers protected by thick wooden shields. They fired shaft after shaft and took out many of the enemy. Before long they used up all of their arrows and pulled out their swords. Flashing them at the Koosti, they yelled curses and challenges. The Koosti responded with arrows and the barge soldiers were forced to take shelter behind their wooden shields. As Tesra had foreseen, the enemy archers moved forward to get better shooting points. Now exposed, the archers on the city walls rained down a heavy volley of arrows and eliminated them.

A trumpet blared and the soldiers on the barge ran to the rear and jumped into the water. Unbeknownst to the Koosti, several logs floated just below the surface. The soldiers found them quickly and took hold, then unhitched the logs from the barge and signaled the gate men. Stout horses inside the city pulled on the ropes and swiftly brought the soldiers back inside the city. The gate plunged down and sealed the entry once more.

From the wall, Tesra pointed down at the river. "Look! The barge is heading toward the south bank. The Koosti are readying to secure it. Now we'll see if our main plan will be realized."

Sure enough, the easterners pulled the barge close and tied it to a post. A score of them rushed aboard and searched the deck while others attached a ramp to the bank. Archers nocked arrows as another soldier pounded twice with a large hammer on the storage deck lock. It flew into the water, and the Koosti were nearly stampeded by a herd of terrified hogs issuing from the storage deck and down the ramp. A riot of joy erupted from the Koosti as they herded the hogs toward their camp. Their rations had been so low for days that fresh hog meat would be a veritable feast. The hogs squealed as knives ended their time with the living.

Tesra nodded and spoke gravely. "It is such a horrible shame that such creatures would be forced to endure the company of Koosti. But they shall serve a great need."

The duke laughed. "Calling someone a pig may come to be complimentary." He looked over the city and saw the fires dwindling, but could not force the scenes of men, women and children being burned alive from his mind. "There is no curse strong enough for these Koosti scum. I'd rather see a thousand of them slaughtered than one of the hogs."

Tesra slowly shook her head. "It just goes to show what evil brutes people become when they follow foolishness and abandon the truth. The truth is what they shall encounter tomorrow morning. Let's get to the meeting chamber to see to it."

She and the duke met with the captains and advisors for several hours, and repeated their plan until even the weariest could recite it after two full glasses of wine. Messages from other fiefs arrived and testified to the resilience of the Seven Lands to their enemies. Clarens had suffered large losses of people and buildings, but greater by far were the losses of the enemy. Rockhounds kept the Koosti paranoid by attacking silently during the night and then disappearing before the enemy realized it. The easterners were so on edge that they killed one another in fitful accidents. Some were so demoralized that they surrendered and begged to be made slaves. Of great importance was the fact that several blue dragons had been killed. At first they struck fear into the hearts of the people of Clarens with their eerie songs and hypnotic eyes. However, the captive Koosti were immune to these effects by the magic arts of LeAnre and took great delight in sinking arrows and spears into the terrible beasts.

Starhaven was a far sadder story. Duke Roland was lost somewhere in the wilderness between there and Grandshire, and his mother had been brutally tortured and cannibalized for all to see. The city was now totally under the control of the enemy, and its citizens enslaved. Many were butchered to feed the enemy.

A long note arrived from Tolemera describing their situation. No doubt they had the largest enemy force sent against them. Some strange man named 'Forest' was instrumental in destroying a score of dragons. His chief weapon was purity. Arrows and spears of the purest steel laced with pure oils caused the dragons terrible pain, leaving them susceptible to weapons of deadly consequence. Very brave men volunteered to serve as bait for the traps that Forest arranged. Only one man had been lost. The nocturnal raids carried out by the Rockhounds under Treybal's lead were taking a heavy toll on the enemy. Along with the guards wearing the special armor that made night vision possible, they sent the Koosti into turmoil almost every night. The enemy troops were denied sleep and became sluggish in the day. They avoided destroying the city buildings and used them for their troops. However, the Rockhounds operated with such stealth that they easily penetrated the enemy defenses. Between the nightly raids and Yanbre's lightning cavalry strikes during the day, the enemy came closer to breaking with every sunrise. As expected, they requested reinforcements from those besieging Neidburg, so Tomius was able to break the siege there and cut off the Koosti supply lines. He received an unexpected windfall of help when the Sudryni army arrived under Marquises Amilla's banner and pounded the southern flank of the Koosti force. Tomius ordered the gate opened and charged the Koosti, sending their army into total confusion. Only a tiny remnant of the easterners was taken captive, the rest being slain or committing ritual suicide. Tomius and Amilla hurried to organize the city for repair, but decided to assist Tolemera by engaging the rear elements of the Koosti forces.

Tesra and Heilson, along with their captains, agreed that when they broke the siege on Grandshire they would head straight for Starhaven and wrest the city from the enemy. Then they would head for Clarens, followed by moving north through Rosea to wipe out any Koosti forces remaining along the west coast of the empire. They would then return to Grandshire for resupply before heading for Tolemera. Time was the great issue. The enemy force at Tolemera was huge and could not be stopped by raids. It would take a large force to attack them directly and bring them to their knees.

The next morning came with a chill, but the sun's light turned the ground into a red-orange landscape. The army of Grandshire lined up on the main street leading to the southern gate. They felt no cold since anger and revenge burned in their blood, eager for release. Up on the fortress wall, Tesra and the duke looked out on the plain to the south, the aging Mother of the Academy taking in every detail.

"Look, my lord; the fires of the Koosti are constantly tended and surrounded. It looks like the sickly hog meat did its job. The number of men standing watch is nearly halved, and even they are not moving around much."

Heilson's hands tightened into hard fists. "The only movement they'll be making is into the cauldron of judgment. I envy the soldiers striking them down."

Tesra sighed. "There will be more than enough of the enemy for us once we head for Starhaven, so don't get your sword stuck in its sheath. The biggest concern will be what to do with the captives. There are many slaves who will be liberated and need looking after. Their families are no doubt being held captive by the Koosti, so the slaves may not turn against their captors."

The duke snorted contemptuously. "Don't worry about that; we will destroy them so quickly that no message of their defeat can get back east in time for them to kill the hostages."

"I hope you are right." She took a deep breath and looked at the duke, her face and voice as hard as stone. "Are you ready?"

"Yes!" He waved to the signalman, who swung his flag up and down three times. The gate clanged open and the horsemen raced out to engage the enemy. Just as expected the resistance was weak. Enemy soldiers felt as much pain in their bellies and muscles as they did from the swords and knives of the duke's men. The stench of the diseased swine made it difficult for everyone to breath, but the horsemen methodically pushed back the enemy. The duke smiled viciously. "All too easy; if they succumb this readily elsewhere we may be back to normal sooner than we thought."

Tesra frowned as she looked down onto the plain. "It does seem easy; so far we have not lost a single man. I wonder if we have overlooked something."

"You've simply been sealed up in this city so long that you can't believe that you've broken out."

"Maybe." She gazed out at the battle once more before saying, "I'm going down to the field to see if I can get some useful information out of the captives. I'll be back in..."

She and the duke landed hard on their sides when the flagman shoved them down. The duke was ready to yell a curse when the flagman shrieked in agony. He erupted in a ball of flame and fell over the wall to the ground below. Tesra rolled to her feet and looked up to see a yellow dragon forty feet away, eying her for its next blast. Swarms of brown dragons came out of the light of the dawn carrying a score of Koosti warriors each. The horses of the cavalrymen went wild and threw their riders.

The yellow dragon smiled as he caught Tesra's gaze and froze her limbs with his song.

Limbs so weak and hearts that quail;
Tongues a'stilled as boasts now fail.
Cries are mute as doom awaits;
You are mine, now meet your fate.

Tesra stood motionless before it's maws, unable even to blink. The yellows held the greatest power in their songs, and she berated herself for letting the beast catch her eye. All she could do now was surrender her body to the beast and her soul to the Creator. She calmly prayed, "Dear Creator, maker of all and giver of life, I am yours."

Immediately she fell to the walkway, as if a tightly stretched rope between her and the dragon suddenly snapped. The beast flew back as though batted away like a ball. It tumbled through the air and took a moment to gets its bearings before heading for Tesra again, full of rage.

Tesra screamed at the duke, who was still rummy from the dragon song, "Get up! Get the bowmen ready with arrows made of pure metals and slicked with pure oils. Move!"

He ran down the stairs and headed for the armory as he shouted orders, while Tesra grabbed a spear from a dazed guard and dipped the point into a pot of boiling oil.

On came the dragon, its anger stifling its reason, working up a great blast in its nostrils to burn her to a crisp in one short second. Rows of razor sharp teeth glistened as the scaly monster closed in on the small, elderly woman, its jaws wide to exhale fire.

Tesra burst forward and let the spear fly with all of her might. It slid right over the beast's tongue, the point slicing it open to reveal the fire-goo glands. It exploded in a bright yellow ball of flame, a second sun illuminating the battlefield. The shock wave knocked Tesra back against the wall and the flames singed her hair and clothing.

Heilson crept up the steps slowly, wondering what he would find. When he saw Tesra shaking her head and trying to stand he ran and helped her up. "Tesra, you wonderful old goat! Thank the Creator you're alive, and that that horrid, yellow worm is destroyed. The brown dragons now seem confused."

Tesra shook her head and clothes. "The yellow was their leader and held the others with its song. Browns are strong but dumber than the rest. Our only hope is to use their confusion against them. Tell the archers to dip their arrows in pure oils and try for the eyes or heart. Make sure that all arrows at least hit the beasts."

Heilson relayed the instructions to his aides and soon the air above the wall was filled with deadly shafts speeding toward the huge beasts. One sank deep into the side of a dragon loaded with enemy troops. The pure oil burned hot, causing the dragon to pull up reflexively. The troops could not hang on and fell to their death as the dragon veered recklessly for the archers to avenge itself.

Tesra grabbed Heilson's bow and one of the steel arrows from his hand. She aimed steadily and let the shaft go. Due to its wound the beast was too slow to evade the shot. The arrow slid home to its heart and it exploded. Several nearby dragons were stunned and fell to the ground, their wings and limbs smashed. The enemy troops they carried were either crushed or thrown through the air to their death.

On the field the soldiers brought their steeds under control and regrouped to assault the enemy troops landed by the dragons. They formed into four companies and rode to attack where the dragons were fewest. Nearly a hundred enemy died before long and the gruesome brown beasts reacted in rage to drive the soldiers away. One of the captains seized upon an idea and ordered the troops to retreat toward the city wall. Off they galloped, their fear growing. Sure enough the dragons pursued them, diving and gliding up behind them.

Tesra watched for a moment and figured out what the captain was trying to do. She yelled for the archers to ready arrows. As a dozen dragons, some of them still carrying troops, closed on the horsemen, Tesra yelled to the archers, "Fire!"

Thirty bows twanged on the wall and others from the horsemen. Many of the arrows penetrated the dragons' scaly armor and sent them into an irritated frenzy, while some hit true to target. They exploded in balls of fire, setting off a chain reaction that took in all twelve. The flames and noise caused the horses to stomp madly, but after a few minutes the captains rallied the troops to deal with the Koosti remaining on the field. Soon the plain was silent.

Heilson put his arm around Tesra's shoulders. "I am so glad that this part is over. It has made me feel weary as never before. When I saw you nearly become dragon fodder my heart almost stopped. I cannot, we cannot, thank you enough for helping us fight off these curs."

Head hanging down, Tesra leaned against the wall and waved the comment away. "My lord, I only played a small part; it is the soldiers who deserve the praise. Now they must rest and prepare to scour the land clean of the Koosti scum on the north side of the city. Let us hope that they shared the hog meat."

Heilson sighed deeply. "Yes, let's hope. But speaking of rest, I want you to get a meal and relax for a bit. You have had a hard day and need to catch your breath. I will see to the details of burial and wounded, then join you later. Do not argue with me; just get going."

A brief smile flashed across her face. "Yes, my lord." She made her way down the stairs feeling so tired that she almost stumbled. A young guard held out his arm for her to lean on and called for people to make way. The people along the passageways and streets cheered as she passed by, yelling out, 'Tesra the dragon slayer, Tesra the dragon slayer.' All she could do was nod thankfully.

Inside the castle she went to her room and bathed. By the time she was dressed, a knock came on the door and a servant rolled in a tray with hot stew, bread, tea, wine and dessert. The stew made her mouth water and the dessert made her curious.

"I've never seen anything like this, miss…uh, I'm sorry, but I don't know your name."

The young woman was dark of complexion and her deep blue eyes gleamed as she spoke. "My name is Vendae, my lady. The dessert is something that the master chef fixed especially for you in honor of your slaying the dragons. He is calling it 'dragon's breath,' and hopes that it will delight your tongue like nothing else."

"It smells delicious. I wonder if it has some type of brandy mixed in. Ah well, first things first; the stew is always good and I feel famished. Dish me up a healthy bowl full, please dear."

She sat in a cozy, cushioned chair and savored every bite. After a cup of tea, Vendae brought her a goblet of wine and a helping of the strange dessert. At first it chilled the tongue, but a moment later and her whole mouth felt warm and her cheeks went red. "Ah, that feels wonderful. The flavor is hard to guess, but I do taste cinnamon, some kind of liquor and something else I cannot put my finger on. The chef has outdone himself."

Vendae chuckled softly, an ominous glint showing in her eye. "The chef had nothing to do with it, old woman. You think you are so smart, but I have subdued you more easily than a dove. The Great Lady will take much pleasure in giving you to the dragon, and seeing your adopted daughter grovel at her feet, begging for mercy for you. All shall be as it should then, and you shall serve the dragon the rest of your days." She laughed louder now, a hideous bark of triumph.

Tesra tried to get up from the chair but could not move, nor could she yell for the guard. Her head spun and she fell into a deep sleep.

Vendae rolled her cart to the chair and opened the doors on the lower cabinet section. Strong for her size, she loaded Tesra easily enough into the cabinet and closed the doors. Rolling the cart out of the room she stopped and left a note on the chamber door requesting no disturbances, then headed for her wagon on the loading dock. There were few guards, and those present were tired and sore from battle; they passed her through the gate without a second thought.

Down into the city she drove and headed for a tall building on the north side, where she removed the cart to a service lift attached to the back of the building. A boy looked out the back door, and Vendae ordered him to operate the lift to the roof. He bowed, gave the horse attached to the gears a sharp slap on the rump, and the lift slowly rose until it came to the top. Vendae loaded the cart off and yelled to the boy to lower the lift. She then wrapped her cloak around herself and slept next to the cart until nightfall. She pulled Tesra out, wrapped a net around her and secured it with a rope that she also tied around her own waist. Dark clouds covered the single moon's pale light, hiding the presence of a large, dark-brown dragon from sight. It flew over the building, a deeper darkness against darkness, and Vendae twirled the rope before casting it into the air. The dragon caught it easily and lifted them up until Vendae was able to climb onto the base of its neck, then flew speedily into the east, clutching the prize.

CHAPTER FIFTEEN

RECOVERY AND DISCOVERY

D uke Roland and his small band of men rested in a cave, hidden in darkness deeper than night. He hated the darkness, for his mind could not stop replaying the horrid abuse of his mother. It refueled his rage and denied him much needed sleep. The enemy scouts and roving patrols they had encountered offered little respite from his woes. Their agonies failed to compensate his boiling need for revenge.

The captives had at least provided some information before he and his men sent them to the Creator. Captured food was stale and mostly inedible, but it was better than nothing. Clarens was holding them off and Grandshire was fighting so well that the enemy there required reinforcements. The Koosti knew that Roland and his men were causing them trouble in the wilderness, but considered him merely a pesky fly to be swatted.

Roland cursed the Koosti and gnashed his food slowly. *I'll be more than a fly pestering them; I'll be a swarm of wasps that stings them into the grave!* He could feel his blood rising to his head, the pressure straining his eyes and giving him a headache. He decided to calm his mind and pursue more useful thoughts.

Yesterday, and the day before, they had seen an eagle circling high in the air. It stayed overhead for hours as they made their way to the hillside cave. As the sun went down it flew off to the northeast only to return the next morning. Tomorrow morning he hoped to be away before the bird came and revealed his position to the enemy. He could not afford to be the prey; he had to be the predator and choose his times to attack.

Sitting back against the cave wall he stared at the glowing embers of the fire, wondering if they burned as hot as the brand upon his soul. Without realizing it sleep overtook him. His dreams whisked him away to look upon the courtyard of the castle in Starhaven. A large fire burned in the center as enemy soldiers reveled in destruction. He noticed a group of them gathered around a woman. They drove their knives into her flesh before throwing her onto the fire. The woman screamed and writhed as the flames burned her to a crisp. Roland let out a blood-curdling cry of anguish and ran to her, hacking down the enemy in his path. He reached the fire but could not get close enough to drag her from the blaze. He turned and cursed the enemy and saw a vast crowd of them ready to strike him down. He cared not and raised his sword to chop at them as a logger clearing a forest. Just as he started to swing at the closest foe, a hand gripped his wrist from behind. He spun around and saw the woman who'd been thrown on the fire. It was his mother. Her body was restored and her face beamed with radiant beauty. A royal dress of pure white formed around her and she smiled at him. Love and contentment shone in her eyes as she spoke sweetly.

"Roland, my dear son, be assured that I suffer no more. The Creator has given me new life and rest from all of my troubles. The Koosti cannot ever take that from me. Do not let them take away the joy of life from you, but see them for what they are: Dupes for the one they call their Dark Master. I am restored and have relinquished all hate. Your time will come for you to join your father and me in the Creator's blessing. Be at peace. I do not say to never grieve, but simply point out that grief shall last only for a little while and then vanish in the renewal of life in the Creator's wisdom. Goodbye, my son, for now, and joyfully anticipate the day when we share all things anew."

He stared at her as tears of joy and relief flowed down his cheeks. The light around her increased as she raised her arms and sang a song of praise and adoration to the Creator. The light enveloped her and she rose into the sky, her song echoing across the land as she disappeared in the clouds.

A shout of alarm suddenly woke him. He looked around and saw his men scrambling out of the cave with their swords drawn. The bright light pouring in told him that the sun was well into the morning sky. Jumping to his feet he ran out onto the modest slope and looked around to see what was wrong. Several thousand people, men and women on horse and foot, dressed for war, were spread out on the slope and at its base. The morning sun made their knives, spears and swords glitter like a galaxy of stars. He realized that they had no chance against a force this size and prepared to die, taking as many with him as he could, when a familiar voice shocked him to wonder.

"Blast, Roland! You look a total mess. Haven't you ever heard of taking a bath once in a while?"

The young duke bounded forward, his joy driving away fatigue and despair. "Kreida, you blessed little shrew, thanks be to the Creator that you are here!" He embraced the young Genazi woman and patted her on the back, noticing another familiar face beside her. "Karsten! It has been over a year since I last saw you. How are you, old friend?"

The two of them shook hands and embraced, then Roland signaled for his men to relax and greet the Genazi. One question popped into his mind as he turned to Kreida and Karsten again. "How do you come to be here, in the middle of nowhere?"

Karsten pointed up at an eagle circling overhead. "The empress sent us to look for you, and the eagle led us. We would have reached you sooner, but a few units of enemy soldiers caught our attention. We lost a handful while they were destroyed. We have horses to spare and thought you might like to join us for a ride to your fief. We have an appointment with some Koosti, there."

Roland's jaw tightened to a grimace. "I would not miss it for anything." He shook his head and looked at his guard unit. "These are all that is left of my soldiers, and my chief counselor, Yargen, as well. We may look a scraggy lot; however, these men have fought like bears and deserve the highest praise."

Kreida flashed them a sly smile. "Give them a bar of soap, a shave and a haircut and I just might have to give them my full attention."

The men clapped and cheered, as they demanded soap and razors immediately. Roland could not help but laugh. "Be careful, men; you are outnumbered." He gave Kreida a quizzical look. "Aren't you and Treybal married? He would be upset hearing you speak like that."

With exaggerated precision she said, "No, we are not yet married. And, if he knows what is good for him he will keep his mouth shut." She walked up to one of Roland's men and tugged on his beard. "Isn't that right, fleabag?"

The man put on a serious face. "Aye, my lady, for true!"

Kreida gave the man a playful slap and then took Roland's arm in hers. "The empress wants you to come with us back to Tolemera. She probably thought that you were taking too long to arrive for her wedding; she and Karsten are a bit slow in some things. Now she has to let a war get started just to get you to show up. That is mighty sorry form, my lord."

Roland felt as though he were on a wilderness adventure. "I apologize, my lady. I look forward to seeing Karsten running around with a delirious smile on his face." His own face suddenly went sad. "I just wish that my mother could be there to see the wedding."

Kreida put her other hand on his chest and a fierce light shone in her eye. "Did the vermin scum get to her?" When he lowered his gaze and shook his head, she read some of the pain running through him. She pulled out her knife and yelled toward the south, "Vengeance shall be taken on all of you rats! Slow shall come your ends as you expire in agony. The Genazi shall show you no mercy!"

Karsten was grim, but soft spoken. "That is the way it will be. My lord, you, Veranna and I have all lost our parents to the treachery of evil men. We will teach them a necessary lesson." He then ordered the cooks to prepare breakfast and assembled ten units of twenty men each to scout out the surrounding land. "Find us some Koosti to kill. If you take any prisoners, get them back here immediately for questioning." The men nodded and rode off to the south at different angles, eagerly desiring to find some enemy troops for Lord Roland to take vengeance on.

An hour later the scouts returned with two bound captives. The squad leader reported directly to Karsten and Kreida. "These two were part of a company heading back toward Starhaven. They fought like sickly old men, so we did not lose any of ours. They look like they are not feeling too well, either. All that they seem to know is that they were ordered to regroup at Starhaven and told not to eat any of the food from the area of Grandshire."

Karsten smiled knowingly. "That means that Grandshire has successfully thrown back the Koosti. Did they mention anything regarding their illness?"

"No, but one of them griped to the other that he should have simply been satisfied with the flesh of captives and not eaten any of the hog flesh."

Kreida gave the prisoners a quick looking over. "Swine fever, eh? That is good; I hope that a lot of them suffered miserable deaths. I wonder if they took any of the pigs to feed their army in Starhaven. If so, Roland and his men could handle them all by themselves."

Before anyone could comment, a shout went up from the sentries at the rear. Horsemen approached, riding hard. Karsten ordered everyone into a defensive setup, and to hold their fire until they were sure of who was coming.

Two minutes later and the point man for the oncoming force slowed to a stop just outside of bowshot of the Genazi sentries. Seeing their banners he waved at them and then galloped back to his main host. A unit of ten men then rode out from the host and raised the banner of the Duke of Grandshire. Karsten, Kreida and Roland mounted and rode with a squad of guards over to the newcomers and received a salute of welcome from the duke, himself.

"My lords, and my lady, this is wonderful. I never expected to find you here. We have just broken the Koosti from around Grandshire and are pursuing them back to Starhaven. How have you fared?"

After relating all of the news, Heilson took Kreida, Karsten and Roland aside. "Our victory is very bittersweet. Tesra helped us to defeat the enemy, especially their dragons. After the battle she retired to her quarters and has not been seen since. The guards reported nothing unusual, so our only suspicion is that her absence is tied to the disappearance of a serving woman and her cart."

Rage and concern burned inside Kreida. "Is this cart large enough to hold someone Tesra's size?"

Reluctantly, the duke nodded his head. "We have even tested others like it with people her size. One of the guards posted on the castle loading dock reported that this girl rolled her cart onto a wagon and drove into the city." He shrugged and held up his hands in exasperation. "That is all we know. A few people in the city claimed that on that night they saw a shadow pass over and it scared them to the bone. Such reports are far too crazed to be taken seriously."

Kreida jumped into her saddle and whistled sharply. Two large, light brown dogs ran up and sat staring at her. She turned her horse to the north and spoke angrily to the duke. "Maybe a crazed notion is all you've got. I am going back and find out what happened if I have to tear the city apart with my bare hands. I want one of your lieutenants who really knows the city to come with me."

The duke was taken aback by her ferocity, but simply pointed at one of his officers and ordered him to go with her. "Remember, she is a sister to the empress; make sure that she has everyone's cooperation."

The man nodded and moved beside Kreida, who raced off as if demons were chasing her. Alongside of her ran her two dogs.

The duke shook his head as he spoke to Karsten. "I should see to it that each of my soldiers marries a Genazi woman. I would have an invincible army."

Karsten chuckled. "Kreida is a woman of strong passions, my lord. Your men would be too exhausted to fight." They all laughed and Karsten signaled for everyone to listen up. "We go to liberate Starhaven. As we near the city you must remember to carefully distinguish between friend and foe. Duke Roland, and his men, will direct our forces since they know the land. After that we may need to head west to Clarens to assist them. We cannot allow the enemy to come at us from behind. If Clarens is able to hold it's own we will return to Tolemera and take the battle to the enemy. No doubt the empress will receive news from the other fiefs and direct us where needed. Remember, we fight for what is right and for the future of our empire. Weakness will betray, and mercy will preserve us. Wisdom must be our guide. Move out!"

He directed the scouts to head south, and then positioned the vanguard. He, Heilson and Roland rode abreast, with Roland's advisor, Yargen, close at hand. The young duke of Starhaven directed the army along the best route toward his city and all weariness drained away. He looked at Karsten and felt a tremor of good-natured envy. The young Genazi lord was strong, intelligent and engaged to the most remarkable woman of the age. It was amazing how she had united the Seven Lands into a brotherhood by her noble character. The two rulers would provide a fine succession of leaders in the generations to come. In three days he would know just how much would be demanded of his own generation to recover from this brutal war.

Kreida pressed hard until her horse could not take anymore. Her dogs proudly kept up with her but did not refuse a time of rest. The lieutenant assigned to her followed at a distance since his horse just could not match the endurance of Kreida's. The rest time allowed him to catch up, and he felt beaten and stiff as he dismounted. Kreida, hands on hips and scowling, could not resist a shot.

"If you are so worn out from a little horse riding, you'd never satisfy a Genazi woman." Before he could respond she went back to her horse and pulled out some dried pieces of meat for her dogs. They gulped them down and lapped up water from her hand. Speaking loudly enough for the lieutenant to overhear, she said to the dogs, "Boys, you have one hour to rest and then we are off, again. I want to reach Grandshire before sundown. Got it?" Both dogs gave their tails a quick swing and lay down in the grass.

An hour later they set out at a trot and stopped at noon for a meal and rest. The lieutenant, thinking he served her graciously, brought his brandy flask over to Kreida. "Would my lady care for some brandy?"

She snatched the flask from his hand and put it to her lips, but then suddenly thrust it back at him. "Trying to shake me loose here in the middle of nowhere, eh? Don't even think about it; we don't have time, and you need your strength. Besides, I have not had the chance to train you properly."

The lieutenant blinked and bowed. "My lady, I meant nothing licentious; I just thought you might like some. Forgive me, please!"

She laughed to herself, but put on a wearied face. "Ah, forget about it. I would not want to give my fiancée a reason to skin you alive." She then became all business. "When we reach the castle I want you to take me to Tesra's room right away, while my horse is being stabled. Then I want a fresh horse and some food I can eat in the saddle. My dogs and I will be searching the city streets. While you rest your tender frame, I will need someone to replace you to assist me. Now, shut up and let me get a half-hours' rest."

The man gladly moved away a bit and lay down for a while, thankful that Kreida's tongue had ceased its lashing.

Five hours later they arrived at the castle's southern gate. Kreida had again outpaced the lieutenant and sat glaring at the guards who held their spears across her path. "What do you think you maggots are doing? I am Kreida, sister to the empress and Princess of the Genazi. Get out of my way or I will make sure that your toes are longer than another part of your bodies!"

One of the guards was ready to retort when an officer walked up behind him. "Private, is there a problem?"

The two guards came to attention. "No, captain; this woman just rode up and demanded to be let in."

The captain gave Kreida a quick glance and then shouted at the guard. "Don't you have enough sense to let in a guest of honor? She represents the imperial throne."

Kreida gave the guard a smug look as she passed through the gate, and then spoke to the captain. "Grainger, the last time I saw you, you were a lowly sergeant wanting an innocent Genazi maiden to dance for you at the *Goose Inn.*"

He laughed and replied, "Genazi yes; innocent, no! But now that I am a captain, I have to conduct myself with a bit more refinement. I see you have brought your dogs with you. The men might be a bit jealous about that."

It was Kreida's turn to laugh. "They will just have to recognize their superiors." The lieutenant arrived at the gate, he and his horse looking exhausted. "This one, here, can't seem to withstand a little bit of exertion, and if the rest of you are so frail I had best not excite you with any dancing."

"Such a pity. What brings you to Grandshire, my lady?"

"I am here to see if I can find out what happened to Tesra. The duke says she just disappeared after going to her room a couple of days ago."

"That's right. We have not been able to locate her even after looking just about everywhere. I am amazed that such a woman as she could be overcome by anything less than a brigade of warriors."

"True, but then I haven't devoted any time to her training. Take me to her room; I want to see if my dogs can pick up the scent of the old prune."

"Aye, my lady. Do you have need of the lieutenant's assistance?"

"Did I ever?"

Grainger harrumphed and sent the lieutenant to get some food and rest then escorted Kreida to Tesra's room. The dogs sniffed around for a moment before heading down the corridor to the loading dock. Both jumped down and headed for the gate toward the city. Kreida told them to stop, and then ordered Grainger to get a horse for her and himself. In minutes they proceeded with an armed escort into the city. Kreida ordered them to let the dogs lead by a good margin, and then commanded the dogs to begin. Out they went, both confident that they were on the right trail. Ten minutes later they halted in front of a tall building on the north side of the city.

Grainger looked it over. "It used to be an inn, but a few years ago it was sold to some outlanders. I don't know much else about it." He ordered the guards to dismount and go with him to the entry, then knocked hard and commanded the occupants to open the door.

A moment later the door opened and a young, teenage boy looked out. "Yes, sir, may I help you?"

"Yes, lad; we are here on the authority of the duke. We are conducting a search."

Kreida barged forward and pushed the door wide open. "Hey, kid, get out of my way. I want everyone down here in the main room, right away."

The boy cowered in fear, but seemed reluctant to follow orders. A second later a woman in her mid-thirties entered the room. Her dark hair and complexion were not the norm for Grandshire's citizens. Kreida's dogs sniffed at her and started barking. The woman froze, her eyes darting between Kreida and the dogs.

"Get the dogs away from me; it is not lawful for you to harm citizens for no cause."

Kreida pulled out her knife and approached the woman, who staggered back against the wall and held up her hands. Before Grainger could restrain her, Kreida grabbed the woman's shirt at the collar and sliced it open down to her waist. Pulling it open she pointed at the fading, dark patches on the woman's body. "If you were a citizen you might have an argument, Koosti."

The woman screamed something in her own language and feet could be heard stomping in the inner hallways. Kreida slapped the woman hard and threw her out the front door. From inside the building there issued several Koosti men with scimitars drawn. Grainger ordered in his men and they quickly dispatched the Koosti warriors. The teenage boy tried to bolt out the door, but Kreida nabbed him by his shirt.

"Hold it, little one. I want some answers." She ordered the soldiers to search and remove the bodies and to bring the woman in and sit her down. "My knife is sharp, woman, and thirsty for Koosti blood. You will tell me what I want to know, or I will let it have a real good drink."

The woman's eyes bulged and her lips quivered, but she said nothing.

Kreida held her knife across the boy's throat. "Is this your son? Get your tongue moving or he will experience my anger."

Hatred for Kreida gleamed in the woman's eyes. A second later she mumbled a plea. "Do not hurt him; he has done no wrong."

"I will be the judge of that. I want information, and I want it fast!"

The woman looked down at the floor. "We only follow our mistress's will. The boy knows nothing else."

"Yeah? Well, just what is the will of your mistress?"

"Simply that we serve those she sends here."

"Did one of them come here two days ago, and then leave suddenly?" When the woman darted her son a glance, Kreida's eyes smoldered. "My patience is running thin."

The woman cringed and tears poured from her eyes. "Do not hurt my son! I will tell you what you want, but please, spare him."

The son suddenly blurted out, "No, mamma, no! They will kill him."

Kreida understood at last. "You don't want to speak because they are holding the boy's father as blackmail if you do not do as you are told. I do not blame you for being stubborn, and can tell you that Koosti have a hard time keeping their bargains. Where are they holding this rat of yours?" The woman pointed down at the floor. "In the cellar? Do they know that we are here?"

The woman shook her head frantically, but was unable to take her eyes off of her son. "There was no time to warn them, and they are two levels down."

Kreida removed her knife from the boy's throat, but held him fast by his collar. "I will make a real bargain with you. If we get this idiot of yours away from his captors, alive, you will tell us everything."

The mother and son looked at each other for a moment, and then the mother shook her head in agreement. "It will be as you say."

Kreida ordered the boy to be taken outside and then commanded the mother to take them to the cellar stairs, pointing at Grainger and another guard to assist her. "Grainger, I will go first, but we will probably need your bulk to bash the door open. While the door is swinging, I will move into the room and take out any Koosti. Got it?"

"Aye, my lady; but how do you know how many will be in there?"

"We dealt with the reserves upstairs, and a secret outpost cannot afford to draw attention with a lot of people running around. I just hope that there is a lamp burning in the room."

The three of them moved silently, but quickly, down the stairs. The hallway was wide enough for two of them to walk abreast, with a floor of solid stone. Kreida crept up to the door, placed her ear against it for a moment, then readied her knife. Grainger gauged his distance, and in a blur, kicked at the door. It smashed open and Kreida leaped in just in time to stop a Koosti soldier from driving his knife into the throat of a man tied and gagged in a chair. Grainger and the guard bounded in and engaged three other Koosti, two of whom were women.

Kreida grappled with her foe, each trying to restrict the other's movements. The man was stronger and obviously a trained wrestler. He managed to place his foot behind hers, and then pushed her backwards. They both went down, the Koosti man landing on top of her. The impact knocked the wind out of her and she saw stars for a moment, but did not feel the man move to slice her throat. In fact, he did not move at all. It became clear to her when she felt her right hand drenched with warm fluid, unaware of the fact that she still grasped her knife, and that the hilt was deep into the man's guts. She rolled him off and looked around. Grainger held the two women at bay while the guard floundered against the Koosti man. The man swung his sword in a quick combination and the guard fell to the floor. Kreida screamed with rage and the man turned toward her, but not soon enough. Her blade slashed across the front of his leg. She swung her left leg around and knocked his good leg out from under him, then rolled and brought her knife down and into his chest as he hit the floor.

The Koosti women fought desperately, but Kreida jumped into the fray and slammed her fist into the forehead of the nearest one, sending her down and out, then kicked the leg of the other, grabbed her by the hair and yanked her off of the floor. She fell hard and was disoriented for a bit, but Kreida was on top of her in an instant and choked her until she lost consciousness.

"Grainger! See to the guard, and then get some help down here; and more light."

The captain quickly ascertained that the guard was dead, and then ran up the stairs for help. Seconds later a thunder of boots sounded through the hallway.

Kreida forced open the mouth of the woman she had choked and felt around the inside of the cheeks. Sure enough, she found a bump and jabbed her knife tip into its edge, then pulled out a small capsule. She ordered a guard to tie her up and take her upstairs. The other woman started to stir. Kreida leaped on top of her and slapped her hard across the cheek. "Go to sleep, Koosti tramp!" She then removed an identical capsule from the woman and had her taken upstairs as well.

The man sitting tied and gagged in the chair seemed barely conscious. When Kreida brought a torch closer to look at him, he screamed in terror, thinking that she wanted to torture him.

"Shut up and listen! Your wife and son are, unfortunately, alive and well, which you won't be if you give us any trouble. Understand?"

The man shook his head as well as he could, and flinched when Kreida sliced off his gag. When she cut the ropes binding him to the chair he still did not move.

Kreida frowned and yelled, "Get out of the chair, maggot!"

The man could barely whisper, "I cannot; I have no strength."

She grabbed his arm and it felt lighter than a bird's wing. "Holy Wahweh's shrine, you are a stick man. Guess we will have to carry you out. Guard, take sticky, here, upstairs and get him some water. He can have his tramp wait on him; their time of serving the Koosti is over." She searched the room for anything of interest, and angrily kicked the chair. It hit the wall and fell apart, revealing a hollow leg with a parchment rolled up inside. She pulled it out and saw writing, but could not make anything of it in the poor light. Once upstairs she ran outside to get a better look. The writing was in a foreign script that she guessed was Koosti. She ran back upstairs and found the wife of the tortured man bathing him. Without knocking, Kreida burst into the room and demanded that the woman read the document.

The woman wiped away her tears of happiness and gratefully did as she was told. "My lady, this writing is from the Great Lady of the Koosti. She ordered her soldiers to capture someone named 'Tesra' and bring her back to Banaipal. She is to be mated to a dragon and used as bait for empress Veranna, if the empress is able to find her way through the maze of chambers to where the dragons mate and nest. Only herself knows this mission and the warriors charged with the task. The warriors are commanded to kill themselves when done."

Kreida's eyes flashed with anger. "Did they do their job, or not?"

The Koosti woman looked at her son, who said, "My lady, the day before yesterday one of the Great Lady's servants came here and ordered me to operate the lift at the back of the building. There was only she and a cart of some kind. I never saw her after that."

"Take me to the lift!"

The boy scrambled out of the room and out the back door of the building. Pointing at the lift, he offered to operate it for her.

"That is exactly what you will do, boy." She whistled and her dogs came running to her. They sniffed the carrier and barked. On the roof sat the empty cart, and the dogs barked excitedly that Tesra's scent was there. A cold chill ran down Kreida's spine. *That woman has meant trouble ever since we met, and now she needs rescuing before she is turned into a dragon wife. Blast! Veranna will be crushed.*

She wiped tears from the corners of her eyes and went down the lift. She and Grainger raced back to the palace where she decided what to do.

"I want to sleep until before dawn. Make sure that food is ready then and not waiting to be cooked. In fact, I want some food now, too. I want my horse groomed and saddled, and four strong spares ready when I finish my breakfast in the morning. I ride for Tolemera. You will send a message to Karsten, of the Genazi, that he needs to head for Tolemera at once, and that the duke must as well. Tell them that Tesra is a captive and has been taken to the Koosti's chief city, Banaipal. We will need every man possible on the eastern front."

Grainger bowed and felt a healthy respect for the fiery Genazi woman. "Aye, my lady. The messenger will be out the gate in ten minutes, and I will see to your food right away. Would you care for the masseur before sleeping?"

Her face brightened for a moment, but she then let out a reluctant sigh. "Naw; my fiancée thinks I get excited too easily. He forbade me such pleasures. Can you believe that he would be suspicious?"

The stalwart captain nearly broke out laughing, but kept his voice level. "Why, it is ludicrous, my lady. I will send the food service in immediately." He bowed and exited the room quickly to see to her orders.

Kreida went to the balcony and looked toward the northeast. The setting sun glowed red, but could not match the burning anger welling up inside her. *Those Koosti scum will pay a high price for taking Tesra. No matter how many there are I will cut them to pieces and feed them to the pigs. If they have harmed her in any way, then I will really be mad.*

CHAPTER SIXTEEN

THE CREATOR'S DREAMS

General Saccar-jah stood atop the tallest building of Tolemera viewing the layout of the city and the castle compound on the northwest side. The Koostis' assumption that they would sweep away the Emeraldians in one fierce wave was totally unrealistic, but LeAnre y'dob could not be convinced otherwise. She had planned poorly and gotten into a great deal of trouble; now was the time to try and salvage whatever good was possible in the whole affair. Fortunately, Saccar-jah had arranged his attack to allow for this situation. Winning the city, and then the Seven Lands, would help compensate for the political turmoil at home.

The man who said he owned the building on which Saccar-jah stood was named 'Eifer,' who had provided a good amount of intelligence about the imperial forces. But what he had not told them was how fierce the Emeraldians were. No progress had been made against the castle, and even the dragons were afraid to fly close to it. Many had already been lost. Even though they attacked at night the castle guards fired arrows and spears as if it were broad daylight. If the weapons did not kill the dragons, they caused them horrendous pain. Wounded dragons killed many of his men when they writhed in painful spasms. Eifer had deserved his eyes being taken; his lack of vision cost them greatly.

What grated on Saccar-jah's nerves most was the situation with his troops at night. Many were paranoid to sleep since the Emeraldians carried out phenomenal raids in the darkness. They never faltered in picking out weak points; even the traps set for them seemed useless. How could they pick out hidden men in total darkness? Hundreds of his men had been lost to them. And where did the enemy go when chased back to the castle? The gate remained closed, and no ladders or grappling lines were used. They just disappeared somewhere near the wall.

Another serious problem was that the Emeraldian army outside the wall was somehow communicating with the nighttime raiders. How could that be, since the castle was virtually surrounded and very few pigeons had been used? The raiders would kill a number of sentries and then turn the camp into a state of total bedlam. The troops chased them but were hit blindside by cavalry rushing on the now poorly manned units, getting his men to act hastily. The Emeraldians operated as a well-oiled machine, while his own troops seemed like drunks chasing whores.

One of his subordinates, a man from a tribe conquered three generations before, adjusted his posture and purposely cleared his throat. General Saccar-jah spoke to him without interrupting his survey of the battle site.

"Yes, Malakite, you may speak."

Malakite was a man of average height and build, but his mind was sharp, and he had proven himself a valuable part of the general's command force. His dark eyes missed very little. "Sir, you ordered me to notify you of any messages right away. One has just arrived from Banaipal, and is being unlocked."

The general nodded and maintained his scan of the castle compound. 'Unlocking' the code used for messages usually took a couple of hours, so he could study it after dinner. He might even have time to dabble in his harem if everything went as he hoped. Ah! That would distract him blissfully and ease his mind for a while. A glass of silk fire, made from the same plant as *geistlos* powder, and a while being pleasured by his concubines would help him regain his strength like nothing else. It would be as an oasis in the midst of the Garaga desert back home. These barbarian Emeraldians did not know the meaning of pleasure.

He clasped his hands behind his back, satisfied that he had come up with a plan to reduce his losses to the nightly raids. Garrisons of troops in overlapping watches should accomplish the task, leaving the bulk of his army to achieve a night of sleep without worry. *Yes, then we will take the barbarian's castle, and this foolish girl calling herself an empress. She will be trained appropriately to kiss the feet of her new master, DeAndre. Naked, with a rope tied around her neck, I will drag her before him to serve his will!*

Saccar-jah felt a sense of newfound purpose; his goal, and his master's, would be met. He heard a short, raspy shriek and looked up. Out of the sun dove a green eagle. Before he could react, the eagle flared its wings a bit and extended its talons. In a blur the talons swept across his face and throat, and the bird was gone, climbing back into the sky. The general felt no pain, but warm ooze now flowed down his chest. He grew dizzy and his vision dimmed. Voices behind him sounded far away. He saw the edge of the roof and fell forward, taking with him two others who had grabbed his arms, and smashed into the street below.

✳ ✳ ✳

The empress of the Emeraldian Empire sat near the fireplace in her private chambers. Candles and oil lamps cast a warm glow around the room, providing enough light for her to read the reports that Treybal delivered to her earlier in the evening. The successes of the nocturnal raids were proving so effective that she often managed a few hours of sleep at night. But the strain and tension affected her nonetheless.

A light knock sounded on her door, taking her attention away from the reports. The hourglass over the fireplace showed a little sand left, and she marveled at how quickly the evening stole away. Grateful for the interruption, she called for whoever was at the door to enter.

Reiki flowed in with such smooth grace that Veranna was reminded of a cat. The Felinii woman carried an earthenware pot in one hand and matching mugs in the other. She walked over to Veranna and bowed before setting the pot down and handing a mug to her.

"Highness, it late; you must sleep. Drink help."

The aroma of hot-spiced wine wafted into the air and Veranna wondered if anything had ever smelled so wonderful. "Oh, thank you, Reiki; this is so kind of you. It is delicious. Please, sit down and join me for a while. I have been so busy that I just have not had time to speak with you since we first met. However, I am very interested to find out how you came to Tolemera, and about your people."

The Felinii woman stared at her for a moment. "You much deefrent from other, uh, nobles I meet. No talk with Reiki, just hit with stick."

Anger flashed across Veranna's brow. "I will not allow anyone to abuse you, Reiki. You are not a slave; I hope to call you my friend."

Reiki bowed in her seat, her voice sounding a bit choked. "I am much happy and, uh, how you say, honored, highness. Reiki no have friend for long time. Friend from Deeri tribe is used by Koosti ruler. He sell me to Eifer."

Veranna sat up straight and wagged her finger for emphasis. "I want you to understand very clearly, Reiki, that you are a free woman. No one owns you; you may leave at any time you wish. If you want to try to return to your homeland, I will help you. You are now responsible for making your own decisions."

"You like father of me. He say much about me doing like older people. Koosti come and kill many older people in our pride. Two older sisters slaved to far away, younger sisters given to dragons."

Veranna gasped. "They were fed to dragons? That is horrible, Reiki. I am so sorry."

"You no understand, highness. Sisters not for food; they are used to make baby dragons."

Veranna nearly screamed, "No! You must be mistaken; that cannot be possible!"

Reiki burst into sobs as she recounted her sister's agony. "No make mistake, highness. Koosti dogs make me see. Yellow dragon put his seed in them and they grow fat with baby dragon. Sister's skin turn like dragon, face too. They now think like dragon. All day lie down on egg like mother chicken, and fright all coming near. Only Potentate and Great Lady of Koosti come near."

Her jaw tight and back straight as a board, Veranna pounded her fist on the arm of her chair and hissed, "LeAnre y'dob! I should have had her jailed at the first sign that she was capable of such evil. But I was naïve, or, maybe stupid would be the better term. I will not repeat that mistake again!" She rose from her seat and paced in front of the fireplace a moment, then spoke in anguished tones. "Why does she think that she must be evil to attain greatness? Is not a good reputation worth far more than that?"

Reiki smiled and spoke softly. "You like priest of Wahweh at shrine. They are much wise. Koosti hunt them and kill them, saying that Dark Lord against them."

Curiosity interrupted Veranna's anger. "I have read of the priests of Wahweh in ancient books. And, a friend of mine uses the name as an oath. She is a Genazi woman named 'Kreida.'"

Reiki nodded knowingly. "Ah, Wahweh know to tribes on all lands. Deeri tribes keep shrines until Koosti come. My friend, now used by DeAndre, come from Deeri. She very angry because Wahweh let Koosti kill her people and make her slave. She lose faith."

Veranna closed her eyes and sighed. "That is so sad, Reiki; I wish that I could snap my fingers and make everything right again. But quick answers often have serious side effects. That was how LeAnre tricked me into allowing dragons to return to this world."

Reiki cocked her head slightly as she recalled something from the past. "You make Great Lady much angry."

Indignant, Veranna crossed her arms over her chest and shook her head in disbelief. "The nerve of that woman! She uses us for her own sinister purposes, kills and tortures thousands of our people and makes slaves of many others, then has the gall to be angry at us. She has no conscience."

Reiki chuckled, a knowing laugh escaping before she realized it. Veranna frowned at her.

"What could possibly be so amusing about all of this?"

"You, highness."

"Me? I do not understand."

Reiki chuckled again. "I no say she angry at people; I say she angry at you."

"Me? How can that be? I accepted her as a friend and we saved each other's lives. She dealt treacherously with me, not I with her."

Reiki smiled in appreciation of Veranna's sincerity and modesty. "She beauty; you more. She smart; you more. She powerful; you more. She slave people to her; you people follow you for love. Her brother rule her very mean; you have Wahweh rule your heart. She much angry."

Veranna just stared at her for a moment. "You are saying that she is doing all of these evil things because she is jealous of me? That sounds absurd. She was planning her rise to power long before she even knew of me."

"Yes, highness, but you no know all of her. She have much torture from yen-Kragar. She deep in black faith of Dark Lord. She drink dragon blood and strange plants. She, like say you, very jealous of brother's bed slave, my Deeri friend. Her head all, uh, how you say…mixed up."

"That may all be true, but she knows right from wrong. She knows faithfulness and treachery. The Creator's laws are stamped on every heart and cannot be erased."

Reiki closed her eyes and chanted, "*Keeya shin Wahwehso; Wahweh basilei watrono.*"

Veranna frowned. "I am sorry?"

"You talk like priest, I say back."

"So then, this is part of the worship of Wahweh?"

"Yes, highness."

"I recognized three of the words since they sound very close to the language of my ancestors. The Erains and Gelangweils destroyed all of the congregations of the Creator in the Seven Lands, but could not take Him away from the hearts of many. He has delivered me from great peril more than once, even if I never had an opportunity to attend a congregation."

"Cannot be stopped, highness. Wahweh always win."

Veranna put her hand on Reiki's shoulder. "That is very reassuring. Thank you for strengthening my faith."

"I servant and help."

"No, you I hope to have as my friend, and we can save one another, if you are willing."

"Yes, me willing. You queen like Reiki's mother. Strong and smart."

"Thank you for the compliment, but I am not nearly strong enough and can be very stupid, at times."

Reiki laughed and poured them some more wine. "You so not like Great Lady. She not hear any hard words."

Veranna smiled and changed the subject. "Reiki, if your mother was a queen, then you are what we call a 'princess.'"

"I hear word, but not know. My father chief male of pride; Felinii have many pride. Father lead elders in meetings. He want give me to mate with son of chief from other pride."

"Do you love this man?"

"No, but Felinii take mate and learn. Reiki no have chance. Koosti come and cut him to pieces and burn for dogs. Say to me I no mate; just slave. Great Lady use brothers of me for mates. She no get baby, so kill them."

"Are there any of your family still alive?"

"No know; some sold as slaves. Koosti, after yen-Kragar dead, say all no worship Dark Lord must die or be slave." Her teeth tightly clenched, she raised both fists as she exclaimed, "I never worship! Die first." She fought to come up with the right words. "I let my words freely; I walk way of straight."

Veranna recognized the phrases Reiki recited from an old book about Wahweh, and responded in kind. "As sisters united, Creator we serve."

"In life or in deaded, to the One we bow down."

The two women smiled at each other, and Reiki suddenly sprang forward to embrace Veranna. Tears ran down both cheeks. Reiki said many words before Veranna was able to calm her down and get her to use the common speech.

"Forgive, please...sister. I so happy to have sister of faith I forget you no speak Felinii. You be priest of Seven Lands to know ritual words."

"No, I am not a priestess or religious authority, but the rulers of Emeraldia have all been expected to lead lives worthy of the Creator. That is where our strength lies." A quiet moment passed, and then Veranna gave her a short curtsy. "Dear sister, may the Creator bless you with a soothing night of rest. I must try to get what sleep I can since Treybal and Lord Yanbre will be launching another coordinated attack just before dawn."

Reiki bowed and said, "Good night, sister highness; Creator give you much wisdom. Reiki ask to help. Get tired just sit and look."

"Please forgive me for overlooking your needs, Reiki. I will give thought to where we need help and let you know tomorrow. Will you join us in the dining hall for breakfast?"

"Reiki honored, highness." She crossed the room to the door with speed and grace, and with barely a sound she was gone.

Veranna could not help but compare her to Kreida. Reiki was smooth and quiet like a lioness hunting in tall grass, while Kreida was a wildcat scattering the herd. Kreida's absence was deeply felt, for the Genazi woman was full of boundless energy and enthusiasm. She could grate on your nerves, but never allowed a dull moment, and was closer than a sister, providing a strong contrast to Veranna's sometimes melancholy moods.

The empress changed into her nightgown and put two fagots of wood onto the fire. Lying in her bed, surrounded by the fire's glow, her thoughts turned to Karsten. She longed for his gentle touch and soothing words, for the day of their wedding and for the family she had never experienced. Her eyelids slowly slid down and she fell fast asleep.

She found herself sitting in a chair opposite the fire. Hot sun filtered through the blinds, but no sound other than her breath could be heard. After opening the door she noticed that she now wore the travel clothes that Tesra had made for her two years ago. No guards stood in the hallway, but Reiki suddenly appeared, running around a corner, an oak stick in each hand.

"Highness, you late. Must go; now!"

"Go where, Reiki?"

"Get others. Come."

She grabbed Veranna's wrist and pulled her along down the hallway, nearly running to the next turn. They stopped short of the corner. Reiki held a finger to her lips and signaled Veranna to stay where she was. She then readied her sticks and jumped around the corner, screaming a war cry. The cry turned into a lion's roar, and Veranna moved to see what was in front of Reiki. Three snarling hyenas stood ready to pounce, but Reiki transformed into a lioness and sprang at them. Loud and furious was the fray as jaws snapped and claws swiped through the air. The hyenas were forced back and suffered many wounds from Reiki's powerful blows. They scampered down a side hall with Reiki in pursuit.

Veranna looked down the main hallway and noticed that it led to a large open area drenched in sunlight. Passing through the doorway the heat touched her skin but failed to give her any sense of warmth. Opposite the hall door was a huge entryway between two knolls in the face of a hillside, in and around which stood a palace complex. To her left and right spread a large city teeming with people. On each side of the pathway before her stood heavily armed guards. As she passed them she noticed that their faces showed wonder, fear and enmity. None raised a weapon toward her, but they watched every step she took. The entryway stood open and the doormen pointed that she could enter. Another long corridor headed deep into the mountain, but it took only a second to traverse the distance. As if she had been there all along, Veranna spoke to a woman on her left.

"Tesra, why are we going in here? Shouldn't we be getting home?"

Tesra laughed and patted her on the back. Sharp points nicked her back, causing Veranna to comment that Tesra should cut her fingernails. The older woman ignored the remark.

"Veranna, I have always told you to never be afraid of who, or what, you are. Why should I be any different?"

The young empress frowned as she studied the ancient corridor. "Why are you saying that now?" She turned and looked at the older woman whom she had adopted as her mother and recoiled in fear. "Tesra, what has happened to you? You look terrible!"

Tesra's face was longer, and sharp fangs protruded past her lips. The pointy tips of her ears were hard, and her skin looked like shiny plates of overlapping leather. She wore no clothing and her hair had formed into a row of spiked ridges. On her fingers and toes, sharp claws glistened with fresh blood. The most frightening feature was her belly, which stretched the scaly plates of her skin.

Veranna backed away in horror, but the woman she knew as Tesra seemed unaware of her turmoil. "I think that I have never looked better, my dear. Furnasco, my wonderful dragon mate, tells me that I am his favorite. I am going to bear him a son." She patted her belly and smiled, then continued down the corridor to an opening that was easily ten feet wide, and had large, bronze doors. "Come, dear, and meet our new masters."

Veranna's fear strove against her curiosity and kept her from looking inside. Seemingly against her will, her feet slowly moved toward the door. A walkway of dark, polished stone ran from the door to a dais on the far side of a circular room carved out of the rock. On the dais sat a man with bright bronze skin, and a tall woman stood behind him. On her head danced red flames and around her neck was a set of amber stones glowing more strongly as Veranna approached. The woman's eyes glowed as well, but the radiance showed envy and wonder mixed with resentment. To the man's right lay Reiki with an iron collar and chain attached to her neck. Numerous welts showed on her body as she mewed in agony. At the man's feet sat LeAnre. Heavy scars showed across the front of her body, and she gave Veranna a quick, sidelong glance before lowering her gaze to the floor.

The man on the dais spoke calmly, as though everything happening was simply as expected. "It is good that you have arrived. The war between us has been costly, and I have need of the vast resources of the Seven Lands. I apologize for LeAnre's ineptitude in bringing you to me, sooner; she is now your slave since she can no longer rule as an y'dob. My chief concubine shall instruct you in how to please me at all times."

Before Veranna could respond, a tight collar clamped around her neck and guards placed fetters around her ankles. The woman behind the dais came and stood before her, satisfaction and sympathy competing for control of her face. "It is useless to struggle. Your Creator has abandoned you, and you must learn contentment in serving the Potentate. My people and yours are united in this once more." She nodded to the guard, who dragged Veranna over to the harem section.

Reiki screamed, "Fight, highness! No let them have you. Fight you mu…" LeAnre slapped her hard and tied a leather strap over her mouth.

Veranna struggled against her bonds, but the chains were too strong. "I will not surrender my people to you, nor will I be your slave. The Creator will judge between us and…"

Her voice failed when the concubines kicked, slapped and spit on her as they yelled abuse because of her mention of the Creator. Tesra smiled and held out a large, black egg for her to see.

"Look, dear, I have delivered a dragon. Keep it warm while the father starts another in me."

Veranna screamed as Tesra walked away to the dragon chamber. "No, Tesra! Mother, no! NO!!"

She awoke to see Reiki leaning over her as her maid shook her shoulder. "Be awake, highness; no scream. You have bad dream."

It took a moment for Veranna to get her bearings as she sat up. "It was a terrible dream! You and I were captives of the Koosti, and Tesra was mated to a dragon. Dear Creator, do not let this be a prophecy."

Her maid brought her a cup of tea and inspected her head and neck. "My lady, you have a bruise around your neck and your eyes are red from crying. Did you get out of your bed in the night and injure yourself?"

"No, ma'am, but I have had this type of reaction to dreams before. It seemed so real. What time is it?"

"It is nearly the end of the sixth watch, your highness. Lord Treybal is in the mess awaiting your arrival."

"Oh! I have overslept and missed his report. Please, run over to the mess and tell him I will be right there. Reiki, I want you to go to our tailor and tell him that you need attire befitting a princess at court. Mrs. Gruntun will go with you."

The plump, older maid took Reiki by the hand. "Come, my lady; we will go to the tailor's after we stop by the mess."

Veranna thanked them and then rushed to get washed and dressed. In the mirror she saw the bruise encircling her neck and winced at how tender the raw skin was when touched. She looked down and saw that both ankles were bruised and raw. Nearly two years before she had had a dream while in Tesra's home that involved flying with eagles. She fell to the ground and woke up with badly bruised legs. The bruising vanished after Tesra pointed out that the Creator was supplying them with a sign that He was with them in their quest. Now, she wondered what these signs would entail. In the washroom she knelt and prayed that the Creator would keep Tesra safe. She also asked that the Creator would give her strength to carry out the Divine will, and gave thanks for all of the blessings poured out upon her. When she arose and started brushing her hair she noticed that her neck bore no sign of injury, nor did her ankles. She breathed a sigh of relief and headed for the mess.

Pausing to look out a window facing east, she noticed a ring of light moving down from the sun. It impacted the ground heavily, causing the castle to shake violently.

She shook her head and closed her eyes for a moment, then looked out again and saw everything back to normal. Scurrying down the hallway, her heart yearned for those days that would bring a measure of peace. If only she knew exactly what the Creator wanted her to do, she could usher in those days and settle down sooner.

But duty called; others had their hopes shattered or delayed for the sake of the community, and so must she. Duty she knew well, and it supplied its own agenda.

CHAPTER SEVENTEEN

TALENTS AND TURMOIL

Treybal arose and bowed as Veranna strode over to his table. Apart from his clothing needing a thorough wash and his eyes a bit of sleep, he seemed in a surprisingly good mood. Veranna nodded and motioned for him to sit down.

"I am sorry for being so tardy, Treybal; I woke up from a bad dream later than I had planned. I could use a strong cup of tea." She signaled for a serving girl and requested the tea and some yogurt with fruit. "You seem uninjured and well; does this mean your raid was successful last night?"

He smiled and sipped his own tea. "Your highness, successful is too lowly a word for the mission. It was outstanding, and went off almost exactly as you said it would. The Koosti are still in ferment over who is to blame for their losses. Their attempt at a counter-trap flew back in their faces and cost them dearly. Only one of our own was injured, and the healers say he should recover nicely. Our only tight spot came when the wind shifted and blew the wretched smoke from the burned out building over our waiting point. The men became sluggish and fought against sleep. Once the wind shifted, the garlic and onion bag woke them right up."

Veranna nearly spat at the mention of the smoke. Since the day that the Koosti started their attack it had been a thorn in their side. The castle, however, had some unknown ability to filter the air and allowed the people inside a welcome relief. "If it were not for this amazing building we would have been overrun by now. It sounds as though the Koosti got a bit of their own medicine."

"They did, and it proved to be very bad medicine. Since a large portion of our target was sleeping, we shifted our attack to several buildings on the northeast side of town. My men scaled them and entered from the roof doors, while the soldiers took out their sentries and attacked through the ground level doors and windows. The Koosti are so spooked that they hack at anything, often killing each other. It was more like a slaughter than a battle."

Veranna thanked the Creator for the victory, but the thought of so many people dying left her nauseous. "How many?"

Treybal sat back and sipped his tea, staring up at the ceiling as he tallied the night's results. "I would say that my men easily eliminated over three hundred of theirs, while Yanbre's cavalry strike put down more than twice that many. All told, it has to be around a thousand."

Veranna was stunned. "A thousand! Treybal, were anyone else saying that to me I would think he was joking. We can start planning our frontal assault and, hopefully, break the siege. Our only problem will be finding a way to stop the cursed smoke from blowing over the gate area. Then we can..." She was interrupted by someone pulling on her dress. "Elly, dear friend, what are you doing here?"

The little girl did a quick curtsy and then jumped onto Veranna's lap. After a hug she spoke as if on a picnic outing. "My mother sent me to get some breakfast, so I brought Alicia and Tyrzah with me. When I saw you I remembered that you told me to visit you any time."

Veranna saw Alicia across the room sitting next to another girl with fine, light brown hair and bright smile, then gave Elly a serious look and nodded. "As a matter of fact, I recall saying that to you. I am glad that you are here. Have you been playing outside on the castle grounds?"

"Uh huh, but I fall asleep a lot."

"Ah, that is due to the smoke."

"It smells yucky! Alicia's kissy-friend thinks he knows how to stop it, but all he does is look at rocks and dirt."

"Is he with you?"

Elly turned and yelled across the room, "Hey, Alicia, come over here, and bring 'dirty' with you."

Two youngsters of about ten years old got out of their seats, walked cautiously over to Veranna's table and bowed. Alicia led the way.

"Good morning, your highness. I pray that all is well with you this day."

"Thank you very much, my lady. And, I hope the same for you and your family. I am glad to see you again. Is this your special friend whom you mentioned to me before?"

Alicia grabbed Jeremy's wrist and pulled him forward. "Yes, your highness, this is Jeremy Thakay."

Eleven or twelve years old, Jeremy was of average height and lean. His fair skin had dried dirt on it at several points, but the red of his blush contrasted sharply with his bright, blue eyes.

"Good morning, your highness. Alicia said that she spoke with you before, but I found it hard to believe."

Veranna smiled and put her hand on Alicia's shoulder. "Alicia strikes me as a very reliable young lady, and it speaks well of you that you chose her to be your special friend. She tells me that you like to read and study many things."

"I love to read, and to see how things work."

"That is excellent, my young sir, and exactly what the empire will need for the future. Elly mentioned that you believe you know how to stop the sleepy smoke."

Jeremy fidgeted and looked at the floor. "It is just an idea, but I have not tried it on anything big, yet."

In a patronly tone, Treybal leaned forward and asked, "What does your remedy involve?"

Jeremy did not hesitate in the least. "It relies upon making the fire hotter."

Treybal frowned. "Hotter?"

"Yes, sir. It would cause the fuel to be spent much more quickly."

Veranna's eyebrows rose in admiration. "That is a very interesting idea, Jeremy. How would you do that?"

Sounding like a teacher from an academy, Jeremy spoke in precise terms. "When studying various rocks a few months ago, I noticed that a certain type had veins of material that would produce more heat in a fire, especially when mixed with other veins in the right proportions. Through a lot of testing

I found ratios of the materials that performed the best for producing heat. I have a small amount of the mixture with me if you would like a demonstration."

Feeling as though she were back in a classroom, Veranna set Elly into a nearby chair and asked Jeremy to proceed. He found an unlit candle and brought it over to the table where Veranna and Treybal sat, and then took out a small leather bag from one of his pockets. He then sprinkled some of its contents onto the stone floor, rolled the candle in it, and then squeezed the gray-white powder firmly into the wax. Sitting upright on the floor, he carefully lit the wick with another candle. It caught slowly, but when the flame reached the wax it flared with a great deal more light and heat. The wax was consumed in half a minute and the ceramic stand was too hot to hold.

Veranna stood and bowed to Jeremy. "Young sir, that was very impressive. Are you thinking that this will work on the enemy's smoke mound?"

"I am sure that it would, your highness, but I cannot say how strong the reaction will be since I do not know what is in their smoke mix."

Treybal stood and shook the boy's hand. "It is worth a try; the hard part will be finding a way to get the powder onto the smoke mound without getting ourselves killed. Have you also thought of a way to do that?"

A voice full of humored exasperation cut through the room. "Of course he has!" Lord Forest strode in and plunked into a chair at their table, picking at leftover food.

Veranna was no longer shocked at his audacity. "My lord Forest, you speak as though you know all there is to this bright, young man. Have you met him before?"

"Yes, and no."

Frustrated and amused, Veranna growled through clenched teeth while maintaining a smile. "Perhaps you would not mind elaborating upon that answer."

"Perhaps I wouldn't."

"Blast it, man, get on with it!"

Forest's teasing laugh made Veranna and Treybal feel like dunces under the tutelage of a pedagogue.

"Are your eyes still so blind that you miss the obvious? You are dealing with one of the Talents."

Veranna's eyes popped open wide while Treybal and the others looked at him in confusion.

"Lord Forest, you are familiar with the Talents, but we are not. Are you sure of what you speak?"

He looked at Jeremy and motioned for him to move closer. "Tell me, boy, when did you start getting interested in studying things around you?"

Jeremy shrugged his shoulders and shifted nervously. "A couple of years ago, sir."

"Where were you when you first noticed this interest?"

"When our family went to the western hills with the Resistance movement against Duke Weyland."

Forest nodded triumphantly. "You see, your highness? His gift was activated when yours began to blossom, but remained dormant until you opened the Curtain of Power."

Veranna frowned in thought. "But I thought that one had to be of a particular blood line in order for..." She stared at Jeremy and assessed him anew. "I see! Jeremy, do you know what this means?"

The boy looked like he wanted to simply disappear. "No, your highness."

She gave him a hug and said, "It means that somewhere back in time we have the same relatives. The Talents were associated with the royal bloodlines either by birth or marriage. We are distant cousins."

Jeremy became even more nervous as he bowed. "I ...am, uh, honored, your highness."

"The honor is ours, young sir. Would you care to be a member of the imperial court?"

Fear of the unknown caused him to lose his sense of etiquette for a moment. "You wouldn't keep me holed up inside the castle in pretty little silks, would you?"

Veranna laughed. "No, not at all. Your value lies in what you can learn of the world around us. I am assigning Lord Forest as your primary tutor, and I am certain that he will have plenty to show you in the Lands. However, there will be occasions when your presence is required at court. Is this agreeable with you?"

Jeremy hardly knew what to say. "Why, yes, your highness, but I will have to ask my parents, first."

"I agree. After this war with the Koosti is over I want you to bring them to the castle to dinner so that I may present my plans for you to them. You should bring Alicia, Elly and Tyrzah with you. Now, what is your idea for delivering the fire powder to the enemy's smoke mound?"

Thankful that the conversation turned away from him personally, Jeremy gave Forest a curious scowl as he spoke to Veranna. "As Lord Forest says, I do have an idea, and it came to me when I saw the messenger service attach notes to the legs of the eagles. The birds can carry fairly heavy loads so it should not be too difficult for them to drop bags of the powder right onto the smoke mound. It might be best right near dawn."

"That it would," answered Treybal. "It will provide an excellent diversion for our troops to muster and send the Koosti running." He gave his forehead a light slap. "Oh, that reminds me, your highness. One of the captives we took says that an eagle killed their commanding general. Apparently they have an underling directing them now."

Veranna paused in thought. "That could make things worse for us. An underling often has fresh ideas and less pride. Be prepared for a shift in their tactics. Jeremy, please have your materials ready for tomorrow morning, and make sure you get enough sleep, tonight. For now, I want you to get to the royal tailor and have a suit of clothing made for you that will be appropriate for court. That goes for Alicia and Elly, as well. I will speak with you again in the afternoon, Jeremy."

She suddenly held up her hands and requested silence as she closed her eyes in concentration. Her lips moved silently as if in response to something the others could not hear. A few seconds later her eyes opened slowly and she yawned. "I am sorry for the interruption, but Lord Yanbre just sent a message through his armor. He says that Kreida just joined them and wants to see me right away. We cannot get her into the castle until after sundown, and will have to try to sneak her past the enemy units and sentries. Treybal, see to the planning before you rest. I am going to the wall and take a look at the enemy placements."

"Yes, your highness."

Forest and Treybal sat and exchanged ideas while Veranna made her way to the outer wall and climbed up into one of the parapets facing the city. Even at a distance she could see the enemy moving like ants through the streets, and marveled that so many were left after their horrendous losses against Yanbre and Treybal. No doubt many had arrived after the siege of Neidberg broke, but it would take a lot of fighting to push these Koosti out of the city. Many buildings served as their barracks, and they used various trade shops, as well.

She lifted her hands toward the sky and prayed that the Creator would help her to end the siege and the war.

Leaning back against the wall, she held her face in her hands. Karsten had not returned with Kreida, and she needed his calm, reassuring presence to help guide her through the terrible decisions facing them. Kreida, for all of her brash ways, buoyed her spirits with her humor and fierce loyalty. She had insights regarding people who were often outside of Veranna's experience, and was closer than a sister, even if she was a brat at times.

The enemy soldiers kept a respectful distance from the castle wall after many fell to the expert archers in the castle. At moments of increased activity, Veranna would take part and the enemy soon believed that spirits guided her arrows. Even the most brutal Koosti commander knew not to send troops on forays when it was a given that she would eliminate them once they entered her range.

Making a circuit along the wall, she inspected both the inside and outside of the castle grounds. At various points on the outer side foliage still stood. She made it a point to defend them since her men used the brush and trees to help hide their nightly excursions. Inside the wall stood many tents filled to capacity with city folk. It was fortunate that they kept themselves in good order, but it would not be too much longer and tensions would erupt. Work helped alleviate the stress, especially for those helping directly with military tasks. Fletchers, blacksmiths and weavers supplied the troops with quality weapons and clothing, while cooks and artisans handled the domestic chores.

Rounding near the main gate, Veranna prayed again for a sign that an end was near for the siege. Just as she said the closing words to her prayer a horn sounded across the field from the Koosti forces, and a rider came forward bearing a flag of parley. Veranna called for the soldiers to hold their fire, then told the signalman to flag the party forward.

Just behind the Koosti flagman rode a man wearing the robes of an officer. He looked to be about thirty years old and had fine, dark features. His skin was not as bright as the other Koosti, and when he spoke he demonstrated a cadence and style that Veranna thought unlike the Koosti she had heard. The flagman held up his right hand and yelled, "Malakite, master of the army of the Koosti, comes to speak with the empress of the Seven Lands. Is this agreed?"

As in the past, the ancient castle amplified Veranna's voice. "It is; you may proceed."

Malakite passed the flagman and approached the gates, stopping about thirty feet away. "I represent the Great Lady of the Koosti Dominion, LeAnre y'dob. It is her command that you cease all resistance and submit yourselves to her rule."

Veranna, along with her people in the castle, laughed. Once they quieted down she said, "Master Malakite, the Seven Lands have never been under the rule of the Koosti Dominion, nor any other eastern tribe. LeAnre has no authority here and her actions against other peoples demonstrate that she has abused what authority she now holds. Many are the terrible crimes she commits; they are in direct defiance of the will of the Creator. As long as this continues we are enemies."

Malakite tried to sound like an old sage. "That is not wise, for she will deal with you more harshly. This applies not only for you, but also for those you love."

Veranna answered him matter-of-factly. "Those I love will fight beside me to the death to oppose the madness of LeAnre; no doubt you have seen that we are quite capable of repelling your army even though you have far more soldiers."

Again acting the sage, Malakite dismissed her reply. "The hardest stones are worn away by the ever flowing waters. You have shown strength so far, but you cannot continue for long." He paused, and when he spoke again the hairs on the back of Veranna's neck stood up. "The process has already begun with one who is dear to your heart." He reached inside his robe and pulled out a wadded up cloth. "Perhaps this token shall convey reality to you far better than mere words."

Veranna nodded to one of the guards, and he extended a long pole with a small basket attached to its end. Malakite placed the cloth in the basket and a few seconds later it rested on Veranna's palm. Pulling back the cloth, she gasped and nearly fell to her knees. Tesra's Academy ring shined, the jewel's rays piercing Veranna's very being. The world around her went dark and Malakite's voice seemed to pound on her very soul.

"This one named Tesra thought herself beyond our grasp, but she was taken very easily and now serves our black dragon. The Great Lady has decreed that you will be taken to serve DeAndre in his harem. He will decide the fates of all your subjects, as well."

The horrible vision of Tesra as a dragon mate flashed into Veranna's mind. She felt like vomiting and her mind froze at the idea that the woman she loved as a mother was now a tortured slave given to a dragon's will. She did not even realize that Treybal stood beside her, holding her steady. She thought of offering herself as an exchange for Tesra and serving DeAndre in whatever way he desired.

Revulsion at the idea of giving herself to him sent a wave of nausea through her, but it left a seed of anger that quickly grew in strength. The rage in her voice caused the castle to tremble as she proclaimed, "Now you hear me, Master Malakite." She did not yell, but the mysterious connection with the castle transformed her voice into one of dire warning. "Mercy has been my way all of my life, but you and your evil masters have removed any hope for it. I want you to count each breath, for you have few left. Notify your master that I shall come for her, and the Power of the Creator is with me. No longer shall LeAnre be immune from my wrath. She will either die or submit to those whom she has oppressed. The blood of all whom she has killed cries out for justice, and they shall have it. Get you gone and prepare to meet your Creator."

Her eyes blazed with emerald-green light, causing Malakite to cringe. Eagles circled overhead and screamed war cries as the ground trembled. Malakite spun his horse around and galloped back to the city, ordering his forces to prepare for a full attack. Horns sounded and banners rose, marking the call of Koosti troops into the city. No raids by their enemy would do away with any of them this night. The castle, and therefore the Seven Lands, would fall into their hands.

Veranna's eyes still gleamed as she marched to her planning room. Treybal and Forest followed, saying nothing that would interfere with her thought processes. "Lord Forest, you will monitor the enemy's positions and try to pinpoint their troop concentrations. I want to know where they are most heavily gathered." A knock came on the door and Veranna answered sternly, "Come."

Reiki started to enter, saying, "Highness, tailor say..."

Veranna, her eyes still agleam, cut her off. "Not now, Reiki."

The Felinii woman grimaced and exited quietly, full of wonder at the emerald glow of Veranna's eyes. The Deeri were the only others she knew with legends about glowing eyes and special powers, and Veranna had both. The Creator was with her, and Reiki, of the Felinii, knew better than to interfere.

The empress dismissed Treybal and Forest, her voice showing a hard edge of fear and determination. The only other time Treybal had seen her like this was when they fought their way through the Ravines of Renfroun, and Veranna vanquished the spirit of Renfroun to the Creator's judgment.

She put her face in her hands and cried. The woman she had adopted as her mother now suffered terribly in the hands of her enemies. Good news and results seemed to bring bad news like a wagon behind a horse. Prayers answered turned into fears realized. She solemnly vowed that the Koosti would not have even a prayer.

CHAPTER EIGHTEEN

TRANSFORMATION

Tesra opened her eyes and groaned. Pain shot through her skull and neck as she lifted her head to look around. A large shock of her hair fell from her scalp, leaving her nearly bald. The only heat in the mountain cavern came from the lamps and torches mounted on the walls, but she felt warm enough. Her skin was changing into hard, dark scales and was cool to the touch. Her head spun as she forced herself into a sitting position. When the spinning dissipated she opened her eyes and saw that her toe and fingernails were growing into sharp claws. Her jaw and the front of her face had elongated, with sharp teeth protruding slightly past the lips. All of this change had taken only a little over a week, and she wondered how much more would occur. In her abdomen she felt the growth of something and realized that the black dragon had impregnated her. Terrible had been that day, both from the dragon's merciless lust and LeAnre's evil arts. She shivered at the memory of the pain, but longed for the dragon to use her again.

That thought caused her great dismay, for she realized that her mind was being taken over by dragon thought. Around her in the cavern were those under the dragon spell longer than she. They sat in their nests made of furs or blankets waiting to lay an egg, or lying on one until it hatched. Most of them were totally transformed into dragon mates and past any recall of ever being human. The closest one, on Tesra's right, noticed her looking at her, and rose up on all fours as she snarled and hissed a warning for Tesra to stay away from her egg. Without thinking, Tesra bared her fangs and growled a warning of her own. Each seeing the other make no aggressive moves, they broke their stares and huddled back into their nests.

The rapid growth of the dragon egg inside her, along with the changes to her body, required a lot of food. Tesra's stomach ached from hunger and she knew that feeding time was near. All twenty of them in the room fidgeted in their nests as they anticipated the arrival of the handlers with fresh meat.

A moment later they walked in leading a line of ten slaves. The handlers, seven men and three women, wore leather shorts and sandals, while the slaves were naked. The handlers positioned the slaves in front of the dragon mates and left the room, but the slaves simply stood still and stared their vacant eye sockets straight ahead, awaiting a command.

DeAndre y'dob, the Potentate of the Koosti Empire, walked into the cavern flanked by two guards in red and black leather, with stout spears in their right hands. Seeing their highest master the dragon mates smiled and quivered in their nests, letting out growling purrs as he walked among them patting their heads.

Tesra wanted to scream out that they should kill him since he had caused so much death and suffering. However, when he stopped and patted her head, all she could do was purr in response. If she had a tail she would have wagged it in response as he stepped back, studied her and spoke.

"I hope that you are still able to understand my words, beyond simple commands."

Tesra nodded her head even though it caused a spinning sensation. The fear of losing herself to dragony gave her enough strength of will to gasp, "Help me, please."

DeAndre sighed and looked at her with great sympathy. "I am afraid that I cannot help you, now. Once the transformation begins it cannot be stopped. It is said in our ancient writings that the Deeri or Emeraldians had the power to do so ages ago, but the Deeri are a people no more and the Emeraldians survive only in the one you call 'Veranna.' LeAnre has vowed to subdue or destroy her and see if she cannot absorb her powers. She set these things in motion before

I had a chance to stop her. Were I now to call a halt to the campaign we would lose much face."

The eastern tribes deemed saving face above other ethical principles. Whole dynasties had been cast down due to embarrassment. A lack of resolve to finish a battle constituted one of the greatest shames possible.

LeAnre walked in and fell to her knees in front of her brother. After bending down to kiss his feet she kept her gaze at the floor and spoke softly, "I have come, as you commanded, my gracious brother."

Without looking at her he snapped, "Get up."

She stood quickly and swept her reddish-brown hair away from her face. Her red wrap-around skirt was fastened at the hip with a jeweled clasp signifying her status as the Great Lady of the Koosti, but the plain, black leather halter top she wore left her belly and shoulders in full view. All could see the scars marking her as one unfaithful to her brother and people.

DeAndre's voice was cold as he spoke to LeAnre, but he looked down at Tesra. "This woman is the one that the Emeraldian Empress calls her mother, and she is a great warrior. I have been told that the empress helped you escape from the Gelangweil's, and that she treated you as a friend. And this is how you treat her mother!"

LeAnre trembled at the wrath lacing his words. Her mind raced to find a way to ameliorate the situation. "My great brother, this woman, named Tesra, has been the reason that we have lost so many warriors. The city that they call Grandshire has broken the siege we placed around it, and destroyed most of the dragons aiding our army. The enemy now marches to another city called Starhaven, and this will cost us more soldiers. Clarens defeated us as well. This woman is the reason."

DeAndre considered her words for a moment. "I have no doubt that what you say is true. However, you have greatly erred in giving this woman to the dragon. She should have been kept as an honored captive. The *kemicka* could have made her able to bear children again, and I would have produced sons to be great warriors."

The *kemicka* were a class of highly trained potion makers who utilized the black arts for extra effectiveness.

DeAndre's voice changed to a flat tone of simple truth. "This woman, Veranna, now has a just claim over your life. Only a total victory and her death will release you from her control. Should she walk The Way and survive the mazes she may stand before me and demand your life. I would have no choice, as your brother, but to strike you down with my own hands. Your eyes would be hers, and you would be a blind soul under the Dark Ones' merciless punishment."

LeAnre shivered and fell to her knees, bowing her head to the floor. 'The Way' was the long walkway made of some mysterious, dark stone that led from the gate in the wall around the front of the palace and down into the palace proper. Once a person reached The Way they were immune from attack since they had proved themselves worthy enough to reach it in the first place. Specially selected guards were stationed along the five hundred foot-long path at twenty-foot intervals on both sides. Eight people could walk abreast along its length with ease. The Koosti, along with every other eastern tribe to ever occupy the palace, held The Way in great respect, as well as with a sense of eerie fear. None of them had built it, and it looked as smooth and polished as ever.

After that came the maze. Once one stepped through the entryway he had to prove himself worthy to come before the Potentate. Only those invited by the rulers were led straight to the reception hall by guides born into a special caste of palace servants. Otherwise, one needed to find their way through an exceedingly complex maze of hallways and catacombs where warriors would unexpectedly ambush you. If you made it through the maze, you were considered worthy to enter the Potentate's ruling chamber, and hope that he might allow you a chance to address him.

LeAnre begged her brother not to give her up to their enemies. "Great Master, it would be far worse than torture for you to give me up to those barbarians. It would be like slaves handling gold and imagining that it was lead. I am born to rule and will do so by your will. We are family, Great Master, and I will prove to you my loyalty and worth."

DeAndre snorted and looked down at her with disgust. "You have shamed our family and proven yourself disloyal already. You bear the scars of an outcast and have no offspring to pass your inheritance onto. A tenth of the empire, here in the west, was yours to rule, but in your greed you were not satisfied. You rushed to conquer the Seven Lands and take the empress as your slave before you thought of all that would cost us in soldiers and supplies. Now, we will be weak on our eastern border and our enemies might exploit that opening. You will be fortunate, indeed, if the Emeraldian empress is satisfied with simply sawing your head from your shoulders." He paused and shook his feet free of her fawning hands. "You have carved out a cave, and now you must dwell in it."

He gave Tesra one last pat on the head before leaving the chamber. "I am so sorry, and can only hope to make your days as comfortable as possible. My sister knows to give you only the best feed. Farewell, for the next time I come here you will have been totally consumed by dragonhood." He walked toward the entryway, but before passing through he said to LeAnre, "Feed them," then disappeared around a bend with his two guards.

LeAnre stood up slowly, wobbly with fear and resentment. Her own brother despised her and his concubines treated her abusively. For them it was only a short time until she was the lowest of the concubines, or dead. The turmoil in her mind made her feel sickly, which she had been that morning after a full nights' sleep. Because of her dishonor only Kaesean would enjoy her in his bed. Those men of the noble families who frequented the public mating chambers refused to mate with her, calling her a barren traitor.

She felt as though she stood near a dock to board a boat, when the boat detached from the dock and floated away. She was powerless to stop it and soon it was gone. Sinking to her knees once more, she let out a frustrated scream of impotent rage and buried her face in her hands. Weeping bitterly, she yelled at Tesra, "This is all your doing, you heap of rat dung! Being a dragon mate is too good for you, but I at least will know that you are reduced to being an animal, a senseless, brute beast of instinct and obedience. I will feed you well not out of mercy, but because it will make you live longer as one totally debased. And, I vow to you now that Veranna shall suffer a hard and cruel life as my slave before I give her to a dragon as a mate."

Tesra's heart pounded in terror, but some instinctual power kept her from attacking LeAnre. Her dragon nature took over, setting off a cascade of emotions ending in a frenzied desire to satisfy her rage in blood. LeAnre clapped her hands twice and the zombie slaves turned toward the dragon mates. The one in front of Tesra was well muscled and handsome but for the heavy scar across the left side of his head. A tattoo on the side of his neck marked him as a Koosti soldier, and the scar was evidence of a horrible punishment. His empty eye sockets stared straight ahead.

LeAnre stood and yelled, "Dragon mates, eat!" She clapped her hands sharply, twice, and the dragon mates sprang like leopards at the slaves. In a matter of minutes nothing remained of them, save for a few pools of blood that the dragon mates licked up casually.

Tesra's belly was now full, but her rage was less. The only rational thought she could muster barely came to mind. *Veranna, my dear child, stay away. Dear Creator, help keep her safe!* At the thought of the Creator a searing pain burned through her head, and she released an agonized roar at the cold, stonewalls.

CHAPTER NINETEEN

HOT, TEMPERED

A great mass of Koosti troops filled the huge central square of Tolemera, awaiting final instructions from their commander about the siege of the castle. All of the cavalry they could muster stood ready to attack, but kept a very respectable distance from the walls. The smoke pile had burned low, and this was a cause of concern. Their enemy would not be hindered by the smoke and could fire arrows and spears more effectively. On the other hand, their own archers and spearmen would be able to see their targets more clearly.

Malakite smiled to himself as a new part of his plan rolled along the main street from the eastern section of the city. The large catapults made of thick oak and cast iron had teams of six horses pulling them toward the western side of the city to set up on the edge of the clearing opposite the castle. There they could operate without having to worry about enemy archers taking out the handlers. The wagonloads of rocks and oil bags would be safely sheltered among the trees along the edge of the clearing. Some of the oil bags had the special sleep-smoke powder added in. The enemy would find it hard to man the walls with sleep coming over them.

With his back to the smoke mound, Malakite looked up and saw his troops bulging from every window in the buildings surrounding the public square three blocks deep. Thousands waited in eager anticipation for him to give the order to attack, knowing that they had an overwhelming numerical advantage, and more thousands standing on the rooftops cheered him and led all of the army in shouting curses toward the castle.

Yes, he thought, *I will crush the Emeraldians and take the survivors back to Banaipal to grovel before the Potentate. He will reward me for helping him save face, and for salvaging the Great Lady's foolish plan. He may even give me this empress as a war prize. My family will be among the most powerful in the entire empire of the Koosti.*

When the sun cleared the eastern mountains, this land would all be his for the taking.

Veranna and her advisors had labored far into the night discussing contingencies in their offensive against the Koosti. The lookouts reported that the enemy troops on the western side of the castle had thinned out, and that the city had swollen into a solid mass of soldiers. Accordingly, Yanbre organized a strike force to misdirect the enemy on the western side of the castle so that Kreida would be able to reach the wall and enter through one of the secret openings. The plan worked flawlessly, and the Genazi woman ran through the corridors to find the empress, catching up with her in one of the armories where Lord Forest was demonstrating a weapon he had designed. Opening the door to the room, the two women saw one another and embraced. Tears squeezed out of the corners of Veranna's eyes as she told Kreida about Tesra's capture.

"I know, kiddo; that is what I was racing here to tell you. It seems that a Koosti woman passed herself off as a servant in Heilson's kitchen and slipped Tesra something that knocked her out. They flew her by dragon in order to upset you. Apparently, they think that you will not be able to resist the urge to go after her."

Veranna's hands clenched tightly as she exclaimed, "In that they are right. Tesra is my mother and friend; I will not abandon her to being a dragon wife."

Kreida wondered if Veranna's mind had not slipped into insanity. "Girl, if you try that you will be captured and enslaved. I don't care if you are the greatest fighter ever, you cannot last against their numbers."

Veranna's eyes smoldered and her voice sliced through the room. "This is not a matter for discussion; I am going to free Tesra if I have to go alone."

Kreida, for all of her spunk, knew that she could not make any headway in the argument. All she could do was accept. She bowed and said, "Yes, your highness," in a reluctant, weary tone. "If you can manage to make it out of this castle in one piece then I guess you have earned the right to die in theirs'."

Veranna glared at her in reproach, but turned to Forest. "What is this weapon you have been speaking of, my lord?"

Forest patted a solid wooden shaft larger than an arrow but smaller than a spear. "It is this bolt, your highness." He gave her a knowing wink and went on. "I invented this a long time ago. It is very effective, if I do say so, myself."

After the exchange with Kreida, Veranna was in an irritable mood and nearly yelled at Forest.

"You are wasting my time with showing me a small spear? We have those aplenty, my lord."

Forest scowled but kept his voice calm. "It is not just a spear. Do you see these ten small dowels through the shaft? Each will hold an iron ball with multiple, razor-sharp protrusions laced with poison. The shaft is launched from a large crossbow and reaches high speeds as it flies. When it hits a tree, large rock or even hard soil, the speed is transferred to the balls and they fly out with great force in a tight arc from the shaft. They can kill or wound an enemy immediately, but even a slight nick to the skin will send the poison into the blood. The poison typically takes anywhere from ten to twenty seconds to down a man."

Veranna was impressed with the idea, but was in an anxious mood. "How many of these weapons are ready for use?"

Forest reminded himself that she was under great pressure both personally and for the empire. Now was not the time for humor or his temper. "We have nearly two hundred of these ready."

Veranna turned away from both Kreida and Forest as a thought came to her. "Have you any idea of how to locate all of the metal balls that will lie on the ground after the battle? Innocent children playing around might step on one and die from the poison, or simply become diseased from a small cut."

Forest had not considered the after-effects of the weapon, and pondered a solution. "The poison lasts only a few hours once it is applied to the balls, and the razor points will rust away as well. We can take a tally of all the balls that strike an enemy, as well as all those recovered from the ground. That way we will know how many remain to be located."

Veranna looked at the weapon again. The hard, shining metal and design had a hideous gleam that sent a shudder through her. All thoughts of remorse faded as she reminded herself that the enemy outside the wall was one with those who held her adopted mother prisoner. "Ready the weapon for use, but only on my direct order shall you fire one of them."

Forest nodded and calmly replied, "Yes, your highness."

The empress went quickly through the doorway and, without looking back, said, "Kreida, come with me."

The feisty Genazi woman exchanged glances with Forest as she shook her head and followed. "Poor kid." She had to hurry to catch up with her and was surprised once more to see the change in her friend. One could berate, tease or insult her and she would take it all with humility. However, if one threatened one of those close to her she transformed into cold steel. Kreida could not make up her mind as to which aspect of Veranna's personality impressed her more.

They headed up three flights of stairs and went through an embrasure that opened onto a fair-sized barbican about a third of the way up the main tower. It allowed a broad view facing east toward the city, and near the parapet stood Treybal and Jeremy with eight small, leather bags. They bowed as Veranna approached, but could see that she was all business by the set of her jaw and the determined look in her eye.

"Sir Jeremy, Lord Treybal, are you ready?"

Jeremy felt uneasy under her intense gaze and was grateful that Treybal answered first.

"Yes, your highness. All that we need now are the eagles."

Her answer came out as a cold chop. "Excellent. I shall summon them."

She closed her eyes and started to focus on the lead eagle when Kreida surprised them all by walking up to Treybal and slapping him on his left cheek.

"That is for all of those lurid thoughts you entertained while I was gone. And get that silly pipe out of your mouth and kiss me, you fool." She wrapped her arms around him and pressed her lips against his before he could get set. The two of them nearly fell over the parapet.

Normally, Veranna would have blushed at Kreida's brazen manner, but in her present mood, she was irritated.

"This is no time for brothel bantering! We have work to do, so be quiet."

Kreida glared at her, but said nothing. She looked at Treybal and saw his eyes urging her to remain silent, so she turned and stared out at the city.

Veranna leaned back against the hard stone of the castle and closed her eyes again. After a few seconds, a view of the land southwest of the castle came into her mind, and a craggy voice-impression sounded in her ears alone.

We soar before sky fire flies over mountains.

Veranna felt a surge of exhilaration as she experienced the wonders of flight through the eyes of an eagle. *Yes, you who helps guard my aerie. I have need of this many of you here.* She held up her fingers without realizing it. *Each must be strong to carry dead cow skin with dirt, and let fall on fire hill in many aerie place.*

There was a few moments pause and Veranna felt a sense of disdain from the eagle toward the idea of carrying dirt. It called to its fellows and circled around, slipping effortlessly through the air back to the castle. In a minute, five of the larger eagles sat along the parapet staring at Veranna. She held out her left arm for the leader to perch on and locked eyes with him. She pointed at the leather bags, then grabbed the top of one in her right hand and imitated an eagles' claw clutching it. *Cow skin with dirt must go on fire hill in many-aerie.*

Three more large eagles flew onto the parapet and bowed. Veranna nodded to them before continuing. *You must drop all cow skins together. It must be a surprise like swooping on a rat in a field. Can you do this?*

The leader spread his wings and bowed. Veranna swung her left arm up quickly and the large bird jumped off, climbing into the sky. The other eagles watched as their leader circled around the castle and gained speed. As it approached the barbican, Forest picked up one of the bags and lobbed it into the air. The eagle grabbed it with its talons and lost altitude at first, but beat its wings and quickly rose above the highest point of the castle, going into a holding pattern until its fellows joined it. The seven other eagles flew into the air and formed a line as they came toward the barbican. In rapid succession Treybal and Jeremy tossed the other bags up for the birds to grab.

Veranna saw the sun clear the eastern mountains and sent her thoughts to the eagle leader. *Attack from where the sky fire flies.* The eagles flew off to the south for a ways, and then headed east toward the dawn, passing out of sight.

Veranna frowned at Kreida and could not pass up the opportunity for a bit of scalding humor. "At least even a bird-brain can understand directions."

Kreida opened her mouth to retort, but Treybal quickly overrode her. "Let's keep our eyes on the city and see what happens."

Kreida scowled at him and said nothing, crossing her arms over her breasts as she turned to look toward the smoke mound.

Malakite raised his hands in salute to the sun as its rays broke over the distant eastern mountains. Thousands of Koosti warriors yelled all the louder, swaying in their battle lust. Malakite then turned back to face the crowd on the western side of the smoke mound. Raising his right hand to call for silence, his bronzed skin shined with the orange light of the dawn. The people gazed at him and wondered if he was a living flame of fire that would burn away their enemies. Gradually, they quieted enough for him to speak.

"Servants of the Dark Master, today has come in order that we may destroy our foes. Let nothing stop you from enjoying the opportunity to kill them. Let their blood flow like water over the ground!"

The crowd roared as blades rose in salute. Malakite raised his hand again, silencing them.

"Among the Emeraldians are Genazi. If possible, take them captive so that we may enjoy a victory feast this evening and have their torture for our entertainment. Their screams shall be music as we dine on their eyes and livers."

The crowd erupted once more in frenzied glee at the thought of torturing the captives.

"Our great Potentate commands us to be victorious, and we will not be disobedient. Our enemies are holed up in the castle and can do nothing. We will reduce them to rubble and show no mercy. Even if they fight hard they cannot prevail, for we are too many. We shall..."

He was interrupted as a number of the people pointed up at the sky behind him. He turned and saw eight green and gold eagles fall out of the sun and swoop over the smoke mound. Each dropped a bag and flew in different directions away from the city center. The last fell from the sky as an arrow pierced its body. Malakite wondered why they would do something so strange, and then turned back toward the crowd.

He opened his mouth to cheer on his soldiers, but it turned into a scream that was abruptly cut off. Intense, white-hot heat pounded into him and melted the flesh from his bones, and the bones fell as ashes to the ground. The heat wave exploded out from the mound faster than the people could react. In seconds the city center resembled the inside of a potter's kiln. The only buildings that survived were those made of dragonstone. The others were heaps of white ash, and those not destroyed became ovens for anything inside. Everything left intact looked freshly whitewashed.

Those on the castle walls covered their eyes from the bright white light and wondered if a star had fallen from the sky. Then came a powerful vacuum effect that nearly sucked them over the parapet. Wind rushed in, forcing Veranna and the others to drop down beneath the walls to keep from being blown over. A few moments later the howling winds dissipated and a fine, white ash floated down from above.

Veranna, Kreida, Treybal and Jeremy all stood and looked out toward the city. Except for the ancient buildings made of dragonstone, the city square was now a large circle nearly three blocks radius from where the smoke mound had been. Veranna wrapped a scarf around her nose and mouth to keep out the ash, but did not even realize that she was hardly breathing. She stared in mute astonishment, and then let out a long breath.

"Holy Creator," she whispered and blinked to clear her eyes of the ash. She heard someone sniffling next to her and looked down to see Jeremy wiping tears from his eyes. "Jeremy, are you hurt?"

The boy barely mumbled, "I am sorry, your highness; I did not mean to destroy the city. I had no idea that the heat would be so great. All of those people dead because of my idea! Forgive me, please!"

Veranna's heart nearly broke as she pulled Jeremy close and put her arm around him. "Jeremy, you did nothing wrong. You simply did what I ordered you to do, so the responsibility for what happened is mine. The enemy knew that what they were doing was wrong, and they have paid the price for it. Justice is not easy and too often not very enjoyable. But you have helped deliver us from their evil and saved the lives of many of our people. For that everyone will be grateful."

Jeremy nodded somberly, then looked over to see Kreida saluting him with her knife drawn and Treybal bowing respectfully. The fiery Genazi woman then spread her arms wide and bowed in the traditional Genazi form for apology.

"Hey kid, a while back I called you a weakling. I am sorry. If any bully gives you trouble, just let me know and I will take care of him."

Jeremy was grateful for the support, but hung his head. Veranna glanced at Treybal and motioned with her head toward the embrasure before speaking to Jeremy. "Go with Lord Treybal; he will need your assistance to describe to the others what just happened. Try not to think about those killed in the city, and seek the wisdom and comfort of your family and friends. I had to do so when I was required to kill. The Creator's guidance has been a must ever since."

He nodded and followed Treybal as he exited the barbican. A moment later, Forest emerged through the embrasure and let out a low whistle as he looked east.

"Whoa! A skew of dragons could not have caused so much damage. I guess you will not be needing the other new weapon, now."

Brushing ash from her clothes and shaking her hair, Veranna said simply, "That is correct. Store the weapons away safely; we do not know when we might need them again. In one hour we will meet in the conference chamber. I want all the lords, ladies and captains there." She closed her eyes and concentrated on Yanbre.

Yes, your highness? came the reply in her head.

Bring the army back to the castle; the Koosti are gone.

Gone?

Yes; the bright light you no doubt saw was part of the reason. I will explain the rest later. For now I want you to report to the conference chamber in an hour and have one of your lieutenants take the troops to hunt down any remaining Koosti east of the city. Tell them to keep going until they are told to stop.

Yes, your highness.

She broke the connection and looked at Kreida. "We need to get back to our rooms and clean up. Be swift, for we only have an hour."

Kreida gestured that it was unnecessary. "A little dirt does not bother me. I would rather use the time eating."

Veranna wrinkled her brow and her nostrils flared. "You smell worse than a horse. I do not want to have to gag in the conference chamber. Let's go!"

Kreida looked at Forest for some support, but the enigmatic man gave her a teasing sneer.

"I was going to say that you smell worse than something else, but it would have been redundant."

The Genazi woman glared at him, but did not know exactly how to respond. Her face went beet red as she heard Veranna chuckle and walk back inside.

Adding salt to the wound, Forest said dryly, "If the horse smells better, it probably rides better, too."

Kreida stomped back inside and down the hallway.

CHAPTER TWENTY

UNSTOPABLE

The conference chamber buzzed with conversation and the rattle of knife and fork. Eggs, sausages, bread and cooked grains were in abundance. Even Kreida felt full after fifteen minutes of uninterrupted consumption. When Veranna walked in they all started to rise, but she immediately motioned for them to sit. Ignoring the food on her plate she got right down to business. Washed up and with her long braid wrapped around the crown of her head, her regal countenance contrasted sharply with the dull, practical clothing she wore. Kreida immediately recognized the sturdy travel tunic and pants that Tesra had made for her. The empress clapped her hands sharply and waited for them to stop all other activities.

"My mother, Grand Dame Tesra, is being held captive by the Koosti in their capital city called 'Banaipal.' I am going to retrieve her. The level of danger involved requires that any who assist me do so purely on a voluntary basis."

Kreida snorted and shook her head in disbelief. "What she is asking is, 'Who wants to be tortured and killed by Koosti scum?'"

Veranna glared at her, but knew that her words conveyed a good deal of reality. "As Kreida has so directly pointed out in her highest level of skill, the odds are definitely against success. However, my duty as an empress, and as a daughter, requires me to try. Who will go with me?"

Sounding exasperated, Kreida blurted out, "Okay, fine! It has been pretty boring around here lately."

Veranna reached over and gave her hand a thankful squeeze as she saw hands raised all around the table.

Yanbre looked at Veranna and said solemnly, "I would go even if she were the most lowly of our people."

There came many 'ayes' of agreement, and Veranna felt such a strong kinship with them that a tear nestled in the corner of each eye. "Thank you so much. If I die in this quest I know that I will at least have done so in the company of the very finest." She paused to collect her thoughts and thank the Creator for such steadfast companions. Fear swirled around her as she contemplated how to go about rescuing Tesra. Few of them had ever been beyond the borders of the empire, except for Lord Forest, and his adventures were hundreds of years past. She felt confident that someone in the room would come up with an idea.

"As we have never been to the Koosti Empire we are at a loss as to how to proceed. Who has an inkling of how we should go about this mission?"

Kreida blurted out, "Hah! All we have to do is turn into cats and we might make it at least partway through their lines."

Veranna started to reprimand her when Treybal spoke up.

"Your highness, she may have a valuable contribution hidden in that inane remark. It seems evident that a large-scale invasion is out of the question since even if we fought our way through it would consume a great deal of time. The alternative is stealth. If we move by night, we will be harder to spot. Yanbre and a few of his knights could guide us in the darkness just like cats. We Rockhounds would help when it comes to traversing difficult terrain. If we go by unexpected routes and maintain stealth we can move much more quickly than trying to fight our way through."

Veranna looked at each person for his or her reaction to his plan. They seemed as impressed as she.

Forest raised a few chuckles as he stared at Kreida and said in a deadpan tone, "That means no yelling, slapping, dancing or drinking."

Kreida sat up and readied a retort, but Veranna squeezed her hand hard.

"Lord Forest, please keep your remarks to the subject at hand. Do you have any knowledge of the Koosti city of Banaipal?"

Leaning back in his chair, he shrugged his shoulders and bit off a large chunk of sausage. "Um, no, but um, gulp…you do have someone who might know something about it." He stopped and chewed his sausage, and then took a drink of his tea.

Veranna knew his eccentricities, but her mood did not allow as much leniency as before. She slapped her right hand hard on the table and jolted them to fresh awareness as she snapped, "Get on with it, man! To whom do you refer?"

Looking at her as though the answer were obvious, he frowned and said in an overly simple manner, "I am talking about Reiki."

Veranna wanted to give him a thorough tongue-lashing, but was brought up short by the fact that he had a very valid and useful point. Her face showed irritation, but she spoke to one of the guards with as much control as she could muster. "Bring the lady Reiki, here."

The man bowed and hurried off, glad to get away from the sudden tension in the room.

Yanbre brought them back to business. "Your highness, I believe that it would be a good idea to have the army move on to Neidburg and then head east as if it were beginning an invasion of the Koosti empire. This would draw off their forces from other points of entry and make it easier to slip in quietly by another route."

The young empress felt a sense of relief as the discussion got back on track. "Thank you, Yanbre, that is an excellent idea. I will utilize the eagles as scouts; in that way we will be able to avoid roving patrols and accidental contacts."

Just then, Reiki entered the room. In her dress with a low-cut neck and deep amber color, she caught everyone's attention. Her lions' mane of hair was swept back and tied with a slender string of leather at the nape of the neck. She kept her eyes on Veranna as she flowed gracefully over to her and bowed.

"You send, highness, I come."

Kreida stared at her as though transfixed, a skeptical wonder skewing her features. Her voice was soft and wispy as she said, "This cannot be real."

Veranna raised an inquiring eyebrow at Kreida and gestured for her to continue. Kreida's face changed to a humored grin.

"It is a kitten!"

Veranna scowled at her. "Kreida, I want you to try showing some respect for our honored guest. Her name is 'Reiki,' and she comes from a tribe of people called..."

Suddenly sitting forward with her elbows on the table, Kreida blurted out, "Yeah, yeah, I know! She comes from those we called *Felinyiyeh*. My people have not come across one of them for hundreds of years. They were thought to have died out long ago when the Genazi migrated out of the east. They helped our ancestors fight through the mountain passes controlled by the Koosti and Sudryni. What is she doing here?"

Veranna's irritation grew at this diversion from their agenda, and she addressed Kreida as if talking to an irksome child. "They refer to themselves as *Felinii*, and she was sold by the Koosti to the guilds man named Eifer. Lord Forest found her in one of the buildings in the city. She had already dispatched many Koosti and helped save the life of one of our Rockhounds." The anxiety she felt over the situation with Tesra caused her to speak more harshly than she intended. "Be quiet now, and do not interrupt."

Kreida's head jerked back in response to Veranna's tone, but she said nothing.

Reiki wanted to speak with Kreida, but Veranna's insistent voice did not allow for it.

"Reiki, we need to ask you about the Koosti city called *Banaipal*. As you know, my mother has been taken captive by the Koosti and made a dragon wife; am I correct in guessing that she is in *Banaipal*?"

Reiki nodded. "That correct, highness. Banaipal chief city of Koosti. Very old. Palace cut in hill, not by Koosti. They make, uh..." She felt embarrassed at not knowing the word she needed. "How you say hole in rock?"

Veranna calmly replied, "Cave?"

Reiki brightened and hurried to finish her sentence. "Yes, highness; they make cave more big. Many cave. Cannot keep in head all cave. Special slave lead people right way."

Yanbre commented that it was likely a deliberate maze for security purposes. "We will have to be very careful about ambushes along the way once we get inside, but getting inside to begin with is more to the point."

Veranna agreed and asked Reiki to take a seat before continuing.

Reiki grabbed a napkin and folded it into the shape of a hill, then placed it on a plate, covering half of its surface. She then rolled another napkin tightly along its length and laid it a few inches away from the plate and parallel to its rim. She laid another napkin a few inches away from the other but left it straight. She pointed at the napkin on the plate and proceeded to explain the illustration.

"Highness, this Koosti palace. It in hill. Front much carfed."

"*Carved*," corrected Veranna. She gave Reiki a reassuring smile so that she would not feel too self-conscious.

Reiki smiled back to help cover how nervous she felt. "*Carved*; it funny word."

Kreida, feigning serious intensity, flashed Reiki a feral grin. "It is way more pleasing when it refers to your knife in the guts of your enemies."

A few soft chuckles sounded around the table, but Reiki felt confused. Veranna gave Kreida a hard look and told Reiki to continue.

"Highness," and she pointed at the plate again, "here is long walk from front of palace to high wall. Many guards. Koosti have very, uh..." She struggled to find a word. "Uh, not right custom on long walk. If even enemy come they no fear. Guards protek them."

"*Protect*, Reiki." Veranna had to forcefully remind herself that the alien woman was trying hard to be helpful.

"*Protect*. If enemy come to door in wall and open, they go no fear to palace door. On other side of wall is long way from small hills. Many soldier, many things in way make dead."

Treybal looked over at Reiki, and then turned to Veranna as he rubbed his hands in thought. "It sounds as though they have a dead-zone between the hills and the palace wall. It is probably so lethal that they figure anyone who can fight well enough to reach the gate deserves to enter the palace grounds. We will have to scan the zone from up in the hills to try to figure out where the traps and weak points are. If neither of the three moons are out we can send in a team of Rockhounds during the night to find the safest route through."

Veranna thanked him for his input before turning back to Reiki. Feeling a sense of progress, her voice lost its hard edge. "Reiki, what is there after one enters the palace? Is the maze controlled by guards?"

"Yes, highness, special guard people everywhere. Guards from Koosti best. Attack, then gone. Kill one, then come more kill. Caves very long. No can sneak through. Dragon room special hide. You must find mother soon; too long and she all dragon. No can come back."

Veranna sprang out of her chair. "Treybal, get yourself and eleven other Rockhounds ready to move out in an hour. Yanbre, you will remain here and oversee the castle while I am gone, but I need a dozen knights ready to go right away. Lord Forest, you and young master Jeremy are to get busy with drawing up plans for the rebuilding of Tolemera, and assist the citizens returning from the countryside. Kreida, you I want with us, and you too, Reiki. Do you both agree?"

The two women looked at each other and then back at Veranna. Kreida answered nonchalantly as she stood and stretched her arms.

"Yeah, like I said before, I need some action to inspire me." She pointed at Reiki before saying, "Kitty cat, here, nearly woke me up. Besides, from the sound of things you will need someone who knows how to handle a knife."

Reiki, understanding that Kreida intended humor with her remarks, played along, and glanced at her before speaking to Veranna. "I go with highness. You need woman with right head."

Veranna grinned at Kreida sarcastically. "You have no idea how true that comment is, Reiki." She paused and then addressed everyone in the room. "We move out in an hour; be ready and waiting by the gate. Kreida, help Reiki find some clothing suitable for this mission. Dismissed."

Everyone hurried out of the room to see to their tasks. After operating for so long in a defensive mode, it was energizing to finally take the offensive.

Veranna could not help but relate the situation to some of the games of chess that she and Tesra had enjoyed. She patiently defended against Tesra's relentless attacks while increasing the strength of her own position in minute ways. After the strength of Tesra's attacks waned, Veranna would take the initiative and turn the tide of the battle.

She quickly reached her private chambers and went into the large closet, selected a one-piece dress and undergarments appropriate for a Mother of the Academy and folded them carefully before stowing them away in her pack. Her rapier shined as though newly made, and the bow that Tesra had given her was ready for action. She held up the sword before her face and vowed, "Until my mother is free, you and I shall be as one, my friend."

The steel of determination in her mind matched that of the blade, but the clay around her heart broke, fear and sorrow wanting to flood her being. She fell to the floor and poured out her heart to the Creator, begging for mercy and strength.

An hour later she mounted her horse and set her face toward the east. The gate opened and she snapped the reins to set her horse to a quick trot. As she and her company passed through the streets, she remembered the powerful blasts from the sun in her vision. The buildings made with dragonstone still stood solid, but everything else lay burned up, leaving the city hollow. Soldiers patrolled the streets and searched the standing buildings, the noise they made echoing ominously.

Veranna wished that she could return and find everything in order, with life teeming not only in Tolemera, but also throughout the empire. *My dear mother Tesra, please hang on and do not leave me, or I will be emptier than the buildings.*

CHAPTER TWENTY ONE
PLANNING SESSION

DeAndre y'dob, Potentate of the Koosti Empire, sat in his favorite chair in his personal quarters, but it refused to make him comfortable. Sunlight brightened round windows carved through the rock; however, his dark mood failed to abate. Documents lay before him that he had read many times. The words would not change to those he wanted to see no matter how hard he tried. Thousands of troops now lay dead or captured by the Emeraldians, and many dragons destroyed.

LeAnre had used only her portion of the troops and materials, but rushing other troops and materials to the depleted zones along the border with the Seven Lands left the northern and eastern parts of the empire with only the bare minimum of strength they needed to defend against the nomadic tribes roaming those lands. Most of them had once been settled tribes, but as the Koosti spread the terror of their conquest into more lands the natives could either surrender or run. Now the nomads played a deadly game of cat and mouse, attacking those points they desired on a random basis.

His sister presented another problem that could prove more dangerous than ambushing tribes. Her continued barrenness and poor judgment brought shame to the name 'y dob. Coups had taken place for lesser reasons. Taking her into his harem was one way to reduce the damage she wrought with her foolish drives, but having to see her each day in such a lowly state would remind him of his own shame in not keeping a tighter hold on her. She had resumed the bronzing of her skin, but the scars across her body would testify to her dishonor to the day she died. Until then she would always need another to control her as well as answer for her. She still had a legal claim to her portion of the empire, but if she were considered unfit to rule, another person would be required to administer it for her.

Ghijhay entered the chamber and saw him sitting while in deep thought. In her silk dress of reds, yellows and green she looked like a bright flower come to bloom in a dark land. Her rich, red hair cascaded down around her shoulders as she walked smoothly over to DeAndre and caressed his cheek. Knowing that he liked her in the colors she wore, as well as the soft, gentle approach she used with him, she hoped to bring him out of the depression afflicting him lately.

"Is my love not feeling well? If you wish, I will give you a massage that will help you relax." She lifted his chin up to look her in the eye. "I could make you forget all of your troubles."

DeAndre gave her a brief smile and then signaled for the rest of his concubines to leave the chamber.

"Ahh, my lovely *kahlia*," he whispered. *Kahlia* was an ancient Deeri word that literally meant 'heart stop.' The word was used for animals so bound to one another that the joys and pains suffered by one were felt by the other. "You are more than enough to make me forget the entire world. Often times I wish that we had met while your tribe was still intact, and that I had to win your love to have you with me. I would have offered the priests of Wahweh anything to let me marry you."

A tear came to the corner of her eye at the mention of her tribe. She stepped away a few feet and turned her back to him. "My tribe is all but destroyed, and the priests, well, no one has seen any of them for years. You and your sister did your work very thoroughly."

DeAndre nearly cried out because of the ache in his heart. "My love, I am so sorry. We acted in great stupidity. Please, try to find it in your heart to forgive me."

Her jaw trembled as she fought to control her outrage. Being angry with him would not bring her family or people back to life, nor would it make her life any better in the future. The Creator may have abandoned her, but she would not allow her common sense to do so as well. She turned back to him and saw that he was on his knees, with his hands clasped in supplication. On his face was the most distraught look she had ever seen. Her heart nearly broke as she knelt in front of him. She removed her top and gently reached out and pulled his head down against her breasts.

"My love, I am the one who should ask for your forgiveness. I have told you so many times that I have forgiven you for the slaughter of my people. Try to understand that I cannot simply forget. Their faces locked in agony are still fresh in my mind after all these years. You have been so kind to me and given me children, but I am shamed by not bearing the honor of being called your wife. Were any of my people to see me with you, they would call me a traitorous whore, a slave who brings them great shame."

DeAndre's face went red with frustration and anger at the technicalities of Koosti law. As a concubine, Ghijhay could not become his wife unless LeAnre were to be discredited from the line of imperial inheritance. Koosti law was swift to assign succession in the lines, so the inheritance would pass to one of LeAnre's children regardless of her status. To fail to provide an offspring for succession was a serious weakness. DeAndre would then be far more vulnerable to a coup, and facing destruction if his sister lived, yet destroyed if she died. Fierce guards surrounded her lest anyone be tempted to assassinate her.

All he could do was try to give Ghijhay some hope. "I am trying, my *kahlia*. The troops were ordered not to kill anymore of the Deeri, nor should they molest them in any way. As for LeAnre, I will find a way to deal with her so that you may become my wife, and have the title you deserve: Empress of the Koosti. All that is mine shall be ours, and will pass to our children. You will have a real chance at rehabilitating your people. I hope that your priests devoted to Wahweh have not all been killed, and that they would agree to bind us as husband and wife before your tribes."

Ghijhay sighed and bowed her head. "I hear your words, my husband to be, and believe you. Until then I remain your lowly slave. Do with me as you will."

DeAndre could not take anymore. He reached out and embraced her, pulling her tightly against his own body. Enraptured by the thrill of physical love, he lifted her off of the floor and carried her over to his bed on the other side of the room. He quickly removed his robe, shirt and pants, and the two of them were locked together in an insoluble union.

The other concubines took their places around the bed, for they were required by law to serve as witnesses to DeAndre's virility, and keep track of those whom he enjoyed in his bed. They exchanged knowing smiles and were confident that Ghijhay would keep her promise to them. The concubines were from leading families, or were the most beautiful of the women taken captive. They were not in love with DeAndre, and hoped to lead lives of their own, especially in choosing lovers. Ghijhay made a promise to them that she would keep DeAndre satisfied so that he would not desire the use of any of them. She had done her job so well that DeAndre became generous toward them, giving them money and privilege enough to lead semi-independent lives. In return, the concubines always spoke well of DeAndre, and this fueled a positive image of him among the general populace.

He lay on his back and tried to catch his breath. The exhilaration of primal urges waned slowly and he felt as though the rest of the world had fled, leaving him in peace with the love of his life. He wondered at Ghijhay's ability to adapt to a foreign culture even after the cruel slaughter of her people. The woman had done more than survive. Although technically a slave, she had increased her influence to become one of the most powerful people in the empire. She had done it all in the weakness of surrender to him, opening her heart and allowing him in. Likewise, he had opened himself to her, the only one since his mother, and she held him captive with chains stronger than any made of steel.

The empire needed strength such as hers if it was to remain the greatest power on Treluna. His sister wanted power, but she knew only the methods of brutality to achieve her goals. LeAnre was an iron axe that could shatter along its faults, while Ghijhay was a steel blade able to bend under pressure and still cut through her foes.

She adjusted her position in the bed and snuggled even closer. Her warm, smooth skin and the rhythm of her breathing were a tonic for his very soul, and even that had no difficulty in being poured out to her.

"Ghijhay," he whispered into her ear. Her breathing became more quiet and an eyebrow lifted, but she kept her eyes closed and said nothing. He rarely called her by her name except when greatly troubled, or intimate. "I cannot have my sister slain without a tremendous charge against her. Foolishness is not enough, and she has been trying to fulfill my will."

Ghijhay wrapped herself more tightly against him and tried to sound carefree in her attitude.

"Do not worry, my love; we have a lifetime ahead of us to accomplish our dreams. Do not rush forward unwisely and jeopardize your power on my account. I will be with you no matter what."

He pulled her on top of himself and gave her a long kiss. In her eyes he saw no fear, only a longing for a future where she would not have to worry about any threats to him or herself. He had to admit that a woman like her made a lie of the notion of Koosti superiority.

"Ghijhay, LeAnre's hatred will grow as you advance in power, especially when the people see you as one of their own. LeAnre promised them victory over the Emeraldians and that we would take their land for our empire. She would have had rule over it since she used her own portion of our troops and could grant rewards to her faithful followers. However, she cannot fulfill her promises. Even in the public mating places she often waits all day without any man wanting to mate her. If her troops still defend her we might have a minor civil war that would cast Tribe y'dob into oblivion, regardless of the outcome."

They both lay silent for a while and contemplated how to approach this complex political problem, when Ghijhay propped herself up on her right elbow to look down on his face. With her left hand she gently rubbed his chest and stomach as an idea formed in her mind.

"My love, you want to save face and spare the empire anymore strife among its people. You say that you cannot order the death of your sister, nor do you wish her for your harem. It would seem that you must not kill the snake, but simply remove its fangs. After that, the snake must be kept at a distance so that it does not influence any of the other vipers wanting to replace her."

DeAndre frowned at her, and wondered what she was getting at with this review of the obvious. "Ghijhay, I do not see what you are trying to say. The most important part is finding a way to be able to marry me. Only in that way can you become empress."

She smiled cunningly and spoke carefully. "It all rests on if she can be made to bear a child. For her offenses against the empire she must be punished by being removed from power, even if she retains her inheritance. That way, those who are hungry for power among the major tribes will hope in vain. You can control her inheritance by conferring it on her child and keeping it in trust. LeAnre will be removed from power and be little more than a figurehead. Her removal shall leave an opening for me to rule her province as your appointed regent. You can then name me as queen over it and proceed to marry me. The powerful tribes cannot object since you will be the guardian and LeAnre will be my ward."

DeAndre's eyebrows rose in admiration as he considered the ramifications of her plan. "My love, I had no idea that you could be so devious." He fell quiet for a moment as he summarized the details. "We face two major difficulties. First, she is having great difficulty conceiving and, secondly, she has the scars of a traitor on her body. No one from the powerful tribes will consider her a viable holder of any inheritance and will use it as an excuse to seize her portion."

Ghijhay laid her forehead down on his chest and let out a soft, frustrated groan. "This sister of yours is one problem after another. I wish..." Her eyes brightened with another idea and she swiftly swung her left leg across him and sat down on his abdomen. "I have it! It may be a very slim chance, but it is the only one. Order a number of your troops to stand for duty in LeAnre's chambers. One after another they shall take their pleasure with her until she conceives. Have a couple of concubines on hand to rouse the men to action, or to render any service needed should she be injured.

"Next, send a special unit of soldiers to retrieve a *pharmakai* from Kreston. Our *kemika* are not succeeding with their potions to get LeAnre pregnant, and her scars must be treated. Refusal must not be an option for the *pharmakai*.

"Send for the leaders of the twenty-six tribes to be present at the next fullness of the first moon. They need to witness LeAnre with child. They will also witness her humiliation and see that her portion is under your guardianship. You can then appoint me as the one responsible for administering your will over her portion and name me its queen."

DeAndre was impressed with her approach, and her enthusiasm drove away all of the dark clouds hanging over him. Her plan rested on two points that were very tenuous and could end up costing him loss of face. However, it was a plan with some real possibilities.

"*Kahlia*, how can I refuse you! You have given me hope where I had stored up dread. Come here and let me reward you once more" He grabbed her around her ribs and started pulling her down on himself, but she pushed away and frowned at him in mock irritation.

"Silly! We do not have time for this; let me get things going while you recover your strength. It should not take me too long."

She bounded out of the bed and hurriedly put on her clothes while two of the concubines helped brush and style her hair. She pointed at another concubine and spoke swiftly.

"Fivey," so named due to the fact that she held the status of the fifth concubine in the order of prominence, "Make sure that no one else takes pleasure with him until I return. He needs strength for when I get back."

Fivey, a full-figured woman with auburn hair, had been taken captive as a little girl and had no memory of which land or tribe she came from. DeAndre had not taken her to his bed since Ghijhay had asked him not to. Fivey had her eye on a young officer in the army and hoped that he would request her for himself. She bowed to Ghijhay, and sprang onto the bed like a watchdog.

DeAndre felt breathless with the speed at which Ghijhay moved and gave commands.

"Ghijhay, I promise that I will not use Fivey."

Her response was crisp and humorously ironic. "And so you will not; she is guarding you against your weaknesses. Besides, she is another witness to your virility. Just do as she says." She walked over to the entryway and summoned two of the guards, and then turned back to DeAndre. "Give me authority."

The two guards marched in and fell to their knees, then lowered their heads to the floor. The fluidity of the maneuver was such that no metal clashed and their thick, leather armor barely squeaked. The leader of the two intoned, "We are yours to command, Great One."

DeAndre managed to sit up, even with Fivey sitting on top of him, and spoke in tones of simple command.

"My woman, Ghijhay, speaks in my name and with my authority. Go with her and do as she says."

The guards were surprised at DeAndre's use of the term 'my woman' for Ghijhay, for it denoted a much greater status than when he referred to her as his concubine. They touched their foreheads to the floor, and the leader called out, "As you command, Great One." They stood and bowed, and then turned and bowed to Ghijhay.

She addressed them in regal style. "Come with me," and headed out and down the corridor.

Inside her private chambers, LeAnre fussed with the cushions to find a more comfortable position. Servants assisted her, but she snapped at them to leave her be. Kaesean she had banished to the other side of the fire pit after he made a few awkward tries at generating some intimacy. She just wanted to be left alone and suffer through her nausea quietly. The servants had no difficulty complying and found good reasons to avoid coming into contact with her.

Kaesean mustered as much tenderness and sympathy as he could. "My Great Lady, let me summon the *kemika* to see if..."

LeAnre did not open her eyes, but her voice was hard. "I will not tell you again to be quiet, Kaesean."

He had seen her in moods before, and wondered if the pressure being applied to her by her brother was not putting her into a permanent depression. The sound of voices at the chamber door sent him running to head off any disturbance that might increase her agitation.

He passed the archway to the entry chamber and came to a dead halt. The Potentate's chief concubine stood in the middle of the room, flanked by two of the Great One's personal guards. According to the legal technicalities of Koosti society, Kaesean was not required to bow to a slave, but everyone knew the power behind this one. He gave her a nod and kept his voice respectful. "Does the Great Ones' servant wish something?"

Ghijhay's tone dismissed him as irrelevant even as she answered his question. "I do; I come on his behalf and require his sister's presence immediately."

A jolt of fear stabbed through Kaesean's guts as he bowed and ran back inside to get LeAnre. He did not know which of the two women was more dangerous to be around. The sour look on LeAnre's face nearly made him run back and tell Ghijhay to leave.

"Great Lady, you must come to the entry room..."

She bared her teeth and yelled, "I do not have to go anywhere you dung worm! Leave!"

Kaesean's large, dark-brown eyes bulged out and his hands trembled. "Great Lady, it is your brother's chief concubine. She demands..."

Anger made her forget any feelings of nausea. She jumped up from the cushions and struck him across the shoulder with a flat-sided stick used for beating servants. "I am going to have you beaten to despair. How dare you defy me for the sake of a lowly whore; she shall join you in the beating."

She stomped out of the room and toward the entry. When she passed the arch to the entry chamber all she saw was Ghijhay. "You, slave, have disturbed me for the last time. You will..."

Ghijhay's right hand smacked hard into the left side of LeAnre's face, sending her to the floor. She saw stars and found it difficult to regain her balance. Ghijhay did not yell, but her powerful voice pierced LeAnre's disorienting fog.

"Shut up. I am here in your brother's name and will not allow you to dishonor him. He still feels a bond with you and is giving you one last chance to obey him. Until I order otherwise, you will have a man using you at least once every hour from sunrise to sunset. Your only deviation from this shall be to eat, bathe or use a chamber pot. You shall have only one thought: Pregnancy. Your servants' first priority will be to keep you ready for the men. It matters not what race or caste they come from. These guards with me have orders to see that you do as you have been commanded."

In shock, all LeAnre could do was grovel blindly on the floor and whimper, "I have been doing as he commanded; I have been trying. I will try harder..."

Ghijhay picked up the stick that LeAnre had used on Kaesean and swung it hard against LeAnre's bottom. LeAnre let out a shrill shriek of pain and started to roll away toward the bedchamber. Ghijhay's voice followed her like a vulture on dead meat. "Oh, you will obey, indeed, and it is not going to be left up to you. We have tried that and you failed us. Believe me when I say that I will not fail to take revenge for how you treated my family if you give me the least excuse for so doing. Your only hope is obedience."

LeAnre wanted to retort, but Ghijhay did not allow her the chance. Another blow smacked across her butt, and Ghijhay's voice pounded in her ears. LeAnre's fear for her own life forced her compliance.

"Get into the bed and get busy!"

Bawling in fear and pain, LeAnre quickly climbed onto her bed and lay down on her back. Ghijhay pointed at Kaesean and then at LeAnre.

"You, get busy with her." He leaped on the bed but his fear made it nearly impossible to perform. She spoke to one of the guards and said, "You next." To the other she gave a short command. "Go and find more men."

The guard bowed and ran down the corridor.

Ghijhay approached the bed and looked down on LeAnre, her eyes and voice showing no indication that mercy had any chance with her.

"Remember, obedience is your only protection." She spun around and strode down the hall back to DeAndre's chambers. He was asleep and had his arm around Fivey. Ghijhay whipped off her clothes and threw them on the foot of the bed, and then gave Fivey's shoulder a gentle shake. The lesser concubine turned and smiled at Ghijhay, then carefully rolled out of the bed and gave her a hug.

"Thank you, Great Mistress. He followed your instructions very carefully."

Ghijhay placed her hand over her mouth and giggled a bit. "You are free to do as you please for the next week."

Fivey kneeled and spread her arms wide. "Thank you, great Empress of all Koosti."

Ghijhay nodded and her eyebrows rose at being addressed as the empress. "Let us hope that it all works out, Fivey. If so, then the fun we are having with these idiot Koosti is only beginning. Now, off with you."

The young concubine donned her robe and nearly ran for the door. Ghijhay plopped onto the bed and rolled DeAndre on top of her, which brought a tired grunt from him. "Do not act like an old man; I need pleasure. Get busy."

CHAPTER TWENTY TWO

EMPRESS OF HIS HEART

Lord Karsten stood on a high balcony of the castle-fortress of Grandshire, deep in contemplation. He and Duke Russell Heilson had helped Duke Roland rid Starhaven of Koosti, and then met up with the army of Clarens to thoroughly scour the countryside of any remaining enemy. Sir Charles, now the general of the army of Clarens, reported that they had done away with the enemy along the western seacoast as far as the northern border of Rosea. They had then headed inland and searched the areas close to the Dividing Mountains, all the way down to the southern border of the empire. They crossed the mountains and chased any Koosti forces northeastward. The enemy was caught in a fearsome smother as the forces of Clarens pressed them from the south while Karsten's and Heilson's forces pounded them from the north. The Emeraldians lost few men while the Koosti suffered a great slaughter. Not many captives remained since Koosti preferred suicide to capture.

Russell and Charles joined Karsten on the balcony for an evening of rest. Deep mugs of fine ale helped them relax after so many days being in the saddle or swinging a sword.

Karsten set his mug down and sighed. "I feel so sorry for Roland; his mother having been tortured and three out of four of his people butchered could drive him insane. An entire generation has been decimated. We can be very thankful that the lands north of the empire have not gathered to sweep down and take control of our northern areas. The nomads still begrudge our presence after hundreds of years."

Russell nodded his head solemnly and, after a long drink of ale, spoke softly. "Roland is very strong of character. He may be in a bit of shock regarding his fief, but he will rise to the occasion and have things going smoothly before long. I plan to encourage settlers to seek out Starhaven and help rebuild the population.

"As far as the northern lands are concerned, I do not fear any immediate trouble as long as they fail to unite. Most of them still fear our empire due to the ancient tales of our effectiveness in battle. They also have reason to be thankful to the Emeraldians for many of the contributions we have made to their survival. The other factor is their healthy respect for Genazi; they know not to push their luck and provoke them."

Charles chuckled softly. "Those geniuses referred to as the 'Talents' in the ancient realm were very clever when they invented the idea of ferocious creatures, the *gregans*, who guarded the mountain passes near the border. It is possibly the best idea ever dreamed up by them; we have not had any trouble worth mentioning for hundreds of years."

The *gregans* were said to be creatures of uncanny stealth and fighting ability. The ancient Emeraldians had propagated the idea that *gregans* haunted the mountain passes along the empire's borders in order to scare off intruders. No one had claimed to ever see them, and only the emperors and empresses were said to be able to communicate with them.

Karsten smiled and shook his head. "Some have accused the Genazi of being *gregans* since we are able to repel any intruders entering the Boar's Spine. It is not much of a compliment though, since the stories about *gregans* always depict them as short, horny and ugly. I like to think that I do not resemble those qualities."

"Ha!" barked Heilson, "you and the empress are two of the finest in all the Lands. The day that the two of you exchange vows there will be many men and women claiming that you have not been fair to them."

Karsten flashed a humorous grimace. "The women of the Genazi nearly started a civil war over who had the right to marry me. I tried to stay away as much as possible just to have some peace and quiet. Veranna came along just in time. I wish that I were with her now. Even a note would make our time apart more bearable."

He nearly fell out of his chair when something landed on his lap and an eagle screeched as it flew to a perch on a stone outcrop above the balcony's embrasure. Charles and Russell both spilled some of their ale on their laps and scrambled for rags. A moment later, Karsten identified the object the eagle dropped on him.

"It is a scroll from Veranna." He unrolled it, and as he read the message his face changed from pure joy to dread and fear.

> *Karsten, my love, I have prayed for the Creator to keep you safe and to bring you back to me with all speed. I have missed you so much and long for your tender voice to dispel all of my fears. You are my strength, and I am so thankful that I am yours. I need your strength and wisdom now more than ever before. As you likely know the Koosti have captured Tesra. She is as my own mother. The thought that anyone would wish to do her harm is enough to make my blood boil. Time is short, for the Koosti have plans to turn her into what they call a 'dragon wife.' A witness has told me that once the process starts there is a limited amount of time to try and reverse it. Only in ancient records is there any report of someone being saved from such a miserable fate.*
>
> *My love, I must try to save Tesra. If I did not try I would say that you have chosen foolishly for a mate. A platoon of volunteers is setting out with me, but I ask for your presence as well. If you are by my side I can have great hope for the Creator's blessing.*
>
> *I have sent the army ahead of us to deal with any remaining Koosti. They shall proceed to Neidburg, and from there they shall head to Curt's Vale and threaten an attack on Koosti lands. We want the army to be seen at the border so that the Koosti will shift their forces toward that point and leave other passes undermanned. The volunteers and I shall break off from the army and head northeast before leaving Loreland. We hope to enter Koosti land without being seen, and race for Banaipal. If the western lords are able to join the army, so much the better. The Koosti must fear us and respond hastily. Their haste shall leave gaps in their defenses, and we must utilize those gaps. We now have the initiative and must maintain it.*
>
> *My dear Karsten, knowledge of the very material of the ground helped deliver us from the Koosti siege. I pray that your knowledge of my heart shall always keep it under siege, for I surrender to you with great joy and anticipation. Come to me, my love, and make me whole. Please, send a reply with the eagle.*
>
> *All my love is with you.*
>
> *Veranna.*

Karsten bolted out of his chair and addressed Charles and the duke. "My lords, you must set out at dawn with your forces for Neidburg. The imperial army is heading there already. You will learn more about your mission once you reach there. My lord duke, I must leave immediately and request enough food and water to get me to eastern Loreland, and I will need some spare horses. For now, I just need a pen and ink."

Heilson nodded and called for an attendant to see to Karsten's requests, but Charles put his hand on Karsten's shoulder and spoke with a tinge of fear.

"Karsten, is Veranna alright? She is as a daughter to me, and I must know if she is being harmed."

The young Genazi lord knew of the great love that Charles and his wife, Kate had for Veranna, for they had been involved in her life from the time she had been brought to the Academy, in Clarens, as a little girl. Charles had a right to know what threatened her.

"My lord, she is setting out to rescue Tesra. This must be kept secret lest Koosti spies gain knowledge of the mission. I am going to join her and protect her in any way I can. Besides, I need you and Tesra to grant me her hand in marriage."

Charles smiled warmly. "The sooner the better. Everyone knows that you will do your best. Just remember to be careful."

Karsten shook Charles' hand and vowed to bring her home. Just then a serving woman appeared with a lapboard, pen, ink and paper. Karsten nodded thanks to her and then sat to write out his reply to Veranna.

My dear Veranna,
I come, my love, and hold you close to my heart.
With all my love,
   Karsten.

He allowed a few moments for the ink to dry and then rolled up the paper and tied a piece of string around it before handing it to the eagle. The large, green and gold bird bowed and then dashed into the air with a great beating of its wings. All three moons were out, even if at less than half, and provided more than enough light now that the sun was sinking in the west.

The duke walked onto the balcony and reported that Karsten's horses and provisions would be ready for him when he reached the stable yard. "Also, a swift sloop shall be ready for you down at the river dock. It will take you up the river quickly while giving you some time to rest. I have given orders to the captain to let you off toward Chenray, since it allows you to go east with the fewest obstacles. The captain and crew do not know your identity, except that you are an important person and are served by me."

Karsten shook his hand and thanked him. "My lord, you have done so much for the empire that we are deeply in your debt. I look forward to seeing you again when we have my future mother-in-law back. May the Creator keep you safe."

"And you, as well," replied the duke. "Remember: Daring is one thing, foolishness another; do not lose your head in reckless gambles."

Karsten nodded and bade the two men goodbye. He and his horses were given an escort to the river dock and within minutes he was aboard and making good speed up the river. The sails bellowed with wind and he even helped with the rowing of the oars. All he could think of was finding Veranna and hearing her voice. After midnight he lay down below deck and fell fast asleep. It was about noon when the captain awoke him.

"My lord, I suspect that you might enjoy a bit of the scenery around here."

Still getting his bearings, Karsten shook his head and followed the captain up on deck. The man pointed north by northeast to the foothills before the Boar's Spine Mountains. The Genazi lord knew those hills very well, especially a particular slope where he first met Veranna. It seemed an age ago in a different world. She had mistakenly knocked him for a loop, but her wonderful spirit took him captive. He longed for his chains to be tightened all the more.

Two hours later he unloaded his horses and materials on a small quay on the easternmost end of Smooth Lake. After sunset he finally reached the town of Chenray and found an inn owned and operated by a nephew of Charle's. A generous meal and night's sleep had him up before dawn and speeding to the northeast to find Veranna.

Chenray had suffered little damage from the invasion, for the Koosti leaders concentrated on Neidburg and Tolemera. However, farms and villages along the Koosti line of travel between the two cities were horrors. Rotting corpses with hollow eye sockets lay all around. Some of the people had been nailed to the walls of their houses and left to die slowly. Most buildings were reduced to ashes, some of which still smoldered, and a foul stench carried far into the fields.

Coyotes and carrion fowl scattered as Karsten rode by, only to hurry back to their feast when he was gone.

Two days later and Karsten knew that he must be drawing near to Veranna and her company. The bodies of dead Koosti steadily grew in number as he pressed east. The Koosti soldiers had obviously made a hasty retreat, with those at the rear paying the price for being too slow. Many had slain themselves to avoid capture, but others fought to the very end. The freshest were at least a day old, and the smell was not yet at its peak.

He changed horses regularly and pressed harder. If there were dead enemy soldiers along the path that Veranna's company took, there might be large enemy units they encountered that could present a great risk.

Three days later he paused on a short slope just below the crest of a hill. Looking east he saw a large bird, likely an eagle, circling in the sky a great distance away. The sighting filled him with hope that he would soon find his love.

CHAPTER TWENTY THREE

JUST RESTING, KILLING TIME

The evening sun cast its sheen across the land revealing both sorrow and beauty. The bodies of Koosti, and their victims, lay along the eastern route, but the land could not be divorced from its touch of the Creator's handiwork. Veranna and her company halted to rest beside a pool at the bottom of a short waterfall. The brush and trees countered the smell of the distant, putrid carcasses, and the waterfall poured into the pool from thirty feet above, giving a steady and smooth background noise that soothed the mind while masking other sounds.

Still sitting in her saddle, Veranna took in the beauty around her, marveling at how a world full of such wonders could harbor so much evil. She lifted up her left arm and the eagle accompanying them glided down and over the pool before fanning out its wings to land easily on her arm. She used her right hand to reach into a pouch for some partially cooked meat and fed it to the majestic bird.

Her companions spread out to search the area while she allowed her horse to edge up to the pool to drink. In her mind played out a fantasy of her and Karsten, alone, visiting this place during a time of peace. The bushes and trees were abloom and the fragrances of their flowers filled the small hollow. Her imagination drifted away to seeing herself in the pool with Karsten, enjoying his touch and voice. They frolicked about in the cool water, chasing each other and splashing when Karsten caught her and pulled her close with a long, tight kiss.

In the back of her mind she heard the quick pounding of hooves, but ignored it, assuming it was one of her comrades moving around the landscape. The fantasy was far more engaging.

* * *

Karsten saw the eagle drop down out of the sky about a mile ahead and knew that Veranna would be there. He gave his horse a swat with the reins, urging it to move faster.

* * *

At the top of the waterfall two dark eyes peered out from a small opening in the dense brush. The eyes watched carefully as Veranna moved her horse to the water's edge and closed her eyes. The noise of the falling water would cover other sounds, and with her eyes closed, she would catch no sight of the arrow pointed at her heart, nor gain a glimpse of the poison-laden arrowhead that would insure her death.

The Koosti assassin had prepared his position well. The heavy brush concealed him better than any camouflage, and the secret cave beneath the stream and waterfall had allowed him plenty of rest before the Emeraldians approached. The cursed westerners had killed so many of his fellow soldiers that none of them could hope for escape as long as the barbarians were in pursuit. Once he took out their empress, the rest of their empire would collapse due to the absence of any driving force for survival. After firing his arrow, the secret cave would provide him an absence that would allow him to survive and collect a reward for destroying this barbarian empress.

* * *

Karsten saw some Rockhounds and knights out patrolling the perimeter of the hollow and waved to them. After a few moments they recognized him and turned their horses about to join him in the hollow. As he began his descent toward the pool he caught a glint of light on metal near the top of the waterfall in a clump of bushes. In horror, he realized that it pointed directly at Veranna, who sat as though asleep in the saddle of her horse. All he could do was spur his own tired horse to greater speed.

* * *

Veranna indulged her fantasy of Karsten holding her in the pool. It was a tonic for all of the anxieties plaguing her heart and mind. She pressed her body tightly against his and kissed him gently, but it turned wild in a heartbeat. A few moments later she pulled away and began a song she had created just for the two of them.

Many long days have we waited;
And toiled through both sorrow and dread.
We long to be one with each other,
And hurry the day when we wed.

Come fill up my hours as a fountain;
Pour sweet flowing waters within.
Life's currents have brought us together.
Oh, hasten our day to begin.

Take me now and enfold me;
Embrace me with all of your might.
We surrender our hearts to each other,
And taste all of love's sweet delights.

Her musings were cut short when she suddenly found herself flying out of her saddle, grasped by strong arms. Something whisked past her head as she and her attacker plunged into the pool. Automatic responses took over as she tried to get her head above water. She kicked at the legs of her attacker and manipulated his finger joints to cause pain. His hands suddenly released her and she sent a hard kick into his stomach. The water dulled the blow, but it drove him away enough that she could push up to the surface for a breath.

Air rushed into her lungs as she wiped water away from her eyes. She grabbed her knife from its sheath and looked for her assailant. Six feet away a head popped out of the water and Veranna thought that her eyes must be playing tricks on her. She could not believe her ears as the familiar voice yelled at her.

"Get down, now!"

From the corner of her left eye came a quick movement. She instantly splashed back and down, barely avoiding an arrow shot at her neck. She went deeper into the pool and swam for the side furthest from the waterfall. Nearing the shore, she pushed off the bottom as hard as she could and tumbled behind a fir tree as another arrow thumped into the ground beside her.

No sign of any other attackers came from the surrounding foliage. Closing her eyes, Veranna communicated with her knights and ordered them to surround the area so that no one could escape.

Karsten splashed out of the water on the side of the pool across from her. He wrestled out of his wet tunic and motioned Veranna to stay put. Running up the short slope to the top of the waterfall, he crouched down and surveyed the area. Trees and thick brush grew along the stream, making it an ideal place for an assassin to hide. One drawback that favored Karsten was that the heavy growth made arrows virtually useless against him.

Pushing the grass and bushes back from the stream's edge revealed tracks at least a day old. They led toward the lip of the waterfall, but another set of the same tracks came back from Karsten's left, near a huge fir tree. A brief glimpse of color in motion took his attention past the tree, and suddenly the movement was gone. Approaching the lip of the fall, he saw fresh tracks heading back toward the tree. They ended right near an especially thick growth of stiff bushes that included nettles. Ignoring their stinging barbs, Karsten pressed through the mass of vegetation and suddenly slid down a shaft into a dark cave. To his right lay a bed of coals that gave the cave an eerie red glow, and to his left was a curtain of water.

A shadowy form lifted a bow ready to fire across the pool. Karsten realized that Veranna had been at that point when he came out of the water. Readying his knife, he moved as quickly as possible in the snug cave and just a few feet away from the assassin he leaped through the air and grabbed him just as he let his arrow fly. The arrow hit the tree that Veranna stood behind, while Karsten and the assassin plunged into the pool.

The killer was taken by surprise. With Karsten's weight on his back he hit the surface of the water hard on his face and chest like a slab of thick, wet leather. His opponent's powerful arms allowed him little movement, leaving no chance for drawing a breath. A fog grew in his mind and he knew he would soon be unconscious.

Panic gave him enough strength to remove his poisoned blade from its leg sheath. All of his remaining power and concentration focused on moving his hand a fraction of an inch. Little pain reported as he made a small cut into the thigh of his left leg, but he smiled at the last, satisfied that he had not been taken alive.

Karsten felt the body go limp. His own lungs screamed for air as he shoved off the bottom and toward the edge of the pool. Still clutching the assassin's body with his left hand, he quickly moved up through the water and finally penetrated to the surface. The butt end of a spear shaft tapped his shoulder and he grabbed hold to be pulled to the edge. Treybal and several knights were there to help him out of the water and pull the body of the dead assassin to shore. Getting the water out of his eyes and ears, Karsten heard and saw Veranna running over to him.

"Karsten; Karsten! Are you all right? Are you hurt?" A frantic look was in her eye as she turned him around to see if he was injured. Seeing the redness and small cuts of the nettles she flew into a rage thinking that he had been poisoned. She stepped over to the body of the assassin and screamed, "You dung heap! You filth! How dare you touch him!" She kicked at the body thinking the man was still alive.

None of them had ever seen her so upset. Karsten had to pick her up and move her away, even as she continued to kick at the body.

"Veranna! Calm down; there is nothing to fear, now. You are safe, and so am I." He still labored to catch his breath, but she was breathing harder than he. She started to yell at the dead body again, but Karsten gave her shoulders a shake and looked directly into her eyes. "Calm down, my love, please."

She suddenly stopped and her eyes filled with tears. Her jaw trembled as she wrapped her arms around him and pressed her face against his neck. Karsten returned her tight hug and rubbed her back, soothing away her fears with his gentle touch. All she could mutter was, "Thank the Creator that you are safe."

After a few moments, Karsten led her over to a fallen tree and had her sit down. In her wet clothing she felt chilled and asked for a blanket. The

Rockhounds and knights scoured the area around the pool and waterfall, poking their spears and swords into the thick clumps of brush. A Hound soon had a fire burning brightly and prepared some hot tea, which helped Veranna and Karsten warm up and dry off.

Kreida, with Reiki behind her, trotted up and scanned the area. Kreida gave Veranna a sly grin. "I see you got him to take his clothes off. The others must have shown up just as you got down to business; the interruption must be aggravating you to death. At least you had some entertainment killing Koosti."

Reiki scowled at her. "No talk, dog breath. She upset and cold."

Kreida snarled back, "Listen, kitty cat, I have told you before not to call me..."

Veranna found the exchange humorous, but after the jolt to her emotions from the assassin she was in no mood for silliness. "Kreida, please be quiet. We will make camp here, so find a place to set up our tent. Then help the Rockhounds with the food preparations." Before the fiery Genazi woman could respond, Veranna turned to Treybal.

"Would you please bring me the skin balm and a small flask of rum? I will also need a piece of clean cloth."

Treybal nodded and went to one of the packhorses. In a minute he returned with the requested items. Veranna turned Karsten around and inspected the small wounds scattered along his torso, brushing away dirt and debris. She then balled up one end of the cloth and soaked it with rum. Without comment she moved from one wound to another and pressed the rum-soaked cloth against them, then followed up by rubbing some balm onto each. After a final inspection, she leaned forward and gave him a quick peck on the lips before flashing him a mock scowl.

"Be more careful next time, you silly oaf. You are lucky that the killer did not scratch you with his knife. He might have..." She paused as a thought came to her. "He gave up far too quickly. He must have deemed it necessary to avoid capture at all cost. That means he knew something vital. Did you see where he was hiding?"

Karsten pulled on a dry shirt and pointed toward the top of the waterfall. "There is an opening to a cave beneath the stream that is hidden behind some heavy brush and nettles. If we chop away the brush there should be little trouble getting inside. The other opening is behind the waterfall."

Veranna turned to Treybal. "Find the opening up above and clear away the brush. Then, do a thorough search of the cave. Take Reiki with you; she has good eyes for dark areas."

Twenty minutes later, Reiki returned with a piece of parchment that was mostly burned.

"Highness, Koosti no burn all. Some message left. Reiki read Koosti, if need."

Veranna studied the scrap for a moment. "I hope that you can read what is left; it is very damaged."

The Felinii woman chuckled. "Much Koosti talk and write same: Kill and take." She fell silent as she scanned the scrap. A minute later she felt confident to relate the information. "Koosti Great Lady say to kill highness; brother no want attack and say only great victory save her. Last part mad at brother's. . .uh, how you say, whore slave?"

Veranna and Karsten exchanged puzzled looks, but Kreida spoke up first. "Hey kitty, what is the Koosti word that you translate as *whore slave*?"

Reiki frowned at Kreida calling her 'kitty,' and responded in kind. "Dog-breath, the Koosti word is *grayliya*."

Kreida did not recognize the word, but after a few moments, Karsten's face lit up with a look of understanding.

"Of course! The word is similar to an ancient Genazi term for a woman taken as a slave, a bed partner, better known as a concubine."

A thought suddenly blazed into Veranna's mind. "LeAnre and her brother are at odds with one another, and his concubine is causing LeAnre more frustration. There is likely a rivalry between them."

Kreida wagged her finger at Veranna and exclaimed, "You see; I told you that that devil worshiper was trouble. You should have let me kill her when we had the chance."

Veranna closed her eyes and wearily shook her head. "Thank you, Kreida, for repeating yourself for the thousandth time. Now, unless you have something useful to say, please be quiet."

Kreida harrumphed and turned away while the others suppressed grins. Veranna turned back to Reiki.

"Reiki, did you not tell me that you were taken as a slave to the Koosti imperial court?"

"Yes, highness. Reiki made whore for DeAndre. He no want; he love chief whore."

Veranna hurried to correct her. "The right word is 'concubine', Reiki."

The Felinii woman practiced pronouncing the word a couple of times before continuing.

"Chief concubine friend of Reiki. She very much beautiful. LeAnre hate her, fear her. Great Lady must keep part in empire. If not, she then low whore for brother. Other Koosti could buy. Great Lady no have children. Her part in empire go to other ruler."

Veranna smiled at Treybal and asked rhetorically, "What often happens when your opponent becomes desperate?"

Treybal smiled back, a lion seeing his way to attack a leopard. "The desperate foe often commits a serious blunder, leaving himself open to a crushing blow."

"Indeed." She paused to think for a moment, and then headed for her horse. "Let's get something to eat and have a relaxing evening. I want to break camp and be far along our course before dawn." She pulled a towel and comb from a saddlebag to set about drying and combing out her hair, but Kreida took the comb from her and directed her to sit on a large rock nearby. Still thinking of how to take advantage of the new information about LeAnre, Veranna probed her friend's mind for ideas.

"Kreida, if you were LeAnre, what do you think you would be thinking about your situation?"

Kreida shocked Veranna by not blurting out the first insult that came to mind, taking a moment to collect her thoughts. "If what Tesra said is true about the bronzing of their skin making them less able to conceive a child, I would be lining up men at my door to try and get pregnant. Otherwise, she will lose everything if kitty is right about Koosti customs. LeAnre is probably scared stiff of what her brother might do to her. Actually, if he is in love with his concubine, then LeAnre has more to fear from her. Either way, LeAnre goes to the dogs. Her only hope was to defeat us and boast of being a great warrior-ruler. That will not happen, now."

Veranna let out a long breath. "I think you are right. She is caught up in a vicious trap of her own making, and cannot find a way out. She would live among her own people in total disgrace. I can almost feel pity for her."

Kreida threw the comb down and stepped in front of her, wagging her finger like a scolding grandmother.

"Don't you dare let me hear you say anything like that, again! Twice she has tried to kill you, and she betrayed you to the Gelangweils. She has taken your mother hostage and is turning her into a wicked creature. Her evil desires led her to attack us and kill many of our people. She deserves no mercy, and is unlikely to ever appreciate why. She will count on you being weak and giving her a way out."

Veranna looked over to where Karsten was going about setting up tents. She longed to have him take her by the hand and speed the two of them away on a fast horse.

"I am sorry if I seem weak, Kreida, but I just want this all to be done with. Some peace and quiet would be very welcome."

Kreida noticed her glance toward Karsten. "I totally agree with that. However, weakness will not win you any peace; if you compromise what is true and right, you can only expect more trouble. Besides, if you cannot control an empire, how do you ever hope to control a husband?"

The look of mock exasperation on Kreida's face brought out a hearty laugh from Veranna. "Oh, Kreida, how I have prayed for Treybal!" After a moment of silence, she changed the subject. "Let's get some food; I am starved."

Kreida gave her a wry look and said suggestively, "I bet you are after rubbing your hands all over Karsten's bare body."

Veranna gasped and blushed. "You are impossible. Karsten needed attention to his wounds or he would be itching all night long."

Kreida gave her another insinuating look. "Yeah, well, I am sure you will be, too." She laughed and headed for the cook fire as Veranna's face turned redder.

CHAPTER TWENTY FOUR

DEAD END

Marques Amilla, of the Sudryni, turned away from the window that looked out over the public square where criminals were being executed. She could not remember a day when the sound of the headsman's ax did not pound at her ears since returning to Neidburg. Veranna had refused to look out that same window when the late Emperor, Dalmar Gelangweil, was dispatched to the Creator nearly two years ago. Amilla had attended that execution as Veranna's representative, but she felt no pangs of sympathy for Dalmar. Hatred ruled her heart that day, a hatred fueled by Dalmar's rape of her and the many pragmatic murders he saw fit to commit.

The heavy thump of the ax sounded again. It sent a shudder through her, making her all the more sympathetic with Veranna's refusal to watch executions. Amilla cursed her own imagination when it conjured a vision of a dance, corresponding to the beat of the falling ax, through her head. The music in her mind failed to cease, haunting her in the castle chamber's silence. The vision grew in strength and she saw her blue silk gown turned blood red. As she danced with the headsman, blood dripped from the gown's sleeves and hem, and the ballroom floor was strewn with heads. The eyes opened as she danced by, pleading for mercy as more fell and rolled across the cold, yellow marble.

Amilla screamed in terror and her head shook in denial of the vision. Her personal guard rushed in and looked around for any sign of an attacker. Seeing no one, the woman slid her knife into its bosom sheath, her sharp Genazi features showing disappointment that no opportunity existed for combat.

"Lady Amilla, I heard you scream, but there is no one attacking you. What is wrong?"

It took a moment for Amilla to find her voice, and when she did it was a hollow whisper.

"Nothing, Atani; do not worry, I am alright."

Amilla appreciated Atani's attention to her duty. She was a lot like Kreida in her straightforward manner and ferocity. But the no-nonsense attitude toward killing that was bred into Genazi increased Amilla's agitation.

"You may go, Atani, I will be..."

She screamed again as the sound of the ax doing its work came through the window. She tore through the room and into the corridor. Atani followed her through the halls and down the front steps of the palace, wondering if she was dealing with a madwoman.

Large crowds always attended the executions. The captured Koosti, criminals and mercenaries had been found guilty of multiple heinous crimes and refused to show any remorse. Those in the crowd were affected by the brutality of the guilty and desired vengeance. The noise of their cries made it all but impossible for Amilla to make her way through to the platform. Suddenly the square went quiet, but was filled with an air of expectant tension. She hurried to the steps of the platform, but was frozen in place by the sound of the ax pounding onto the block. What followed seemed to happen in slow motion. The head of a man bounced off the deck of the platform and flew through the air. It twisted around enough for Amilla to see the crazed grin on its face. Before she could react it struck her on the chest, smattering blood all along the front of her dress, forehead and cheeks. The roar of the crowd drowned out her shriek of horror. She collapsed to her knees before crawling up the steps to the deck of the platform.

Her legs felt so wobbly that she feared a slight breeze might whisk her away. Hanging on to the railing, she stepped onto the deck and forced herself to stand up straight. The guards and executioners bowed to her, but they were puzzled by her sudden appearance. She studied their faces and wondered how much they had suffered in order to become so grim in their duties.

At the rear of the platform stood the condemned. Over thirty awaited death, their hands tied behind their backs, with tight fetters greatly limiting their mobility. Men and women, young and old, made up the group. Each wore only a brief loincloth, for the prisoners would use any piece of cloth to choke a fellow whom they suspected might divulge information to their enemies. The men were shaved bald, and the women had hair barely to the bottom of their skulls. Hair was another tool they used against informers and guards. They had no shoes or sandals, for they could be used as weapons, and it made it easier to dispose of the bodies in the mass graves.

The headsman signaled for another prisoner to be brought forward. He cleaned his axe blade and sharpened it as the guard captain stepped in front of the prisoner and proclaimed the man's judgment.

"You, of the Koosti, have been found guilty of murder, torture, rape, wild destruction, theft and invasion of the Empire of the Seven Lands. You showed no mercy toward any of your victims, nor has remorse been witnessed from your mouth. We offer you this last chance to admit your crimes before these people, and before your Creator."

At the mention of the Creator, the man's face twisted into a frightening mask of contempt, and his voice came out in a snarl.

"The Dark One knows my service and will reward me with power. I have no fear of your blades, and I fear your Creator even less."

The captain, a man of almost fifty years, did not bother to argue with the captive. He shook his head and signaled for the man to be positioned for execution.

As the man was forced to his knees and strapped down, Amilla knelt and looked him in the eye as his head lay across the block.

"Do not be a fool! I can grant you a pardon from death if you will renounce the Dark One and swear never to harm another person, again."

She recoiled as the man spat at her. An eerie countenance came over his face, a smile of wicked anticipation.

"Only a fool would give up great power in the next life. I have no doubt that the Dark One will give you to me, and I shall do anything I please with you. So shall it be for any who oppose him. You but send me to my reward sooner than I had foreseen. Were I to continue in this world, I would serve the Dark One by killing you, and any others who tried to stand in his way."

While he spoke, Amilla saw more clearly the nature of the battle that the Seven Lands now fought, and the deliverance that she, and her people, had been granted by the ascendance of Veranna to the throne.

"You of the Koosti presume too much power for the Dark One. He has no place granting you power in this world, let alone in the next. My people, the Sudryni, were under his spell for years, but the Creator sent a servant to open our eyes, and she made known to us the Creator's mercy. We live free from the Dark One's tyranny, and can enjoy a great service of transforming the world around us. That is true power, for it is the power for life. All that you have with darkness is death and destruction, whether in this world or the next. The Dark One has cheated you, for he knows that the Creator shall bring him to judgment, and vanquish all evil so that life may be lived to the full."

A pang of fear shot through the man and his face showed his trouble, but a moment later he broke out in a hideous, ranting laugh. "We shall see, you Emeraldian scum. It will not be long before I have you, body and soul, in my power. Your screams shall be my music, and your never ending wounds my pleasure."

Amilla stood and looked down at him in mute horror, astonished that he could be so given to corruption. As she stepped back, she raised her hand to the headsman, and then let it fall limply to her side. It seemed to happen in another world as the headsman raised his ax and swung it down in one swift, fluid blur. The prisoner's head plopped into the basket, bounced out and rolled to a stop on the deck, facing up.

The Marques at first felt numb, but terror seized her and the crowd. The sun grew dark, and they all stood rooted in place as the eyes on the severed head focused straight at Amilla's. Its mouth opened and a voice slithered out from depths unknown. Time seemed to vanish, and Amilla realized not that she wet herself. The voice from the head held her captive.

"You think to persuade my servants to abandon me? They will not, for they know their place. Your ideas about mercy and judgment are pointless; I shall be the one who judges all others. Mine is the mastery, even if you refuse to see it. Observe."

The head rolled to face the prisoners.

"You, Jirmey, kill yourself."

The Koosti man obeyed without hesitation. He sprang through the air and fell onto the reverse blade of the headsman's ax, neck first. His wife, who had stood beside him, screamed as his blood poured out and took the life from his body.

The head rolled back toward Amilla, and the voice seemed stronger than before.

"You must understand that pathetic creatures such as you cannot hope for any victory against me. My servants dwarf your forces, and I shall give your empress to the foulest and cruelest of despots. She walks blindly into my trap, and there is no saving her. The one you call 'Creator,' has abandoned her, and you shall be under my sway as you were before. The Creator will submit to me, and all of your petty policies will be for naught."

Utter fear nearly made Amilla pass out. Her eyes would not focus and her voice failed. Bone-chilling laughter rumbled forth from the Pits of Perdition, and Amilla's limbs shook to its timber. Insanity threatened to overtake her, and she wondered if it had not already done so. The crowd wailed in despair, expecting the ground to rend and swallow them up.

Amilla, desperate to escape, tore her gaze away from the possessed head and looked up at the sky. A shaft of light pierced the darkness and brought a remnant of reason into her mind. It grew stronger as its import clarified. She looked back at the head and found the faintest whisper of voice she could ever imagine.

"No."

Barely audible, the word struck like a thunderclap through the public square. The crowd went silent and looked at her to see if fire would erupt from below and consume her in an instant. The evil face drew into a frown, and then broke out into derisive laughter.

"Foolish woman, you have no power to resist my will. Your ridiculous attempt at bravura shall end in your humiliation. Your faith is useless."

The light grew brighter as Amilla remembered discussions she and Veranna had pursued after the fall of the Gelangweils.

"I make no claim to power, and freely admit that foolishness is ever near me. For I did not bring myself into being, and wisdom is no creation of mine. I must simply accept both. And, one piece of wisdom that I recognize is that whatever is made is not greater than its' maker. The Creator made you, but you were not content, and fell into denial of the truth of what you are. I make no denial that I am a mere woman, nor will I join your folly in doubting the Creator's supremacy. It matters not that you could slay me, for I know that my destiny is not in your hands."

The sun shone to the full as she stood tall and confident. She cried out, "Be gone, for we do not serve you, no matter how many others satisfy their lusts in your lies."

The Dark Ones' voice turned cold as ice.

"Enjoy your childish resistance today, for it shall not be long before all that you are is mine. Your beloved empress shall learn the futility of her ways as my snare tightens around her. That which she seeks she will find, but it will prove to be her destruction."

Amilla blinked and the world came back to normal. She felt the passage of time again, and the crowd of people wondered if they had awakened from a dream. The oddest sight was the group of prisoners. Many of them wept and fell to their knees, crying for mercy. A barrier was gone from their minds, one that kept them from seeing their evil deeds. They realized that they deserved death many times over, and knew that their captors would be swift to punish them.

One of the women pointed at the head through which the Dark One spoke. Its eyes were glazed over in the finality of death, but no one wanted to touch it, lest the evil spell that had possessed them return. The woman looked up at Amilla, a different type of fear coming over her as she spoke to her comrades.

"That woman faced the Dark One and survived. She sent him away in humility. Even the Great Lady never had such power."

A murmuring buzz went through the group, and a moment later five people stood separate from the others, looking at them with malice and contempt. Amilla saw the division and hurried to exploit it.

"You Koosti, do you now see the reward that the Dark One grants? It is only death and destruction. Simple truth is all that is required to show him for the liar that he is. You do not need to fear him anymore. You are free, and can live lives that are not dominated by irrational slavery to evil."

One of the five separatists, a tall, muscular man in his early thirties, snarled back at her, "You will not succeed in trying to draw us away from the Dark One. We do not heed your notions of truth. These other weaklings are not worthy to be called Koosti; the Dark One will repay their stupidity forever."

Amilla stood in front of the others and said simply, "You have seen the truth with your own eyes. If you deny reality there is no hope for you. And, if you listen to these followers of the Dark One, you will never be free. Renounce the Dark One and live."

A woman at the front of the group looked quickly at the man who spoke for the separatists, and then back at Amilla, before looking down. Shame, guilt and fear were written on her face and posture.

"Lady, we have no life. The Dark One is all we know. And now he has brought us to death by your executioner. We deserve it, but we have no hope for anything better. Your people want our heads for vengeance, and we would do the same in their place."

Amilla studied the group for a moment before turning to the crowd. They bowed as she held up her hand for silence.

"People of Imperia, you have witnessed an amazing event. The Dark One, who spurs our neighbors to be our foes, openly showed where his weakness lies. He cannot bear the truth, and fights against reality, itself. These prisoners were under his sway all of their lives and just now have been delivered from his grasp. They admit their terrible deeds and beg for mercy. What say you?"

Angry grumbling erupted, and a woman raised her fist and shook it crossly.

"They killed my husband and ate my babies. Their men raped me day and night, and had no concern for me. Why should I care a whit for such mad dogs!"

The crowd yelled at the Koosti, cursing them in every way. Amilla let it go on for a moment before raising her hand once more.

"Dear lady, I have great sorrow for what you have endured and agree that your claim is just. Your hunger for justice is a tribute to your Creator, and no one here shall deny it. Has anyone forced you to seek justice?"

The woman was taken aback by the question, and her face twisted in confusion.

"No one forced me, my Lady; I do so on my own."

Amilla sat on the deck and put her feet onto the second step down. "Would you consider it right for me to force you to seek justice?"

The woman grew more wary of where this line of questioning was going, and her voice came out in a suspicious tone. "I do not need anyone to tell me to seek justice; I am perfectly capable on my own."

The Marquis shook her head solemnly. "That is true. For your concern over your loved ones to be sincere, it must be chosen by you, just as love cannot be forced upon you.

"As you have seen today, these Koosti were dominated by the will of another. While not inescapable, that will held them in its powerful grip. For my part, I am willing to commute their sentence from death to servitude. In this way they can help to rebuild that which they have torn down. Wars cease, and treaties are made between the parties. Shall we not try to make peace with those who were enslaved when they repent and seek to make restitution? Can we not put an end to killing when it is both just and practical?"

A man near the back of the crowd yelled, "How can we trust them? You speak as though they will simply stop murdering and raping."

The woman who had spoken first shook her fist in anger, again. "He is right! Those mongrels would slit our throats in the middle of the night and run off to kill more. They are rabid curs!"

Amilla's face fell into a sad smile. "That is the same rationale that they used to justify attacking us. It is amazing how hate and pride can make us so much like our enemies. They have been fed stories telling of how barbaric we are, and how we seek to slaughter and abuse them simply for pleasure." She turned to the group of captives and motioned for the Koosti woman in front to step forward, then gestured to the woman while facing the angry crowd.

"This woman killed one of our people during combat, according to the rules we allow for war. Her death sentence came from her aiding spies and murderers." She turned to the Koosti woman, and said, "Tell us why you aided murderers."

The woman's jaw trembled and tears squeezed from the corners of her deep blue eyes. She looked down at the ground, and her words shot out as one tortured.

"I wanted my children to live!" She fell to her knees and sobbed, sputtering words as best she could. "We came on orders from the Great Lady to spy and hide warriors. When Koosti army defeated, warriors hide where we live. My husband was killed by Genazi. We have no food. Warriors take my three children and eat them. The children scream, and screams stay in my ears till I die. Genazi kill warriors in battle. I captured and sentenced to death. I dead to you, I dead to my people and I dead to my children. Kill me, I care not."

A hush came over the crowd, as they looked upon the woman and her comrades in a new light. A number of them turned and walked away, but the one who had argued with Amilla was not finished.

"She deserved what she got; she should not have been aiding those murderous dogs. We did not kill and eat her children; her own people did."

Amilla placed her right hand on the kneeling Koosti woman's shoulder, but spoke to the woman in the crowd.

"That is true. However, she was forced into doing as she did. I am, therefore, commuting her punishment to servitude."

The face of the woman in the crowd was red with anger, but after a moment, she gave Amilla a short bow and said, "Yes, my Lady. But, since she and I are alike in our fortunes, I demand that her servitude be to me."

Amilla looked at both women before agreeing to the demand, trying to gauge the level of animus each held for the other. She prayed that her decision would prove fruitful, then announced her conclusion.

"So be it." She motioned for the court scribe to approach, and then said very clearly, "This Koosti woman, whose name is…" She paused and looked questioningly at the woman.

The woman took a moment to understand what was expected of her. "My name NeLamay."

Amilla continued her sentence straightaway. "…NeLamay, shall be the personal servant to…" Here she pointed at the city woman.

"Cebra," said the woman, her tone firm, but level.

"…Cebra, of the city of Neidburg." Amilla paused to see that the scribe had the names written down. "This shall be for no more than one year, and no less than one month. NeLamay shall be housed in the castle servant's quarters, and go each morning to Cebra's home to serve her needs. She shall cease one hour before sunset and be free to visit the markets until sunset, when she shall return to the castle. No physical or verbal abuse will be used, and NeLamay shall perform her service faithfully, without complaint. Is this agreeable to you, madam Cebra?"

Cebra's hair was a mixture of gray and brown, but her face was grayer by far. Her jaw line softened a bit as she nodded resignedly. "It is."

Amilla turned to the scribe. "A copy of my decision shall be made for each party. As for those prisoners who beg for mercy and repent of the Dark One, they are to be sent home with sufficient supplies for the journey. They must also swear never to attack the Empire of the Seven Lands, nor aid any who try. If any refuse these terms, they are to be executed outside the city where I cannot see or hear the process."

She swiftly went down the steps and hurried back to her chambers in the castle, dreading to hear the fall of an axe, or the vicious glee of the crowd savoring death. Downing a goblet of wine, she noticed an imperial message lying on the table next to her chair. Affected by the wine, she had to focus her mind to take in the information. In short sentences it relayed to her that Veranna was setting out to rescue Tesra in Koosti lands, and that the imperial army would be passing by Neidburg in about a week. They would have complete instructions for her.

She poured herself another goblet of wine and asked the servants to prepare her bath. One of the three serving girls asked if Amilla wished her dress cleaned, and Amilla told her to burn it.

The wine and hot bath nearly made her delirious. She looked at the water and noted that any move she made caused small, rippling waves. After a long swallow of wine, she could not help but wonder what waves she had caused by stopping the executions. It could result in a tidal wave that destroyed them all.

The blood of the executed man had dried over her breasts and in the warm water it slowly dissolved and flowed between them as a river between mountains, dissipating until it could be seen no more.

CHAPTER TWENTY FIVE

PRELUDE

Nearly a week had passed since Veranna and her company camped at the pool. They saw no sign of Koosti soldiers as they moved through a number of small villages in the dales and valleys they crossed; the inhabitants were mostly women, children and old men. Fields and flocks appeared depleted and neglected even though the people worked desperately to survive. Mud brick houses comprised the vast majority of dwellings, with timber-frame buildings usually at the center of both towns and villages.

Since entering Koosti lands the Emeraldian Company traveled by night. Veranna, and her knights in their special armor, had no trouble picking out a path. They now looked out across a wide valley at the foothills of the main mountain range encircling the high mesa on which sat the city of Banaipal.

Veranna was reminded of the strange feelings that ran through her when she first saw the Wheaton Plateau in western Loreland. Although she had never been there before, she felt the land telling her that she had come home. It was not exactly that feeling now, but she had difficulty thinking of the land as alien. The dirt, trees and climate bore a familiarity she could not explain. Kreida's voice broke the silence as the sun fell behind the mountains far to the west.

"What a dreary place! No wonder these Koosti slime are madder than rabid dogs. On top of it all, the women have no men to give them satisfaction."

Veranna gave her a dry look. "I am sure that the women here think only of satisfaction."

Kreida shrugged her shoulders and looked at Treybal, disparagingly. "What else are they good for?"

An odd, cat-like chuckle came from Reiki as she looked at Veranna and Treybal. "Dog-breath no satisfied. Much women, no many men, mean man make much women satisfaction. She fear man no satisfaction her."

Veranna smiled sickly and rolled her eyes, but Treybal laughed.

"Ha! You are probably right, Reiki. Maybe I will just have to take care of them all and see what I have left for her."

Kreida's face turned beet red, and she pulled out her knife. "Do not even think about it, you rock crawling pig! You even try such a prank and I will ensure that you do not have the necessary parts for satisfying any woman." She stepped in front of Reiki and placed her finger on her chest. "I am way more satisfaction for one man even in my sleep, so do not fill his mind with idle notions."

Veranna could not help but give her another little dig. "We have no fear of Treybal entertaining idle notions."

Being as upset as she was, it took a moment for Kreida to catch on to Veranna's sarcasm. Before she could respond, the empress brought them all back to the business at hand.

"We have been blessed by the Creator with not being detected, so far. Make sure that all of your gear is secured and does not rattle. So close to our destination, it would be a travesty to be found out just as we reach our goal. Reiki, have you ever been here before?"

The Felinii woman gazed at the valley and shook her head. "No, highness; Reiki slaved far north and east of here. Come to Seven Lands by road south."

Veranna frowned in thought before asking, "Does anyone have a suggestion as to which direction we should go in order to find a suitable pass through those mountains? Time is short; we cannot delay with looking for paths."

After a few minutes of discussion about the terrain, Karsten looked at Veranna and gave her a slight smile.

"You have the blessing of the Creator, and this will aid you in deciding our course. Remember, your ancestors traveled this land ages ago."

She stared at him for a moment, and then turned back to scan the eastern mountains. After a quick, silent prayer, she focused on two sharp peaks separated by a small gap. The peaks were nearly identical in height and shape, and evergreen trees grew higher up on their slopes than on the others. She raised her right arm and pointed, then said in a resolute voice, "We shall head for that gap. Treybal, take your Rockhounds and scout out the trail until night has come in its fullness. After that, the knights shall take the lead since they can see in the dark. Let us hope that the three moons are dark. Move out!"

Treybal bowed and called for his men to take the point position, giving the reins of their horses to the knights. Ten minutes later the sound of an owl hooting four times came floating up the slope towards the company.

Eight knights nudged their horses forward, followed by Veranna, Kreida and Reiki. The other four knights brought up the rear, guarding the packhorses.

An hour later and the knights took over the point position. Two of them rode to each side of Veranna, and the Rockhounds devised ways to get past natural barriers along their path, such as streams, tree and shrub growth too thick to penetrate, and marshy ground. They made good time once they reached the floor of the valley, for established paths criss-crossed the land. The locals kept to their homes and feared to venture out lest a disgruntled warrior find them and take their eyes.

After three hours they reached the foothills of the mountains. No one lived in the area, and the terrain showed little evidence of use. Boulders, both large and small, littered the path and talus aprons were plentiful. A number of them showed signs of being visited and their stones carried off, but the winding trail up took more time to traverse due to the obstructing boulders.

The company dismounted as the trail became steeper and narrower. Two hours of hard progress brought them to a tiny dell before the saddle of the mountain peaks. Veranna called a halt and requested that the Hounds make a small, sheltered fire for some hot tea and food. A half-hour later she sat with her back against an old log sipping her tea. As she looked up at the stars she noticed that she could see all three moons. The first and third were aligned and dark, but the second was northeast of the others and its bottom rim was lit.

The moons typically aligned at momentous times, the Creator showing the people signs of providence. Veranna wondered what might be coming, for the foreshadowed events were often full of great sorrow and struggle.

Drifting into a fitful sleep, she found herself atop a tall pinnacle of a grand palace. Rays of sunlight perforated the light-gray clouds and revealed the surrounding countryside. Dark lines rippled along the ground leading to and from the palace. She looked more closely and saw that the lines were not ants, but people. They had a sense of order, but no sense of purpose. Effort was poured into the futile pursuits of various clan areas where sat small castle villages. The people worked hard, but saw no increase in the quality of their lives.

Veranna looked to where many of the moving lines joined and disappeared into rugged hills, but the light of the sun did not penetrate well enough to allow her to see where the people went.

She gazed up at the sun and saw a large, dark ring speed down at the palace. It impacted the ground and shook the buildings, nearly knocking her from the pinnacle. Another ring sped out from the sun and blasted the people in the moving lines. Many died, and the rest scattered in frenzy. Boulders rolled down from the hills and crushed others, their cries carried on the wind, causing Veranna deep anguish. From the corner of her eye she saw another ring loosed from the sun. As it approached, she saw a dark shadow leap up, faster than lightning, from the center of the rugged hills. Too late she saw the ring turn dark from the shadow, its impact demolishing the castle villages and pounding the life from the land. A strong wind gusted from the west and lifted Veranna into the air above the rugged hills. Without thinking, she transformed herself into a great eagle and rode out the wind, but it swept her far to the east.

Another ring spewed out from the sun and a shadow leaped again from the hills and infected it. Veranna knew that when it impacted the ground, it would destroy the palace and all of the people. She beat her wings against the wind and turned toward the hills. The ring gained speed, and she knew that it would hit before she could get to the ground. Folding her wings tight against her body, she dove like a falcon for the center of the hills. At the last second she spread her wings wide to slow down, but she slammed into the hills with great force.

Pain consumed her, and she knew that she would be destroyed, as she lay helpless on the ground. All she could do was pray.

'Oh, Creator, all that I am is nothing. Forgive me if I have failed you. But save these people, I pray, even if they do not know You. Take me and do as You will, but do not leave them bereft of hope.'

Immediately, she saw the Curtain of Power open in the sky and a beam of soft, green light shone down upon her. Her bones knit together and she was filled with new life. She sprang to her feet and ran for the center of the hills between the highest peaks. Boulders and rock-hard soil had accumulated over the centuries, but she tossed them aside as if they were pebbles. She looked up and saw the dark sun ring over half its way to the ground, and feared that she would not be quick enough. She leaped into the hollow she had made by clearing away the boulders, and started spreading away the soil. Several feet down she came to a red granite layer with a slight curvature. Gathering her strength, she screamed and pounded the granite with her bare fist. The ground shook and slender cracks laced the stone. She pounded again and the cracks went deeper and wider. The third time and a hole opened up as rock shards flew in every direction. A ray of pure sunlight beamed into the hole, and a shriek came back out. The darkened sun ring halted just before hitting the ground, the contaminating shadow disappearing like a mist in the wind.

Veranna managed to stand, the pain from her smashed and bloody hand threatening to send her tumbling down into the rocky crags below. Through her tear-drenched eyes she noticed that people were moving on the plains far below, and the dry brown of the soil was being replaced with verdant green. She forced herself to ignore her pain for a moment as she raised her hands and looked up. From deep inside her there welled up a song of thanks and joy.

We thank You, Creator, for breaking the sway,
Of darkness and terror through night and the day.
Your mercy and kindness to all we shall know,
And all through the land shall new life now flow.

We thank You, Creator, for giving us life.
And for helping us stand through all of our strife.
Your mercy and love, no evil can mar,
And cause us to shine like the night's brightest star.

The wind blew and lifted her up, taking her to the high pinnacle and gently setting her down. She raised her destroyed hand to the sun and felt power run through her. All pain left her and she felt as spry as a fawn. Her dress turned to a brilliant white and her eyes gleamed with emerald green. Her hand was healed, but bore the scars of her travail; the hard rock had cut like the teeth of a fearsome beast. She cared not, for she had done the Creator's will.

Veranna awoke to Reiki's gentle touch and voice.

"Highness, Master Treybal say no sleep; must leave for Koosti palace."

The young empress shook her head once and wiped her eyes as she yawned and stretched. Although she slept only a few hours, she felt refreshed and full of energy. The passing of the darkness and late moon showed that the night was waning.

"Thank you, Reiki. Have the scouts returned from searching out the other side of the mountain?"

"Yes, highness. All back; I go with. I show main gate to palace. They look for hide places."

Veranna stood and brushed off her clothes, then turned and greeted Karsten, who held out a cup of hot tea for her.

"Hello, my love." She gave him a quick peck of a kiss before he could respond. When he did, his voice was smooth and pleased.

"Hello, my sleeping beauty; did you rest well?"

Kreida strode over to them and frowned. "If that is all that she can put in a kiss for you, her dreams must have been very boring."

Veranna smiled reproachfully. "Not at all, but at least in my sleep I get some rest."

Not to be outdone, Kreida smirked and turned to Reiki. "Yeah, and I suppose it took a lot to wake you. Isn't that right, kitten?"

It had, but being called 'kitten' made Reiki want to disagree with Kreida all the more. "Not lot. If dog-breath like you, then wake all land."

Kreida's face drew up in a snarl as she replied. "I have told you many times not to call me that! If you think..."

Karsten cut her off. "Save your strength for when we rush the Koosti gate. The distance between the last foothill and the gate is about a half-mile. We will not be able to take the horses over to the other side, so we will be on foot. We will run for the gate, and have the knights on each side as we proceed. Their armor can stop virtually any arrow. Rockhounds will be placed at the front and rear of the formation, each with a small spear. When we reach the gate, we will have to figure out how to open it. The knights and Hounds will form a defensive circle around us while Treybal deals with the gate. After we get inside we will decide what to do next. Any questions?"

Feigning seriousness, Kreida said, "Yeah. If the little kitten, here, gets an arrow between the eyes, do you want me to pull it or leave it in as an improvement?"

Veranna groaned. "Kreida, this is dangerous business, so stop acting like a little child." She called for everyone to gather around her, and then said a prayer to the Creator, asking for success in their mission. She then thanked them all for participating and named Karsten as her successor if she were killed. "I am not the empire; I merely serve it. If I am gone from this world, then I expect everyone to strive for the ideals that Emeraldia stands for. Now, let us go and see if the Creator's will is that we should rescue Tesra, who is as my own mother."

They all bowed and went about their tasks. The horses were tethered where they could reach grass and water, and the knights took the lead as they passed through the gap to the other side of the mountain. The Rockhounds held their bows ready, and after an hour the company made their way down to the lower third of the mountain.

As they neared the place where they would wait for dawn, a knight called a halt and told them to keep quiet. He crept back to report to Veranna and Treybal, his blue eyes and ruddy complexion visible even in the limited light. His barely audible whisper could not avoid a note of tension.

"Your highness, I have spotted a Koosti sentry crouching down in a small hole about a stone's throw northeast of us. He has not shown any sign of reaction, so I do not think that he knows we are here. The use of an arrow would be risky since it would have to hit well enough to kill him instantly. Otherwise, he will sound an alarm."

Veranna and Treybal conferred for a moment, and then Treybal spoke to the knight.

"Chimael, return to your post and keep us informed of any of the sentry's actions. We will have to get closer to take him out."

"Aye, sir." Chimael quietly headed back to the front of the company, keeping his eye on the sentry every step of the way.

Veranna asked Treybal whom he had in mind to send after the sentry.

"Jannan, your highness. He is stealthy, and should be able to locate the Koosti before too long."

Veranna started to agree when Reiki interrupted.

"Highness, this one for Reiki. Felinii great masters; guard no know I come."

Veranna was a bit taken aback at Reiki's confidence.

"Why, Reiki, that may be so, but this is likely a seasoned Koosti warrior. If you make even a slight mistake he will kill you. My head tells me to deny your request, and my heart fears putting you at such great risk."

"Highness, Reiki know Koosti; have much revenge to give. When Felinii no honor, Felinii no good for nothing."

Veranna hated making such decisions, and would have preferred doing the task, herself. However, her intuition nagged at her, telling her to preserve Reiki's honor.

"Very well, Reiki. You shall go, but Jannan shall come behind and be ready to assist you. Be careful!"

The Felinii woman responded with a grim smile and untied her hair, letting it hang down around her arms and face. Crouching close to the ground, she asked Treybal for the direction in which the guard was placed. With surprising grace and silence, she quickly darted wide to the left and disappeared into the tall grass. Even Veranna, with her gift of night vision, found it difficult to differentiate her from the terrain, and realized that Reiki's hair blended in perfectly with the grass.

Several minutes seemed like ages, and Veranna could hardly breath. She prayed that Reiki would come to no harm.

Reiki moved through the grass in total silence, the only sound those of the natural workings of the breeze over the slope. She caught the scent of the sentry before she saw where he was, took out one of her fighting sticks and placed it in her mouth. The other she held ready in her right hand. On her hands and knees, she crept closer to the sentry. His scent was typical of Koosti, and strong; she estimated that he was no more than fifteen feet away. Feeling along the ground, she found a pebble, and then crept a few feet closer. At the very edge of where the sentry had batted down the grass, she sat back on her heels and cocked her right arm with a stick ready in her grasp. After a long, calming breath, she tossed the pebble at the sentry with her left hand, and as his head jerked in her direction she threw the stick with great force directly at his throat. Just before it impacted she sprang forward, a lioness hunting her prey.

The sentry had no chance. The stick pounded directly into the hollow of his throat and ruptured his windpipe. A second later and the silhouette of an attacking feline loomed over him. One swift blow with another stick across his temple and he knew no more.

Veranna saw Reiki's attack and was amazed at her fluidity and precision. She thanked the Creator for keeping her friend safe, and nearly jumped when Reiki suddenly emerged from the grass right in front of her.

"Reiki! Are you alright?"

"Yes, highness." She paused to take in a deep breath. "It long time since Reiki hunt, but still no forget."

Kreida was impressed, but could not allow too much in the way of praise.

"Not bad, kitten; one day you might do well enough to stand beside Genazi."

Veranna smiled at Reiki. "You did a superb job Reiki, but I am so relieved to see that you are unharmed. I wish that that were the end of it, but there are five more such sentries to get past before we reach the bottom of the slope. Can you do it again in grass that is not so tall or thick?"

Reiki made a dismissive gesture. "Pah! Reiki can do in no grass."

"Good. You and Kreida shall take the next two, and the Rockhounds will be able to take the other three out with arrows. Then, we will all move to the bottom and prepare for the sprint to the gate. Let's go!"

With dawn not far off the sentries were tired and less aware. Reiki slipped past the nearest sentry and headed straight for the next, waiting for Kreida to take care of the first. When a slight yelp, followed by a gurgling sound came from the first, the second sentry quickly turned to try to hear more. Reiki's first stick hit him across the mouth, and he bent down to cup his mouth in his hand. Reiki's second stick did not hit flush, but glanced off the top of his head. She jumped down to smother any noise he might make, but her left knee drove straight into his groin, bringing a clear gasp of pain. She hurried to press her stick across his throat and choke him out, but he had enough strength to strike her ribs. Pain shot through her and she brought up her other knee to help block anymore blows. Reaching up between her arms, he grabbed her by the throat with his left hand, and the contest now centered around who would go unconscious first. Just when she felt herself slipping away, Reiki saw Kreida jump out of the darkness and slice into the sentry's bicep. He tried to yell with pain, but Reiki kept her stick across his throat. His hand released its hold on her throat, and he thrashed to try and gain some maneuvering room. With the loss of blood from his arm and the lack of oxygen to his brain, he suddenly collapsed.

Kreida helped lift Reiki off of the man and then made a swift stab down into his throat. She then grabbed both of Reiki's sticks and handed them to her, while saying, "Do not make so much noise, kitten; you are supposed to be silent."

The noise actually worked to their favor, for the other three sentries rose high enough above the rims of their pits that Veranna and the Rockhounds were able to take them out with arrows.

Even with the ability to see in the dark, the company decided that the path to the gate would likely have traps and hidden sentries that they were not able to detect without the light of day. Treybal ordered them to hide where they would complement the shadows, and try to get some rest before dawn.

The sky was clear, but fog arose and obscured their view. As Veranna looked up at the pass where they had cleared the mountains, she saw all three moons align, orbs darker than the background sky. The eastern sky grew lighter, revealing guard towers, barracks and patrols dotting the divide between the hill line and the palace wall on the plateau. The huge gates of bronze stood fast between forty-foot tall towers manned by archers, net and oil throwers. The oil pots steamed as the soldiers moved them into place, and the squad leaders practiced sending messages to the mounted guards outside the wall.

Veranna understood, now, why Yanbre had referred to the divide as a 'dead zone.' It was hard to imagine anyone traversing the nearly quarter mile gap between the hills and wall and remain alive. Even if they tried to turn around and flee the way they had come they would be spotted and face a horrible battle to escape.

There was no going back. Veranna had only to picture Tesra in agony to bolster her resolve. From the hills behind them a cold breeze blew down on their backs, giving them a chill. Veranna set her gaze on the guard towers and felt not the breeze, for in her determination she was far colder.

CHAPTER TWENTY SIX

BAD COMPANY, GOOD MORALES?

Tomius the Hammerhand, Lord of Imperia, sat on his horse looking at the wide plain that lay in the southwest corner of the Koosti Empire. Beside him were dukes Russell Heilson and Roland Nepsin. Lord Charles, of Clarens, stood beside his horse and whistled softly at the sight before them, commenting without realizing it.

"How can there be so many of them! With all that they lost attacking us there should hardly be a one of them to muster."

Tomius tried to keep the atmosphere calm around the western army. Fear could ruin their confidence and discipline. His voice came out in carefully modulated tones.

"We Genazi thought the same about the Gelangweils. Empress Veranna came at just the right moment to give us assurance that the Creator had not abandoned us. I, for one, will remain confident that her timing will prove true even in the face of this host of enemies."

"Well said," barked Charles, as he crossed his arms over his chest. "It's likely that this lot has been mustered from across the Koosti Empire, just as Veranna hoped. I wonder if it reduced the guard around the Koosti palace enough to allow her to get inside."

Duke Roland's low and iron-hard voice brought their heads around. "I envy her. She will have a chance to smash the leaders of these hideous jackals. I must be content with slaughtering their minions. My blade is thirsty and may never be satisfied."

Tomius understood the source of his rage, but feared for him lest that rage betray him to foolishness. He spoke to all of the assembled leaders.

"Remember, our assigned task is to draw off their forces and keep them occupied until the empress has accomplished her mission. Do not take risks that remove you from the battlefield. We must remain an imposing, threatening force. As usual, Genazi shall take the flanks, and the knights will take the center. We have an advantage in horse and bowmen. If we hold them on the flanks we can pound them down the center and reduce their numbers more quickly. Trust in your Creator, and use your heads." He turned his horse eastward and yelled, "Forward!"

The knights moved out in a phalanx formation with the bowmen close behind. Many of the Genazi also carried bows, readying arrows while riding. Their formation spread out as they trotted onto the plain, looking like a giant bird with its wings outstretched.

Tomius signaled a reduction in speed, bringing many of the soldiers to glance at him, questioningly. He called the leaders close and spoke in a loud voice. "The Koosti are not moving, at all. This is totally contrary to their tactics at any other time we have engaged them. I am not sure what this means."

One of the knights suddenly called out, "Parley! A dozen of them ride out bearing a flag of parley!"

Tomius and the others stared at the Koosti in disbelief, while Heilson laughed.

"Maybe they fear that their three-to-one advantage is not enough, and they want to declare the contest unfair."

Roland snorted, "After what they did to my mother and people, nothing that is done to them can be considered unfair."

Tomius felt uneasy about the situation, and brought them back to the matter at hand.

"We will honor the flag of parley and see what they wish to say. It cannot be too much since Koosti consider it an insult to be addressed by Genazi. Keep your eyes and ears open."

He selected a dozen knights to accompany the lords as they rode forward to meet the Koosti. No enemy soldiers broke from the lines, nor were there any traps along the path to the parley. Fifteen feet away from the Koosti, Tomius came to a halt and nodded at their leader.

"I am Tomius, Lord of Imperia and the sworn servant of Veranna, Empress of Emeraldia. We have come to serve justice upon the Koosti Empire for invading our lands, and for killing, raping and torturing many of our people. If you lay down your weapons and surrender, it will be noted in our mercy toward you. To resist is to face total destruction. Who speaks for you?"

The Koosti leader shocked the western lords when he gave them a short bow. His eyes were wary, but cautious, and his voice calm, if reluctant. His royal red robe and purple headdress marked him easily.

"I am Garyain y'dobin, cousin to the Great Lady, and chief of the tribe under her command in this region of the empire. Her brother, the emperor of all Koosti, has ordered us not to engage you in battle unless you attack us. We neither surrender nor attack. We await further orders from the Potentate in Banaipal."

Roland nearly spit suspiciously, "Koosti do not use reason in settling issues. Are you not simply delaying to get more time to move in troops behind us?"

Garyain looked at him contemptuously. "Were it my choice I would already be devouring your eyes and liver. But I am a servant of the Potentate, and know how to follow orders."

He turned back to Tomius and continued in a calm voice. "Part of my orders are to see to your supply while we wait for further instructions. Food and water for both your people and your horses shall be provided upon request."

The western lords wondered if they had not accidentally entered an enchanted land. Koosti offering to suspend aggressions was one great shock, but offering to serve the westerners with supply nearly knocked them from their saddles. Tomius signaled for his comrades to gather close to him for consultation.

"I honestly believe that the Koosti are sincere. Could it be that the empress has taken the Koosti emperor hostage, and that she threatens him with death if he does not cooperate?"

Roland's eyes burned at the mention of Koosti held hostage. "Let us hope that her torture of such a worm far surpasses what they did to my mother!"

Charles ignored Roland's heat and brought the discussion back to a calmer level. "I cannot imagine Veranna holding anyone hostage. It may be that the Koosti are flustered by the strength we showed in repelling them. Now, they fear a conquest with so many of their warriors gone. These may be their last soldiers sent to oppose us."

Duke Heilson rubbed his chin as he stared at the Koosti army. "Whatever the reason they are acting so odd, it cannot be denied that they are standing down. Their army is in total encampment mode; this would make it so easy for us to cut right through them in a charge. They must be awaiting something, as they said."

Charles folded his arms across his chest and looked at Tomius. "I say we play along with them, for now. We can get some much-needed rest and wait to see what happens. We can keep up regular scouting patrols, and the knights will be able to see what is going on at night." He smiled as he recalled a fair memory. "Once, when Tesra and Veranna were playing a game of chess, Tesra tried a risky sacrifice of a pawn. Veranna took it and proceeded to defend against Tesra's fierce attack. With an extra pawn, Veranna managed to win the game. I asked Veranna what made her decide to accept Tesra's risky play, and she said, 'The best way to refute a gambit is to accept it.' I believe that we are facing the same type of situation, here."

Tomius nodded. "So be it. Order the troops to stand down, with one out of five on active sentry duty. We will wait and see what their next move will be. As long as we keep them here, we keep them away from the empress and her company."

He looked over the troops before nightfall, encouraging them with his sense of confidence. Sitting with his back to a fire outside his tent, he gazed at the stars and noticed that they shined more brightly this night. He realized that the moons were dark, except for the second, and that only its bottom rim was lit. Just to the east of it, he saw the other two moons in alignment, and that the third was on its way to join them. Veranna and Karsten had noted that the alignments of the moons were connected with important events that the empire experienced. Lying on his back, he drifted into a fitful sleep and dreamed of an eagle battling a sleek panther. The eagle screamed and beat its wings, rising into the air. The panther swiped at it, but the eagle was too quick. While concentrating on the eagle, a dragon swooped down and bound the panther's legs with steel chains. After a quick scorching of fire, the dragon flew off to sit on a mountaintop where it could eye the panther from a distance. The eagle soared above the panther, reminding the wily cat that it could easily sink its claws into the hampered beasts' neck.

Tomius did not awaken after the dream; he rolled over and fell fast asleep.

CHAPTER TWENTY SEVEN

CHIEF CONCERNS

DeAndre y'dob, emperor of the Koosti Empire, walked slowly into his court, avoiding the eyes of those surrounding his throne. The group was made up mostly of his concubines and personal servants, but today he felt as though all were testing his intelligence and resolve.

Along both sides of the center aisle were the chiefs of the tribes comprising the vast majority of the empire. They strove to keep their faces inscrutable, but their stiff backs and shoulders belied the tension in the room. Many of them were quite a few years older than DeAndre, and thought of him as an inexperienced youngster requiring their advice. In fact, the bolder among them conspired to bring down the tribe of Y'dob to that of a minor ranking. LeAnre's province would be taken from her since she had proven herself unsuccessful in her campaign against the westerners, and it would be given to the most powerful of the chiefs.

The emperor could smell their greed and conniving as he stepped up onto the dais. Adjusting his red, gold-fringed royal robe, he stopped and turned to face the people. An officer of the Imperial Guards barked the word 'submit', and everyone in the room went to their knees, bowing down before him. The officer then barked *'serve,'* and they all sat back on the floor, servants scurrying to make sure that their masters had cushions.

Ghijhay sat on the floor next to DeAndre's throne. She and the other concubines had preceded him into the large, oval throne room. Tradition demanded that the servants await the arrival of their masters. As she entered, all eyes fell upon her. Tall and slender, soft-curled, golden-red hair trailed down to the middle of her back, complementing her rich, tan skin and bright blue eyes. Even as she bowed to the assembled chiefs, it was apparent that they were in the presence of a powerful and intelligent woman. The golden browns, yellows and reds of her silk dress conspired with the natural beauty of her figure to keep the attention of the people on her; their being so distracted would aid DeAndre.

The emperor slowly swept his gaze across the assembled chiefs, and thought, *Let me see even one of you try to find a woman like mine! You may be a pack of ravenous wolves, but you will never match her in the least. She will cut you up like a shark among minnows.* He felt her hand come to rest on the top of his right thigh, and his voice came out firm and calm.

"My servants, you have come as I commanded. We have issues to address, and I must console you with my will for the empire. I shall answer your questions, and you shall be blessed with knowing how to serve me best."

He felt a small thrill as Ghijhay gave his thigh a squeeze. She did not look up at him, but he could see that she was pleased with how he spoke to them. She had drilled him for hours, pelting him with questions that would likely arise during the session. Other men may have been irritated with her demanding regimen, but DeAndre was too amazed with her knowledge and cunning. She pounded into him the need to subdue any thoughts of disrespect or rebellion by setting the proper tone of master and slave right from the start. This he had done well.

The chiefs, however, had made some preparations of their own, even if not with one another. The greater chiefs would refrain from asking questions or speaking until the lesser ones had set DeAndre up. As his patience waned, he would be easier to confuse and manipulate. He may be a fearsome warrior with knife and sword, but extensive use of craftiness had not been his forte. They would maintain the decorum of respect lest a guard put a javelin through their hearts, while maneuvering him toward concessions that would weaken his power over the empire.

Ghijhay advised DeAndre on how to deal with this tactic, since it had been used before. He had suffered loss of face, and Ghijhay had expended a great deal of thought and effort in damage control.

From the furthest point along the central aisle, and to DeAndre's left, a lesser chief arose and bowed deeply. He looked to be in his later twenties, and his long braid of russet-brown hair hung down over the back of his yellow robe. Being so low in the hierarchy, he could not wear red while among the other chiefs, and he felt awkward speaking to his Great One without having been spoken to first.

"Great One, has the Great Lady destroyed the westerners once and for all?" He lowered his head immediately so as not to show impropriety by looking DeAndre in the eye.

The emperor grimly said to himself, *And so it starts. This insolent pup has chosen a difficult path, and who knows what branches the others will choose to follow?* His tone of voice dismissed the topic while replying according to the etiquette of the court.

"My son, the Great Lady has ceased her efforts in the west, and is striving to do my will above all else."

Ghijhay had to suppress a proud smile. DeAndre answered the question while planting a small diversion. The next chief to ask a question, sitting to DeAndre's right, followed the bait. His heavily lined and tanned face showed that he thought DeAndre had provided them an opportunity. He tightened his yellow-brown robe after bowing.

"Great One, has the Great Lady proven obedient to your will? It is said that the people of her province love her greatly."

DeAndre nearly sighed with relief, seeing that the course of the discussion was centering in on LeAnre's obedience. "She is taking every step possible to see that she obeys." He paused for a moment, before saying, "And yes, her people love her."

The next chief, about half-way up on the left, asked, "Great One, we have heard that the Great Lady refuses to bear a child. Have you decided to proclaim her unfit to lead her province?"

The question bordered the limits of propriety, but DeAndre decided to maintain control over himself and the meeting. "The Great Lady is urgently applying herself to see that she bears a child. If she does not, she shall be removed from power."

The chiefs showed a noticeable reaction in their postures, and their eyes widened a bit. The question before each resolved into how to get LeAnre assigned to his own harem, and then how to take power over her province. A chief on the left, closer to the throne than the last, hurriedly stood and bowed, his light brown skin flush with eagerness.

"Great One, I stand ready to serve you in your plans for the Great Lady." He pulled his gray, red-bordered robe tight and bowed smartly.

DeAndre's tone fell flat, as he looked away from that chief to the other side of the room. "My son, your willingness to serve is noted. However, if she persists in her barrenness, I shall deal with her, myself."

A chief on the right with a light red robe fringed in scarlet, asked, "How can such a decision be justified since she is your sister, Great One?"

The emperor felt Ghijhay's hand tighten on his thigh, warning him to be careful in how he replied. "I shall reckon her lineage from her mother's side. We share only a father, and I must protect the interests of her mother's family." Ghijhay squeezed his thigh more tightly and then relaxed. She clearly considered his reply very good.

A great chief on the left, his bushy, gray beard contrasting well with his solid-red robe and silver cap, bowed and spoke like a snake.

"Great One, we are awed by your magnanimous concern for your family and people. Which of us shall you appoint as guardian of the Great Lady's province?"

A bit too quickly, DeAndre replied, "I shall appoint one whom I deem most able to serve in my stead," sounding both anxious and defensive.

One of the greater chiefs to his right, who wore a bright red robe with blood red fringe, nodded sagely before bowing, and asked, "Great One, we have heard that the Great Lady bears the marks of treason on her body. How is it possible that she has not been executed for this offense against the empire?"

DeAndre felt a drop of perspiration form on his temples. The chiefs were gradually applying more pressure to corral him into a corner where he would be forced to make concessions. He had to direct the flow of the meeting toward that which gave him the most options. "The Great Lady did not intend any insult to the empire; she was caught between what she thought were opposing demands, and did not choose wisely. Her primary goal was the continuance of our people."

It was not exactly true, but it was close enough that it would allow no rebuttal. The leader of the chiefs, a man of sixty-plus years, arose and bowed. His robe was totally blood red, as was his cap. On a finely woven gold cord draped around his neck hung a knife with a pure silver handle and a white ivory blade. It was the symbol of power that DeAndre had passed on to him when the Great One had slain yen-Kragar. He wondered if the chief planned on passing on the knife to a successor, soon. This chief was the only one allowed to argue openly with DeAndre, and he and his tribe, the Tarkani, guarded it closely.

"Great One, your forbearance instructs us all." He paused, allowing the double meaning of his words to penetrate to the others. "Are we to assume that the Great Lady will receive no punishment? That would be a severe violation of our laws."

The challenge was now clear for all to see. They would try to claim that DeAndre was in violation of Koosti law, and could not save face without giving in to their demands. Fortunately, Ghijhay had prepared him for this tactic.

"Indeed, the Great Lady shall be punished, but she shall not be deprived of her inheritance. It shall be kept in trust for her while being overseen by the one I choose. Should she decide to bear a child, her inheritance shall be passed on to it, and the child shall assume all of the inheritance upon its coming of age. LeAnre shall be the Great Lady no longer, but shall serve the empire in whatever duties I assign her."

The chief cocked his head slightly, and said, "Would it not be better for her to finish her campaign against the westerners? She could maintain her honor even if she lost control of her province."

It was a tricky question that forced DeAndre to speak of LeAnre's failure. "The Great Lady will not be allowed to lead the campaign, for she has proven incompetent in its execution. Her poor judgment led her to capture the mother of the Empress of Emeraldia, and put her through dragony. The mother is a wise woman and mighty warrior. She should have, at the least, received the gift of death befitting a warrior. Now, the Empress, her daughter, has a claim on the Great Lady."

Simply out of curiosity the chief asked, "What is the name of this mother of the empress, and why is she not the empress?"

DeAndre welcomed the change of topic, and answered, "The empress is of the pure lineage of Emeraldia, and her true mother was killed by those of the House of Gelangweil. This empress destroyed that House in a great battle, and then adopted this other woman as her mother. The bonds are deep between them. As to her name, it is 'Tesra.'"

The chief's eyebrows shot up and his head snapped around toward DeAndre. His fists clenched tightly on his belt as he gasped, "Tesra!"

Total silence gripped the room, and the chief's face turned nearly as red as his robe. DeAndre, along with the others, wondered what spurred such a reaction in him. Such an emotional upset could work to the Great One's advantage.

"My son, you look vexed. What is it that concerns you?"

The chief closed his eyes a moment and gathered his thoughts. After bowing once more, he said, "Great One, my tribe is pledged to defend this one named Tesra."

DeAndre was stunned, and wondered how to reply. Ghijhay's voice came to his ear, but he did not consciously grasp that it was hers. It was loud enough to be heard only by him.

"Assure him that you will not allow him to suffer loss of face, and that you will provide a remedy. Inquire as to how such an obligation came to be."

DeAndre blinked and said, "My son, I shall honor your pledge and aid you in serving it. How is it that this strange oath came upon you?"

The chief felt a sense of unexpected leverage. The Great Lady had provided him with the key to her own destruction.

"Great One, the woman named Tesra came to our province nearly forty years ago, when our tribe fought the Arbori. They raided our lands and killed our people, making us wary of any outsiders. When Tesra came to our leading city, Tarkane, our soldiers arrested her as a spy. She fought off a dozen of them by the time I came along. Bowmen surrounded her and she was forced to surrender. All of the people were awed by her skill and ferocity, so I dismissed the soldiers and told Tesra that she would not be harmed if she followed me to our palace. She did, and my father told her that she would be punished for trespassing our land. He gave her the choice of being my bed slave for two years, or to join in the fight against the Arbori."

The chief's face showed admiration and fond memories. "She chose the latter and proved tremendously effective. We repulsed the Arbori within three weeks and they fear entering our land. I longed to have her for my bed, but she was not of the bronze. My father granted her safe passage and protection as an honorary member of our tribe."

DeAndre responded immediately, "Your father's will shall be honored. The Great Lady shall pay for her lack of respect." He commanded the scribes, who were dressed in white and yellow, to draw up a decree of recompense for Tesra and the Tarkani. As he turned back to face the chiefs, he, along with the others, were stunned when the tall, bronze and steel entry doors began to open, and no servants were there to open them.

CHAPTER TWENTY EIGHT

BEATING DOWN THE DOOR

As the dawn broke over the city of Banaipal a mounted guard headed out through the low fog to check on the sentries situated on the slopes west of the gate. Attempts at penetrating the defenses were so rare that the guard patrols had become simply perfunctory. When he called for a response from the first sentry, he paid it no mind that the proper password was not used in response and the fact that the accent in the voice was unusual did not register either. He continued down the line, his mind as misty as the air around him.

The fog rose high enough to obscure the vision of the guards in the towers. As the mounted guard neared some large boulders near the foot of the hills, he stretched his limbs and called out to the sentry posted just up the slope. He did not even know what hit him when an arrow slammed through his chest and into his heart. He fell to the ground dead, and his horse stepped around in confusion.

From behind the boulders, three Rockhounds crept stealthily and caught the horse's reigns. They broke off the arrow in the dead guard's chest and placed him back into the saddle. Aiming the horse once more toward its routine course, one of the Rockhounds gave it a light tap on its hindquarters, sending it along the normal path and procedure.

Two knights with shields hurried out from behind the boulders, followed by four more Rockhounds. Five more knights went in line to the left, and the other five moved to the right, providing a secure barrier for Veranna, Kreida and Reiki. Karsten placed himself to Veranna's left while the last five Rockhounds brought up the rear.

Karsten swept his gaze right and left, and then signaled with his right hand, 'Go!' The company surged forward and headed into the fog, the Rockhounds used short spears to slap the ground in front of them, looking for any traps. Nearly invisible trip wires could not be avoided, the slightest pressure loosing arrows from concealed firing points. The knights closed in tightly, using their shields as a shell around the company. Some of the arrows were heavy, their momentum shaking the knights as they impacted the shields and special armor. Several of the hidden firing points had trip flares attached to them, which combusted with red or yellow flames and smoke.

One of the knights suddenly fell into a pit. A fraction of a second later came the sound of thick metal points biting down into armor. Veranna screamed as the terror and pain of the knight resounded in her mind, the metal teeth gashing him to pieces like a dragon's maws.

Arrows flew around them from the guard tower, landing randomly in the fog. Veranna yelped as Kreida slapped her hard on the butt.

"Move! You cannot help him now; he is gone to the Creator. We must get to the gate."

Veranna's anger at the Koosti burned anew at the sight of the dead knight. She jumped over the pit and ran beside Kreida, readying her bow.

They passed the trap zone and increased their pace, but a new sound now haunted them. The pounding of hooves came from right and left, leaving little time before they were caught between the hammer and the anvil. Without conscious effort, Veranna concentrated on the fog, and it grew thicker around the company. She waved her hand toward the left and the fog opened up to reveal them to the forty horsemen on that side. They raised their spears and galloped forward, screaming their war cries. She then closed the fog on that side and opened it on the right. The forty horsemen on that side saw them and charged forward. She closed that side and yelled, "Run!"

At a full sprint, they just cleared the spot where the horsemen on each side slammed into each other, the fog interfering with their ability to identify friend from foe. Each side fought without mercy, thinking the others to be enemies.

Treybal yelled back, "One hundred yards to the gate. Ready all bows and fire on the towers and wall."

Guards on the wall and tower shot arrows into the horsemen thinking that they were eliminating enemies. When the company emerged from the fog the guards were confused for a moment, leaving them vulnerably exposed. Arrows streaked up and felled a dozen sending the others back under cover. They scrambled for new positions and screamed for the oil throwers to ready their pots. They hurled down stones and pieces of wood with metal spikes, but the shields of the knights and the nimbleness of each member of the company kept them from injury.

Treybal and a knight reached the gate and pressed as close to it as possible. Hot oil fell from above, but the knight's shield was just large enough to protect them. The rest of the company reached the wall and fired arrows at anything that moved. Oil and stone continued to fall, keeping them occupied, and Veranna knew that they could not last long before exhaustion overcame them.

The fog blew away, revealing the scene in stark reality. The remnant of the horsemen gathered their wits and formed into a unit of seventeen. Sighting the company, the leader ordered his men to attack.

Veranna felt a cold stab of terror as the horsemen closed on them. To her left came a sudden scream of horrible agony when a Rockhound failed to evade a falling stream of oil. His flesh popped and crisped as if in a deep fryer, and when a fire arrow landed near his feet he was engulfed in flame in an instant. He fell and writhed for a moment, then died in sight of them all.

On the verge of madness, Veranna screamed at the tall doors, "Open!" She wondered if she might be hallucinating when they swung inward. The company ran in, but Kreida and Reiki had to grab her by the arms and yank her inside, for terror had disoriented her.

The Rockhounds and knights shoved the doors closed and turned to face any attackers. Reiki cried, "Stop! No fight here; only if you fight."

Kreida had to give Veranna a slap to bring her out of her emotional trauma, the wretched deaths of her two companions stark in her mind. Karsten took her in his arms and soothed her, giving her a chance to recover her composure.

After a few minutes she wiped her eyes and looked around. No one else had any debilitating injuries, and they all caught their breath. She then looked at the palace entry, which was about two hundred feet away, and saw guards by the doors. Along the path to the doors stood more guards. They were stationed every twenty feet and armed with spears, knives and swords. Each wore a blue headband with a snake symbol over the forehead. Their tunics and pants had yellow and red tiger stripes, and they wore open sandals.

Karsten ordered the knights and Rockhounds to form into an official escort formation, then held Veranna's arm in his as they marched across to the palace entry. When they arrived, a guard held up his hand and stood in the way. They halted, and Karsten walked forward to speak with him. The guard said something in the Koosti tongue, but Karsten did not know enough of their language to make sense of it. Reiki stepped forward to help.

"He say, 'Only...ah, stupid ones...go no asked in Banaipal...ah, caves. Death for all.'"

Veranna stepped forward and asked Reiki, "How do you say, 'Step aside,' in their language?"

Reiki answered with precise diction, "Lene mwa."

Veranna then placed herself directly in front of the guard and stood up to her full height as she commanded, "Lene mwa!"

The guard's head jerked slightly, but he bowed and moved out of the way.

With Veranna leading, the company entered the maze of corridors carved into the ancient palace. Craftsmen had smoothed the stone over the centuries, and the shiny copper veins in the rock reflected the light in all directions, illuminating the corridors with surprisingly few candles or torches. To Veranna, the path to follow was clear. The turns to reach the throne chamber called to her in some strange fashion, like a flute playing in and out of tune as she tested which way to go. Reiki urged her to slow down, saying that deadly traps would kill them all. However, the empress felt at ease just as she had when she first walked the halls in castle Grandshire.

A minute later they came to a long, straight section at the end of which stood tall, bronze and steel doors. Guards lined the walls, staring at them in disbelief. These strangers had no official guide leading them, but they had come through the halls of deadly traps and must have been allowed through by someone. Veranna called a halt and took off her backpack, then asked the men to face away. Pulling out the dress that Tesra had made for her coronation, she removed her travel clothes and stowed them in the pack, and then slipped on the dress. Kreida and Reiki helped her with the buttons on the back, while Veranna placed the necklace of emeralds, which Duke Heilson had given her, around her neck. After brushing the dust from her hair, she donned the slender tiara of gold, emeralds and diamonds, and Kreida handed her a damp cloth to wipe her face. Feeling a bit refreshed, she turned to Kreida and Reiki. The two women shrugged their shoulders and nodded their approval, but Kreida could not restrain herself.

"You will do for now, but with me along, they probably will not even notice you."

Karsten responded with a smile, "You look wonderful, my love. Just keep Kreida close for contrast."

Veranna's eyes glowed all the more against her tanned skin, and her hair showed reddish highlights from being out under the sun. Standing tall and fair, she gave Karsten an appreciative smile and then turned to face the doors.

"Now comes the hard part. Karsten, Kreida, you will need to stay near the center of the group. Koosti do not care for Genazi. Knights, you will form up on both sides, with the Rockhounds right behind me and at the rear. Stay calm, but be ready for anything."

Her eyes gleamed bright, emerald green, and her voice came out as hard as steel. "Open." The doors slowly swung inward.

CHAPTER TWENTY NINE

OH, WHAT A MEETING

All eyes turned toward the doors as they parted. Ghijhay stood on her knees and leaned closer to DeAndre. The necklace of amber stones around her neck felt strangely warm, and her senses peaked as they probed the shadows in the hallway beyond the doors. A vibrant energy unlike any she had ever experienced ran through her, giving her a feeling of new life. No fear assailed her mind; rather, an exhilarating awe and expectation riveted her to the form emerging from the darkness.

Guards poured out of antechambers and surrounded the dais, then spread among the chiefs, who were left fumbling for knives among their robes. A few felt a sense of helpless doom as they remembered that weapons were not allowed when in audience to the Great One. The lesser chiefs rose to their feet, determined to fight with their bare hands, if necessary.

From the darkness of the doorway came a glow of emerald green light. It resolved into individual points as a person entered the light of the throne chamber. A beautiful woman, with emeralds around her neck and in a tiara on her head, stopped as she scanned the room. The brightest points of green were her eyes, which centered on DeAndre.

Ghijhay leaned closer to DeAndre and whispered into his ear, "Tell the guards to stand down. This is a royal embassy, and will not harm us."

At first, DeAndre did not hear her. When she gave his thigh a sharp pinch, he twitched and blinked, and then blurted out, "Guards, withdraw to the walls. Chiefs, be seated."

The guards were well trained and backed off, but slowly, for they could hardly believe their ears. The Great One, addressing them directly instead of through a subordinate, was a shock. Two guards took up station to his right and left.

Veranna noted the placements of the guards with her peripheral vision, but kept her gaze on the throne. Head high and back straight, she stepped onto the center aisle made of some dark, smooth stone. In an instant she recognized it to be the same as that which lay in the corridors of the castle in Tolemera. In her mind she commanded, 'Awake, and give light.' The aisle immediately began to glow in soft green. The chiefs on each side hurriedly shuffled away from it, wondering if the light would burn their flesh.

Stopping three feet from the dais, with her company behind her, Veranna spoke directly to DeAndre, after a shallow curtsy.

"I am Veranna, Empress of the Seven Lands, and heiress of Ergon, of Emeraldia. You hold my mother, the Grand Dame, Tesra, captive, and by the Creator, I demand that you surrender her to me immediately."

DeAndre's eyes nearly popped out of their sockets as she identified herself, and there was no denying the great authority in her voice. The chamber shook as her words echoed through. Ghijhay pinched his bottom, and he sprang to his feet, the first Great One to do so for a guest in over a thousand years. His voice quivered slightly as he responded.

"I am DeAndre y'dob, Great One of the Koosti, and I welcome you to Banaipal." His lips trembled and he looked down as he searched for the right words.

"As to your mother, I feel great shame and obligation, for I did not learn of my sister's doings with her before it was too late. Your mother has been transformed into a dragonwife, and even our priests cannot undo the spell. Just before you entered I learned from my leading chief that his tribe is sworn to her defense. The Great Lady is yours in recompense. I am so sorry, for the woman, Tesra, is one of great renown. I would spare you the grief of seeing her as she is now."

Veranna eyed him coldly, but kept her voice in check.

"I appreciate your concern; however, after all of the horrible deeds committed against my people by yours it is hard to imagine suffering any greater grief." She saw the concern on the face of the woman kneeling at his side, and knew that he strained under some internal burden. She fixed her gaze on the woman and addressed her respectfully.

"You, lady, are named Ghijhay, are you not? Am I right in saying that you come from the people called *Deeri*?"

Many of the chiefs frowned at the lack of honor Veranna showed DeAndre by speaking directly to his slave, but the Great One gestured for Ghijhay to respond.

"You have spoken correctly, your highness. My people fared poorly against the Koosti army, and there are few of us left. My father was the ruler of all the Deeri, and a priest before the altar of the Creator. I fear that I am the last of my family."

In spite of her own trauma, Veranna felt a deep stab of sorrow for the woman and a sense of kinship in the distress they both shared.

"I admire your strength to survive and ask that you arise and stand with me as one of your family. Far back in time we share some forebears, and I count you as my cousin."

Ghijhay was stunned by the request, but surprised even more when DeAndre brought her to her feet and propelled her gently in Veranna's direction. The two women embraced as family and gave one another a kiss on the cheek. When Ghijhay saw Reiki, the scene was repeated between the two friends.

Veranna turned back to DeAndre, her jaw tight with conflicting emotions. "Thank the Creator that there is some small measure of joy amidst my sorrow. If what you say of my mother is true, I shall have little joy the rest of my days. I say again: Bring her to me!"

DeAndre reluctantly agreed and sent servants to bring Tesra to the throne chamber. The look on his face belied his regret, and Veranna knew that he was sincere in his concern for her own troubles. She heard the chiefs exchanging subdued conversation and decided to assure her own Company that she was all right.

Ghijhay saw her linger with Karsten, and her intuition quickly informed her that they held deep affections for one another. When Reiki confirmed her appraisal and informed her of Karsten's Genazi background, Ghijhay's face showed alarm, and she hurriedly told Reiki not to even mention the Genazi.

After several interminable minutes the guards could be heard returning along the hallway. Veranna resumed her position at the head of the Company, but could not help fidgeting as the image of Tesra from her dream flashed in her mind.

She staggered in muted horror and despair as Tesra, flanked by four guards, one of whom held a leash attached to a collar around her neck, was led into the chamber. The scene was more unreal than her dream, for at least the character in the dream had obvious human personality traits. The dragonwife now in the chamber looked and walked like a dragon, with shiny black scales for skin, a long snout with fangs protruding past the lips, armored plates along the spine, and long, thick claws on all four powerful feet. Burning red eyes looked at Veranna, and a snarl of hatred and warning formed on its face, telling her to stay away and not threaten the egg developing in her belly. Veranna gasped, and then screamed, "No!! What have you done, you pack of vile brutes! How could you do this to my mother, or to anyone? Dear Creator, have mercy." Her voice trailed off, and she did not even hear the wailing and cursing of her own company.

Karsten, seeing Veranna sway on her feet, stepped behind her to support her with his strength. His own fury he subdued for her sake, lest he draw his knife and slay every Koosti in the room.

Likewise, Kreida came to her side; counting the number of guards she would drive her blades into.

Treybal and his Rockhounds, along with the knights, prepared to draw their weapons and hack the head off any Koosti who attempted aggression.

From a portal behind the dais a woman, escorted by two guards, walked in and fell before DeAndre, bowing her face to the floor while eying the astonishing scene in the room. There was Veranna, along with her followers, being allowed to live in the presence of her brother!

"I have come as you commanded, oh Great One." Wearing a simple loincloth and a wide strap of linen around her breasts, LeAnre y'dob, the Great Lady of the Koosti, looked hollow-cheeked and wasted, with only a feral glint of self-preservation in her eye. She preferred to remain close to the floor to hide the stark scars of shame across her body. The tone in her brother's voice made her cringe, for it held the satisfaction of finality.

"Get up, turn around and face your new master."

234

LeAnre would have burst out in laughter were it not for the serious look on his face as he pointed at Veranna. Crazed fear contorted her features, her head twitching back and forth from her brother to Veranna. Desperate that some opportunity to escape would arise, she slowly stood and stepped toward Veranna.

The empress's body trembled at the sound of LeAnre's voice, a volcano on the verge of eruption. In one blindingly fast motion she spun around, her left hand streaking up to clamp down on LeAnre's throat. The Koosti woman could not have screamed if she tried, for the grip was near to crushing her windpipe and spine. With super-human strength, Veranna lifted her from the floor and roared, "You filthy vermin."

The dragonwife, Tesra, felt a stab of painful memory in her mind. The woman with the glowing, green eyes seemed familiar. But she was attacking the Great Lady, her mistress! Instinct took over and she sprang at the woman, baring her fangs for a kill. The guard holding her leash was surprised and had no chance to restrain her as she flew through the air, growling.

Veranna heard the commotion behind her and threw the limp form of LeAnre onto the floor. She immediately turned around and held up her right hand at Tesra as she screamed, "Stop." A green nimbus surrounded her and Tesra hit the barrier just beyond Veranna's hand, knocking her to the floor.

Four guards drove their spears into the dragonwife. She let out a hideous yelp as she crumpled into the spasms of death.

Hysterical frenzy overtook Veranna. She motioned with her hands and the four guards flew away and slammed into the walls. She dove onto Tesra's limp form and cried, "Oh, Creator, do not let it end for her this way. Please, I beg you!"

The Curtain of Power opened and a shaft of emerald green light pierced the ceiling of the chamber, landing directly on Veranna and Tesra. The empress sensed that Tesra's life was not flowing away as quickly now, but something hindered her from healing Tesra's wounds. Her mind raced for a solution when suddenly a thought rang through it. Her head snapped around and her eyes locked onto Ghijhay's as she said, "Come here!"

The Deeri woman went over to her quickly, but spread her arms in confusion.

"Yes, your highness, but what can I do?"

"Pray," barked Veranna.

"But I am not a priestess. How can I..."

Veranna glared at the woman. "Your father was the high priest before the Shrine of Wahweh, and as his daughter you have an inheritance in it. Open your mind and heart, and pray!"

Ghijhay felt totally lost and ill-equipped, but closed her eyes to concentrate on the memory of her father officiating at the shrine, raising his hands as he pronounced a benediction upon the people. The words came to her slowly, but surely.

"Creator of all, Maker of all things fair and wonderful, grant us your love and mercy. Heal us this day from all ills of mind and body. Help us to realize our blindness and folly when we stray from your paths. And help us to stand against all that opposes you. Kae rhen shayiyah! (Let it be as ordained.)."

At the last word the amber stones of her necklace blazed with golden-yellow light, filling her with euphoria. She placed her right hand on Veranna's shoulder and knelt down. Then, she touched the side of Tesra's head with her left hand, and blinding white light engulfed the three of them. The others in the room had to shield their eyes, but after a few seconds the light faded, revealing Veranna, Ghijhay and Tesra. The Mother of the Academy was fully healed and smothered in Veranna's embrace.

Veranna managed to say to the Deeri woman, "Please, bring me my pack." In a moment she pulled out the dress that she had brought for Tesra, and hurried to help her put it on. It fit well everywhere but around her stomach, which was swollen large with child. "Tesra, you are pregnant!"

The Mother of the Academy swayed and blinked, a bit dizzy from all that had happened. "Yes, my dear. It seems that being transformed into a dragonwife rejuvenated me in some ways. Look, my hair is mostly black again and my face does not feel as lined. I am wondering what effects this will have on the baby."

Veranna looked at her with shocked concern, and all she could say was, "Dear Creator!"

A sharp yelp came from behind her. She turned to see LeAnre on her feet with her arms spread wide and fists clenched. Ghijhay stood in front of her, holding her head with a hand on each cheek, speaking in a commanding tone.

"I am a priestess of Wahweh, the Creator, and in that name I forbid you to dwell in this woman any longer."

LeAnre writhed and shook, and would have fallen to the floor if Ghijhay were not holding her up. In one final convulsion her mouth and eyes opened wide. A dark, empty mist issued forth like a tight cork from a bottle, wavering on the brink of being torn out. Ghijhay, Veranna, Tesra and all of the Emeraldian Company yelled to it, "Be gone!"

The ghostly presence burst, let out an agonized screech, and then was gone, dissipating into nothingness. LeAnre jerked and fell forward into Ghijhay's arms, unconscious. Her scars were gone and a golden glow slowly faded on her abdomen.

The guards did not know what to do. Their master had bidden them to withdraw, but this foreign woman who led their enemies had joined Ghijhay in opposing the emissary of the Dark One. The foreigner could do as she wished to the Great Lady, since DeAndre had given her into the empress's hands. But were the Great One, or the chiefs, in danger from the strange woman? Was the Great One's concubine conspiring with the foreigners?

DeAndre stepped down from the dais and called out, "Peace! The Emeraldians have not harmed any of us, and have helped in healing the madness and marks of disgrace of the Great Lady. They are to be honored among us. We shall enjoy a great feast to celebrate an end to the destruction wrought by LeAnre, and judgments shall be pronounced upon her. I say to you now, LeAnre is removed from power in her province and is given as a slave to the Empress of the Seven Lands. If the glow on her belly is a sign of a child, her province shall be held in trust for it. The Empress, as recompense, shall have power over LeAnre's province and may choose anyone she wishes to administer it."

A hard murmur spread among the chiefs. Each wanted to add LeAnre's province to his own, and a foreigner over it was outrageous. Finally, one of the high-level chiefs stood and bowed, his voice oily and conniving.

"Great One, we obey your every wish, but this strange woman has not shown us that she is a worthy warrior, which she must be if she is to rule a province. The law requires that she be tested."

Karsten's voice was hard as he turned to the man and said, "I will not hear any threats made toward her. If it is a warrior you need, then I can satisfy your demand by handing you your head."

DeAndre felt as though his heart had fallen into his bowels. The Emeraldian Empress had shown great courage in coming to rescue her mother, and great authority in healing her. She also provided a means to remove LeAnre without losing that province to one of the other chiefs. And, he could see that Ghijhay was already bonded to her. He had to find a way past this dilemma.

"Hold!" He walked over to Karsten and put his hand gently on his shoulder. "I am sorry, but the test must be made on the one to be the chief. Even I cannot change this law."

Karsten was about to snap at DeAndre, when Veranna placed her hand on his chest and smiled as she spoke softly into his ear. "My love, fear not for me. The Creator has given me strength and ability, and desires that these people chose light instead of darkness. Where the Creator wills, the Creator makes a way."

The two of them conferred with the rest of the Company, and Tesra smiled with total confidence as she asked for some water before sitting on the steps of the dais. Kreida and Reiki complained that they were being left out and should have a chance to kill some Koosti, but Veranna made her will clear.

"I want an end to killing. It is wrong to kill when lesser measures can satisfy the needs." She then turned to DeAndre and said, "Your offer of a feast sounds wonderful, and I accept. We have been living on trail rations for too long, and would love some fresh food. Let us finish with this test, quickly."

DeAndre was impressed once more by her courage and calm. He clapped his hands twice and announced, "The test shall take place in the evening, after our guests have had a chance to rest from their long journey. Let all be made ready, and any who need witness of the test must be present." He clapped his hands twice again, and his guards formed around him as he exited the chamber.

Ghijhay walked over to Veranna and took her arm in her left arm, and Karsten's arm in her right as she led them out toward the guest chambers. Shaking her head in amusement, she gave Veranna a knowing look as she said, "That chief, Sharim'tay is his name, has no idea of what he is getting into. He does not realize that the true test will be for him."

Veranna smiled, and she recalled the vision she had seen when downtown in the city of Tolemera with Kreida and Laura. The rings of light emanating from the sun had pounded the earth, while some of them brought healing. This test would open up new ground and make it ready for use in some way that she could not foresee. The Creator's ways were hard to understand at times, but she would do her part, even if it meant being pounded.

CHAPTER THIRTY

ORIGINS AND DESTINIES

In the mid-morning, Banaipal was busier than a hive of bees. Slaves scurried through the corridors of the palace compound trying to please their masters, while Ghijhay escorted Veranna, and her Company to some personal chambers. Thinking in Koosti terms, the Deeri woman showed them to a large bathing pool sunken into the floor almost four feet deep. Scantily clad girls, women and men stood ready along the walls to serve any request, while in the pool waited a dozen men and women, unclothed, to assist the bathers. Ghijhay smiled and waved her hand at them as she spoke to the Emeraldian Company.

"These slaves are here to serve you in anything you may wish. They are yours to command whether in or out of your bed chambers."

Kreida bounded forward and yelled, "Great," as she hurried to remove her top. But Veranna's voice stopped her in her tracks.

"No!"

The Genazi woman's shoulders slumped and she rested her hands on her hips, knowing what Veranna was going to say.

The empress turned to Ghijhay, who looked confused, and said, "We appreciate your concerns for our comfort; however, we do not believe it correct or wise for men and women to participate in communal baths, reserving that honor only for husband and wife."

Ghijhay bowed and said, "Please forgive me. It was the same for my people, but it has been so long that I forget my manners." She clapped her hands and spoke to the servants in Koosti. All but two of the male servants left the room, as well as all of the females. Ghijhay then asked, "Will this be suitable for your men, your highness?"

Veranna nodded and smiled. "Yes. We four women do not need such a large pool. Do you have one smaller and more private?"

"Yes, your highness, and..."

Veranna reached out and touched her arm in a friendly manner. "Ghijhay, as I said before, we are related, even if from long ago. Please, call me Veranna."

The Deeri woman was amazed. Koosti lords and ladies demanded adherence to the protocols of hierarchy to the extreme, but here was an empress of a large empire whose forces had defeated waves of Koosti armies, who desired to be addressed in the familiar! She was unlike anyone, with the possible exception of her parents, whom she had ever encountered.

"Yes...Veranna. Come with me, please, across the way and I will show you a chamber that you should enjoy."

She led them away after Veranna conferred with Karsten and Treybal, and showed the women a smaller chamber with five sleeping cushions and a bathing pool for three, not counting servants. After showing them the closets and toiletries, Ghijhay ushered in four young women and commanded them to attend every wish of the four guests. Veranna astonished the women by introducing herself and shaking their hands. So taken by surprise were they that they asked Ghijhay if it would be permissible to speak with them and ask questions. She promptly agreed, but warned them not to intrude on the guests' time of rest.

Reiki led the way into the bath, for she had been a servant here before being bought by Eifer's Guild. The servants recognized her and plied her with many questions, especially about Veranna. When Reiki mentioned that Veranna did not approve of slavery, they chatted more quickly than anyone was able to follow.

Kreida tried to exude a royal authority, but Veranna asked her to control herself and befriend the girls. The Genazi princess ground her teeth for a

UNDER THE LIGHT OF THE SUN

moment before saying, "Girl, I have serious doubts that you will ever learn how to rule."

After a full scrub, the servants led them to a pool in an antechamber where the water was hotter. Reiki again went first, stepping slowly into the steaming liquid, beckoning and instructing the others to enter carefully.

Veranna felt self-conscious about exposing herself when rising out of the bath, so she hurried over to the soaking pool and plopped in.

"Yikes!" Very *unself*-consciously she hopped out and sat on the edge to cool off. Kreida laughed, but Reiki and Tesra admonished her to slow down. She placed her feet in and gradually slid into the pool. After calming her heart and breathing slowly and deeply, a thought suddenly occurred to her. "Tesra, do you think that this will harm your baby?"

The older woman shook her head no and said, "Remember, its father is a dragon, even though the Creator transformed it and me back into humans. I would not be at all surprised to see some lingering dragon traits in him."

Kreida smirked at her and commented dryly, "Yeah, children typically take after their mothers."

Even Tesra chuckled, but Veranna scowled at the implication and retorted, "That was very unkind of you Kreida, especially after all that she has been through."

Feigning innocence, Kreida leaned back against the side of the pool and closed her eyes, saying, "I simply mentioned the obvious; why let it upset you, so?"

Veranna smile wickedly, her voice coming out in a fey rasp, "I will give you something obvious!" She reached out and placed her hand on top of Kreida's head, then pushed down hard, sending her totally under. After a few seconds she let go. Kreida popped to the surface, her hair a soggy mask over her face, and she gasped for air.

"You spoiled, royal brat! Why did you do that!?"

Veranna's smile turned sarcastically sweet as she replied, "Oh, was it not obvious?"

Kreida jumped and tried to grab her to dunk her head, but the water made getting a good hold difficult. Veranna spun her around, locked both of Kreida's arms behind her back and plunged her head into the water.

"Are you ready to apologize to Tesra?"

"But I did not…"

"Guess not." She plunged her again. Kreida's face and neck were redder than a lobster's. "Ready now?"

Kreida spewed water from her mouth and snarled, "Ohhh! Fine, I apologize! Now let go of me."

Veranna released her arms and gave her a small shove toward the far side, where she sulked as the other three chuckled.

One of the servants asked Tesra and Reiki if Veranna had to punish her servant regularly, and Tesra brought smiles to their faces when she said, "Never enough. However, they are more like delinquent sisters at times. They have been through many battles and are fiercely loyal, but they each help one another learn in ways that are very different. Veranna learns about vices from Kreida, and Kreida is learning when to shut her mouth."

A petite, curly-haired brunette servant asked a question about Veranna, and soon, Tesra and Reiki were inundated with all kinds of questions about her from each of the servants. One asked if Veranna was as good with men as she was at everything else. Tesra shocked them to silence with her answer.

"I am sure that she will be, but that is still an unknown. Veranna is a virgin."

After a protracted, silent moment, the girl's face turned intent as she asked, "Is she in danger of being punished for not bearing children? The Great Lady is now her servant because she refused to give the empire a child."

Tesra answered in her Mother of the Academy style, "You must remember that those in other cultures often think very differently from you. Veranna is fulfilling the will of the Creator by waiting until she is married to have children. Also, unlike LeAnre, Veranna's body will not be interfered with by the substance you use to bronze your skin."

All five servants did a quick glance around the room before making any reply. The brunette, the oldest at twenty-two, lowered her voice and leaned closer to Tesra.

"What you say is not allowed. One of us could be executed for speaking against the bronzing."

Tesra simply shrugged her shoulders and said, "The evidence is as plain as can be. How many men have each of you been with?"

They exchanged glances, and the brunette again answered for them. "Hundreds. It is the law that we give ourselves for pregnancy."

"How many children have you borne?"

"None."

"And how do you like being used as sex slaves?"

They looked down as their lips trembled, and the brunette said, "It is terrible. We have no say over our own bodies."

"Now you can see: Koosti culture prevents life and destroys the soul. It takes away your right to choose your own life and makes you slaves to base desires. Veranna is powerful precisely because she resists carnal pleasures and is free to use her mind and body for her own good, as well as the good of others."

The women stared at Veranna with renewed wonder before asking, "She can do this because she is an empress?"

"No, it is because she is human."

They gave Veranna another serious look, inadvertently catching her attention. She broke off her conversation with Kreida and asked, "Is something wrong, Tesra?"

"Not at all, my dear. They are simply amazed at you. The Seven Lands operate by a very different set of rules and attitudes than what they are used to."

The brunette pointed at herself as she spoke to Veranna, and said, "Reyiya."

Veranna understood that she was giving her name, and responded in kind, then pointed at Kreida and Reiki, saying their names, also. She nodded graciously and said, "We are very pleased and honored to meet each of you."

The servants' eyes popped open wide as Tesra translated, for no Koosti noble would ever address a slave in such a kind and familiar way. Reyiya suddenly stood and grabbed a towel, then motioned for Veranna to step out of the pool. She wrapped the towel around Veranna's waist, and then took her hand to lead her to a side chamber. In the center of the small chamber was a sturdy table that came up to Veranna's thighs, and the top was padded with a firm, but comfortable cushion. Reyiya lit a stick of incense, and another of the girls sat on the floor, picked up a harp and played a light, relaxing tune. Reyiya had Veranna lie on the table on her stomach, and then sprinkled warm, fragrant oil onto her back. She then gave her a massage from head to toe that had her moaning with delicious pains.

Veranna imagined the parts of her back being eased out and then put back better than before. All muscle tension vanished, and with the soothing music, she drifted off into a sensual dream where Karsten embraced her in the pool where he had saved her from the assassin.

The next thing she knew, she awoke to the touch of someone giving her shoulder a light shake. She stretched and saw Tesra through sleepy eyes. "Hello, mother; what time is it?"

"It is almost three in the afternoon. I brought you some tea to help wake you up. You have two hours before the test starts."

Veranna pulled the down comforter around herself and sat up. "Did you get any sleep, mother?"

"Some, but I had to send Kreida away and stand guard. You were talking in your sleep, saying...ah...various things to Karsten. Kreida heard some of this and is already scheming over how to tease you unmercifully. She and Reiki taunt and prod one another like old friends, and have made quite an impression on the guards. The servants have started referring to them as your 'two spears.'

"However, you are the one making the tongues wag around here. Your natural gifts would have been enough to do so, but your showing of supernatural powers in casting out one of the Dark One's minions from LeAnre has them thinking you could call fire from the sky and destroy them at will. It is what a Koosti would have done. As it is, you are seen as so powerful that you are able to show mercy even to LeAnre."

Veranna looked away for a moment, contemplating how she had come to this point in her life. It still seemed so unreal that people treated her with such deference. She had not chosen her ancestors, nor had she arranged any of the circumstances or events that brought her to be an empress. Fulfilling that role was enough to bring her to the point of hysteria.

"Mother, all I had in mind was finding you. I could not bear the thought of you suffering so. Everything else is no doing of mine."

Tesra smiled and shook her head. "Of course, and that should fill you with confidence. The Creator's hand is behind it all. You sought to do what is right, and the Creator's will was accomplished in that way. Never forget whom you represent, here."

She helped Veranna prepare for the feast, brushing her hair and selecting from among the many garments provided by Ghijhay. Tesra recommended that she try to identify with as many of the people as possible, so she wore black silk pants and an emerald-green blouse. The slave girls would notice the pants, and the nobles would note the fine silk. The blouse would set her apart as the leader of Emeraldia.

Kreida and Reiki walked in, each of them eager to get to the feast. Sounding like a taskmaster, the Genazi woman stood in front of Veranna and placed her hands on her hips in an imposing stance.

"I see that you finally managed to get your carcass off of the floor. After that massage, I don't think an avalanche would have roused you. We had to drag your butt in here and listen to your dreams of how you are going to abuse Karsten."

Veranna's face burned bright red. "Kreida, I…you should not be violating peoples' privacy. I do not want to…"

"Hah! I was not the one jabbering away about my pent-up sensual lusts. And, as far as violating anything goes, I believe that is what you have in mind for Karsten."

Veranna's blush turned even redder and her hands tightened into fists. Unable to find words for a retort, all that came out was a frustrated growl. Even Tesra could not help laughing. After a moment, Veranna scowled and pointed at the doorway.

"Kreida, wait for me out there; I need to calm the desire to choke you to death."

Kreida's smirk and tone of voice told them that she knew far more about Veranna's desires than Veranna thought possible. As she turned to walk away, the empress noticed the low-cut design of her black dress across her bosom, and the slits on the outside of each leg. "Kreida, wait; you cannot go to the feast looking like that. The men will think that you want to entice them. You are a princess, not a concubine."

Kreida groaned and rolled her eyes, and Reiki giggled. Sounding exasperated, Kreida threw up her hands and exclaimed, "Of course I want to entice them! You want them to be like putty in your hands, and this is how you do it, girl. Do not be a dunderhead; improve your odds."

Reiki bowed and smiled, a bit embarrassed for Veranna. "Highness, dog-breath right. Koosti men not use head. Beautiful woman like lioness with kittens. You much power that way."

Through clenched teeth, Veranna said, "Thank you, Reiki. Just remember that wild power injures, or kills. For it to be effective it must be harnessed and stored." She glared at Kreida, then decided to distract herself by concentrating on something else. "Reiki, you look stunning in that tiger stripe gown. You must be quite happy to return here as a free person. It should give the other slaves new hope that they can one day be free, as well."

Reiki bowed and smiled warmly. "Highness, I no do. You make free. Reiki now serve from heart. Creator make much grace to me." She then turned and pushed Kreida out of the room. Kreida objected, but slowly made her way out as Reiki kept prodding her to move.

Veranna had to chuckle seeing Kreida corralled by the Felinii woman. It helped her regain her composure, and a moment later she stood and took one last look in a mirror. Tesra surprised her by placing a necklace, made of solid gold links with a large octagonal diamond, around her neck. It hung down to the top of her cleavage and sparkled in the light.

"Tesra, where did you get this? Is it meant to symbolize my status?"

Tesra put her arm around her shoulders and gave her a hug. "Indeed, my dear. Gohie, the leading chief, is sworn to defend me. Since you are proclaimed my daughter, that pledge extends to you. As we do not have the necessities for ceremonies, he generously provided them. This necklace declares you as promised for marriage. Karsten has a matching one. According to Koosti etiquette, Gohie will sit between you and Karsten to fulfill the role of a father figure."

Veranna looked her straight in the eye and smiled knowingly. "Mother, if I were to bet, I would say that you are smitten with the man."

"The old mare still has some kick left in her? He and I fought many battles together and saved each other's lives. He saw to it that the Koosti showed me some respect, too. They also helped me improve my chess play to master strength. He may be foreign to our ways, but that makes him all the more attractive."

"So, I have to keep my eyes open to look after you, too. Just be careful around Kreida; she is a shameless tease."

Tesra laughed and patted her hand. "She will be no problem for me to handle. After all, I can satisfy a dragon!" She calmed her mirth, and then said, "Let us get going to the feast; I am famished."

"So am I. I can hardly wait to see what the Koosti have prepared for us."

Outside the door waited the rest of her Company. As Tesra and Reiki knew the palace, they took the lead. Veranna, arm in arm with Karsten, came next, followed by Kreida and Treybal. The Rockhounds and knights marched proudly behind them, their eyes looking straight ahead while watching everything.

CHAPTER THIRTY ONE
FEASTING AND FIGHTING

Veranna expected the feast to take place in some large chamber of the palace. When they passed through a high, arched portal into a huge outdoor pavilion, she breathed slowly, in awe.

"This is magnificent, Karsten; I have never seen anything like it."

They stood on a landing overlooking an oval area larger than any arena or horse-training yard. Twenty steps led down to the floor, and on the periphery were short cedars fronted by a bay leaf hedge. In four terrace levels innumerable roses, dahlias, lilies and many other flowers in full bloom cast their fragrances and colors for all to enjoy. At the center sat DeAndre and Ghijhay, while the chiefs were spread in a wide arc to each side of him, with servants running to and fro to serve their masters. The center area was paved with smooth, tan stones and bordered by the same mysterious material as the hallways in Veranna's own castle. As she walked along, it changed from black to a glowing emerald green.

The center area easily took up half of the floor space. Acrobats, martial artists, painters, jugglers and musicians stood ready to perform. As Veranna and her company approached the center all of the Koosti, except for DeAndre and Ghijhay, went to their knees and bowed their faces to the ground. DeAndre and Veranna exchanged regal nods while Ghijhay performed a deep curtsy.

Spreading his arms wide to indicate the entire pavilion, DeAndre said proudly, "Your highness, welcome to the Imperial garden. I trust that it pleases your eyes and nose. I come here often to meditate and relax when the demands of authority weigh heavily upon me. Please, feel free to walk around or sit. The servants are ready to provide all of the food or drink you desire."

Veranna thanked him before saying, "I am sure that my Company is as hungry as I. So, some food right away would be wonderful."

DeAndre clapped his hands twice and a number of slaves hurried to direct Veranna and Company to firm cushions for sitting. A moment later and long, low tables placed before them were subsequently filled with all kinds of meats, fish, breads, fruits and vegetables. When a serving girl approached with a large pitcher of wine she poured a small amount into Veranna's goblet and waited for her to sample it. The empress first sniffed it and noted that the bouquet immediately reminded her of fresh, ripe berries. A small taste delighted her senses like nothing she had ever encountered, as if a bright, sunny day suddenly appeared in the deep of winter.

"Ahhh, that is wonderful. Thank you very much." She held out her goblet to be filled.

The serving girl did not understand the common speech and turned to Ghijhay for the translation. Her eyes brightened and she smiled, for Koosti did not thank slaves. When she came to Kreida's cup, Veranna caught her attention and signaled for her to give Kreida only two fingers of wine. Kreida gave Veranna a nasty look that demanded an explanation.

The empress kept her voice cool and maintained a smile, but her eyes were full of warning. "This wine is deceptive. It is sweet and smooth, but potent. We do not want any unfortunate incidents due to you losing your wits. Remember, you are an ambassador of the throne."

Kreida glared at her before turning back to her food. Royal life suited her in some ways, but others were just too restrictive. Treybal admonished her to not let it cause her grief, and Reiki could not let the opportunity pass.

"Highness think you not same drunk; all us know better."

Veranna, Tesra and Treybal laughed as Kreida stewed in confusion. "Kitten, one of these days you are going to push me too far, and I will rub your nose in dung to teach you a lesson." She turned to Veranna and snapped, "I am not a child."

Veranna just smiled and replied, "My point, exactly."

Just then a quick beat on drums started up. A moment later came the sound of flutes and strings as a team of dancers, men and women in bright yellows and blues, whirled and pranced by. Singers joined in, and although Veranna did not understand the words, a vision of hard work, love lost and found came to mind. Kreida forgot her ire as the music started, her body responding to its ebb and flow in true Genazi style. One of the dancers bowed and beckoned her to join them. In an instant she was off her cushion and writhing to a sinuous, snake charmer's tune.

The Koosti chiefs, as well as the rest of the men, fell under her spell and followed every move. Her spontaneity and exotic looks stood her out from the other dancers, and her skill in raising a man's desires knew no rival. When the song ended, the people clapped and hooted. The otherwise inscrutable looks on the faces of the chiefs had changed to feral desire. Kreida strutted in front of them and spun around, sending her dress flying up to reveal her legs in one last tease before she sat down on her cushion.

Veranna leaned over and spoke in feigned chastisement, "Establishing relations with these people is one thing, but starting a riot is another. Be careful!"

Kreida laughed and gave her a rascally look. "Now you will be able to wrap the chiefs around your finger. Sometimes you just have to show them what they lack."

Another tune started up and the acrobats leaped to the forefront. Jumping, tumbling and twisting, Veranna was amazed at their skill. When they finished the jugglers came forward and gave a masterful demonstration of coordinated tossing of objects.

When the jugglers finished, the martial artists stepped forward to display their skills with swords, spears and staffs against both armed and unarmed opponents. Veranna and her Company noted the skill of the fighters, but also recognized the same formalized patterns of technique that they had faced on the battlefield. Kreida displayed a yawn, and Veranna's face did not show as much excitement as it had for the acrobats.

The leader of the martial artists found this offensive and sought to remedy the situation by humbling the two foreigners. He picked up a staff, and then went down on his knees and bowed before Veranna, holding the staff parallel to the floor, offering it to her.

She looked at Karsten and Tesra to see their reactions, and both nodded for her to participate. Karsten reached behind Gohie and held her hand before she stood.

"My love, keep in mind that this is a vital moment. The Koosti, just like Genazi, place a great deal of importance on the arts of war. You must show total mastery in order for our mission here to have its full success. Center your very being on what you do."

Veranna felt both challenge and relief in his words. He had always taken her fighting skills simply as a given, but the intensity in his voice called her to demonstrate a greater level of skill than usual. His desire for the mission to be successful showed a strong love not only for her, but also for those of the kingdom she led. Pride and confidence welled up within her, and she smiled in appreciation as she gave him a quick peck of a kiss.

"Yes, dear, I will do my best." She then stood and took hold of the staff, testing its weight and balance as she stepped to the middle of the floor.

DeAndre stood and spoke first in Koosti, and then in the common speech.

"One of the tests that a chief must pass is that of a warrior. My officers have reported the great skill demonstrated by the Emeraldian Company, but the leader must demonstrate skill on his, or her, own. This demonstration shall provide for this point in our law. Is this acceptable to you, Empress Veranna?"

Confident and relaxed, Veranna answered with a smile, "It is, Great One."

"Very good. Master Sarim'tay, you may proceed."

Sarim'tay, the leader of the martial artists, bowed to Veranna and said, "Your highness, this test is one of increasing difficulty. You will start against one opponent, and others will be added at regular intervals. Only staffs are used." He bowed again and stepped back.

Ghijhay noticed her palms sweating, and realized the tension building within her. She noticed that DeAndre, despite his attempt to seem inscrutable, also showed signs of tension in his breathing and the tightness of muscles. It was only natural since a failure on Veranna's part could threaten the plan Ghijhay and DeAndre had for LeAnre's province. The chiefs would see failure as a sign that Veranna was unfit to rule, and that a current chief should be allowed to absorb LeAnre's province.

As Veranna lifted her staff in salute to her opponent, she thought back to all that Tesra had taught her. The main lesson was concentration on the task. As her mind settled on what she needed to do, her limbs loosened and her senses became more focused. Energy flowed through her, and only Ghijhay and Tesra could see the faint nimbus of green that surrounded her.

Sarim'tay barked, "Begin."

Veranna eyed her opponent, studying his build and movements as he maneuvered counter-clockwise. She paralleled his movement for a few moments and made no overt displays of her ability to handle a staff. Faster than the eye could follow, she jabbed her staff and connected right between his eyes. Stunned, his pupils dilated and he fell flat on his back, unconscious.

Tesra laughed and clapped her hands, and in a second the whole room joined the applause.

Sarim'tay hurriedly commanded two warriors to the floor and ordered them to begin. They stayed back further from Veranna than the first warrior, and placed themselves on opposite sides of her. The one on her left struck first, jabbing his staff at her stomach. She stepped back and deflected the blow with one end of her staff, and then swung the other around from the outside, slapping hard just above the knee. The man grimaced and fell back. But Veranna spun around to face the other warrior, letting her staff carry around and strike the downed one just above the right ear, while deflecting the swing from the second man. Continuing her spin, she swung her staff in a sweeping blow to the second man's leg, and when he jumped up to avoid it she slammed a back kick straight into his chest and sent him flying into the crowd of chiefs and servants.

Applause filled the room again, and Sarim'tay's face shed its inscrutable mask. With an angry command he directed three warriors to the floor.

Veranna saw the three communicating with their eyes, and knew that a coordinated attack was coming. Rotating calmly, she picked out the one whom she judged to be the least skilled and waited for them to pounce. A second later they did. She sprang instantly at the one and blocked his angular swing, then sent him out with a trio of swift blows ending with him unconscious outside the ring area. The other two had missed their blows and closed in on her. She flanked the one on her right and forced him to interfere with the other. A quick jab with her staff on the top of his foot caused him to shout in pain and hop on his other foot. She whacked the shin of that leg and he dropped to his knees. A sharp blow to the chin knocked him into the land of dreams.

So great was Veranna's skill that the Koosti looked totally inept. Sarim'tay suffered great loss of face when the onlookers started laughing and jeering at his warriors. Enraged with humiliation, he ordered four more warriors onto the floor.

Veranna now had five warriors circling her. Ghijhay noted how the nimbus around her became more intense as she focused on her strategy, her breathing calm and muscles flexing smoothly. Her senses detected a slight movement from behind. She hesitated a fraction of a second to allow the man's motion to commit him to his attack, and then spun around faster than a mongoose to grab his wrists. Adding her strength and motion to his, she sent him flying through the air, relieved of his staff, and into a pool past the chiefs.

The other four attacked simultaneously, swinging their staffs at different angles. Veranna evaded them all and came out on the flank of the man to her immediate left. With a quick flick she tossed the staff, taken from the previous man, over to Sarim'tay, and then surprised the four warriors by launching a lightning assault. Blows rained down on them too quickly to follow. One man barely had time to note that his staff was gone before a blow to the temple knocked him out cold. Veranna tossed his staff to Sarim'tay, and then made the warriors jittery by aiming super fast blows at nerve points on their bodies. In one great finale, Veranna leapt at the three. *Whap!* Out went one, and his staff was tossed to Sarim'tay. *Whap!* The same happened to the next, his nerves temporarily paralyzed by a precise blow. Veranna tossed his staff, and her own, to Sarim'tay, and engaged the last man without any weapons. Fixing him in a semi-hypnotic gaze, he wondered what she planned to do with bare hands. Did she wish to take his eyes? Fear ran through him.

In desperation the man swung recklessly, simply trying to hit her in any way. Veranna grabbed the staff and flowed with its motion. Continuing and augmenting the force, she took advantage of the fact that the man had a death grip on the staff. She directed the motion down, then pulled up and back, flipping the man into the air. He landed flat on his back and she immediately applied a chokehold until he went limp.

Veranna stood, held up his staff to the crowd in salute, tossed it to Sarim'tay, bowed and went back to her seat.

The crowd roared in awe and shouted her name while Karsten hugged her close and Tesra patted her on the shoulder. The crowd rose and bowed to her, calling upon DeAndre to reward her in some way, which he did after conferring with Ghijhay for a moment. He stood and raised his hand, calling for silence.

"Once more we have been given a tremendous demonstration of the skills of the Empress of the Seven Lands. Let it be noted that she has defeated ten of our best warriors while suffering no injury to herself. For this we have no equal in our time or in the history of the Koosti. Receiving the *Shenqah*, which would translate as, 'Supreme Master's Blade', will honor her. Let all Koosti warriors esteem her skill."

The crowd cheered again as Veranna arose and bowed. Sarim'tay, keeper of the *Shenqah*, slowly removed the strapped sheath from his shoulder and knelt before Veranna, offering the ancient blade up to her. He tried to remain expressionless, but the bulging of his eyes and the stiffness of his movements belied his resentment. In the realm of warriors she was now his master. It was bad enough that she was a foreign barbarian who had easily defeated his warriors, but it was excruciatingly humiliating that she was a woman. He would now be known as the first Koosti Master of the Sword to have been displaced by a woman. He nearly swooned as he bowed and then returned to his seat. He had no desire for food, and drink set his mind reeling. A shadow engulfed him and set an idea into his mind.

DeAndre and Ghijhay sat down across from Veranna and Karsten, joining them in conversation over the delicious foods. Chief Gohie moved next to Tesra and before long the two of them were laughing like old friends. Veranna commented to the chief about some of Tesra's deeds over the years and his eyes went wide with awe. After relating how Tesra had done in two assassins in the halls of the Academy, in Clarens, the chief bowed and spread his arms wide.

"Most noble woman, the offer of marriage that I made to you over thirty years ago still stands. I beg you to honor me so."

Tesra scoffed at him playfully. "Gohie, you already have a wife and many concubines. I would end up as just another pretty face you would flirt with for only a moment each week."

"Ah, no Tesra, you would be special, for none of my other women can fight like you. We would be practicing together and that would fill each day with joy."

"Gohie, it sounds good in theory, but in reality it just is not plausible. Besides, any day now I will give birth, and caring for a child is a lot of work. What is more, I have the daughter of my heart ready to be married. I will need to be near her in order to fulfill my role as a mother-in-law to Karsten."

Gohie pleaded, "Tesra, those are not barriers; they are simply small difficulties. You could travel between our lands, easily."

"No, no my dear Gohie. It is a long and tiring journey. Besides, we would experience a deep conflict of interest since I serve the throne of Emeraldia and you serve the Koosti. You must admit that your political situation here is far more volatile than in the Seven Lands."

"You are a very difficult woman, Tesra; just remember that any piece of armor has its weaknesses. One of these days I will find yours and help you come to your senses."

They all laughed and DeAndre patted him on the shoulder. "Gohie, I know how tortured you must feel, for if Ghijhay was suddenly gone my life would seem a total waste. A woman such as she is a rare find." The others all seconded his remarks and Ghijhay snuggled closer to DeAndre. Turning to Veranna, his face grew serious. "There was a shadow-being that left my sister when you and Ghijhay commanded it. Do you know what it was?"

Veranna's body shivered for a moment before she answered. "Yes; it was a dark spirit, a servant of the Dark One who obviously had LeAnre doing his will. I can now understand how she could do so many wretched things, even if it does not render her guiltless. I mean no offense when I say that the Koosti way of life makes you very susceptible to the influence of the Dark One. Emeraldia, from ancient times, stood with all those opposing evil such as the Deeri and Felinii. We are family in more than blood."

DeAndre's eyebrows rose a bit as he looked at both Veranna and Ghijhay. "There is a great deal that the two of you share. Before today I never knew that anyone had such special powers."

Tesra, her voice coming out in her Mother of the Academy lecture tone, quickly downed some of the fruit liquor and said, "Do not chide yourself for your ignorance, Great One, for in reality neither Veranna or Ghijhay has 'powers.' They do not belong to them in the natural sense. All power comes from the Creator for accomplishing a divine purpose. Both of these ladies represent a gift and obligation before the Creator. Ghijhay's line was to never let the worship of Wahweh die out, and Veranna's line was entrusted with defending the truth of the Creator. If Wahweh gives you a task or responsibility, then Wahweh gives you the means. Were either of these ladies to reject their Creator they would have no more powers than anyone else."

Karsten's eyes glowed with pride as he looked at Veranna. "I must disagree with you, Mother Tesra. Even if Veranna were a milk maid she would still have total power over my heart." He gave her a lingering kiss that made her blush.

DeAndre laughed and said, "We are in agreement, Lord Karsten. At times I feel as though Ghijhay has me bound faster than a prisoner, even though she is a slave."

Ghijhay's eyes burned into him, and she gave him a poke in the ribs. "That is a designation which should no longer apply, my love."

Before he could respond, Veranna asked, "Why have you not declared her free before today, DeAndre?"

Ghijhay answered for him, a strong tone of disgust evident in her voice. "According to Koosti law I could not be free since there was an active campaign against the Deeri in progress. Also, Koosti law requires him to marry a woman high in the ruling caste, which a slave is not." She gave Veranna a look of expectation and pleading as she continued, "If I were to be named as the ruler of a province I would then be able to marry DeAndre."

Veranna wondered why Ghijhay would give her such a strange look, and what she might be missing in the subtle clues the woman gave her. Then, it dawned on her. She stood and clapped her hands twice to draw attention.

"Excuse me please, for interrupting, but I would like to make an announcement." Tall and fair, she swept her gaze over the crowd and paused for a moment. In a clear, royal tone she said, "As the Empress of the Seven Lands, I cannot abandon my ruling city to tend the typical demands of individual provinces. So it is with the province ruled by LeAnre y'dob. It is under my rule until all recompense has been made, and I am appointing my distant kin, Ghijhay, of the Deeri, as my lieutenant over that province. In the courts of the Seven Lands she is given the rank of Marques, with all of the rights and privileges thereof."

She turned and requested a sword from one of her knights, and then turned to Ghijhay. "Lady Ghijhay, do you agree to this?"

Ghijhay bowed and said, "Yes, your highness."

"Then come and kneel before me."

Both of them moved to the center of the floor, and Ghijhay went to her knees, facing Veranna, who set her sword first on Ghijhay's right shoulder and then on the left.

"I, Veranna of Emeraldia, appoint you, Ghijhay of the Deeri, as a Marques in the Seven Lands, and as my representative in the province allotted to LeAnre. This shall remain so until specifically revoked by me, or my successor, or until the world's end. Arise and be recognized, Lady Ghijhay."

Ghijhay stood and curtsied to the rest of the room. The chiefs and servants all bowed, as did Veranna's knights and Rockhounds. Even as the chiefs calculated the new political situation, DeAndre stood and made a pronouncement of his own.

"To all my loyal children of the Koosti, and to our honored guests, I declare Ghijhay to be my wife." The room went still, and DeAndre looked at Veranna. "Is this acceptable to you, your highness? You are her liege lady and distant kin; Koosti law requires your permission."

Veranna nodded and said, "I agree to this totally, but only on the condition that Lady Ghijhay agrees as well. This is the law of the Seven Lands."

Ghijhay's face beamed with delight. "I agree." She sprang over to DeAndre and the two of them embraced, giving one another a long kiss.

The chiefs bowed once more and DeAndre ordered the servants to pour more wine and resume the music. Veranna, Tesra, Kreida and Reiki surrounded Ghijhay, giving her hugs and congratulations, while Karsten led the room in a toast to the newlyweds. After they finished the toast, Karsten spoke again.

"The empress, Veranna, and I are betrothed and would be greatly honored by any of you who would desire to attend our wedding ceremony in our capital city, Tolemera. This shall take place," and here he glanced at Veranna, who held up two fingers, and then flashed five fingers three times, "on the ides of the third month from now."

The chiefs were slow to respond, for the Emeraldians had been enemies for so long that such niceties as social engagements with them were totally foreign. DeAndre helped them along by raising his goblet and toasting Veranna and Karsten.

"We shall be there, my Lord Karsten, and I grant permission to all of my subjects to do so." He drank the toast and swept his eyes over the chiefs. Some showed signs of serious reluctance to join in, but he realized that change did not always come quickly or easily.

Sarim'tay waited until the feast was nearly over before approaching DeAndre. He stayed on the outskirts of the people during the feast, speaking with various other chiefs for a few minutes as they passed by. Now, he felt more confidence after contemplating what he would do to reduce the damage caused by DeAndre. After all, LeAnre's province should be under his control, as well as LeAnre.

"Great One, many of the chiefs and I find things moving far too quickly. The safety of the empire is our highest goal, and we wish to have the Empress of the Seven Lands undergo a test of reason. She is not of our land and must have a strong mind to assess Koosti in order to rule them well."

DeAndre stifled an angry outburst, for Sarim'tay had a valid point according to Koosti law. Inheritance rights had been revoked for those sons, or other men, whom the chiefs or Great One deemed too young or stupid to rule a province.

"My son, what you say has sense to it. Arrange your test for the later morning, and be sure that no harm can result to the empress or her people."

Sarim'tay bowed low and started to turn away when Karsten, his brow tightly knit with suspicion and concern, stepped into Sarim'tay's way.

"What is this test you speak of?"

DeAndre answered, "It will involve a few problems of thought that the person being tested must resolve successfully. No one but the testers may know what is involved until the actual time of the test."

Karsten looked to Veranna. She simply shrugged her shoulders and said, "Why not?"

Karsten bowed slightly and returned to her side, but Sarim'tay went back to his place among the chiefs, a small, devious grin overtaking his face.

As the evening passed, Veranna, Karsten, Ghijhay, DeAndre, Kreida, Tesra and Reiki exchanged family histories and anecdotes. Ghijhay brightened all the more when Reiki mentioned that her people could likely find Ghijhay's brother. Veranna added that if he was located he had a standing invitation to come to Tolemera and officiate her and Karsten's wedding. Ghijhay immediately ordered official courier units to spread out to the north and northeast, to announce the end to any hostilities against the Deeri or Felinii, and that she and DeAndre were now married.

Tesra leaned over to speak softly into Veranna's ear. "My dear, it is time that we got back to our room. Whatever the test of reason may be, I want you to get a good night's sleep so that your mind will not be foggy."

Veranna noted an anxious tone in Tesra's voice. "Mother, are you feeling well?"

"Let us simply say that all things have their own timing. My time has come. It seems that the Creator greatly shortened the time of my pregnancy when He healed me."

Veranna arose and the others scrambled to their feet, wondering why she wanted to leave. She bowed to DeAndre and Ghijhay, then to the chiefs. "Please, excuse me for interrupting things, but I must get Tesra back to our room. It looks as though her time to give birth has started."

Ghijhay clapped her hands twice and ordered the maid servants to summon the midwives, then led Veranna and her company back to their rooms.

Veranna was more nervous than Tesra, flitting about the chamber adjusting every little detail of furniture and decor. After one too many times asking Tesra if she was alright, the older woman rolled her eyes in exasperation.

"My dear, please, just sit down and calm yourself. You have participated in many births and should handle this without a problem."

"I am sorry, mother, but it is not everyday that you give birth. This child is special; a blessing from the Creator."

"That may be true, but remember that his father is a dragon. One never knows how any child will turn out." A sudden contraction brought a grimace to her face, and when it passed she asked for a drink of water.

Veranna looked at her and wondered if she would be as composed when it came time to deliver her own children. It seemed as though she had been giving birth ever since she left the Academy. Time would tell what had just been born with this new relationship between her empire and the Koosti. She hoped that the pangs would be minimal.

CHAPTER THIRTY TWO

MOVES AND COUNTER MOVES

C hief Sarim'tay strode back and forth in front of the group assembled before him. Three women, and the rest men, sat and listened as he gave his instructions. He ordered the slave girls to pour more tea now so that he would not be interrupted with a request later. An especially voluptuous slave took her time finishing her task, bending and twisting to ensure that the men would notice her attributes. The men were, after all, considered higher caste, and any of them would provide a comfortable living for her as his concubine.

The chief walked swiftly up to her and backhanded her hard across the face. She went flying toward the chamber entry and fell to the floor, her split lip splattering blood in every direction. She managed to get to her hands and knees and made her way out of the chamber. Sarim'tay paid her no mind as he continued speaking to the men and women.

"Remember, complexities are what you must aim for. Your opponent is a daughter of dogs, and you must demonstrate this to everyone. Be strong and attack all weaknesses. Subtlety and crises will be too much for her, and she will lose her powers of reason.

"We enter this conflict for our empire and for the glory of the Dark One. If we are faithful to the darkness we will reap many rewards. Go, and do battle to the utmost."

Kreida walked into the sleeping chamber she shared with Veranna, Tesra and Reiki. The empress was fast asleep, nestled on cushions and a down comforter. Tesra lay furthest into the room, a small bundle wrapped up next to her. Kreida checked to make sure that the newborn boy was breathing properly, and then walked quietly from the chamber.

She decided to let Veranna sleep for another hour. For as long as she had known her, Veranna always seemed to need more sleep than she. The Genazi woman wondered if growing up in a structured environment, the Academy, had instilled this pattern. Regardless, staying up into the wee hours of the morning would make anyone tired. Veranna's 'test of reason' was not due to start for another two hours, so why not let her get more rest.

The birth of Tesra's son went off with remarkably little difficulty. His body and head were slender, offering minimal resistance as he slid through the birth canal. He barely cried, and enjoyed the bath and fussing over him by the women. Kreida commented to Tesra that she would need to keep a close eye on him because his deep black hair and dark sun-tan colored skin would make him very attractive to the ladies. His dark eyes and fine features gave him a serious and dashing look, and his limbs were surprisingly strong.

She took up post at the chamber entry to keep anyone from disturbing Veranna. Reiki joined her and was able to explain to the servants why Kreida did not want them to enter. She directed them to prepare a rain-wash for Veranna and to have some strong tea and fruit ready for her when she awoke. An hour later, the serving girls returned with the tea and fruit. Kreida awakened Veranna by shaking her shoulder, but avoided speaking lest she awaken Tesra and the baby.

Veranna groaned and stretched. "Kreida, what time is it? I feel as though I could sleep for several more hours."

"Shhh! You might wake the baby. Get your lazy butt out of bed and into the washroom. Hurry up!"

Veranna felt a bit cranky and was tempted to reply. For the sake of the baby she said nothing, and held out her hand for Kreida to help pull her off of the floor. When they reached the washroom, she mentioned that a strong cup of tea would taste wonderful. Kreida clapped her hands twice and yelled for the servants to bring it. In seconds she had her tea and downed it quickly.

Kreida then grabbed the cup from her hand and set it aside, yanked Veranna's robe from her, shoved her toward the wall and said, "Stay right there."

Confused and embarrassed at suddenly being naked in front of others, she covered her breasts and turned away as she cried, "Kreida, what do you think you are doing?"

Kreida motioned for one of the serving girls to proceed and a moment later a shower of water fell from a device full of tiny holes located a foot above her head. She was startled by the first touch of the water, for it was very warm. After a moment she loosened up and moved around to let the water run down every part of her body, this time eliciting from her a smooth 'ahhh' of satisfaction. The serving girls scrubbed her down, and the effect was like getting a massage during a bath. After drying off and donning her robe, she sat in a padded chair and ate fresh fruit while the girls dried and styled her hair.

"Kreida, you should have warned me before shoving me into the rain bath."

The Genazi woman said, matter-of-factly, "No time for that; you know how slow you are to get going in the morning. I had to make sure that you would be awake for this 'test of reason' that they want to put you through. Only the Creator knows how hard I have tried to get some reason into that head of yours."

Veranna had to laugh. "I am so sorry for being such a poor student; maybe I will never be warped enough."

Just then, Tesra entered the room. "Are we speaking of Kreida, again? I just heard the word 'warped' mentioned."

"Pah!," snorted Kreida. She pulled Veranna's long braid up and wrapped it around her head, then pinned it fast. "If anyone can be referred to as warped, it is you, Mother. After all, you are the one getting intimate with dragons."

Veranna chuckled at the exchange, but Tesra affected a concerned look and said, "Can I help it that I have so much power over males? Besides, I have to have some fun, too."

They all laughed, and Tesra gave both of them pats on the shoulders. "Thank you, dear daughters of my heart, for coming and saving me from that wretched fate. It was a dangerously foolish decision to do so, but it seems as though the Creator watched over you."

Veranna's eyes watered up. "Oh, mother, you would have done the same for either of us. We are just so happy to see you well. You look fifteen years younger, now."

"Well, as I have said before, the Creator does not do anything second-rate." She paused and took a sip of Veranna's tea. "That is precisely what you will be demonstrating to the Koosti, today. I do not know what type of test they have in mind; just remember that reason is a universal standard, and that it does not change from one culture to another. The starting points from which they reason may differ from yours, but reasoning does not."

Veranna stood and requested the serving girls to bring her some clothing, then said to Tesra, "Thank you, mother; I will try to do you proud." Tesra smiled and patted her shoulder, and Veranna then turned to Kreida. "Would you go and let the Company know that we will be going to this test, shortly?"

Kreida smirked and started off. "Handling the men is easy; I have more powerful tools than reason for motivating them."

While she left the room, Ghijhay showed up with a variety of dresses for Veranna to choose from. After ten minutes looking them over, Veranna asked Ghijhay what type of dress would suit the test.

"I do not yet know what the test will be, your highness, so I..."

Veranna motioned with her hand that she should pause. "Ghijhay, please, just call me by my name."

Ghijhay smiled appreciatively. "Yes, Veranna. As I was saying, the test is still unknown to me, but it will likely involve men. I would wear something that will catch their eye and distract them, like this." She reached out and grabbed a dress made of flame-red silk, with gold embroidery and shiny, forest-green borders. It was tighter in places than Veranna was used to, but it was not uncomfortable, at least not in the physical sense.

"Ghijhay, this dress is beautiful, but it makes me feel as though I am on display."

Tesra commented, "You are on display. You would be on display even in sackcloth. Take her advice and use your attributes to distract your opponents. I am sure that Karsten will not mind."

Veranna's eyes filled with worry. "He will think that I am some type of brazen hussy. I do not want him to be ashamed of me."

The other women laughed, and Ghijhay shook her head in wonder.

"You are the most unusual woman I have ever met. I hope that it will work to your advantage in the test. We had best be getting to the garden; a late arrival might be seen as a sign of fear."

Veranna swallowed more tea, and then turned to Tesra. "Are you coming, mother?"

Tesra put her arm around Veranna and walked her to the doorway, bolstering her confidence. "Yes, but not right away. The baby will awaken soon and will need feeding. I will be along after that."

"Alright. By the way, have you named the baby?"

"Yes; I believe I will call him 'Draco.' It will be a reminder of his origin and more than a few of the ancient Emeraldian nobles bore that name."

"Hmnn, Draco; it is an intriguing name. He certainly has the look, and it will be easy to remember." She gave her a quick kiss and then headed out of the chamber with Ghijhay. They met up with the Company and Karsten's eyebrows rose as he saw her coming.

"My dear, I am sure that it will be you who does the testing, today. The Koosti will not be able to look at anything else."

Blushing and anxious, she asked, "Are you sure that it is not too, uh, extravagant?"

"You were made for extravagant."

She blushed all the more, and when she saw the rascally grin on Kreida's face she hurriedly turned and motioned for Ghijhay to continue on to the garden.

The doors opened and Veranna gasped softly. Along each side of the walkway were nine tables. At the far end stood two more across the walkway, forming a long 'u' shape. On each table sat two chessboards with the pieces in place. At all but three tables stood two men, the three women having been separated out to each of the three sections.

DeAndre walked in from a side entry just as Veranna neared the tables at the open end. The people went to their knees and bowed their faces to the floor, but Veranna and her Company bowed from the waist. DeAndre bade all rise, and then sat on a high-backed chair.

On the inside of the tables, Veranna walked toward the other end slowly, studying the people standing opposite her at each table. They kept their faces expressionless, which made them seem more intimidating. She stopped at the end where the two tables stood, and faced DeAndre, whose seat was on a raised platform a few feet away from the side of the table opposite her. She gave him a brief nod of a bow and swept her left hand around at the tables.

"Is this the test? I was expecting something a bit more conventional."

DeAndre nodded his respect and spoke in a curious tone. "It seems that Chief Sarim'tay has a Koosti tradition in mind. This is considered not so much a game as it is a part of training for our officers in the army. Chiefs are expected to be able players, and disputes have been settled in this way. But, like you, I thought there might be something more straightforward for the test." He paused as if his mind wandered for a moment, and then asked, "Are you familiar with the game?"

Veranna, still a bit taken aback, frowned as she said, "Yes, but this format is one that I have never encountered before. What is its purpose?"

DeAndre called Sarim'tay over to explain the set-up to them.

"Great One, highness, this is a test to see how she manages in solving numerous problems at the same time. A kingdom or province has many demands that must be tended to, and decision-making must be swift and effective. She is not the Great Lady, so she does not have the heritage or gifts of your line when it comes to ruling. As a woman she will express emotions and flights of fancy that will interfere with effective ruling. This test will help us determine whether she is worthy to rule a Koosti province."

Veranna bristled at the insinuation that as a woman she would be unable to effectively rule a province or kingdom. "Let me tell you, Chief Sarim'tay, that I have been ruling the Seven Lands quite effectively, and that I come from a line of rulers just as old, or older, than LeAnre's. I have a number of outstanding men who aid me in all types of decisions, but in the end I am the one responsible."

A slight smile passed over Sarim'tay's face. Veranna realized that he was trying to unbalance her mind before the test, so she forced herself to concentrate on the task at hand.

"What do you have in mind for the rules in this test?"

Sarim'tay answered, "You shall have the choice of colors. Your opponent at any given board will make a move only when you are present, with any disputes over the rules to be decided by the Great One. To pass the test you must win three-out-of-four games, with a win counting as one point, a draw as one-half of a point, and a loss as zero."

Veranna's tone was indignant. "Three-out-of-four is a very demanding result. I am sure that you have chosen only the best players to place against me. Do you consider this a fair test?"

Sarim'tay responded with an oily smile. "The chiefs of the provinces are the best warriors out of all those in the province. This test follows the same Koosti tradition."

Putting on an air of unaffected confidence, Veranna said, "Very well; we shall see just how good your best are. I would like to request that tea, water and finger foods be placed at the end of the table line, and that my guards be allowed to oversee the boards and watch for cheating."

Sarim'tay's back went stiff at the suggestion that one of his players might cheat, but he kept control of himself and bowed in agreement.

Veranna nodded to DeAndre that she was ready, and he commanded the servants to fulfill her wishes. Kreida and Reiki sat next to Ghijhay, while Sarim'tay sat on a cushion to DeAndre's right. Kreida helped herself to a generous serving of food and drink, requesting a full flagon of the liquor served the day before. One hard flash of Veranna's eyes curtailed that request, so Kreida contented herself with imagining escape scenarios in case of hostilities.

Starting at the far end to DeAndre's left, Veranna said to the players, "On every third board I will take the black pieces."

The players counted down the line and turned their boards for the proper color. Veranna knew that she had likely given a slight advantage to the players having the white pieces since white had the first move. However, she also knew that some people were not as comfortable with opening a game as they were to responding.

When the players were all set, she addressed them once more.

"In our land it is customary for people to show respect and sportsmanship by shaking hands before and after the contest. I shall do so with the first table, and he shall represent you all."

She held out her hand for the man to shake, and he looked at Sarim'tay as though confused. DeAndre spoke directly to the man.

"Respond in kind, my son; the empress is showing you great honor."

The man's eyes went wide and he reached out stiffly to shake Veranna's hand. Such a ritual was very uncommon in the eastern lands. Opponents were enemies to be destroyed, but here was this outstandingly beautiful woman, the leader of his nation's foes, showing him great respect. He could not help but follow her every motion.

Veranna closed her eyes a moment to try and recall everything she had learned about chess from Tesra. No doubt certain basic principles would go a long way in helping her decide on a move, but these players were very likely lifetime devotees of the game and would have preplanned responses to different starting moves. She decided to follow common sense and let each game present its own possibilities.

With the first game she started by moving her king's pawn forward two squares, the second by moving her queen's pawn, and the rest by alternating between the two. On those boards where she had the black pieces she responded by paralleling her opponents moves. After ten minutes of making her way around the boards and moving pieces almost automatically, she received her first surprise. Her opponent on the fourth board used one of his priest pieces to capture the pawn next to her king. Capturing the priest would expose her king to a flurry of checks and could end with her being checkmated. After analyzing the situation, she decided to accept the risk and capture the piece. She would be minus a pawn and her king would be exposed, but she would have the advantage of an extra piece and would be able to move her other pieces to good squares while defending her king. However, the refutation would require exacting calculation.

The rest of the boards went on in conventional modes. Veranna noted that boards nine, eighteen, twenty-seven and thirty-six had players whose lines of play were more reserved and complex. She realized that they must be the strongest players and that the games would be tougher. They were also boards where she had the black pieces and would need to counter their advantage first.

She came around to the first board again and saw Tesra enter the garden area. The older woman gave her a big smile and nod, then made her way around the guards, many of whom gave her a congratulatory hug and kiss, to take a seat next to Kreida and Reiki. She asked for a glass of dark beer, saluting Veranna as she passed the boards nearby.

Seeing her adopted mother whole and happy filled Veranna with joy and confidence. It showed in her play as she made a number of bold sacrifices on some boards, and double-edged complications on others.

The players began exchanging worried looks as it became clear that they had underestimated Veranna. On attack she was ruthlessly methodical, and on defense she was as solid as a rock, neutralizing attempted combinations with amazing simplicity and taking the initiative. On one of the boards she exchanged her most powerful piece, her queen, for a knight, priest and castle of her opponent. With many lines of attack opened up, the assault of her lesser, but more numerous pieces threw her opponent into totally passive defense.

Tesra was the only one of the Company who fully understood the games. When Veranna glanced up at her as she came around, Tesra gave her a wink of approval. The Mother of the Academy recognized the gleam in Veranna's emerald-green eyes that testified to the fact that the gifts of the Creator were at work in her.

The opponent to whom Veranna traded her queen for three pieces sweat noticeably as Veranna made her way down the line of tables. When the empress finally stepped over to his table, she smiled at him, regretting having to deal out defeat. He trembled as she reached out, took hold of one of her castles and moved it to capture the pawn in front of his king, placing him in check. The empress moved on, knowing that she had him in an attack that could not be thwarted.

He laid down his king to indicate surrender, then slowly started to walk toward an exit. Tesra caught his eye and signaled that he should come to her. He bowed, and she asked him many questions about the game. Her last question made him shiver.

"Now that your game is done, what will Sarim'tay do to you for losing?"

The man was in his mid-thirties, but he was more nervous than a young teenager awaiting a paddling from his father. "Selling those who lose into slavery, including our mates and children."

Tesra's eyebrows rose and she turned calmly to DeAndre. "Great One, Sarim'tay plans on giving those who lose to Veranna a great punishment. This should not be so, for Veranna is gifted and is likely to win every time. To kill, torture or enslave the players would be totally unethical."

He looked sorrowful as he responded. "Koosti culture has an ancient tradition that says that one person does not interfere with another's disciplining of his slave. It may be unfair, but authority structures must be maintained."

Tesra wanted to yell at him. Obvious injustices should be dealt with swiftly, and Koosti culture was not just slow to progress, it was stuck. She checked her temper and took a few minutes to come up with a solution. Leaning close to DeAndre, she smiled craftily and said, "Have the players gather in a chamber where you can address them. Congratulate them for playing well against such a demanding opponent, and then tell them that you want them to get plenty of rest and study for the next time they play Veranna. They will serve as ambassadors of good will for the empire. I will talk to Gohie and get him to show enthusiasm for this idea. Sarim'tay will be obliged to treat the players well for the sake of the empire."

DeAndre let out a quick bark of a laugh. "Tesra, you are slier than a dragon." He spoke to a servant who led the player to an antechamber large enough to hold all of the players, and then turned back to the games as Tesra made her way through the crowd to find Gohie.

One after another, Veranna forced the submission of her opponents until only four remained. The four were the strongest players and each game balanced on a razor's edge of tension. One less than perfect move by either side would spell their doom. She reviewed each game to find a stylistic trait in the opponent's moves, and then walked to the refreshment table for a refill of her tea.

Sarim'tay glared at her, knowing that she had already passed the test with ease. His eyes remained on her throughout the event, full of lust and malice. He knew that he could not provoke a fight since DeAndre had given them sanction. He also had no doubt that she and her followers could likely fight their way out of the palace and escape, for she was aided by this power she referred to as the Creator. It would take someone equally gifted by the Dark One to defeat her. Maybe not today, but her time would come. It would take time anyway for the proper tool to be prepared for the task. One blow after another and he would have her, like water wearing away a stone.

Veranna returned to the play and watched as the only woman left made her move. Her style of play was subtle, always trying to offer Veranna situations that allowed reasonable responses that were actually loaded with peril. The empress surprised her by making a move that made no immediate threat but allowed for serious lines of attack in the next few moves. Now, the Koosti woman only had moves that would weaken her own position. Realizing the situation, the woman laid down her king to signal surrender. Veranna started to step over to one of the remaining three boards when she noticed the woman try to stand, but fell forward across her table. Veranna rushed to lift her off the table and back into her seat.

"Lady, please, just relax; try to take some deep breaths."

Sarim'tay approached and clapped his hands twice. Immediately, two young male slaves jumped forward and fell to their knees in front of him. His command was quick and sharp. "Take her to be revived, and then begin her punishment."

Veranna eyed him coldly. "What do you mean, 'her punishment?' She has done me no wrong, and conducted herself honorably during our game."

Somewhat bemused, Sarim'tay bowed slightly and said, "For you that is true, but not for Koosti. She has dishonored her master by performing poorly. Her children and home are forfeit and she shall spend the rest of her days in painful labor. The same is true for all of these losers."

Fear and outrage knotted up in her stomach. She turned to DeAndre and started to speak when Tesra arrived with Chief Gohie. The Mother of the Academy dispelled the tension with a simple statement.

"The players are summoned by the Great One to an audience with him. He commands that you, Sarim'tay, attend as well."

Sarim'tay looked past her to Chief Gohie for confirmation. Gohie nodded and pointed in the direction of the chamber for the audience. After Sarim'tay bowed and departed, Gohie turned to Veranna.

"Your highness, if you are finished the Great One requests your presence also. Do you feel up to it?"

She frowned in puzzlement and wondered what was going on. "I will be finished in a moment, my lord, and will attend promptly. If you will pardon me for asking, is there some food ready? I am very hungry."

"Yes, your highness; all is prepared."

She smiled her thanks and then turned to the three players waiting patiently at their boards. "I apologize for the delay, and am willing to offer a draw to each of you."

Two of the three accepted immediately since their positions were shaky. The other, a man in his mid-forties, with reddish-brown hair and a serious air, said, "I will accept only on the condition that you show me how you planned to finish the game."

Veranna obliged and demonstrated the strategy she had in mind. The man bowed and stepped away from the board, struck by the simple, but irrefutable logic of her approach.

The audience was dominated by stiff, formal Koosti tradition that allowed DeAndre to save the players from harm. Tesra and Ghijhay devised a plan whereby the players would need to have an opportunity to regain face, and Sarim'tay could not find a way around this use of Koosti honor.

When DeAndre asked Veranna about the possibility that the Koosti players would do better in the future, she decided to get in a dig at Sarim'tay.

"Great One, virtually every player can perform better when not under such foolish compulsion. If it were one of my lords or ladies treating people in that way I would sit them down and give them an earful regarding the mistreatment of others. If they refused to change I would remove them from office. Crass egotism always brings destruction."

After more discussion of the games, Veranna, Karsten, Tesra, Kreida, Treybal and Reiki joined DeAndre and Ghijhay for a tour of the palace and the city of Banaipal. The network of slaves had spread news of Veranna far and wide, and throngs of them crowded the streets to catch a glimpse of her. They gazed out of the windows of multi-storied, mud brick buildings and tossed flowers, while others rushed to present her with gifts of food, cloth, jewelry and many other items. DeAndre was amazed at the peoples' reaction to her presence and ordered wagons to be brought for all of the gifts.

The Great One kept Sarim'tay close by to show how well kindness could motivate people. When they returned to the palace the Koosti chief was near to bursting with what he perceived to be DeAndre's humiliation of him. Food and drink he ignored while the others feasted, and his brittle manner was evident.

Deep into the evening, Veranna stood and thanked all of the Koosti for their hospitality. She then urged them to consider fresh thinking about the way of life in the Koosti Empire, and to keep in mind the fact that it was necessary for everyone to work together for the common good.

"For the good of our own empire my fellows and I must return home. Let us all hope and pray that from this day on we shall have peace and friendship between our peoples." She looked directly at Sarim'tay as she said, "For this opportunity to come to know one another let us thank the Creator."

DeAndre, and all of the Koosti, bowed and thanked her for coming, while Sarim'tay moved close enough for only Veranna to hear what he said.

"Make no assumptions, for you do not know me."

Veranna's eyes glittered as she gave him a frosty smile. "I make no assumptions about you, for your mind is obvious. I doubt that you will ever know my mind, even though I know you. Or, maybe I should say that I know both of you." She turned her back to him and strode from the room with her arm in Karsten's, the rest of her Company following. Ghijhay accompanied her, and many of the servants begged to wait upon her needs. Along the way the Deeri woman thanked Veranna for all she had done while among them, but the empress shrugged her shoulders in a self-deprecating gesture.

"Ghijhay, I came to retrieve someone I love. Many people died along that path, and each of them shall be upon my conscience as I stand before the Creator to be judged."

The queen of the Koosti looked at her with all seriousness and grasped her hand. "You know that is an oversimplification. By the gifts given you by the Creator, you defeated the Dark One and shook the foundations of Koosti culture. DeAndre received a message that says that since it has become known that you will be ruling LeAnre's province, thousands are already streaming there. You have filled them with hope."

She paused as tears welled up in the corners of her eyes. "I had lost my faith in the Creator, and many fond memories of my father in service at the shrine. I thank you for restoring my faith and for helping me remember my family."

The two embraced at the entry to Veranna's guest chamber. Afterwards, Ghijhay thanked the rest of the Company. Coming lastly to Karsten, she admonished him to take good care of her cousin.

He bowed and said, "Indeed; rare gems need close guarding. I just hope that I can keep up with her."

They laughed, and Veranna did a quick curtsy. "You and DeAndre are invited to attend our wedding. If any of the young ladies whom you have had serving us wishes to come, then, by all means, bring them."

The new Koosti queen curtsied and said, "We would be greatly honored." Having now a handle on Kreida's sense of humor and bluster, Ghijhay gave her a withering glare and said, "Leave her man alone. You would not do very well with both of your arms cut off."

Kreida feigned innocence, and then put on a harlequin smile. "A girl has to do what a girl has to do. Besides, I have a hard time already just keeping the wolves away from this sheep." She jabbed her thumb at Treybal, but did not look at him. "This fuddy, old smoke blower is always reminding me of how a civilized, married woman should act. I swear, he is driving me to drink. Men are such idiots when jealousy takes them." She turned and gave him a quick slap. "Do not go eying the serving girls!"

They all laughed and said goodnight. An hour later, after a soak in the pool, Veranna lay on the massage table, half asleep as Reyiya kneaded all of her muscles into relaxation.

Tesra, holding her baby in her arms, gave Veranna a thoughtful look. "This new relationship with the Koosti Empire will be very difficult for many to accept. Do not be surprised if some of your lords want to take DeAndre and shred him."

Veranna took a deep breath to help Reyiya smooth out a knot of tension in her back. In a faint, wispy voice she said, "We will work it out, mother."

She fell asleep and a dream arose in her mind. The castle in Tolemera was one huge emerald gem with banners snapping in the breeze. The people in and around it shined like stars against the green background. The three moons aligned and a warm, golden blaze poured out from an altar set up in the castle pavilion. The flame grew and reached into the sky like a pillar, disappearing in the heavens. The Boar's Spine Mountains to the west were capped in bright white, while the lands to the east could hardly be seen. From between the two highest peaks to the north in the mountain chain could be seen a tiny, but intense red dot. Or was it an eye? It sank below the mountains and out of sight before it could be identified. She approached the altar, but several times she turned and looked east. Her arm was ready.

CHAPTER THIRTY THREE

AND SO IT STARTS

Veranna and her company headed south to meet up with her army led by Lord Tomius. It was almost a week since leaving Banaipal, and they made good time with the wagons DeAndre supplied them. The seats and beds were well cushioned and the road smooth, and as they cleared the last hill bordering the plain where her forces were encamped, the empress could hardly believe her eyes.

Multitudes of tents stood in the midst of the plain, a small city teeming with activity. From the largest tent located near the center, a red and green banner flew atop a tall pole, with the surrounding tents each displaying a banner of their fiefs' colors. The red and green signified Tomius, silver on sky blue for Starhaven, gold and green for Grandshire, deep red on pink for Rosea, and gray on purple for Clarens.

The strangest sight was her own army working together with Koosti to dig an irrigation canal from the hills to the east down to the plain. When the horns blew to announce her arrival, the thousands of soldiers from each empire rushed out to greet her, yelling and clapping as they bowed low. A rhythmic chant of, *Veranna, Veranna of Emeraldia*, started and she had to cover her ears as she looked around in amazement.

Her lords rode out, bowing in their saddles as they made their way through the crowd. Veranna could not hear her own voice over the noise so she simply stood up in her wagon and bowed several times. When Tomius came near and surrendered his scepter of office to her the crowd's roar nearly knocked her over. She handed the scepter back to him and designated him as her chief lieutenant, then motioned with her arms for the people to clear the road for her Company to pass. Several minutes later she dismounted in front of Tomius's tent. People bowing and begging to serve rushed forward like a tidal wave, and the western lords and captains greeted the Company with hugs and slaps on the back.

Kreida, wanting to make an impression, looked at a well-muscled Koosti man and ordered him to bring her a large mug of ale. In less than a minute he was back with a full mug. She purposely ignored him as she grabbed the mug, looking at the others as though he had done nothing. She noticed Veranna giving her a hard, accusing stare, her green eyes boring into her conscience. The only thing she could do was surrender. Turning to the man she said dryly, "You have served me adequately for now," and walked on. The man beamed with delight that he had received such recognition and stayed close enough to hear even the slightest wish of one of the nobles.

Tomius's tent became Veranna's, the wise Genazi leader insisting on the change since such symbols were very important to Koosti. An hour later the empress had freshened up and sat down with her lords to relate what had happened in Banaipal. Some things they already knew since messages had arrived, but other details were new and fascinating. They marveled at how the Creator had healed Tesra and opened up the Koosti to receive the Emeraldian Company in peace. Veranna and Tesra answered as many questions as they could about Koosti politics, but the empress wanted to wait until they returned home to discuss future policy regarding the Koosti.

Veranna conveyed her condolences to Lord Roland regarding the death of his mother and people, and promised to help in whatever ways possible to rebuild his fief.

Roland thanked her solemnly, and then gestured toward the Koosti noble sitting next to Tomius. "Your highness, it will take time for my people, and me, to recover from the horrors done to us by the Koosti. However, I can say that I no longer crave their slaughter. The slaves simply follow orders or die, and this extends to their spouses and children. I do not know that I will ever love them, but I do pray for the strength to forgive them."

The empress smiled and nodded slowly. "I have no doubts about your progress, my lord, for such prayers always seem to be granted." She addressed them all as she asked, "Why the aqueduct project? Were you in danger of running out of water?"

Tomius answered, "No, your highness. We thought it best to give the troops something to help them learn to work together. Also, the soil around here is good, but dry. It will make fertile farmland with readily available water. Lady Amilla impressed a number of the captives we took by showing them mercy, and Duke Heilson pointed out that helping them rebuild their lives in this land would engender peace and appreciation for us. I believe that he is right."

Veranna's eyes glittered as she smiled. "Well done, my lords! I cannot thank the Creator enough for surrounding me with such wise and noble counselors. I suspect that what you have done will have a positive impact for an entire age of this world. Getting both sides together in a common cause builds unity, and we will need that more than ever in the years to come. As I mentioned before, we will have control over this province belonging to LeAnre for a generation. If we are diligent we can develop permanent bonds that will be to our benefit."

To her right sat General Garyain y'dobin. He was intrigued with the way in which these westerners interacted, and wondered how it might affect Koosti culture. One thing that he knew well was the mind-set of his people. He raised his hand to request a moment to speak and was surprised again at the courteous recognition he received.

"Ah, General Garyain, we are honored to have you with us. Please, feel free to speak."

He bowed in his seat and tried to show the full respect due to his ruler. "Your highness, Koosti can be very practical. It would serve your ends to show the Great Lady in homage to you. Some of the people may not really believe that she is your slave if they do not witness it. She holds the power of the Dark One; the people fear her still."

The empress thought about what he said for a moment, her eyes seeming to focus on something far away. Then abruptly, she said with finality, "No. I am sure that what you say is true when it comes to Koosti culture, but I wish to demonstrate a new way of doing things. We do not believe in slavery in the Seven Lands, and recompense for crime is not to be construed as such. The Dark One no longer possesses LeAnre, so I am praying that she can now come to a new way of seeing her own life. Subjecting her to humiliation would only burn her hatred deeper into her soul. She is with child, so my goal is to gain respect and friendship with the child and have it endure indefinitely. If LeAnre can have nothing but good to say of us then she will have a hard time filling her child with hate."

Garyain thought her idea simplistic but tried not to show it in his voice. "Your highness, as the Great Lady's cousin I thank you for such great mercy. However, I hold great reservations about conforming her mind to a new pattern. Years of effort may prove vain."

"I agree, sir, but we are obligated to at least try. Her child will need the support since its father will not be present. As one who grew up without father or mother I can tell you that role models are absolutely essential." She paused as a sudden decision solidified in her mind. "Tomorrow morning, before we depart for Neidburg, LeAnre shall address her people. I expect them to show her the respect due her station." She stood, bringing everyone else in the tent to their feet. "That will be all for now, my lords. We have need of rest before resuming our journey home, so I bid you to prepare for departure and get a good night's sleep. Thank you for your attendance."

They bowed and calmly filed out of the room, leaving Veranna alone with Tesra, Kreida and Reiki. Kreida sent a servant to fetch four large mugs of hot, spiced wine, and soon the women were chatting about old times. The subject of Veranna's wedding came up and two hours quickly passed as they discussed a few aspects of it to the nth degree.

Tesra called them to a halt. "It is time I nursed my boy; you all should see to turning in before too long."

The empress just smiled and said, "Yes, mother. But, if you do not mind, there is one more thing I need to do before retiring. I have been dreading it all evening."

"LeAnre?"

"Yes, mother."

Tesra just shrugged and sat down. "Let us be done with it."

Kreida sent a servant to bring LeAnre to the tent. When she stepped in, Veranna wondered at the change in her. The confident and defiant look on her face was gone, replaced by dejection and humiliation. She seemed shorter than what Veranna recalled from previous encounters. LeAnre was used to being seen as a very seductive beauty, but now she reminded the other women in the room of a worn out prostitute working alehouses for another drink. The worst part was her skin. The old, bronzed sections were peeling away slowly, leaving a patchwork of white, red and brown splotches. As the old skin loosened it caused an itching sensation. Abrasions and dried blood showed where LeAnre had scratched furiously. Adding to the woeful sight were the plain, brown shorts and tunic allotted slaves. The tunic had been cut short to reveal the shame of scars and lack of bronzing. The scars were gone from her flesh, but they lingered deep in her demeanor, especially her voice.

"I have come as you commanded, Great Mistress." She fell to the floor to kiss Veranna's feet, but the empress's voice brought her to an immediate halt.

"Stop!" Veranna could see LeAnre's body trembling with fear of sudden punishment. With her brother, LeAnre presumed leniency when he judged her. However, Veranna was a foreigner whom she had betrayed and assailed. Koosti culture demanded hideous torture and execution. Veranna let the fear work on her for a moment. "Get up, LeAnre, and pull yourself together."

The Koosti woman moved swiftly to stand, wondering if the empress wanted her in an upright position for her Genazi slave to drive a knife into her back. She had done as such, herself, to maintain a high level of terror among her people. A cold sweat came over her and she flinched at the sound of Veranna's voice.

"LeAnre, you have earned your execution many times over, as well as disgrace before all of the people on this world of Treluna. While I delight in the death of no one, your death would not bring me regret. What shall be upon my mind until I die will be the images of people murdered and suffering due to your evil ways.

"However, as much as I would not deem execution undue in your case, there are two mitigating factors. The first is that you are with child. I will not murder the child in my desire to dispatch you to the Creator. The unborn deserve every effort to grow and realize their destinies among the people.

"Secondly, it is obvious that your mind and soul were possessed by the Dark One. This drove you to commit unspeakable horrors that the forces of evil used to hold your people in bondage. No doubt you were, at some point, complicit with this agenda, but for now I must withhold the ax until I am able to determine how much guilt you bear even though possessed.

"Here then is my decree: You shall represent the Koosti people and testify to your guilt while among us. That shall last no less than the day that your child reaches his, or her, majority. Among us that age is eighteen years. Your child will be raised in the Seven Lands, but shall be taken several times to visit its province to see how the people live. By the Creator's mercy it shall grow to be a wise and just ruler. Only then can you have any hope of a heritage other than infamy.

"You will attend court regularly and conduct yourself in the dignity befitting a member of a noble house. Always keep in mind that this judgment can easily be modified should your behavior require it. Have I made myself clear?"

LeAnre could hardly believe her ears. Not only was she going to live, she would be living the life of a noble. She might even find a way to escape exile in this foolish woman's empire. Veranna had so much to learn!

"Yes, your highness," said the Koosti woman, trying to make her voice humble and submissive.

Kreida moved over to stand only a foot away from LeAnre, hands on hips and eyes smoldering as she spoke. "You are alive only because the empress commanded me not to draw and quarter you. The instant that she gives me the command, my blade will have cut you in half. She may seek the healing of your soul and your repentance before the Creator, but I do not. Never presume me to be lax or sentimental; it will prove to be a fatal error."

LeAnre felt like a mouse surrounded by a pride of lions. The stone-cold stares of Tesra and the Felinii woman were more than enough evidence of their agreement with Kreida. She fell to her knees and bowed down until her head touched Kreida's feet.

"I hear you Mistress, and will obey. I have my brother's will to follow, too. I will give you no reason to kill me."

Kreida pulled her feet away in disgust, and Tesra retorted firmly, "You have made promises before, and will understand if we simply disbelieve what you say. As for a reason to kill you, we need no more than what you have already provided. Keep in mind that you live under a sentence of death, and that grace is the only reason you live."

In a resigned and weary tone, Veranna echoed Tesra. "That is true for us all. It will be a grace to get a good night's sleep." She yawned before addressing LeAnre in a neutral tone. "Arise and get to your bed. We depart tomorrow morning. Servants shall be assigned to you, but not in the manner that you are used to. They are to be paid and not abused in any way. Do not confuse them with slaves. Treat them well and they will serve you well. Good night."

LeAnre bowed and said, "As you command, your highness." She bowed to the other women and then backed out of the tent as she kept her head down.

Tesra gave Veranna a kiss and bade her goodnight, followed by Reiki and Kreida. The Genazi woman paused just before moving through the door flap and gave Veranna a serious look.

"You would not let me gut her the last time I had the opportunity. I warned you then and repeat that I told you so. Let us hope that I do not need to repeat it again." She slipped through the doorway and into the night, leaving Veranna to contemplate the future.

CHAPTER THIRTY FOUR

CONSTRUCTING THE FUTURE

Veranna and her forces reached Neidburg, now called Zishiye by the Genazi, after several days of steady riding. Tired and sore, they all appreciated taking a few days rest. The empress had agreed to take the Koosti servant, Reyiya, with them, and thanked the Creator that she knew how to give an excellent massage.

Marques Amilla had made tremendous progress in organizing the people and getting repairs made to the city's buildings and walls. She and Veranna spent many hours discussing the situation regarding the Koosti, as well as the future of the empire. With so many people killed in battles over the last few years it was obvious that marriage and children must take precedence in their considerations.

Veranna, overlooking the city from a high balcony in the palace tower, commented on the noticeable reduction in traffic. "The last time I was here was when Dalmar was executed. There was a hustle and bustle to the city that was almost deafening. We must build up the population once more or risk falling into a state of decline that could leave us severely weakened in manpower." Her face brightened as she turned to Amilla and asked, "Have you found that special someone who will help you increase the population?"

Amilla grimaced and looked away. "Since being used by Dalmar, I find it difficult to think about such things without cowering in fear. Besides, what man with his head on straight would want to acquire damaged goods?"

Struck by the awful finality of Amilla's statement, Veranna gasped silently. Wondering how to help her friend toward healing, she could only think of buttressing the positive.

"Amilla, any man worthy of the title would see you as a great treasure. You are very intelligent, noble and beautiful. What Dalmar did to you was not your choice; you had to survive in order to help others. Your innocence and privacy may have been stolen from you, but he was totally unable to take away your virtue and dignity. The Creator made men and women for each other, and you will find the one who complements you for a lifetime."

Closing her eyes and hanging her head, the Sudryni woman forced herself to hold back tears. "I pray that you are right, and that foul memories will not haunt me the rest of my days."

Veranna lowered her own head as she caught a fleeting glimpse of where the gallows once stood in the city square. "I have memories that love to pop into my mind and make me cringe with grief. I vanquish them by reminding myself that my duty to the Creator required the actions I undertook. Better a grief observed for that which is right than regret unending for that which is wrong."

After a protracted silence the empress put on a beaming smile and stood up straight. In a crisp, friendly manner she said, "How about some lunch? Do you know of a decent inn or café in the city?"

Amilla found Veranna's enthusiasm infectious. She was thankful for the change of subject matter and marveled at how her empress seemed to bring the best out of virtually anyone. "Yes, I do. It is a café that has been around for ages, but seems to have taken on a whole new life. Both the service and food are excellent."

"It sounds wonderful. Are there many shops nearby?"

Amilla stepped briskly to the door and opened it, gesturing for Veranna to follow. "There are many; we will not be able to visit even half of them before closing time, so let's hurry."

The two of them scampered down the corridor, stopping at their quarters only long enough to retrieve their purses and let the staff know they would be out and about. Heading through the main gate they passed Duke Roland, who bowed and greeted them warmly.

"You two look like you are on a mission. May I be of assistance in any way?"

The women exchanged a conspiratorial glance. Veranna thanked him for asking, and said, "Why yes, my lord, you may. Would you join us at…," and she looked at Amilla, who supplied the name of the café, "…*The Leopard's Spot* café in about one-and a half-hours?"

Roland could see that something was being left unsaid, but decided to wait to find out what. "Yes, your highness; I will be there."

"Thank you, my lord. We will see you then." She nodded and headed through the gate, but was surprised when she had to give Amilla a little pull to start her moving. "We have got to hurry, Amilla."

The Marques smiled as she watched Roland walking away, then said in a hazy voice, "Yes, your highness."

Making their way down the street, Amilla, with a twinkle in her eye, caused Veranna to burst with laughter when she said, "He is sooo yummy!"

After lunch the two women shopped well into the evening. Roland felt exhausted after the first hour and ordered a soldier to bring him a small wagon to carry all of the purchased items. He was overjoyed when he found a wine shop that carried several brands produced in Starhaven, and invited the women to join him for an evening of song and drink after their return to the palace.

The time came soon enough and they all gathered to celebrate friendship and plans for the future. Karsten, Reiki and Tesra were there as well as Duke Heilson and Lord Charles. Veranna saw to it that Roland was always near Amilla, and was not surprised when he reported that he would be staying in Zishiye for a few more days before returning to Starhaven.

A week later, Veranna and her army came to Tolemera. The early afternoon sun revealed a dramatic change since the time they had left a month before. The ash and rubble were gone, and the buildings made of dragonstone were freshly painted and had new windows. The streets now ran as close to straight as possible, the old, meandering ways giving way to a far more organized layout. Many were paved with brick and slightly curved to allow water to run into drain lines. New buildings both complete and in the process of completion, lined the streets. The builders took care to blend the styles of the ancient buildings with more modern techniques. Trees, bushes and flowers had been transplanted along the new sidewalks, and the central park already showed a new lawn. Several of the huge, ancient trees that had been burned to stumps showed new shoots reaching for the sky, and lampposts were evenly spaced along its walkways. They matched the ones posted along the city streets and would provide much needed light on long nights.

A great cheer arose as Veranna rode along the main street toward the castle. Young and old alike bowed and waved as they called out the Creator's favor upon her. As she reached the end of town closest to the castle, Yanbre and Lord Forest stepped out of a three-story building under construction. Although covered with sawdust, crusty mortar and paint, the castellan put on a dignified air as he bowed and greeted Veranna.

"Your highness, welcome home. If you had given us a bit more time we would have gotten things nearly finished. As it is, you will have to endure the sound of hammers and saws for a couple more weeks."

Veranna jumped down from her horse and rushed to give him and Forest a hug and kiss. "My lords, it is wonderful to be home. You have done an amazing job of restoring the city. The noise of building will be as music to our ears."

Forest could not help spouting some dry humor. "Yes, well we heard that Kreida was singing as you rode along, so we had to come up with something to counteract the torture."

Joining in on the humor, Treybal shook his head solemnly and said, "I will have to keep that in mind, my lord."

Kreida shot him an angry look, and then jumped in Forest's face. "You had better hold your tongue, you old goat, or I will see to it that you have no means for pleasure. Besides that, your voice will sound like a young boy's."

She turned florid when Forest's face wrinkled up and he took a deliberate sniff of her. "I think your horse smells better."

Reiki took his arm in hers and resumed walking toward the castle. She affected a disgusted look as she passed by Kreida. "He right."

Kreida ground her teeth and vowed revenge on them, but Treybal lifted her up onto his horse before she could say anymore.

Veranna laughed and grabbed Karsten's hand, then called the others to proceed to the castle for the midday meal. In the evening, Yanbre took her for a tour of many of the new buildings. She was curious as to the differences in technique used in the construction of some of the structures. He explained that he had hired craftsmen from many parts of the empire and that they had different ways of doing things. He also warned her that the treasury would be very tight for some time after the construction was done. Veranna simply dismissed any worries over the situation.

"I could not sleep if I knew the people's needs were not being seen to; they are more than worthy of out best efforts. Besides, once things are running normally we shall be back to a reasonable budget in no time."

Yanbre shook his head in amazement. "Well said, your highness. Weyland and Dalmar would have been loath to spend any funds on such charitable causes. They would be demanding tribute and selling into slavery those who did not pay."

The next morning started early, for Veranna wanted to assist with organizing the work crews. When Kreida caught sight of her in plain clothes she rolled her eyes and groaned.

"Where are you going dressed like that? I thought that I had made it clear to you that you should not go around acting like a commoner!"

Veranna's response nearly floored her. "Why thank you, Kreida; that is a great compliment. Would you care to assist us?"

Kreida looked sick to her stomach as she asked, "Us? You are referring to lugging sausages around, aren't you?"

Veranna smiled and nodded. "Not exactly." Just then Karsten, Charles and Heilson passed by and helped load a wagon being readied in the courtyard. "In fact, if you wish to join us we will be eating breakfast in Master Dufer's new café."

Kreida covered her eyes and spoke as if in prayer. "Please, let this be a bad dream that I will awaken from." She lowered her hands and looked around. Seeing Veranna the same as before, she let out a wounded howl. "I have got to find Treybal. This is unbearable!"

Veranna had to force herself not to laugh, but maintained her smile and sweet voice. "Treybal is with the Rockhounds. They are surveying the city for defense planning and should be in the northeastern quarter. Would you like to ride with us?"

"No! I would rather crawl." She spun around and dashed off toward the stables, muttering how Treybal would hear about this, and how he would suffer if he did not get some sense into Veranna's head.

Two months later the city pulsed with new life all the more. Veranna and her advisors lowered taxation to help stimulate trade, and before long the royal exchequer had his hands full keeping track of all the monies coming in. The empress decided to maintain an ongoing program of public works while advocating the growth and contribution of the private sector toward community projects. One such effort was a large stone monument dedicated to all those who died in the war with the Koosti.

Treybal took the lead in training recruits for the city constable force, utilizing Lord Charles whenever possible. Kreida often terrorized the candidates with sneak attacks and ferocious sparring. She also set up tests involving beautiful women who would distract them while someone else committed a staged crime. It took many drills before she was able to thoroughly imbed in their brains the idea that they needed strict mental discipline so that they could appraise a situation properly. A tithe of the best students was sent off to Clarens for the rigors of Rockhound training.

A week before the wedding of Veranna and Karsten, an alarm bell sounded from the castle's high tower. Guards and soldiers rushed to their stations while the city constables cleared the streets and armed for action. The guard tower reported that a beacon had flared from a lookout tower to the east of the city, warning of a potential danger. A few minutes later a sentry galloped into town to deliver a report to the castle. A Koosti force of nearly two hundred approached led by a unit composed of forces from Neidburg, Sudryni and Starhaven. Lord Yanbre immediately understood that this was a royal procession and authorized their entry. The Emeraldian forces were greeted with a mighty roar of welcome while the Koosti caused suspicious silence.

Horses and wagons filled the castle stable yard. DeAndre and Ghijhay brought with them many wedding gifts, but they also delivered many gifts for the people of Tolemera. Clothing, household items and rare artifacts were unloaded into a warehouse in town. Veranna assigned Reiki to oversee their distribution.

The empress greeted all of the guests and bade them enter the castle. The Koosti soldiers were taken to a guest barracks for lodging and DeAndre, Ghijhay, Chief Gohie and another man were given rooms to use inside the castle. When they reached the room for Ghijhay and DeAndre, the empress personally gave them a tour and explained the services at their disposal. However, before Veranna exited to allow them time to unpack and enjoy some privacy, Ghijhay took her hand and escorted her over to the other man in their party.

"Veranna, allow me to introduce to you my brother, Garjhan, ruler of the Deeri and High Priest before the Shrine of Wahweh."

Veranna's eyes went wide as the man drew back the hood surrounding his face, which was longer than Ghijhay's, and his skin was darker due to more exposure. However, his eyes were even more intensely blue than his sister's. His hair was a mixture of golden-red with gray, and he was tall, with long, lean muscles that were as hard as rocks. A short, well-kept beard gave him an air of pious dignity. Veranna immediately fell to her knees, clasped her hands together and bowed her head.

"Thank the Creator that you have survived! And we thank you, Father, for journeying so far to visit us."

Garjhan smiled and shook his head. "Please, your highness, do not bow down to me. I am simply a servant before Wahweh, as are you. In fact, I am in your service for having helped my sister be delivered from shameful treatment. However, that is nothing compared to the fact that you helped her find her faith once more." He took Veranna's hand and gently helped her to her feet.

"Father, I did little in that regard; the Creator is the one who gave her new life." She paused and then pulled Karsten close to her side. "Father, if it is not too much to ask, would you perform the ceremony for our wedding?"

He bowed graciously and said, "I would be greatly honored, your highness."

Veranna thanked him and immediately she and Ghijhay began exchanging ideas about the wedding. The men knew better than to interrupt, so Karsten led them to an eatery near the castle pavilion for some refreshment.

The day before the wedding was filled with activity. The cooks had to prepare not only for the wedding but also for all of the nobles residing in the castle. They came from every part of the empire and were used to being served. Veranna put Kreida in charge of seeing to them, knowing that few of them could equal her tenacity if it came to petty complaints. All she had to do was glare at them and they dropped their fussy manner.

The empress worked through the day setting up for the ceremony and into the night for changes to the dresses that the ladies in the wedding party would wear. Kreida caused Veranna a great deal of embarrassment by joking about her lack of experience with men. Everyone laughed when Ghijhay retorted that there was no one who did not know of Kreida's experiences, and then feigned pity as she said to Veranna, "Is Treybal sad at getting used goods?"

Kreida threw a spool of thread at her and said, "At least I know what to do with the goods. Imagine getting into a fight if you do not have any training; you would be worthless."

Tesra gave her a skeptical look. "Are you equating being with a man with being in combat?"

Kreida did not flinch. "Of course! You cannot let things turn dull."

"Poor Treybal!"

"Poor my foot! I am going to find that pig-headed pipe puffer and remind him of a few things." She sprang to her feet and stomped out of the room.

Tesra closed her eyes for a moment before saying to Ghijhay, "Make sure that you ask your brother to pray for Treybal."

They laughed again and went on with their work. A half-hour later they finished and decided to get to bed. Veranna thanked them for their help and wished them goodnight. Ghijhay and Tesra both noted a nervous quality in her voice, and knowing smiles formed on their faces. Ghijhay nodded to Tesra and wished her a night of good sleep. "I will talk with Veranna for a bit."

Tesra gave each of them a kiss and headed for her own room, while Ghijhay took Veranna's arm in her own and walked her to her chambers. Once inside they sat down in a private reading room and Ghijhay ordered a servant to throw more wood on the fire and bring them two crocks of mulled wine. When the servant left, Ghijhay took a deep breath and said to Veranna, "Tomorrow you enter into a life-long commitment as a wife. To be nervous is perfectly natural; so do not scold yourself for that. You are intelligent and wise in many ways, but Kreida does have a point about knowing how to deal with men. Her idea about marriage being like battle is bizarre, so try to think of it more in the sense of training two horses to work as a team to pull a wagon. Some of the things you accomplish as a team are most enjoyable."

An hour later and Veranna's cheeks glowed redder than her wine.

CHAPTER THIRTY FIVE

UNITY

Trumpets blared and drums beat as the tall bronze doors opened to the castle pavilion. Eagles circled above, their cries calling all to come and observe the wedding ceremony. Lords, ladies, rich and poor crowded every niche of the pavilion to see their empress wed. The small orchestra behind the dais struck up a proud march, bringing everyone to bow as Veranna proceeded along the center aisle.

Dressed in a gown of ice-blue silk with delicate, beaded sleeves of lace, Veranna walked nobly, arm-in-arm with her foster father Charles. Behind them walked Elly and Alicia holding the train of her mantel. Made of emerald-green velvet, it had a fringe of muted gold and a shoulder piece of silver-gray. The bodice panel of her gown was made of creamy-white silk with a lace border that rose to her collarbone. Over her left breast was fastened a green and gold feather pin, and on her head rode a slender circlet of silver that held her gauzy veil in place. Her dark-brown hair was braided and wrapped around her head in a natural crown with woodland flowers woven in, and her eyes shined like bright, green stars.

To the left of the dais stood Kreida, Ghijhay, Laerha and Reiki, and to the right were Karsten, Treybal, DeAndre, Tomius and Forest. Karsten wore a dark-green suit with a broad, golden ribbon draped from his right shoulder to his left hip. On it was sewn a knife badge symbolizing his Genazi background, and a badge bearing a scroll to mark him as the court chronicler. On his head was a crown matching Veranna's. The four men with him wore black with gold trim and the bridesmaids wore silver gowns.

On the dais stood Garjhan in a simple, white monk's habit with a piece of rope for a belt. Behind him were four nobles who would serve as the official witnesses of the marriage covenant. Marques Amilla, Duke Heilson, Duke Roland and the Countess Petalia of Rosea all wore plain, white clothes without insignia, as was the custom for all who served as witnesses in any legal court of the Lands. Petalia was a short, petite woman in her early fifties with a full head of bright white hair.

Behind Elly and Alicia walked Tesra and Kate, the wife of Charles. Both had served as mother figures for Veranna and rejoiced that the Creator had seen fit to join her in marriage to such a fine man. Following them came Yanbre and his wife Yakhia, with Baron Lenarde of Clarens, the last of the party, escorting Rita, the daughter-in-law of Charles and Kate, down the aisle. LeAnre stood in the second line of the crowd, her face devoid of joy or excitement. However, the constant frown she wore was gone as she observed the ceremony taking place around her.

Charles and Veranna stopped at the foot of the dais and bowed. The orchestra ceased playing and a hush came over the room. Garjhan raised his hands high and invoked the blessings of the Creator, then turned and looked at Charles.

"You, sir, bring this lady before the Creator and this realm to give her in marriage to Karsten, son of Tomius and Laerha. Do you bear witness that she is ready to undertake such a holy calling?"

Charles nodded and said, "I do, as do my wife and the Grand Dame, Tesra."

"So be it." He stepped back and motioned for Veranna and Karsten to step up onto the dais. As they stood hand-in-hand before him, he said in a very serious tone, "Hear the words of the song that my sister shall sing. It has survived the centuries and counseled newlyweds from the beginning of the empire of Emeraldia."

Ghijhay stepped up on the dais and turned to Veranna and Karsten. As the young lady, Emily, began a solemn melody on a harpsichord, Ghijhay's sweet and powerful voice carried across the pavilion.

Times of joy and times of pain.
Summer and winter turn again.
A tear or smile in labor true,
So many days; so few, so few.

A past to fade, a future bright.
A bond that's woven ever tight.
Tender love and hearts laid bare,
A union sweet we now declare.

Ears perceive and eyes behold,
Vows now made that won't grow old.
Two lives as one, to life invest;
Creator led, Creator blessed!

Many a woman's eyes teared up, and those married nodded sagely at the words. Garjhon slowly swept his gaze over the assembled crowd and addressed them.

"From the day that the Creator saw fit to give life to our ancestors, the union of man and wife was ordained. Those who malign this holy institution blaspheme against the Creator and cause untold grief to their neighbors and themselves. This union shall serve as testimony to the fact that those bound together for a higher good shall have great strength. Kingdoms rise and fall on the unions made between people. In such manner there is no greater or lesser, for all are servants to the One and to one another. The act of marriage therefore exalts and humbles at the same time."

He turned his attention to Karsten and asked, "Do you, sir, take this lady to be your one and only wife, until the day that the Creator takes you home?"

Karsten smiled at Veranna as he said, "I do."

Garjhan then spoke to Veranna. "Do you, lady, take this man to be your one and only husband, until the day that the Creator takes you home?"

Her voice trembled a bit as she responded, "I do."

Garjhan raised both hands high and looked up toward the heavens as he said, "In light of your pledges made before the Creator, I now proclaim you troth-plighted before all in this world. May the Creator be pleased to bless you throughout all your days." He paused, and then ended with the Deeri words, "Xre thani," *The Creator's will be done.* He then took Veranna's left hand and placed it in Karsten's right before having them turn to face the crowd. With a hand on the shoulder of each he said, in a loud voice, "People of the Seven Lands, and those from afar, I present to you Karsten and Veranna Emeraldia, as husband and wife. Bless the Creator!"

Deafening applause struck like thunder, and many were the blessings invoked on behalf of the newlyweds. The eagles screamed loudly and flew in circles around the castle. The orchestra struck up a quick march as the married couple started to step down from the dais. But Kreida raised her voice above the crowd and chanted, "Kiss, kiss, kiss!" In a moment the whole room took up the chant and Veranna's face blushed bright red.

Karsten put his right arm around her and lifted off her veil with his left before drawing her close to give her a long, passionate kiss.

The crowd roared all the louder and swarmed around the two with hugs, kisses and congratulations. The eagles swooped down into the pavilion and dropped twigs into the hands of the newlyweds as they said to Veranna, *For your aerie, Wind Mother.* Their leader landed on Karsten's arm and bowed to him before turning and bowing to Veranna, who locked eyes with the large bird for a moment as she spoke mind to mind.

Is all made ready, dear friend?

Yes, Wind Mother, the Great Ones shall serve you.

Thank you. We have prepared a feast for you and your fellows. May your aeries be full!

The eagle bowed once more and then flew away with his comrades to an area set aside for them on an upper balcony where various meats lay ready for their enjoyment.

The orchestra struck up a waltz and the people gave Veranna and Karsten ample room for their first dance. The empress hardly felt the floor as she stepped and whirled across the room. Karsten marveled at her grace as they moved in expert unison, but longed for the reception to be over so that they could be alone together. Each of them had to dance with many others before they were led to a table set for just the two of them. Their goblets were filled with the finest wine, and Treybal led the crowd in a toast. Food and drink seemed endless, and when Veranna turned to help the servants, Kreida grabbed her wrist and stopped her.

"Not today, you ninny! Just let them do their job." She shoved her into Karsten's arms and motioned for him to take her out onto the dance floor.

A few hours later and Tesra called for silence. She then directed the servants to bring Veranna and Karsten each a glass of mead. "According to tradition you shall enjoy a glass of this drink every day for one month. May it give you vigor and joy as you celebrate your marriage. Now, go to your chambers and enjoy some time together, and may the blessings of the Creator be upon you each and every day."

They all drank the toast and echoed her sentiment, then parted to form an aisle to the doors. Karsten picked Veranna up in his arms and carried her out to the castle fountain area, sat down on a bench and placed her on his lap.

"You said to me over a year ago that you needed me to be with you. Here I am."

She smiled and ran a finger along his eyebrows. "I see that. What took you so long?"

"I have been waiting for you. Now that you are here it seems like I am in a dream. I do not ever want to be awakened."

"I must say that my dreams have taken a definite turn for the better. I used to have nightmares about the murder of my parents. But since I met you, I have been having dreams of a very different sort."

He gave her a wry look. "I hope that you did not relate any of them to Kreida."

Veranna's face turned into a mock glare of horror. "Bless the Creator, no! I may be naïve in some ways, but I know better than to court disaster." She took a swallow of mead and said, "Besides, we are a bit late addressing some of the things about which I am, ah, naïve."

Karsten's eyebrows rose as he laughed. "I am getting the impression that you are anxious about something. You told me a few days ago that you had a plan for our honeymoon. Is that what you are getting at?"

Her fingers clamped down firmly on his arms and her voice became raspy. "Definitely!"

They drained their goblets of mead and set them on the bench, then trotted quickly into the castle. Veranna willed the castle to open a secret passage up to her chambers and a door suddenly swung out from what had seemed a sheer stonewall. Thinking it would be dark inside, they were surprised at how light made its way through the passage. The door closed behind them without making a sound and they started up a circular stairway. After a number of turns they came to Veranna's chambers. A doorway stood open into her bedroom and they could see a multitude of gifts piled on tables and chairs. However, the oddest sight was a typically sized book resting on a small table just inside the doorway. The last light of the sun fell on it from some mysterious shaft, causing the gilded title characters to glow like burning embers.

Karsten lifted the book up and examined it. "It looks like a volume of the *Analecta Imperia Emeraldia,* but there is nothing but the title, *Mysterium Konsequenter Ergonum,* 'The Powers of Mysterious Consequences.' The language is ancient and will take time to work through."

Veranna always found books interesting, even on obscure subjects. However, the mead and her excitement took precedence. She gave Karsten a rascally smile and said, "Set it on my nightstand; we will study it when we get back. We are now married, and that has its own consequences."

Karsten's eyebrows rose. "I think that you have been spending too much time around Kreida. What is there I do not know about you, my love?"

"I hope to remove all confusion." She gave him a quick peck of a kiss and headed into the bathroom. "Hurry up and change into your traveling clothes; I had them delivered here. They are next to the dresser. I will only be a minute."

Karsten wondered what was going on, but figured he would find out soon enough as he changed quickly. A few minutes later Veranna emerged from the bathroom dressed in the travel clothes that she had worn when they first met. She pulled on a heavy, wool coat with a hood, and then hurried toward the receiving room in her chambers. She closed her eyes and took a deep breath as she concentrated. A moment later an opening appeared in the wall, right behind a large candelabra.

"Come on; I want to get going before anyone comes to bother us." She grabbed his hand and entered the secret passage. A few flights of stairs later they emerged from an opening in the exterior side of the castle wall where two horses stood ready to ride. "I had Reiki place them here about an hour ago."

Karsten shook his head in disbelief. "Veranna, you are scaring me. I am wondering who I married."

"My dear, you will appreciate my scheming. I dare say that the best is yet to come."

He helped her into her saddle and then mounted the other horse. "Lead on, dear schemer."

She gave her horse a neat swat with the reins and sped off toward the forest southeast of the castle. Karsten had to press his steed hard to keep up with her, and wondered how she could see a path in the darkness of the evening. He recalled her ability to see in the night and relaxed, marveling at how lucky he was to be her husband.

About two miles into the forest they came upon a large glen. The moons were out and cast an eerie glow on the land. The second moon was much brighter than usual, bringing Karsten to question if it might be a bad omen. He tensed noticeably and moved in front of Veranna to survey the glen.

She grabbed his arm and spoke softly. "Karsten, do not worry, my love. I just have one more great surprise for you, but I need for you to relax and allow me to concentrate. Please?"

He was slow to heed her request, for his instincts screamed at him to beware. "As you wish; but something is not right. The moons are strange."

She felt the same sense of the unknown, but knew something he did not. "My love, everything is alright; we are simply not used to what we are about to do. We will be the first to witness what is coming since the time of the Old Empire. We shall meet some Masters of the Air."

He blinked and frowned, for the term was familiar. Rolling it over in his mind he finally realized that the words came from ancient children's stories. "Veranna, if this is part of some plan to amuse me, I..."

A great shadow passed over the moons and circled above the trees at the edge of the glen. They could feel the wake of its breeze as it set the leaves to rustling. As the shadow came closer they could see that there were two objects. Huge wings flared out, catching the wind and slowing them down for a landing. Their feathers were golden brown, the larger of the two having glints of silver along its neck and back. The smaller one bowed toward Veranna and touched its beak to the ground while the larger gave her a respectful nod.

Karsten had to grab the reins of the horses to keep them from bolting in terror. He quickly drew a sword from a saddle sheath and stepped in front of Veranna, pushing her back toward the horses.

"Karsten, these eagles are friendly and will not harm us. Put the sword away."

He was reluctant to do as she requested. The beaks on the eagles were large enough to snap a man in half in one swift bite. Fearsome yellow eyes watched every motion, but he was stunned when words formed in his mind, words not his own.

Have no fear of us, for we know that you are the mate to the Creator's chosen servant. We serve along side you, even if you know it not. We gladly grant her aid since she is held in high esteem among us. We served her ancestors and are in their debt.

Karsten was amazed and looked to Veranna to see if she received the same message. She stepped forward and gave him a quick peck on the cheek before addressing the majestic bird.

"We are greatly honored by your service, Master. We have been mated today and seek to go away together for a time. Will you help us?"

The eagle bowed and responded, *This is a day of great joy, for the days were long ago when the Emerald Throne ruled and raised chicks. How may I be of service, your highness?*

She closed her eyes and said, "I request that you fly us to a small oasis located between here and the Koosti border. I will remember what I can about its location." She summoned the place in her memory and allowed the Master to see it.

The eagle nodded his recognition of the place and laid himself on his belly to the ground. *The place you desire is known to us; we should arrive there when the sun shines in the morning."*

A look of disbelief came over Karsten's face. "Veranna, are you thinking of flying with these eagles?"

As if she had done it a thousand times, she said simply, "Yes." She threw her right leg up and over the upper shoulders of the giant bird, then adjusted her position. "Come dear, you ride the other."

It took him a moment, but her enthusiasm helped him overcome his reluctance. "I feel as though I have entered a children's tale. How do you stay on?"

The Master answered, *Lean down against my back and grab hold of feathers where they enter my flesh. Make no sudden moves as we fly.*

Once they were situated Veranna said aloud, "Let's be off!"

The Master trotted a few steps and beat his wings. In a second he was clear of the ground and swiftly gaining altitude. Veranna screamed with excitement and recalled the dreams she had about flying with the eagles. The wind rushed over her face and rustled her clothes, but she felt no cold. Hunkering down into the feathers was similar to sleeping under a down quilt. The eagle's body heat added to the warmth.

She looked around and saw Karsten on the other eagle. Even in the night she could see him relax as he grew accustomed to the experience. Looking back west she saw the lights of Tolemera shining in the dark. To the southwest was the Gap of Grandshire, where the Boar's Spine Mountains ended and lower hills surrounded Smooth Lake. She thought her eyes were playing tricks on her when she saw what looked like hundreds of torches running among the hills hundreds of miles away. It seemed absurd that she would be able to make out individual torches from such a distance. They would have to be enormous fires to be visible. After a moment's thought she put her curiosity aside and concentrated on her honeymoon.

The eagles did not fly at their normal speed out of concern for their passengers. The wind rush would cause them great stress just to hang on. However, eight hours later they arrived at the place Veranna had chosen. They circled the area twice and saw no sign of people for many miles in all directions. In a moment the eagles swooped down next to the still pool and let their passengers off. The morning light shined on the birds and revealed just how large and regal they were.

Veranna thanked them many times and bowed as she requested that they return in a week to fly them back to Tolemera. The Master bowed and promised to return on the night of the seventh day. He also promised to have the normal eagles patrol the area and warn them if any other people came near. Then, with a few swift beats of their wings they were gone, flying off to the southwest.

Veranna turned to Karsten and smiled brightly, the dawn showing a tender blush on her cheeks. "My love, it is just the two of us for one blessed week. I wish it could be at least a year." She wrapped her arms around him and kissed him with a passion that caused his heart to skip a beat.

Karsten lost track of time as they embraced. Finally, he pulled away enough to speak. "You have obviously done quite a lot of planning for this occasion. Did you think of sleep and supplies, also?"

Her eyes gleamed as she replied, "Yes! Come and see." She grabbed his left hand and ran around the western edge of the pool up along the slope to the top to the secret entry of the cavern. Pulling back a façade of tall grass and branches, she stepped into the hole in the ground and climbed down a sturdy, wooden ladder.

Karsten hesitated at first, the memory of nettles and other barbs from the previous time through this opening still fresh in his mind. Seeing that they were cleared away he hurried down into the cavern. It was warm, for the last of the coals in the fire pit still glowed. Someone had started a fire here no more than two days ago, and banked some large chunks of coal that burned slowly.

Veranna hurried to get the fire burning brightly and quickly had a dozen candles lit. They looked around and saw enough food stored in the small cave to last for two weeks, if necessary. Wine, ale and mead were plentiful, as was a supply of books packed in a wood and iron chest.

"Karsten, I selected some books that I thought you would enjoy. Why don't you take a look at them?"

There was a mischievous air about her as she spoke and he wondered what she was getting at. "This is not exactly what I had in mind, but you must have something sly going on in that head of yours." He moved a couple of candles closer to the chest and started looking at the titles. A few moments later, Veranna's voice came to him from the opening of the cave over the pool.

"Karsten, my love, come here!"

There came the sound of a splash and Karsten hurried to the opening to see if Veranna had suffered an accident. His eyes opened wide when he saw her shoes and clothes lying on the floor by the opening. Her voice came to him again.

"Come join me, dear; the water is wonderful."

He smiled and hurried to remove his clothes. In just seconds he was bare and diving into the water. The immediate temperature change caused a slight chill, but it vanished at once as his head came up out of the water and he saw Veranna. Her eyes gleamed all the more as she swam to him and wrapped her legs around his waist, embracing him tightly. He was glad that he was able to stand, for the rush of sudden passion made him giddy. After a long kiss, Veranna sang him a love song; the very one she had imagined when they were here before.

Karsten carried her out of the water and back into the cave. Laying her down on the soft bedding in the back of the cave, he lay beside her and caressed her. She tensed for a moment, but did not hinder him at all. He marveled at her beauty and knew how blessed he was to be married to this gem of the Creator.

"Veranna, I love you so much and am filled with joy that we are finally one."

A tear of joy ran down from the corner of her eye. "Karsten, I love you, too, and wondered if this day would ever come. And yes, we are one."

They could wait no longer, their hearts and minds bursting with fervent desire.

CHAPTER THIRTY SIX

ALWAYS CONSEQUENCES

Veranna and Karsten had been gone for two days when Tesra entered their chambers in the castle. She wanted to see if the servants had supplied enough candles and wood for the fireplaces, and that the rooms were all clean and tidy. She noted the relaxed impression that the placement of objects projected and how it was so like Veranna. Finesse without fuss, dignity without pretense, everything arranged to allow a person to feel warmly received and comfortable.

Reiki was the only other person involved in Veranna's plan to sneak away, and guarded the secret well. She had put away the wedding dress Veranna left in the bathroom, and Karsten's wedding clothes, too. The room looked untouched, otherwise.

Tesra wandered around a bit and then sat down in the receiving room to sip a large mug of hot tea. Paintings of some of Veranna's ancestors hung on the walls alongside precious memorabilia. Over an old student's desk salvaged from the Academy hung Veranna's Sisterhood diploma in an oak frame, and placed over the small fireplace was her ancestral rapier, flanked on each end by one of Karsten's Genazi knives.

Tesra could not keep tears from welling up in her eyes. The image of her dear, adopted daughter newly arrived on her doorstep was still fast in her mind. Innocently naïve and as bright as a morning star, she had passed through terrible tests and come out enriched in knowledge and wisdom.

And now an even greater test was upon her. She held so many expectations about marriage and the future that it could come as a crushing blow if they went unfulfilled. However, the same noble essence of the younger Veranna still identified the older just as a tree remained with the same bole even if new branches formed. The bole had simply grown larger and stronger.

Kreida bounded in without knocking and thought it odd that Tesra would be here alone. "Are you alright?"

Tesra nodded and smiled. "Yes; I just find it hard to believe that Veranna is now married. It seems so long ago that she shared my home west of Clarens. It was a time of such joy and learning that I fear will never be again. Now she has a husband to please and occupy her time."

Very matter-of-factly, Kreida made a dismissive gesture and said, "You might not have too much to worry about. She did not listen to me when I tried to give her advice about raising men, so her time with Karsten may be less than you think."

Tesra could not help but chuckle. "Oh, she heard every word. However, common sense took precedence."

"Really? You think her books gave her any ideas about how to get a man to do what you want? Even I still have to battle every day with Treybal to get his head on straight. Veranna will not accomplish anything if she thinks that being nice is all it takes."

Tesra shook her head and sighed. "Kreida, she will succeed gloriously because the two of them follow the will of the Creator. Besides, being 'nice' is a necessity for anyone who knows they have imperfections, and do not want a life full of hypocrisy."

Sounding unconvinced, Kreida shrugged her shoulders and walked toward the bedroom. "Yeah, yeah; I think you are being too philosophical." She walked back to stand facing Tesra with her hands on her hips. "Just as I thought; the bed has not been used and there is a book on it. What kind of way is that to keep a man interested?"

Tesra laughed and stood up. "They must have been in a hurry to get away; Veranna is very thorough in what she does." She retrieved her tea and went to the doorway of the bedroom to take a glance inside. Curiosity drew her in to see the title of the book on the bed. Lifting it closer she reached out to set her tea onto a table. The mug tittered on the edge, then fell and shattered on the floor. She paid it no heed and felt as though a dark cloud had drifted over the castle. A wisp of a prayer escaped her lips as she translated the title.

"Dear Creator, no!!"

Casey A. Telling

Made in the USA